# FIELD OF BLOOD

## A CRIME THRILLER

CHIEF INSPECTOR HOLT
BOOK ONE

NIC SAINT

**FIELD OF BLOOD**

**Chief Inspector Holt Book 1**

Copyright © 2024 by Nic Saint

All rights reserved. No part of this book may be reproduced in any form by any electronic or mechanical means including photocopying, recording, or information storage and retrieval without permission in writing from the author.

This is a work of fiction. Names, characters, places, brands, media, and incidents are either the product of the author's imagination or are used fictitiously. The author acknowledges the trademarked status and trademark owners of various products referenced in this work of fiction, which have been used without permission. The publication/use of these trademarks is not authorized, associated with, or sponsored by the trademark owners.

Edited by Chereese Graves

www.nicsaint.com

Give feedback on the book at: info@nicsaint.com

facebook.com/nicsaintauthor
@nicsaintauthor

First Edition

Printed in the U.S.A

# FIELD OF BLOOD

**A killer out for revenge. A detective with nothing left to lose. A town on the brink of chaos.**

After catching his boss in bed with his wife, Chief Inspector Holt's once-illustrious career crumbles in a single punch. Exiled to a sleepy countryside town, Holt is forced to move in with his daughter Poppy, who also happens to be a detective—now under his command. Their bond will be tested when a pair of teenagers steal a bus for a joyride, only to turn up savagely murdered.

As the body count rises, this quiet town reveals dark, hidden fractures, and it will take every ounce of Holt's expertise to hunt down a killer whose thirst for vengeance knows no bounds. With tensions mounting, and the town on the edge of civil war, Holt finds himself in a race against time, where every misstep could be his last.

***Field of Blood*** **is the gripping first novel in the Chief Inspector Holt series—an electrifying thriller that will keep you turning the pages until the final twist.**

# PROLOGUE

Like before, the figure stood by the graveside. A familiar sight, since that fateful day, eighteen months ago now. And every time, there was the same mix of profound sadness and intense despair. Even though the priest said the feelings would eventually dissipate and the shrink said it was important to give them a place, that hadn't happened yet. On the contrary, a new feeling had begun to surface more and more: one of anger and rage.

Rage at the injustice and the sheer senselessness of the events that had transpired.

Religion hadn't helped, and neither had therapy. But there was another option, one that hadn't been mentioned by either the priest or the shrink. A remedy that might finally bring some peace of mind—a peace that had proven most elusive these past few months.

The remedy was as old as time. An eye for an eye, a tooth for a tooth. In other words: revenge. Sweet vengeance upon the person responsible for the tragic and senseless death.

All that remained was to find a suitable method.

A punishment that fit the crime.
In other words: as painful as possible.

# CHAPTER 1

Chief Inspector Holt rubbed his eyes. He'd been staring at his computer screen for the past half hour with unseeing eyes, wondering if life could possibly get any more boring. Six months ago, he had a career and a bright future ahead of him, eager to take his Commissioner exams and be assigned his own precinct—the next step in a great career.

Now, all he could do was await early retirement in this tiny outpost—one of the more insignificant precincts in all of Belgium—with only his pension to look forward to, if he ever made it that far without getting the boot.

All it took was one well-aimed punch to end his career and go from being a promising Chief Inspector to being relegated to obscurity.

Of course, he hadn't just punched anyone. The person he had used his right hook on was his boss, Commissioner Terrence Bayton. And it wasn't as if he hadn't had a good reason to punch the man's lights out. He had, after all, just discovered that the guy had been having an affair with his wife. In fact, he had walked in on the couple while they were enjoying carnal relations, so to speak, on top of Commissioner Bayton's desk. An oversight on the part of the otherwise very careful and always prudent police chief, as evidenced by the first words he uttered when he came face to face with his underling:

"Who the hell forgot to lock that door?"

At first, Holt's jaw had dropped, his eyes had bulged out of his head, and he'd experienced that sudden out-of-body experience that many facing these same circumstances would have felt. But when his wife gave him a weak smile and said, "It isn't what it looks like, Glen," he finally snapped out of his stupor, walked up to his boss, and delivered that well-aimed punch to the man's treacherous visage.

The Commissioner had gone down, Holt had left the chief's office and hadn't turned back, even when his boss cursed loudly and demanded he return and face the music.

Face the music he did, though, when he was called into the office of the Chief of Police himself. It was then that he was informed that, contrary to what he had feared, he wasn't being kicked out of the force. Instead, he was being transferred to Loveringem, located smack dab in the middle of nowhere, a place that could only be described as the town where ambitious police officers go to die.

In other words, the end of a most promising career. And all it took was one punch.

In all fairness, he shouldn't have done it. Though even the Chief of Police, after reading him the riot act, had admitted that he might have acted in the same way himself.

There was one ray of light, though: Loveringem was where his daughter was working her way up the chain of command, currently as an inspector. But even though it was a nice change of pace to work with Poppy, he wasn't quite sure if she felt the same about working with her dear old dad—especially now that his marriage was on the rocks.

His son, for one, had picked sides and opted to live with his mom, casting his dad out of his life altogether. It was hard to tell what Poppy thought. Though he liked to think she was on his side, as he was newly disgraced and the butt of every joke in precincts around the country. People had even given him a new nickname: Glen Coopman, after well-known boxing champion Jean-Pierre Coopman, who had once fought Muhammad Ali himself.

He didn't feel like a champion, though. After all, with that one punch he'd lost not only any future prospects he might have nurtured, but also his marriage, the affection of his son, and the respect of his colleagues. Though truth be told, some people had privately told him he had done the right thing. Apparently, Commissioner Bayton's extramarital shenanigans weren't condoned by everyone—quite the contrary. And as some had informed him, Leah wasn't the first woman Bayton had cheated on his wife with.

He looked up when Commissioner Ezekiel Forrester's door swung open, and the Commissioner motioned for Holt to step into his office.

He shared a brief look with Poppy, seated across from him and hard at work on her own computer. She shrugged, indicating she had no idea why her dad was being called into the Commissioner's office.

"Try not to punch his lights out, boss," said Leland Mealing, one of the inspectors assigned to his team. "When you feel that urge, just think: what would Leland do?"

"Very funny, Leland," Holt said as he got up. "Extremely droll."

It was a joke that never seemed to get old.

He passed the desks of his other officers. Apart from Leland, he could count Georgina Gibe and Rasheed Genner as members of his crew. Also Jaime Lett, who wasn't a police officer but an administrative aide handling the more mundane tasks every police station is tasked with.

"Give him hell, boss," said Georgina with a wink. "But go for the gut this time—not the face."

"Ha ha," he said. "*So* very funny, you guys."

"Glen Coopman for the win," said Rasheed with a grin as he punched the air.

He sighed, entered his boss's office, and took a seat in front of the man's desk. At least there were no scantily clad ladies present, unlike in the case of his now ex-wife.

"Yes, boss?" he said dutifully.

"Glen," said the Commissioner with an avuncular smile as he intertwined his fingers on his desk blotter. "How long have you been with us now? Three months? Four?"

"Six months, sir," he said.

"Time flies when you're having fun," said the chief with a wink. "But seriously, have you given any thought to Jaime?"

"Jaime?"

"Jaime Lett? Her birthday is coming up."

He stared at the Commissioner, wondering if this was a trick question. "Oh… I see what you mean," he said finally. "Should I buy her a cake, you think, sir?" Back in Ghent, at his original precinct, birthdays were celebrated with cake, to be bought by the person celebrating their birthday. Here in Loveringem, where they did things differently, it would appear it was the other way around. "What kind of cake does she like, you think, sir?"

The Commissioner gave him another one of those warm smiles he was rightly famous for. The man was alternately described as a teddy bear and the best boss you could ever hope to have. He was almost as old as Holt's dad and close to retirement. "In this precinct, we have the habit of never forgetting a single birthday, Glen. And it's the responsibility of the team leader to make sure they treat the members of their team. I'd suggest buying her a couple of Boules de Berlin or a Couque Suisse. I know for a fact she loves those."

"Right, boss," he said. "Of course. I'll get right on it. A bag of Boules de Berlin and Couque Suisses coming up on the double." Maybe he'd throw in some croissants as well.

The Commissioner leaned back in his chair, interlaced his fingers on his impressive belly and gave him a look of concern. "So, how's it going, Glen? Settling in all right?"

"Yes, sir," he said.

"Moved in with Poppy, have you?"

"Yes, sir," he admitted, wondering how the Commissioner knew about that. After he'd left the family home in Ghent, he needed a place to stay and bunked with a friend for a while. When it became clear he was being transferred to Loveringem and would need to find a place to live there, it was Poppy herself who had suggested he stay with her for the time being—especially as she was dealing with her own relationship crisis, ever since her boyfriend of three years had proven as unfaithful to her as her mom had been to her dad.

It had created a bond between father and daughter, and although it had felt a little strange at first to move in with his daughter, so far the arrangement had proven doable.

"Good," said the Commissioner with a nod of satisfaction. "It's important that my officers enjoy a happy and stable home life, as if reflects on their professional life." He directed an affectionate glance at the framed picture of himself and his wife, occupying a prominent place on his desk. Next to it, another framed portrait of his Lab Daisy stood.

"That's great to hear, sir," he murmured.

"You have a dog, don't you, Glen?"

"Yes, sir," he said. "Harley."

"French poodle?"

"French bulldog," he corrected his boss.

"Pets are important," the chief pronounced. "Did you know that it's been scientifically proven that pet owners suffer less stress-related disorders? It's true," he said when Holt raised an eyebrow. "Pets reduce stress, boost mental health and provide a sense of well-being. They even lower your heart rate, Glen," he added as he patted his chest. "I don't have to tell you how important that is. Do you personally walk your dog, Glen?"

"I do, sir," he confirmed, squirming a little in his seat. He hadn't expected to be quizzed on his qualities as a dog parent. "Every morning and every night."

"Good," the chief. He leaned forward. "I like to hear that. I don't mind telling you that I, for one, don't trust a man who claims not to love pets, Glen." He shook his head. "You can tell a lot about a man when you know where he stands vis-à-vis pets—dogs in particular. And you are sound on dogs, Glen. I can tell. Very sound on dogs."

"Thank you... sir," he said.

The chief leaned back again, that same warm smile wreathing his features. "I won't keep you," he said. "I'm sure you have plenty of work piling up on your desk."

"Yes, sir. I do, sir," he said, even though his work pile was woefully lacking in both substance and challenge. But then such was the life of a cop in the countryside.

He left his boss's office and cast a quick glance at Jaime, kicking himself for completely forgetting about her birthday. He'd pop by the bakery right away and get her those Boules de Berlin and Couque Suisses she loved so much.

Leland craned his neck to look into the Commissioner's office. "I don't see him, boss," he said. "I hope he's not on the floor, out for the count?"

"The joke is really wearing out, Leland," Holt said.

"And I still think it's funny," his underling replied. "Though I have to admit, the idea of the Commissioner doing the horizontal mambo with a member of the opposite sex seems remote, to say the least. I mean, the man is old. Ancient, even."

"He's not *that* old," said Georgina.

"He's the same age as my grandfather," said Poppy. "And he retired years ago—so, yeah. The Commissioner is pretty old, Georgina."

"Yes, but your granddad retired early, didn't he?"

That was true enough. The moment Holt's dad had the chance, he'd signed on the dotted line and bought the boat he'd been dreaming of for years. Ever since then, he and Holt's mom had been happily using Fern, as they had christened the boat, to sail all the rivers and canals of Belgium, Holland, and Germany they could find.

"Okay, I'm going to pop out for a moment," Holt said, grabbing his wallet from his desk. "Be back in a sec."

Just then, Poppy held up a finger. A call had come in, and she was frowning. "I'm afraid that will have to wait, boss," she said. "A bus has just been hijacked, and fifty Japanese tourists have been left stranded by the side of the road."

Glen suppressed a deep sigh. A hijacked bus was probably the most excitement he could wish for today. "Let's roll," he said, and headed for the lockers where he kept his weapon safely tucked away. He didn't think he'd need it, but since it was standard operating procedure never to go out on patrol without it, he had no other choice.

# CHAPTER 2

Boyd Batham cursed inwardly as he took his phone from his pocket and dialed the familiar number.

"Boyd." The voice was curt and crisp, as usual.

"I'm afraid I've got some bad news, Teddy," he said.

"Toilet's clogged again?" asked his boss, referring to a recurring issue.

"It's not the toilets," he said, wondering how to broach the topic without causing the boss to explode.

"Well? What is it? Spit it out, man." Teddy never did have a lot of patience, and it was in moments like these that Boyd wondered if he shouldn't have followed his wife's advice a long time ago and started looking for a different job—one with an employer who didn't snap at him all the time. Then again, after talking with plenty of his colleagues, also bus drivers, he had come to the conclusion that there was no such thing as the perfect boss.

"The bus has been stolen, boss."

Silence on the other end. But not for long. "What?!" Teddy exploded.

"Two kids. I saw them climbing in and taking off.

Teenagers, actually. I called the police, and they should be here any moment now."

There was plenty of cursing on the other end of the call, then Teddy started breathing very heavily into the device, which was not a good sign. "What about the tourists?"

"Oh, they're fine," he assured the man. At least that was one silver lining to the whole terrible incident. "We had just stopped at Castle Coninxdonck and they were snapping shots as usual when all of a sudden I heard a noise. When I looked over, I saw that those two kids had snuck onto the bus and were taking off with it."

"But how?!"

"Well…" He swallowed with difficulty. "I may have accidentally left the keys in the ignition, boss."

Even more vituperation this time, not to mention personal insults. Mention was made of certain parts of Boyd's anatomy being forcefully removed and inserted in other parts, and the entire experience was far from pleasant.

"You shouldn't have called the cops," said Teddy. "We deal with these things ourselves, Boyd. How many times have I told you?"

"I know, but I figured…"

"What did you tell them?"

"The same thing I've just told you. That two kids have stolen my bus and taken off with it and now I'm stranded with fifty Japanese tourists in the middle of Loveringem."

"Mmm," said the owner of Birt Travel. "I guess you can't call them back and tell them you made a mistake? No, I guess not. That wouldn't go over too well with our boys and girls in blue." He sighed deeply. "Okay, fine. Just let them deal with it, and in the meantime, I'll see what I can do on my end. And Boyd?"

"Yes, boss?"

"You're an idiot."

"Yes, boss."

"Not to mention a moron."

"Yes, boss. I know, boss."

The call disconnected and Boyd tucked away his phone, discovering that he suddenly felt a little nauseous.

MOHAMMAD ELMALEH AND BENI IDRISSI, the two teenagers who had taken the bus, were having the time of their lives. It had been a great coincidence that they just happened to pass by, on their way from the bus stop, when they saw a flock of Japanese tourists snapping pictures of some stupid old castle. A bus stood parked by the side of the road, the engine idling, with not a soul in sight. No driver, no passengers—just a big, old empty bus, the engine running and the keys in the ignition.

It had been Beni's idea to take advantage of this rare opportunity to have themselves an adventure.

"I've always wanted to drive a bus," he confessed to Mohammed.

His eyes were twinkling mischievously, as they often did when he was up to no good. It was one of the reasons he and Mohammed had been friends since primary school. Mohammed had always been a shy kid—reticent and responsible—while Beni was the exact opposite. Maybe that's why they had become such close friends. Mohammed had been seated next to Beni by their first-grade teacher, who thought Mohammed was too shy and quiet and could use a little livening up. Sitting next to Beni just might do the trick.

It had done the trick and more. The two youngsters had quickly become the bane of their teacher's existence with their pranks and jokes. Even Mohammed's parents had noticed the change in their son and weren't happy about it, lamenting the bad influence Beni had on him. But by then it was too late. The two boys had become friends for life.

"Let's go!" said Beni as he mounted the steps to the bus driver's seat.

Mohammed hesitated. Stealing a bus was a different beast altogether from their usual shenanigans and could get them into a lot of trouble. Then again, where was the harm in taking a short drive? They'd take the bus for a spin and abandon it after twenty minutes.

And so, he had joined his friend as Beni took the wheel and put the massive vehicle in motion.

"Oh, this is great!" Beni cackled happily as he steered the bus down the leafy road.

Castle Coninxdonck was only one of the many castles, country houses and villas that dotted this part of the province. It was part of the chateau route, making it a tourist attraction for the many visitors hoping to catch a glimpse of how the rich had lived over a century ago. With its castle parks and charming villages, it was a popular destination.

This part of the province of East Flanders had once been home to the captains of industry who owned and operated factories in the provincial capital, Ghent. Most of the castles were still privately owned, but accessible to tourists. They were part of the city's green belt, with municipalities that stretched along the river Scheldt, and comprised several nature preserves, lakes and even a moated fortress dating back to the middle ages.

As Beni stomped on the gas, the two friends zoomed underneath a canopy of trees and along the twisty roads that made up this part of the countryside.

"Let *me* drive," said Mohammed.

"Not a chance!" said Beni. "You don't even have your driver's license yet. You'll crash the bus."

"No, I won't. I mean, how difficult can it be?"

"Okay, fine," said Beni, momentarily pulling over. Parking on the shoulder of the road, the two boys switched positions, and Mohammed felt like the captain of an airplane as he took control of the wheel. It was a lot harder than he thought, though, and nothing like driving a regular car, which he had done with his dad as the old man gave him driving lessons in the family Mercedes.

"Careful!" Beni warned as his friend almost hit a cyclist slowly creeping along the road. It was an old man, and he didn't seem very steady on his bike.

Finally, they left the small country lane behind and merged onto a bigger road that cut through fields that stretched all around them. Sunflowers to the right and corn to the left.

Now the trouble wasn't old men on bikes but other cars.

"Try not to hit anything, Mo," said Beni. "I'm begging you, bro."

Mohammed discovered that he was sweating. "Jesus, this thing steers hard!" he cried, struggling to keep the massive vehicle on the road and not drifting into a ditch.

And then, all of a sudden, it happened. A car came zooming up from the opposite direction, and because Mohammed couldn't confidently gauge the distance between the bus and the car, he oversteered as he frantically tried to keep the bus under control.

"Hey, what are you doing!" Beni yelled as he shot up from his seat and tried to take over the wheel.

But it was too late. The bus had been going at a pretty steady clip and they headed straight for a ditch. There was a swaying motion as the massive vehicle tilted sideways, and then they were going down, the bus sliding a couple of meters into the ditch, the world spinning around them. Both kids were thrown from their positions behind the wheel, and as the bus shuddered to a full stop, they broke out into hysterical laughter.

"Oh, my God!" Beni screamed. "You crashed the bus, bro!"

"Let's go!" said Mohammed.

Both kids climbed through the driver's side window, clambered over the side of the bus, and down to the shoulder of the road. As they ran off, Mohammed glanced back at the vehicle: it was lying on its side in the ditch, like a giant beast that had been felled.

What an adventure—*what a rush!*

# CHAPTER 3

Tim had actually jumped at the chance. Chasing a couple of kids who had stolen a bus? It seemed like a pretty easy job compared to some of the other assignments he'd been tasked with over the years. As luck would have it, he'd been in the vicinity of Castle Coninxdonck when the call came in, dropping off a package. He wasn't the kind of person typically called in to make deliveries, but this was a special client, and the package had been a particularly large one. Since the pay was good, he didn't mind.

And so he'd jumped on his Kawasaki Ninja H2 and gone in pursuit of the bus. Good thing it was equipped with a tracker, so whoever had taken it wouldn't get very far.

His bosses had supplied him with the coordinates, and now all he had to do was track them on the head-up display built into his helmet. State-of-the-art tech that had set him back quite a tidy sum, but had served him well over the years.

It wasn't long before he caught up with his target, and he wasn't surprised to find that the bus was lying in a ditch. Like a beached whale, it was lying with its belly fully exposed where those kids had presumably left it.

He tapped a button on his helmet and connected with his bosses.

"Yeah, I found the bus," he said. "Crashed in a ditch. No sign of the thieves."

"Find them," the voice said. "And take care of them."

"Are you sure?"

"Nobody steals from us. Time to send a message. Is that understood?"

"Loud and clear," he said, getting more and more excited about the job by the minute.

He scanned his surroundings. The road was clear in both directions—no sign of those kids. Looked like they had escaped by taking a shortcut through the fields.

He thought for a moment. Chances were that the cops would arrive soon, and the last thing he needed was to be seen at the scene. So he resolutely steered his bike in the opposite direction. A couple hundred meters beyond where the bus lay stranded, a dirt path forked off the main road, leading straight into a wooded area. He quickly parked his bike behind a thicket of bushes and dismounted. Time to get to work.

MOHAMMED AND BENI WERE CRAZY, but not so crazy they'd risk walking down the main road. Instead, they had decided to head into the fields and make their way to the next bus stop, then hop on a bus—without paying, of course—and head home to Ghent, where they both lived in the Ekkergem neighborhood. Both of them were high-school dropouts and still lived with their parents. Not for long, though. Mohammed was making so much dough lately that soon he'd be able to afford a down payment on an apartment of his own, and the same went for Beni. The two friends had considered moving in together, which would save them some money, especially now that the real estate market in Ghent was so saturated that rental prices were skyrocketing. But since the money was rolling in at a steady clip, that wasn't even necessary. In fact, things were so good that pretty soon Mohammed might be able to afford an actual loft in one of the swankiest parts of town.

The two teenagers were traipsing along when, all of a sudden, Mohammed had a feeling they were being followed. When he looked back, he didn't see anything apart from a herd of cows, looking at them with their typical inscrutable and bored expressions.

"What's wrong?" asked Beni.

"Nothing," he said. "I thought we were being followed."

"Never seen a cow before, city boy?" said Beni as he clapped him on the shoulder.

Mo smiled and hurried after his friend. His New Balance sneakers were already wet from the soggy soil, and streaked with green. It had been raining a lot these past couple of weeks and he had to watch his step. He didn't mind. He'd buy himself a new pair—or a dozen. He could afford that now. As a self-confessed sneaker freak he owned lots of them. He'd even found a site where they sold exclusive sneakers at exorbitant prices. Heaven.

"I'll bet it will be all over the news tonight," said Beni.

"Yeah, right. It's just a bus," said Mohammed. "Nobody cares."

"You're forgetting where we are, buddy," said his friend. "This is where the rich and famous live. They're not used to crime like we are. When a bus gets stolen it's big news."

He smiled. "Pretty soon we'll both be living here. We could buy neighboring villas."

"No way am I moving to Loveringem. I want to be where

the action is. I'm getting one of those fancy new lofts in the center of town. You know, like that former prime minister."

"How much will that set you back, you think?"

"A million, easy. But that's only if you take one of the lofts right at the top. Imagine looking out across the skyline of Ghent, bro. It's the best."

"Yeah, I guess nothing can beat that view," he agreed. And then maybe, when he was settled in, he could arrange a similar setup for his mom and dad. They'd ask him where the money was coming from, but in the end they'd be too happy to ask a lot of questions.

A twig snapped behind them, and he whipped his head around so fast that he felt a crick in his neck. That's when he saw him: a man dressed in black leather from head to toe, black motorcycle helmet covering his face. He stared at the man, who'd approached so fast he was standing right in front of him. As he opened his mouth to speak, something flashed in the man's gloved hand. An arm was thrust forward, and a sharp pain sliced across his chest. He looked down only to see a knife buried deeply into his chest.

He wanted to scream but found that he had suddenly lost control of his voice.

He staggered back as the man pulled the knife from his chest. Casting about, he caught a glimpse of Beni running away as fast as his legs could carry him, the man giving chase.

He collapsed onto the wet grass, next to a pile of cow dung. As darkness closed in on his field of vision, the last thought that entered his mind was that he was cold—*so cold*.

TIM LOOKED AROUND AND CURSED. He should have been quicker off the mark. Somehow, the second kid had managed to make his getaway. But not to worry. He'd been filming the scene from the moment he caught up with the two kids and would watch the footage later on to see if he couldn't identify him. He may have gotten away this time, but he wouldn't be able to elude him for long, and the same fate that had befallen his friend would come to him.

He wiped the knife on a clump of grass and retraced his steps. When he reached the fallen kid, he took off his glove, knelt down, and pressed a hand to his throat, feeling for a pulse. When there was none, he grunted with approval. One down, one more to go. But not now. First, he needed to get away from here before all hell broke loose.

He searched the kid's pockets until he found his wallet. He studied it for a moment. Mohammed Elmaleh. He turned the card around. Place of issue: Ghent. He made sure that the camera got a good look at the identification number of the National Register. That should suffice to get a bead on Mohammed's cowardly friend who'd left his buddy to die.

He wiped any possible prints off the ID card and put the wallet back where he had found it, then glanced around to make sure there were no unwanted witnesses. Apart from those stupid cows, there were none.

He broke into a light trot in the direction of the main road and the location where he had stashed his bike. Moments later, he was mounting his noble steed, and before long was racing away from the scene. As he gave his boss an update on the state of affairs, he could tell that the man wasn't happy.

"I'll get him," he assured him. "Don't worry, boss."

"Oh, I'm not worried," said the icy voice on the other end of the call. "I know you'll get him. And if not…"

Tim grimaced. He knew that if he didn't do a proper job, it was his ass on the line.

"I'll finish him soon," he promised.

"You'd better."

The call cut out, and he tapped another button on his helmet, connecting with one of his associates. Before long, he had transmitted the National Register number of the kid.

For a moment, no information was forthcoming, but then suddenly the voice returned. "Mohammed Elmaleh? Are you sure?"

"Yeah, why?"

"He's Green Valley."

"You're kidding."

"Nope. Low-level street dealer."

He grimaced. "Is that a fact?"

"And you're telling me he took a bus?"

"He did. Him and his little buddy."

A low whistle sounded in his ears. "The boss know?"

"He does. He's the one who told me to finish them off—both of them."

"Muscling in on Phoenix territory, huh? They've got balls, those kids."

"All the more reason to get rid of them."

"I should be able to get you the information on his friend soon," his associate assured him.

"Good," he said. "Make it snappy."

He disconnected and took the onramp, then sped up and raced off in the direction of Ghent. Life had suddenly become a whole lot more interesting.

Which was exactly the way he liked it.

# CHAPTER 4

Even though he didn't think it was necessary, Holt arrived with his entire team in tow. The Commissioner had expressed a wish that it be so—mostly because the owner of the tour company whose bus had been stolen was the mayor's brother Teddy Birt. And since politics mattered in a small town, the detective division of the Loveringem police station was obliged to investigate the theft of the bus.

It seemed like a total waste of police resources to Holt, but then he wasn't in charge of their local police station—Commissioner Forrester was. If it had been up to Holt, he would have simply sent two uniformed officers to take a look. And as he mused on the indignity of having to spend his time looking into a bus theft, he felt Poppy's eyes on him.

"What?" he finally asked.

"Nothing, Dad," she said. When it was just the two of them, she preferred to call him Dad. It was only when there were other people around that she fell back on the more formal 'sir' or 'boss' out of respect for his rank. "Just that you don't look happy. No, sir, not happy at all."

"A bus theft, Poppy," he said with a groan. "Is this what it has come to? That we have to spend our time trying to find out who has stolen some stupid bus?"

"Oh, but it's not just any bus," said Poppy, who was a lively young woman of twenty-five, with an attitude far too cheerful for his taste. Possibly she enjoyed seeing her father suffer to some extent. Before he had moved out of the marital home and moved in with her, he and Leah hadn't seen Poppy all that much, apart from the occasional visit. And now he saw her all the time. Not that he minded. She was, after all, his daughter, and so he loved her unconditionally. But there's only so much cheerfulness a man can stomach, especially when he's feeling as down in the dumps as Holt had been feeling lately.

"I know it's not just any bus," he said with a touch of chagrin. He glanced out of the window at the passing landscape. Fields and farmland as far as the eye could see. They truly were in the sticks now, where the cows and the sheep outnumbered the people. "It's Teddy Birt's bus. And when Teddy Birt's bus is stolen, the entire police force has to be engaged in trying to find it."

"Oh, don't be like that, Dad," said Poppy as she expertly steered the Renault Megane in the direction of the altercation. "You know the mayor is the head of the police. So what if he considers us his personal security detail? That's small-town policing for you."

"It's a massive waste of resources," he grumbled. "Not to mention the police shouldn't play favorites. Especially not with Mayor Birt, who's possibly the worst mayor this town has ever had—bar none."

Mayor Jan Birt, Teddy's brother, had been elected in a landslide victory almost six years ago, as the first mayor representing the far-right Flemish Front party. His election and subsequent nomination as Loveringem's new mayor had caused quite a stir, and still did to this day. *'Not my mayor'* stickers had started appearing all over town, adorning lampposts and mailboxes, only to be removed by the mayor's fanatical supporters. At one point, the mayor's house had been the target of a Molotov cocktail thrown through the window. Lucky for him, whoever had thrown the makeshift weapon hadn't been an expert, and the bomb hadn't caused any damage, except for a broken window. But as a consequence, police had been forced to patrol his house for months on end, until the culprit had been identified and put behind bars.

"Let's just get this over with," said Holt now, "so we can all go back to do what we should be doing: investigating major crime." Not that there was a lot of that in Loveringem. Still, one could live in hope.

"Looks like whoever stole the bus wasn't exactly an expert driver," said Poppy, pointing at a bus lying on its side in a ditch.

"Park here," he said. The rest of his team were following behind: Leland, Georgina, and Rasheed sharing a car. Five detectives to find one hapless thief. Talk about overkill.

Poppy parked on the side of the road, and Holt saw that plenty of people had already joined the usual group of lookie-loos. All of them were being held back behind a cordon instigated by a couple of uniformed officers. As Holt watched one of them argue with a man who wanted to snap a couple of pictures of the bus, he ruefully thought, not for the first time, that he probably should be grateful that the reprimand he'd received hadn't resulted in him being demoted and relegated to the ranks of the uniformed traffic police. Even though his former boss had been livid and had threatened to get him kicked out of the force, in the end the powers that be had decided that he was too experienced to get rid of—and that his expertise and his track record as a detective were too valuable to put him on traffic duty—like he had been at the start of his career, twenty-odd years ago.

"Okay, let's do this," he said as he climbed out of the car and walked up to the bus. He immediately recognized Teddy Birt, who didn't look happy. Next to him, a short, squat man stood sweating profusely, wiping his brow with a white handkerchief.

"That must be the driver," said Poppy. "He does not look happy."

Next to the bus, a group of Japanese tourists stood, taking plenty of photographs of anything that caught their eye: the bus, the crowd of onlookers, the cows in a nearby pasture. They seemed to enjoy this adventure tremendously. Then again, it's not every day that you suddenly find yourself in the middle of a bus hijacking.

The uniformed officer who had been taking the driver's statement seemed relieved that Holt and his team had finally arrived and happily gave them the gist of the situation.

"Mr. Batham over there—that is Boyd Batham—is the driver of the bus. Mr. Batham says that he only left the bus for a moment," he explained as he consulted his notes. "He was showing the tourists—all fifty of them—Castle Coninxdonck when he suddenly heard the sound of the bus pulling away. He says he chased after it but couldn't catch up."

"Did he see who was behind the wheel?"

"Two teenagers, sir, and the footage from the, ah, CCTV cameras on the bus—there's two cameras, actually—confirms this. The footage clearly shows two, ah, young males driving the bus—and, ah, also crashing the bus."

"You saw this CCTV footage?"

"I did, sir. I did see the CCTV footage." He seemed proud of the fact, as if he'd been let in on a secret that nobody else was privy to. He grinned. "It's something else, sir."

The bus driver had decided to join them and now piped up. "I can show you if you like," he said.

"That would be great," said Holt, curious in spite of himself. But before he could follow the driver into the bus, Teddy Birt stopped him in his tracks by putting a heavy hand on his shoulder and fixing him with a steely-eyed look.

"I want these fellas caught, Chief Inspector. I want them caught and punished to the *fullest* extent of the law. I mean, where are we as a town when we condone this kind of criminal behavior? When honest businessfolk like me are forced to watch in despair while our much-valued customers are stranded by the side of the road? These people paid good money for this trip. Not to mention the damage these two *hooligans* inflicted on my bus." He glanced over at the group of tourists. "They'll probably want a refund now. And I don't blame them. They came for a castle tour, not this nonsense."

"We'll get those kids for you, sir," said Holt. "In the meantime, you can give your statement to my inspector."

Teddy Birt didn't seem inclined to be foisted off on what he must have seen as a mere underling. "I'd rather give my statement to you," he said with a sour look. He was a large man, with tiny eyes that peered out of a flabby face. There was something mean about him, Holt thought. Something of a prizefighter who likes to fight dirty. It surprised him how much he resembled his brother Jan, and he wondered if they were twins.

"Can you tell me exactly what happened, sir?" asked Poppy, leading the man away from her dad.

Holt followed the bus driver into the bus, where he showed him the cameras.

"There's one up there, to keep an eye on the passengers, and also one over here," he added, pointing to a small camera that appeared to be aimed at the driver's seat.

"What does that do?" asked Holt, even though it was pretty obvious.

The man grimaced. "So the boss can keep an eye on me," he said as he briefly glanced in the direction of Teddy Birt.

"He doesn't trust his drivers?"

The driver shook his head. "No, he does not, sir." Then he seemed to realize what he was saying and quickly added, "Please don't put that in your report, Chief Inspector. Teddy doesn't like criticism. In fact, he's allergic to it. One wrong word and it's my job on the line. As it is, it'll be a small miracle if he doesn't fire me after today's disaster."

"Okay, show me the footage," said Holt, whose patience was wearing a little thin.

The bus driver took him to the back of the bus, where the toilets were located, along with a technical space. The recording equipment was hidden there, and as he started up the video, Holt had to peer at the small screen. It was still clear enough: just as the driver had said, two kids—teenagers, by the looks of them—got behind the wheel and seemed to have the time of their lives doing so. Laughing and acting silly as they drove the bus.

Boyd sped up the tape to reach the moment the bus crashed. One of the kids yanked the wheel, and that must have triggered the accident. They didn't seem shocked or surprised, laughing it up until they disappeared from view after exiting the stranded vehicle.

"And that's all I've got," said Boyd.

"It's enough," said Holt. "Do you recognize those kids?"

"Never seen them before," said Boyd, and Holt believed him.

"So how did they manage to hijack your bus? They don't look like professional thieves to me. Just a couple of kids taking a bus for a joyride."

Boyd gave him a sheepish look. "I left the engine idling."

"With the keys in the ignition?"

"A stupid thing to do. But there you have it."

"Why didn't you take the keys?"

Boyd shrugged. "We were only going to be five minutes, and Bertha had been giving me a lot of grief lately."

Holt lifted an eyebrow. "Bertha?"

Boyd smiled. "That's what we've christened her. On account of the fact that she's so big and lumbering, see. She's a chore to drive, Chief Inspector. Trouble starting her up, power steering malfunctioning all the time. Teddy should have replaced her ages ago. No wonder those kids crashed her in a ditch." He shook his head. "Poor Bertha. She didn't deserve to be treated like this." He seemed genuinely concerned for his beloved bus.

"Okay, so these kids just happened to pass by, saw Bertha, engine idling, and couldn't resist the temptation to take her for a spin. Is that how you'd describe what happened?"

"That's exactly how I would describe it."

"Apart from the fact that they crashed her in a ditch—any other damage?"

"Not that I can see."

"Anything stolen? Luggage? Personal items belonging to the tourists?"

"Nothing stolen, as far as I can tell."

It seemed like a pretty straightforward case. A couple of kids taking a bus for a joyride, and through sheer lack of experience, crashing it in a ditch. That didn't mean they shouldn't try and track them down. And since they now had the CCTV footage, that wouldn't be hard. A fine and a slap on the wrist, and hopefully they would have learned their lesson. Since the bus didn't seem to have sustained a lot of damage, and nothing was stolen or anyone hurt, no real harm was done. Just as he thought, a minor incident that could just as easily have been handled by the traffic police.

As he crawled out of the bus, he suddenly heard loud screams. They seemed to be coming from the nearby cow pasture. And as a man came running toward them, it took Holt a moment to understand what he was going on about.

"Dead body!" the man was shouting. "There's a *dead body* over there!" He finally reached them and had to catch his breath before repeating, "I found a *dead body!* It's over there, by those trees—a young kid—*blood all over him!*"

Looked like they wouldn't be returning to the station just yet.

# CHAPTER 5

Poppy stared down at the body of the victim and felt a powerful sense of unease. They were in a pasture, surrounded by cows, in the middle of the countryside. The landscape was bucolic, one she always enjoyed on her daily runs, and yet in the midst of some of the most beautiful scenery in the world, there was now this dead kid—a teenage boy.

The person who had made the discovery hadn't lied when he said there was blood all over the place. The boy stared up at the sky with unseeing eyes, his face pale and impassive, his hand clutching his chest, where a spreading flood of crimson had soaked his T-shirt and stained the grass underneath him red.

The coroner had arrived, along with the crime scene experts, to take a closer look at the body, so she left them to investigate.

She joined her dad, who stood a few meters away, looking thoughtful.

"Do you think he's one of the kids who took the bus?" she asked.

He nodded. "I think so. I mean, the screen on that bus's video system was tiny, and the footage black-and-white, but I'm willing to bet he was one of them. He wasn't driving at first, but he was the one who steered the bus into a ditch when he took over the wheel."

"My God, how old do you think he is? Sixteen? Seventeen?"

"Something like that."

She glanced up at him. Unlike her, he didn't seem particularly shocked or impressed. While she hadn't seen many dead bodies over the course of her career, she knew he must have been present at countless scenes like this—some of them much more gruesome. She couldn't imagine what it must have been like for him, working in Ghent, where crime was a lot more prevalent than here in Loveringem, where it was practically non-existent.

"Do you think he was stabbed by his friend? Maybe they had a fight over who crashed the bus?"

"It's possible," her dad conceded, remaining cautious about committing to a theory until he had all the facts.

"Looks like he was stabbed," she said. Of the two, she was the more talkative one, and his lack of communication sometimes drove her up the wall. It had been like this when she was growing up, and she knew it had driven her mom crazy, too. Dad could be like a sphinx, giving nothing away, his face a mask. Poppy had always thought it was because of his profession, but now that she was a detective herself, she wasn't so sure. She had met other detectives—good ones—who were even more talkative than she was, so she was convinced that his stoicism was just an aspect of his personality.

Tomas Lovelass, the coroner, joined them. A rail-thin man with a stoop, he always looked as if he had a dark cloud hanging over his head, his face fixed in a mournful expression. In that sense, he looked more like an undertaker than a coroner.

"Stabbed through the heart," was his determination. "Long, thin blade is my first guess."

"Single knife wound to the chest?" Dad asked.

The coroner nodded sadly. "That's all it took. No other signs of violence as far as I can tell. No defensive wounds either. Doesn't look like he put up much of a fight."

"Maybe the killer took him by surprise?" Poppy ventured. She looked up at her dad. "That would be consistent with the theory that he was killed by his friend. He wouldn't expect to be stabbed by the kid he was having so much fun with only moments before."

Dad didn't even bother to nod this time, averse as he was to what he often called idle speculation. "How long has he been dead?"

"I'd say no more than two hours, no less than one," said the coroner.

Dad frowned. "That would put time of death around the moment he and his friend crashed the bus and fled from the scene." He looked up in the direction of a copse of trees bordering the field. "They were probably heading that way, him and his buddy, and for some reason, our friendly neighborhood joyrider was attacked and killed."

"I'll leave that to you, Glen," said the coroner.

"Did he have any ID on him? Phone?"

"He did, yeah," said the coroner, handing him both items, wrapped in plastic.

Dad nodded gratefully before the coroner removed himself from the scene, but not before instructing his team to remove the body and transport it to the pathologist's office at the Ghent University Hospital.

The rest of the team had also joined them.

"What do you want us to do, boss?" asked Leland.

"What's behind that tree line over there?" Dad asked.

"Um… that's all farmland, boss," said Leland.

"Talk to the farmer," said Dad. "Ask them if they saw something. And maybe widen the search and talk to any of the neighbors. Take Georgina." He turned to Rasheed and handed him the phone and wallet. "You'd better take a look at these. You know the drill. Go through his call log, messages, emails, social media. We need to find his friend—who must have seen what happened."

"If he's not the one that did this," Poppy added.

Dad was staring pointedly at the ground. "Too soggy," he murmured. "No footprints."

He was right. It had been raining a lot these past couple of days, and the ground was a boggy mess of mud and puddles, with plenty of cow patties added into the mix.

"Lots of hoof prints," Leland said. "But I guess they don't count. Cows don't kill."

Georgina groaned. "Very funny, Leland."

"No, but it's true, isn't it?" He glanced over at the cows. "If only they could talk."

"Maybe you can try. They might recognize a kindred spirit."

"Ha ha. You're hilarious."

"You and I will go and give the bad news to the parents," said Dad.

Poppy grimaced but understood it was necessary. "Okay, boss. Where do they live?"

Dad turned to Rasheed, who had donned disposable plastic gloves and was already going through the kid's wallet.

"Mohammed Elmaleh," he said, reading from the boy's ID card. He consulted the police database, also known as the ANG, on his phone, using Mohammed's INSZ-number. It didn't take him long to determine that he was a resident of the Ekkergem neighborhood in Ghent, coincidentally also where the Ghent police headquarters were located—and where Dad had worked for most of his career. It was safe to say they wouldn't be dropping by, as the precinct was still being run by Dad's former boss and Mom's current husband, Commissioner Terrence Bayton.

She and Dad exchanged a look of surprise at the coincidence.

Dad shrugged. "Looks like we're going to Ekkergem."

"Your old stomping ground," said Leland with a grin. "Knock 'em dead, boss." He punctuated the statement by doing some shadow-boxing, complete with fancy footwork.

Dad gave the young inspector a withering look that did little to put a dent in Leland's sense of mirth.

"Okay, we'd better go and talk to those neighbors," said Georgina. As she and Leland started in the direction of the trees, she gave her colleague a gentle slap across the head.

"Ouch!" he cried.

"Smart-ass," she said.

"What did I say?"

"You know."

"No, I don't."

"Dumb-ass."

"Make up your mind. Am I a smart-ass or a dumb-ass? I mean, I can't be both."

"And yet you are. Which makes you something of a medical anomaly."

Poppy smiled, and as she and her dad started walking back to the car, she saw a slight smile play about her dad's lips as well.

# CHAPTER 6

According to his ID, Mohammed Elmaleh was sixteen years old, which was pretty shocking, Holt thought. During the drive to Ghent, he wondered if Poppy's theory could have merit: that Mohammed and his fellow joyrider had fallen out over the crashing of the bus and somehow the other kid had killed his friend during the course of the argument. Somehow, Holt didn't think that was necessarily the case. The two kids, even though they had seemed shocked at first when they landed the bus in a ditch, had burst into hysterical laughter—just more mischief that had cracked them up. To go from that to having an argument that ended with Mohammed being stabbed to death seemed like a stretch. Though they couldn't rule it out, of course. Whatever the case, it was imperative that they found Mohammed's partner in crime as soon as possible. Whether as a witness or a suspect, only time would tell.

"What are you thinking, Dad?" asked Poppy.

"Just trying to figure out what happened to that kid," he said.

"I think Mohammed's friend blamed him for crashing that bus and getting them into a heap of trouble. They got into an argument and he stabbed him. End of story."

If only it were that simple. "Looks like you've solved the case already."

"Well, there were only the two of them out in that cow pasture. So who else could it have been? Not those cows, surely."

"No, I think we can safely assume the cows are innocent."

"Look, Loveringem isn't Ghent, Dad."

"Oh, I know. No cows in Ghent, for instance."

"What I mean is that things are pretty straightforward in our neck of the woods. What you see is what you get. Two kids hijack a bus, crash the bus, have a fight, and one kid kills the other one. Case closed."

He smiled. "Excuse me for not agreeing with you, honey. Before I reach a conclusion, I like to look at all the facts—and talk to all the people involved. First and foremost, the kid you seem to believe is a killer, without any evidence, I might add."

"Trust me, the moment we catch him, he'll confess. I just know he will."

She was probably right. Things in Loveringem *were* surprisingly straightforward, not to mention infuriatingly obvious. Only last month, a farmer's wife had been fatally stabbed in the back. Poppy had immediately gone out on a limb and predicted that her husband was the killer. They had only just sat the man down at his own kitchen table when he started blubbering through a confession. It turned out his wife had been having an affair with the neighbor, and when he found out, he snapped and planted a kitchen knife in her back.

Straightforward, just as Poppy said. And a little tedious.

FIELD OF BLOOD

"Okay, let's first talk to Mohammed's parents and see what they have to say," he suggested. "Maybe they know who this friend of his is and can put a name to the face."

He had snapped a picture of the CCTV footage and hoped that Mohammed's parents would be able to ID their son's fellow joyrider.

Poppy veered along the R4 off-ramp, heading to the intersection with the ring road, which would lead them to the Ekkergem police station and then on to the neighborhood where the Elmalehs lived. As they passed by the precinct where Holt had spent the better part of his career, a welter of emotion bubbled to the surface at the familiar sight. Most of it was good, but was marred by the altercation that had cost him his reputation as a level-headed and experienced detective. Now when people referred to him, it was as some kind of loose cannon, a maniac who went around slugging his bosses, even though it had only been the one time. Then again, once was all it took to ruin a reputation he'd spent twenty years building, only to destroy it in seconds.

Everyone who had ever looked into his mellow brown eyes knew he was no Dirty Harry. No one had ever had reason to be concerned about being slugged by him. And yet. He had certainly taken Terrence by surprise. Good thing Holt had walked away, or he probably would have experienced the full force of Terrence's wrath and been pummeled to within an inch of his life. Though of course you had to add in the fact that Terrence had been hampered by those Calvin Klein underpants stretched around his feet. Also: hard to give chase when your buttocks are out, not to mention other parts of the male anatomy no one likes to see.

Holt vividly remembered the events of that day. For a couple of weeks prior to the incident, he'd had a sinking feeling Leah was having an affair, but he hadn't been able to prove it to himself or to her, as she had been very careful. It had been little things, as is often the case: messages on her phone that elicited a slight smile, unexpected meetings in town with a friend, more attention paid to her appearance—new hairdo, new clothes, a change of perfume. It all led the detective to conclude she was seeing someone else.

So, he had taken a day off work and decided to follow her around—make sure his suspicions were unwarranted. As it happened, they weren't. They were right on the money. But when he saw her enter his own precinct, he had wondered if she was looking for him. That couldn't be the case, as he had specifically told her he was off that day. So he decided to see what she was up to. He had entered the precinct, and saw her enter Terrence's office. For a moment he had paused, wondering if he shouldn't leave well enough alone. But then he had told himself that she was probably discussing her husband's career with the boss. After all, Leah had often told him that he lacked ambition. That he should take the commissioner's exam and move up the ladder, like Terrence had done. But before he could turn back, one of his colleagues had gestured with his head in the direction of the commissioner's office and made the universal sign of people making love. There had been plenty of laughter, and he'd known that everyone was in on the big secret—except for him. And so he'd stormed into the office to find Terrence and Leah in a state of undress on top of the desk. In their haste to be together Terrence had forgotten to lock the door. Oops. He had just stood there, staring at the strange scene, having a hard time believing what his eyes were telling him, with the two of them staring back at him.

For a moment, it was as if time was frozen. Then finally, Leah had produced a nervous laugh, and time had sped up again, his limbs becoming unlocked. And so he had walked up to his boss, told him he was a bastard, and landed a punch on the man's stupefied face.

Then he had returned home, packed a suitcase, and left, feeling as if someone had put his heart in a vice and squeezed and squeezed until it was ready to pop.

And that's how the unraveling of Glen Holt had begun, ending with him chasing joyriding kids in Loveringem and sharing a house with his daughter.

Poppy parked the car on a quiet one-way street not far from the Coupure canal. Most of the houses were row houses that had seen better days, with paint peeling off the facades, gutters sagging, and sprigs growing through the roof. Even the street itself looked as if it could use a spruce-up, with rubbish strewn about and cracks in the pavement giving way to tree roots and clumps of grass. The house where the Elmaleh family lived looked particularly in need of urgent repair—especially the roof, which had plenty of tiles missing and whose chimney stack resembled the Leaning Tower of Pisa.

Holt steeled himself for the meeting, as delivering death messages wasn't the most pleasant of tasks. But he also knew that it was important for the people whose relatives had met a violent death to be informed by the police, and not by reading about it in the paper or seeing it on the local news.

Poppy locked eyes with him for a moment, and he nodded. She rang the bell and they waited patiently. Inside, there were the sounds of footsteps and kids being scolded. Before long, the door was yanked open, and a tired-looking middle-aged woman appeared, a scarf covering her head, giving them a look of suspicion. "Yes?" she asked, none too friendly.

Holt produced his badge and held it up, and so did Poppy. "I'm Chief Inspector Holt, and this is Inspector Poppy Holt," he said, making the introductions. "We would like to speak to Tamara Elmaleh."

"I am Tamara Elmaleh," said the woman, her look of suspicion intensifying.

"May we come in for a moment, Mrs. Elmaleh?" asked Poppy.

"Why?"

"I'm afraid we have some bad news for you."

"Bad news? What bad news?"

"It concerns your son Mohammed," said Holt.

The woman's face suddenly morphed into an expression of deep concern. "Mohammed? Why? Did something happen to him? Tell me!"

"Let's go inside," said Holt, and, not taking no for an answer, pushed past the woman and into the house, followed by his daughter, who murmured her apologies to Mrs. Elmaleh. Holt walked straight through to the kitchen, located at the back of the short corridor. He knew the layout of these houses like the back of his hand. All of them had been built along the same lines: a dark corridor with a staircase leading to a second floor where bedrooms and bathroom were located, a living room on the left or right of the corridor, and a kitchen at the back. The lucky ones had a postage-stamp-sized garden or paved courtyard, and that was it. Many of these families comprised several generations who shared the space with up to a dozen people, crammed into a home not designed for it.

The Elmalehs were no exception, and as Holt glanced through a door into the living room, he saw an ultra-wide television screen, kids playing a video game, some smaller kids playing on the floor, and an old man staring stonily ahead and smoking a cigarette. In the kitchen, he was met by several women wearing the same type of scarf as Mrs. Elmaleh, busy cooking. They looked up when he entered and

## FIELD OF BLOOD

seemed more than a little surprised, starting to talk very rapidly in Arabic, a language he didn't understand.

Tamara Elmaleh hurried in and replied in the same tongue and just as rapidly. The name Mohammed was mentioned, and then they all stared intently at him and Poppy, clearly expecting answers. He didn't feel comfortable addressing the gathering and asked if they could speak in private with Mrs. Elmaleh. She explained that these were her daughters and her sisters, and that whatever he had to say, he could say in front of them.

"I'm afraid something happened to your son, Mrs. Elmaleh," he said, deciding not to postpone the inevitable.

"What did he do now?" asked one of the other women, crossing her arms across her chest.

"Shut up, Aisha," said Mrs. Elmaleh. "Let the policeman speak."

"He's always up to no good," the woman insisted. "Always getting into all kinds of trouble."

"Shut up!" Mrs. Elmaleh insisted, giving Holt a desperate look. "Where is Mohammed?" she asked. "Why didn't you bring him if he did something wrong?"

"They arrested him, of course," said Aisha. "He's probably locked up in jail."

"Is that true?" asked Mrs. Elmaleh nervously. "Is he locked up in jail?"

"No, he's not locked up," said Holt. "He's... well, I'm afraid he's dead, Mrs. Elmaleh."

The woman's eyes went wide, and she brought her hands to her face. "No!"

"Dead? But how can that be?" asked Aisha. "He's too stupid to die."

"Aisha!" Mrs. Elmaleh screamed, and gave the woman a slap across the face. She buried her own face in her hands and started sobbing uncontrollably.

"What happened?" asked one of the other women.

"He and a friend hijacked a bus," said Poppy. "Out in Loveringem. They crashed the bus and fled the scene—ran away. We don't know what happened next, but Mohammed was killed."

"Noooo!" Mrs. Elmaleh screamed. "My boy! My sweet boy!"

"This doesn't sound like Mohammed," said Aisha with a frown. "He gets into trouble all the time, but he's never been killed before."

Holt stared at her, beginning to wonder what was wrong with the woman.

One of Mrs. Elmaleh's sisters had stepped forward and was hugging Tamara. More people were streaming into the kitchen: the old man who had been smoking a cigarette, the children, and also a young man who must have been upstairs. He looked a lot like the dead kid, and Holt suspected that he might be his brother.

"What's going on?" asked the young man.

"Mo is dead," said Aisha. "These people are from the police, and they say he was killed. In Loveringem, of all places," she added with a grimace.

"What was he doing in Loveringem?" asked one of the others present.

Before long, a sort of free-for-all broke out, with people talking over each other in both Dutch and Arabic. Holt wondered if perhaps they shouldn't come back some other time, when the house was less crowded, and they could sit down with Mohammed's mother and possibly get some more information out of her—like the identity of the kid's friend.

But then the young man ushered them out into a small courtyard and closed the kitchen door. "Okay, so can you tell me exactly what happened, please?" he asked. "I'm Mustafa," he added when Holt gave him a questioning look. "Mohammed's brother."

And so Holt repeated the statement they had made in the kitchen, only this time taking the opportunity to ask a few questions of his own.

"No, I don't know what Mo was doing in Loveringem," Mustafa admitted. "He must have taken the bus out there, as he doesn't have a car or even a driver's license."

"Can you tell us something about this friend of his?" asked Holt, taking out his phone to show Mustafa the picture he had taken of the bus's CCTV screen.

Mustafa took the phone and studied the picture for a moment, using his index finger and thumb to enlarge the image. Finally, he nodded. "That's Beni. Beni Idrissi. He's Mo's best friend. They've been friends for many years." He looked up. "He was also there? Stealing this bus?"

Holt nodded. "They both took the bus, and this kid was driving with Mo sitting next to him."

Mustafa shook his head. "Stupid. Neither of them have a driver's license."

"What can you tell us about this Beni Idrissi?" asked Poppy.

"Not much. His family lives nearby."

"Is he violent?" asked Poppy.

Mustafa frowned. "Violent? No, I don't think so. Why? Do you think he killed Mo?"

"We're still trying to figure out what happened exactly," said Holt. "At this moment, all we know is that your brother and Beni stole a bus, crashed it in a ditch, and then ran off. They didn't get far, as your brother was stabbed to death in a nearby field, and there's no trace of his friend, so he probably got away."

"I can't believe that Beni would kill Mo," said Mustafa, handing back Holt's phone. "He and Mo were great friends.

They did everything together, and I've never known Beni to be violent or even raise his voice. Always up to all kinds of mischief, though. This thing with the bus is just up his alley. My brother, not so much."

"Your brother wouldn't have approved, you think?"

"My brother was easily led," said Mustafa. "He didn't possess a very strong personality, I'm afraid. It often happened that Beni got him into trouble at school."

"What kind of trouble?"

"Oh, just your usual type of mischief," said Mustafa. "Throwing paper airplanes at the teacher, stealing their wallet. Stuff like that. Children's stuff, you know."

"Okay, if you can give us Beni's address, we will try and see if we can talk to him."

"I can't believe this is happening," said Mustafa, glancing through the kitchen door. In the kitchen, mayhem ruled, Holt saw, with Tamara Elmaleh having collapsed onto a chair. "Mo was my mother's favorite," he added softly. "In her eyes, he could do no wrong. She spoiled him rotten—which is probably why he got into so much trouble."

After Mustafa had given them any information he had on his brother's friend, they took their leave. Considering the state Mrs. Elmaleh was in, there was no point in trying to talk to her. Mustafa declined the assistance of a family liaison officer for the moment, assuring them that his mother would have all the support she needed.

Holt gave him his card and told him to contact him with any questions he might have or any information that might occur to him that could prove useful, and said he'd be in touch the moment he knew more.

As they stood on the sidewalk, Poppy let out a deep sigh.

"Well, that was quite the emotional rollercoaster," she said.

"You can say that again," said her dad, then glanced up at

the house. A man was studying them from an upstairs window. He looked a couple of years older than either Mustafa or Mohammed, and Holt wondered if this could be another brother. It was important that they got a more complete picture of the victim's family and his life before the tragic events that had played out in that field. But for now, the main thing was to find Beni Idrissi, and get him to talk.

## CHAPTER 7

Tamara's father-in-law seemed to be the only one who wasn't surprised by the terrible message the cops had delivered.

"I've always known he was bad news," he said, causing Tamara to resist the urge to give him a slap across the face, just as she had slapped her sister-in-law Aisha earlier.

"Mo was a good boy," she said. "The best. It's that Beni kid who's trouble. Always has been. *He's* the one who dragged Mo down with him."

"Do you think Beni killed Mo?" asked one of her sisters.

She hesitated. Even though she had never liked Beni, especially when he started pulling those pranks at school that got him and Mo into so much trouble, she found it hard to believe that he would have killed her son. They were best friends, after all.

Mo's sister Amine spoke up. "Beni would never hurt Mo. They were best friends since they were kids. Beni may have been a lot of trouble, but he's not a killer."

Mustafa seemed to agree with that. "Those detectives said that they're not sure what happened. All they know is that

Mo and Beni stole a bus and crashed it. Then they ran away, and Mo was killed. They didn't say that Beni killed him, though."

The family was gathered in the living room, and the gathering had taken on the nature of a family meeting, with everyone giving their opinion on what had happened or might have happened, as they didn't have a whole lot of information yet.

"When can we see Mo?" asked Tamara's husband Aamir. He hadn't been home when those detectives delivered the terrible news, and he was just as shaken as Tamara was. Mo had always been their favorite. Their youngest and their golden boy. Tamara had collapsed in front of those detectives and now felt sorry. She had missed her opportunity to ask the million questions cluttering her brain and causing her to experience the beginnings of a major headache. Good thing Mustafa had kept a cool head and had talked to them. He even had the main detective's phone number and would be able to call him.

"Call him now," she urged. "Ask him when we can see Mo. I want to see him—we all want to see him."

"*I* don't want to see him," said Aisha.

"Aisha!" Tamara said. "Not another word from you!"

"What? All I'm saying is that he's dead. And I don't like looking at dead bodies."

"That's my son you're talking about! My son!"

"I know it's your son, but he's dead, and I don't want to see him. Dead people freak me out."

"How would *you* know?" asked Mustafa. "When have you ever seen a dead person?"

"I saw a dead pigeon once," said Aisha with a shrug. "It was lying in the gutter. It looked terrible. With maggots crawling all over it. It was really yucky."

"My son is not a pigeon!" Tamara screamed.

She had to resist another urge to hit the woman, who had always been her least favorite of her sisters-in-law, but just at that moment her oldest son, Hassan, stuck his head in and announced, "I'm off."

"Where are you going?" she demanded. "Your brother died. You shouldn't be going out!"

Hassan merely grinned and retracted his head again. Moments later, the door slammed, and she saw his silhouette as he passed by the window, en route to who knows where.

"That boy will be the death of me," she said before she realized what she was saying. Then she abruptly burst into tears again, and this time she couldn't stop crying. If she had expected Aamir to console her, she had another thing coming. Instead, the head of the family gave her a stoic glance and announced, "I'm hungry. I want to eat now," before retreating to the kitchen and taking a seat at the kitchen table, expecting to be fed.

"I can't do it," Tamara said, shaking her head violently. "Not today. Not now!" She gave her sister a pleading look. "You do it."

"I'm not serving that man. He can serve himself. There's plenty of food."

But of course, it didn't work like that. Tamara's husband had never fed himself, and he wasn't going to start now, not even on the day that his youngest son had been murdered.

And so finally, Tamara got up from the table, dragged herself into the kitchen, and started ladling soup into a bowl, serving her husband of thirty years.

Instead of giving her the benefit of his thoughts or offering her consolation on what was surely the worst day of her life, he simply started eating his soup in silence.

She excused herself and returned to the living room, where a news bulletin had just started. The main topic was some political nonsense that interested no one, as was mostly the case, but finally the newscaster related the incidents that had taken place in Loveringem. They had even sent a reporter to the scene who had interviewed the bus driver and showed footage of the bus stranded by the side of the road. From a distance, they had also shot footage of what looked like a white sheet draped over a person lying in a nearby field, and mentioned that one of the kids who had taken the bus had died.

"That's Mo!" she cried, pointing to the screen. She turned to her son Mustafa. "Call that detective. Tell him I want to see my boy. Tell him I want to see him now!"

"Mom, it doesn't work like that," said Mustafa. "First they'll have to do a post-mortem, and only then will they let us see him."

"They cut them open," said Aisha with morbid satisfaction. "I've seen it on TV."

"A post-mortem?" Her stomach turned, and she suddenly felt violently sick. "But… they can't!"

She hurried to the bathroom and was sick all over the toilet. The thought of her boy being cut open—it was too much for her. Something no mother should have to endure.

"My boy," she cried desperately as she sank down next to the toilet bowl. "My sweet, sweet boy!"

Suddenly the door to the toilet was yanked open and Aamir stood before her, giving her a furious look.

"Pull yourself together, woman," he hissed as he yanked her to her feet. "This is no way to behave!"

"But our boy!" she wailed as he shook her. "Our boy is dead!"

"I know he's dead!" he growled, and forcefully dragged her from the toilet and then shoved her in the direction of the stairs. "Lie down and get a grip on yourself." He held up a threatening finger. "And don't come down again until you're able to act normal!"

She dragged herself up the stairs and moments later was dropping down onto the bed. It wasn't long before her daughter Amine quietly entered the room, carrying a cup of tea. She sat down on the bed and offered her mother the tea. Tamara took little sips and immediately felt a lot calmer.

"Do you want me to call the doctor?" asked Amine.

"No doctor," she said. It would only make Aamir even angrier than he already was. "I'll be all right."

Amine nodded, and Tamara saw she had tears in her eyes. The two women hugged, and Tamara realized that maybe Aamir had been right. If she broke down now, it would affect the entire family. She needed to be strong—for her children—for Mohammed. The next few days and weeks were going to test them as they had never been tested before. And so she cried for Mohammed and swore that it would be the last time.

From now on, she would be strong.

## CHAPTER 8

Holt hadn't held out a lot of hope that they would find Beni Idrissi at his domicile—the kid would have to be stupid to return home after stealing a bus and possibly getting into an altercation with his friend that had ended with Mohammed being stabbed to death. Then again, there was also the possibility that he wasn't clever enough to realize the police would come knocking on his door. Unfortunately, that wasn't the case, and even though they found the Idrissis, there was no trace of their son.

"What did he do this time?" asked Mrs. Idrissi, a sour-faced lady who looked particularly cross that her son's shenanigans had brought the police to her doorstep.

"He stole a bus in Loveringem," Poppy explained, deciding not to mention the fact that she also suspected him of possibly having murdered his friend.

"And crashed it into a ditch," Holt added, watching the woman's face carefully for any sign of subterfuge. When he saw none, he was satisfied that the kid hadn't returned home, or at least hadn't apprised his parents of what had transpired that morning.

"It's always the same thing," said Mrs. Idrissi. "Always getting into all kinds of trouble. And I blame his friends, you know, especially that no-good Mo Elmaleh."

"You think Mohammed Elmaleh is the one leading your son astray?" asked Poppy, not hiding her surprise. She had been taking notes, which she would add to the file they had started on the young man.

"Oh, absolutely," said Mrs. Idrissi. "He's part of a gang, you know, the Elmaleh boy. Involved with drugs and all kinds of illegal stuff. And I know for a fact that he has been trying to pull my son into his gang, but I've told Beni in no uncertain terms that if he ever brings any drugs into this house, he's dead to me."

"You believe that Mohammed Elmaleh is a drug dealer?" asked Poppy.

"Of course he is! He was dealing drugs to his classmates a couple of years ago and I'll bet he's still doing it now. But like I said, Beni is intelligent enough to know that he should never get involved with that kind of thing. And so he hasn't."

"But he and Mohammed are still good friends."

Mrs. Idrissi shrugged. "I thought Beni had learned his lesson, but clearly he hasn't, if he's going around stealing buses with Mo. But you can bet we'll have something to say to him when he comes home—his dad will put him straight. And if it's true that he's still hanging around with that no-good boy, we'll have to take measures."

Poppy frowned. "What kind of measures?"

"Oh, I don't know. Maybe send him to go and live with my sister in Canada for a year. Just to make sure he doesn't hang around with those kids anymore."

"Well, if he arrives home, please let us know," said Holt, giving the woman his card. He was pretty sure she would throw it in the trash the moment they left, but that couldn't be helped. He was determined to find Beni and ask him some tough questions—preferably before his parents shipped him off to Canada.

He and Poppy got into the car, and for a moment, neither of them spoke.

"We should organize a stakeout," said Poppy. "Make sure Beni doesn't escape us."

"To do that we would have to coordinate with the Ghent police," said Holt, who'd had the exact same thought. "And that means I'd have to talk to my old boss—who will definitely *not* grant my request."

"But he has to. We can't let this kid walk. He's a killer."

"A possible killer. We don't know for certain that he killed his friend."

"Then I'll do it," said Poppy decidedly. "Or maybe you can talk to the Commissioner, and he can arrange things with your old boss?"

Holt shook his head. "If Bayton knows that I'm in charge of the case, he'll find some excuse. No, if we're going to catch the Idrissi kid, we'll have to do it ourselves. And since we're now operating on Bayton's territory, we might get into a lot of trouble."

Or at least *he'd* get into a lot of trouble. The unspoken inference when he had been transferred to Loveringem was that he would never darken Commissioner Terrence Bayton's doorstep again, and organizing a stakeout a couple of hundred meters from Bayton's precinct wouldn't go unnoticed. Not that he minded crossing his old boss. But he didn't want to drag the rest of his team into the fray. They hadn't asked for this.

"We'll have to find another way to catch the kid," he said. "Let's gather more intel first. Both on what happened with the bus and the killing of Idrissi's buddy Mo. For one thing,

I'm interested in this drug dealer business Idrissi's mother was going on about just now."

Poppy glanced across at the Idrissi home one last time, and seemed annoyed that they couldn't simply stay put and wait for the kid to arrive home.

"We don't even know *if* he'll come home," said Holt. "He knows this is the first place we will look. He'll probably lie low for a while. Stay with a friend or a relative."

Poppy sighed. When she was on the hunt for a suspect, she was like a dog with a bone: extremely reluctant to let go. Which is what made her such an excellent detective. He smiled as she put the car in gear. She reminded him so much of himself it was uncanny.

"We'll catch him," he assured her.

She sighed again. "I sure hope so."

## CHAPTER 9

Mayor Jan Birt was in a meeting with his campaign manager, Gwendolyn Lopez, when the call came in that a bus belonging to his brother Teddy had been stolen.

"I'll get right on it," he assured Teddy.

"The police are already on it," his brother said. "In fact, they're all over it—combing my bus for evidence, impounding my CCTV equipment, taking fingerprints, and who knows what else."

Jan nodded. He could see this was problematic. "When will you get the bus back?"

"Soon, they said. And I sure hope they'll keep their promise. I can't afford this nonsense, Jan. I need my bus back in working order."

"I'll see what I can do to speed up the process," he promised his brother. "Any idea who the thief was?"

"Oh, just two teenagers. Probably taking it for a joyride. You know what kids are like. The problem is that they seem to have gotten into some kind of fight after they crashed the bus, and one of the kids ended up stabbing the other one to death."

Jan knitted his brows. "What are you talking about?"

"Murder, Jan! Right here in Loveringem!"

"And nobody's bothered to tell me?"

"I only found out just now. Though a camera crew has shown up, so the news will be all over the place pretty soon. You know what those vultures are like. And if they implicate Birt Travel in this nonsense... That's a lot of negative publicity we don't need."

"I'll talk to the Commissioner," he said, and hung up on his brother. This was a disgrace. He was the head of the police, after all, and he hadn't been told about a murder? What were those idiots thinking?

"What's going on?" asked Gwendolyn, who was seated on the edge of his desk.

"My brother's bus was stolen. Two kids. And then one of them killed the other."

"Oh, my God." But then her eyes started to glitter. "What kids?"

"No idea," said Jan, but he could see that she'd just had an idea. A bright one, if he knew her well. "What are you thinking?"

"We could use this, Jan. Kids stealing a bus, and then one of them killing the other? This could be right up our alley. Depending who the kids are, of course."

He nodded thoughtfully. He hadn't thought of that. It was true that if violence suddenly erupted in their peaceful little town, they could use it to drive a point of their campaign home: that as the mayor of law and order, he needed to pour more money into a camera network that would cover all of Loveringem territory, and also: more police on the streets, one of the mainstays of his campaign.

"Let me get the facts first," he said, and picked up his

phone again. Moments later, he was in communication with his Commissioner. "Ezekiel," he said warmly. "What's all this about a bus being stolen and a kid killed?"

"I was waiting until I had all the facts before bothering you," said Ezekiel. "But it's true. Two kids stole a bus, crashed it in a ditch, and then one of them probably stabbed his friend. Though we're not sure if that's exactly what happened. There weren't any witnesses to the stabbing. Plenty of evidence on the bus being jacked, though—CCTV footage and everything."

"Names of the kids?"

"Mohammed Elmaleh and Beni Idrissi. Both sixteen."

A big smile slid up the mayor's lips, and he gave Gwendolyn a thumbs up. "Moroccan?"

"Yes, living in Ghent."

"Who killed who?"

"Elmaleh is the one that ended up being stabbed to death. Single knife wound to the chest. But like I said, we're not sure if it was his friend who did it. We'll need to investigate further."

"Okay, you do that. But please keep me informed this time, all right? I had to find out about this from Teddy. Oh, and can you get him his bus back ASAP?"

"Will do," said the Commissioner.

He hung up and grinned widely at Gwendolyn. "Mohammed Elmaleh was stabbed to death, possibly by his friend Beni Idrissi. Two kids, up to no good, stole a bus and then got into a fight, and Mohammed ended up dead."

"This is some good stuff, Jan," said Gwendolyn. "We can work with this. In fact, it just might be the making of our campaign. A couple of immigrants invading our town and causing trouble? This will go down real well with our target demographic."

"I know," he said, rubbing his hands. "Four weeks before

the election, I couldn't have wished for a better way to launch our new campaign." He pointed to the young woman. "You get right on it, and I'll go out and talk to some of our constituents."

Gwendolyn leaned in and gave him a lingering kiss. He'd had his doubts about securing a second victory, especially after his name had been associated with some minor scandals these past couple of years, but this bus business was a godsend and might put them on the road to a second consecutive win. He could have kissed those two young punks for selecting his town to pull off their ill-advised stunt.

"Too bad for Teddy," said Gwendolyn.

"Oh, he'll get over it," he said with a wave of his hand. As long as the cops didn't mess around with his brother's bus and released it without delay. And with Ezekiel on the case, he was sure that wouldn't be a problem. And now that they had a murder to contend with, the bus jacking would soon be relegated to the background. A blip on the radar.

He grabbed his jacket from the coat stand, and with a spring in his step, he left Town Hall to go and talk to some of his voters. He'd always been a mayor of the people, who didn't lock himself up in an ivory tower but spent his time where the people were.

He had a good feeling about this.

## CHAPTER 10

Holt had returned to the station and was leaning over Rasheed's shoulder as the latter scrolled through the CCTV footage from the bus, now displayed on a bigger screen.

"They sure were having a great old time," Rasheed commented as he froze the screen on a frame of the kids laughing their heads off as they steered the bus along the deserted country roads.

"And yet, half an hour after this footage was shot, one of them was dead, a knife in his chest," Holt remarked as he studied the faces of both kids. And kids they were—sixteen, and already up to a whole lot of trouble.

"I can't imagine that the Idrissi kid would have stabbed his friend," Georgina said. "Look at how much fun they're having. Now, why would he suddenly turn around and plant a knife in his buddy's chest?"

Rasheed had reached the moment Mohammed had crashed the bus in the ditch, and both kids got off. Georgina was right. There was no friction between the duo at that moment. On the contrary, they seemed exhilarated by the adventure they were having, including the unfortunate end to their joyride.

"According to Beni's parents, Mohammed was the bad influence," said Poppy. "And according to Mohammed's parents, it was the other way around—Beni was the corrupting influence."

"What else did they say?" asked Leland.

"Well, Beni's mom claimed that Mohammed was a drug dealer, dealing drugs at school. And that she had tried to warn her son not to have any dealings with him. She was even considering sending him off to live with her sister in Canada for a couple of years, to make sure he was far away from Mohammed."

"Maybe Mohammed was trying to get him involved in his drug business again, and Beni wanted nothing to do with it?" Leland suggested. "And when Mohammed wouldn't take no for an answer, Beni ended up killing his friend?"

"Possible," Holt allowed. "But let's stick to the facts for now, shall we? Any luck finding a witness?"

Georgina shook her head. "Nope. We talked to an old guy on a bike who saw the bus pass him by, but he never saw it crash. And no other passersby that we could find. The nearest farm is a couple hundred meters away, and they hadn't seen anything either."

"And no cameras, of course," said Holt as he scratched his beard. He placed his hands on Rasheed's shoulders. He was their resident IT guy and all-around tech wizard. Even though regulations prescribed that every member of the detective division had to be well-versed in the technical aspects of the job and able to search a phone, Commissioner Forrester had decided that, for the purpose of expediency, it wasn't a bad idea to select one person to take all the courses and stay up to date on the latest. Since Rasheed had a natural aptitude for tech stuff, he had volunteered for the job.

"Any luck accessing Mohammed's phone, Rasheed?"

"Piece of cake," said the inspector. "Plenty of messages back and forth with his friend Beni. They were really close—chatted and messaged all the time. No sign of acrimony."

"Drugs?"

"Not that I could find," said Rasheed. "But they'd have to be stupid to use their regular phones to arrange drug deals. They'd know Big Brother is watching."

"Anything else?" asked Holt.

"Plenty of activity on the kid's social media but nothing that stands out. Just the usual stuff, you know. They were both into football in a big way. Followed plenty of the top footballers and were active in a football club in the Blaarmeersen. Amateur level, obviously. Though Mohammed seemed to have been the talented one."

"Anything on ANPR?"

"Our local ANPR network is still quite limited," said Rasheed. "We've only got the main roads equipped with cameras, and also the on-ramp onto the R4. I checked, but it's hard to find something if you don't know what you're looking for. Was the Idrissi kid on a motorbike, car? Did he use public transport? It's like looking for a needle in a haystack."

"Beni Idrissi was sixteen, like his friend," said Poppy. "So no car and no motorbike."

"He could have had a scooter," said Georgina. "Some of them have been tuned up and go faster than a car."

"Mustafa Elmaleh thought that his brother and Beni used public transport to get to Loveringem," said Holt. "So most likely that's what Beni used to get back."

"We should probably contact the Lijn," said Poppy. "Their buses have cameras."

"Some of their buses," said Leland. "Not all of them."

"Get on it," said Holt. "Check all the buses heading to

Ghent within our time frame. And you," he added for Rasheed's benefit, "keep looking. Even though he doesn't have a driver's license, it's still possible he made his way back to Ghent by car or bike."

"Or on foot," Poppy added.

"Or on foot. In which case he'll be much harder to track."

"Shouldn't we stake out the kid's place?" asked Leland.

Holt grimaced. It was a sore point. "That's what Poppy suggested. The problem is that it's not our jurisdiction, so we'd have to coordinate with Ekkergem police station."

Leland and Georgina exchanged a knowing glance. "Maybe you could leave things to the Commissioner?" Georgina suggested. "Ask him to liaise with Ekkergem? Have some of their people watch Beni's house and look for places where he might have gone to ground?"

"I don't know..." Holt said as he rubbed his neck. The less dealings he had with his old precinct, the better. Though he could certainly see the wisdom in Georgina's suggestion. "Okay, maybe I'll take it up with the Commissioner. It's a good idea."

"You know who else has been active on social media?" asked Jaime, who had been busy answering telephone calls from people wanting to know what was going on in their town. She turned her computer screen so the others could see. "Mayor Birt."

They all watched as a video message of the mayor walking through town played on the man's Facebook page. In it, he referred to the events of that morning, though he didn't name the kids specifically, but referred to them as 'scum' that had come to cause trouble in his town. He claimed he was going to make sure this sort of thing didn't happen again—if he was re-elected as mayor in October. He ended the message with a raised fist, declaring that he would use a big brush to wipe the streets of Loveringem clean of all the vermin.

"Disgusting," said Jaime, who obviously wasn't a big fan of the mayor. "The kid's body isn't even cold yet, and already Birt is using him to win votes."

"That's politics for you," said Leland.

"This is probably a golden opportunity for him," said Poppy. "He's running on a platform of law and order, after all. So this is exactly what he needed right now."

"Let's not get distracted by the mayor spouting his usual garbage," said Holt. "Let's focus on the case, shall we? We have one dead kid and one at large. It's important for their parents that we find out what happened, exactly. And get justice for Mohammed."

He steeled his resolve and set off towards his boss's office. Poppy and the others were right. The investigation had spread to Ghent, so it was important to organize some form of cooperation with his old colleagues. And since he wasn't the best man for the job, he'd leave it up to the Commissioner to decide how to proceed on that front.

With that, he knocked on Forrester's door, and walked in.

## CHAPTER 11

Beni Idrissi had been loitering across the street from his home. He'd seen the cops arrive—the plainclothes ones in their Renault Megane—and decided to wait them out, in case they returned to look for him.

He was still shocked by what had happened to Mo. Seeing him stabbed like that by that maniac still sent shivers down his spine. Who would do such a thing? An irate bike rider they had somehow crossed paths with during their crazy bus ride? Maybe they had cut him off at some point and hadn't noticed? The guy could have followed them and decided to get even. In other words: a psycho who saw red. So he'd come after them. An extreme case of road rage. Good thing Beni was light on his feet. Alhamdulillah for all that soccer training he and Mo had over the last couple of years. It had probably saved his life.

It had been a big dude, dressed in black leather from head to toe, his face obscured by that motorcycle helmet, so he had no idea what the guy actually looked like, and wouldn't be able to tell the cops anything. In other words: best to steer clear of the fuzz for now, especially since they would probably charge him with stealing that stupid bus.

In hindsight, it hadn't been one of his best ideas. But the bus had just been standing there, idling at the curb, and he hadn't been able to resist. And now Mo was dead—all because of him. Stupid!

He looked up when he heard a police siren, but the car simply zoomed through the street and didn't stop. He wondered if the cops would be back. They had been detectives, or else they would have been wearing police uniforms and driving a police car. That much he knew about the cops —after having run afoul of the local heat often enough.

They were probably investigating Mo's murder, which meant they'd definitely be back sooner or later. He hesitated, but then he made up his mind. He'd fill a bag with clothes and stuff and lie low for a couple of days—or weeks, if need be.

He could stay with Driss—he wouldn't mind if he crashed at his pad.

After glancing up and down the street one last time, he hurried across and let himself in with his key.

MAYOR BIRT WAS BACK in his office, still basking in the glow of his tour of the town center to gauge people's opinions about the events of that morning. He'd dropped by the Hol of Pluto café and had paid for a round for all the patrons, which had been well received. He had mingled and had a beer at the bar, engaging those present in conversation. As he'd expected, the news had already spread, and everyone was aware that Teddy's bus had been stolen that morning and one of the kids had been found dead.

All of them had urged the mayor to do more to make sure

that something like this never happened again, though they had used more saucy language to convey their opinions. The words 'scum' and 'riff-raff' had been freely bandied about, and those were some of the friendlier terms. All in all, it had solidified his gut feeling that this was a rich vein that he should tap to the absolute max.

His personal assistant, Justine Hallett, walked in now—he wasn't allowed to call her his secretary anymore, much to his dismay—and she seemed less than pleased as she approached his desk. "I've seen your latest video, Jan," she announced, fixing him with a look of distinct displeasure, which he decided to ignore.

"Great stuff, huh?" he said. "A thousand views already and plenty of likes and shares. I have a feeling this one is about to go viral in a big way."

"I would very much advise you against using such language," said Justine as she pursed her lips disapprovingly.

He sighed. Justine had been his personal assistant for fifteen years, and in that time they'd traversed a lot of rough terrain. He had been a candidate for the Liberal Party with some success before changing allegiances to Flemish Front, hoping to become their frontrunner, which he had. If it hadn't been for Justine, he'd never have been able to become mayor, and he knew that and was grateful for it. But lately, she had developed this cautious streak that he found positively offensive.

"Okay, so what is it now?" he asked as he settled back.

"The kid isn't even buried yet and already you're accusing him of all kinds of stuff! Telling people that he's scum and filth and vermin and who knows what else."

"He came here to steal my brother's bus. What else can I call him? A model kid? To be admired by all?"

"He was just a kid, Jan. He stole a bus and had a joyride. That doesn't make him a monster."

"Well, the fact that he was subsequently knifed to death by his friend tells a different story." He pointed a finger in her direction. "Rumor has it that both kids were involved with drugs. That tells me this wasn't some innocent bus ride in the countryside. They were probably doped up to their eyeballs. This could have ended badly. They could have taken that bus into town and smashed it into a school or a shop, killing dozens."

She shrugged. "Well, they didn't. All they did was end up in a ditch."

"Oh, come off your high horse, Justine," he said viciously. "I don't know what's gotten into you lately. Do you *want* me to win the next election or not? Because if you don't, now is the time to say so."

She fixed him with a withering look, then shook her head and stalked out. But not before shouting, "Tone it down, Jan —before the kid's parents file a complaint against you!"

She slammed the door, leaving him seething with resentment. He had half a mind to fire her on the spot and find himself a replacement.

The door opened again, and he was about to launch into a stream of particularly snarky vituperation, touching on such topics as loyalty and respect, when he saw that it wasn't Justine but Gwendolyn who had entered.

Immediately his irritation dissolved, and he greeted her with a grateful smile. At least he had one ally in this godforsaken place. And when she locked the door behind her and gave him a lustful look, his mood changed for the better. In the few paces she needed to reach his desk, she had already shed her blouse and was displaying the pink lacy bra he had bought her on the occasion of their first anniversary, just a couple of days ago.

By the time she reached him, he was already divesting himself of his own shirt and felt the stirrings of the kind of hot and sweaty passion he hadn't known since he was a spotty and hormonal teenager.

He had the decency to turn down the framed picture of his wife and son on his desk before he and Gwendolyn got down to business, right on top of the mayoral desk.

## CHAPTER 12

Justine was still fuming when she reached her office. It hadn't escaped her attention that Gwendolyn had entered Jan's office moments after she had left. Part of the reason she was so upset with Jan was that he had been engaging in a romantic relationship with his campaign manager for months now. Neither of them thought she knew, but of course she did. She sat down heavily behind her desk and wondered, not for the first time, if perhaps it wasn't high time she finally decided to call it quits and start looking for another job.

Fifteen years she had spent by Jan's side—through the bad times and the good—but enough was enough. It was humiliating. There was no other word for it. Humiliating and disrespectful to simply cast her aside like a worn-out rag. As if she hadn't loved him all those years and shared his life—not in an official capacity, of course. He had his wife for that. But everyone knew that she had been his life's companion. More so than Anjanette. Justine had taken trips with Jan to faraway places like Burma and Indonesia. They'd shared hotel rooms during all of those trips, and he had spent more time in her apartment than he had in his own home over the years.

And now he had simply cast her aside. She should have known that Gwendolyn was trouble from the moment she laid eyes on the woman. She had recognized the signs when the PR expert joined the team. Gwendolyn hadn't hidden her fascination with Jan and had gone straight for the jugular, completely taking him in. Now it was her apartment where he spent time, and the side of Justine's bed where Jan used to lie had been cold for months.

She was staring out of the window when her phone chimed. She picked it up from her desk to see that it was Anjanette. She answered before she could change her mind. "Anjanette?" It was rare for Jan's wife to call her. They Both knew the score, and over the course of many years had reached a sort of understanding—the wife and the mistress.

"Can we meet? I'm at the Pussycat."

She hesitated, then decided that maybe this wasn't such a bad idea after all. "I'll be there in five minutes." She picked up her purse and left the office, but not before locking it carefully. It wouldn't be the first time Gwendolyn poked around in her private affairs, and she wouldn't put it past the woman to nose around in her desk drawers looking for any dirt she could find on her rival.

With resolute steps, she high-tailed it out of Town Hall and across the cobblestone square to the Pussycat, one of many coffee shops that had sprung up around the small medieval square. Located in the heart of town, the square attracted quite a lot of tourists, as it was still pretty much as it had been for the past hundred years, with the picturesque Town Hall on one side, the steepled church on the other, and plenty of little shops, tea rooms, cafés, and restaurants in between.

It wasn't Bruges or Ghent, or the Brussels Grand-Place,

but it was still very popular and absolutely thriving. Teeming with life just as it must have done in medieval times.

Once upon a time, there had been plenty of other, less touristy businesses, but these had mostly been pushed into the side streets leading to the central square: butchers, bakeries, clothing stores, and whatnot. All in all, it was a lively, pleasant environment to work in, and she would miss it if she gave her notice and found gainful employment elsewhere—preferably as far removed from Loveringem and its mayor as possible.

She walked into the Pussycat and spotted Jan's wife at a table near the door. She walked right over and gave the woman a faint smile, wondering once again whether this was a good idea.

"Justine," said Anjanette, who was looking quite refined as usual. Dressed in designer clothes, her hair coiffed to perfection, and her face as wrinkle-free as a forty-eight-year-old woman with plenty of money to spend on beauty salons and the occasional visit to the plastic surgeon could manage.

In that respect, she could have been Justine's lookalike, if not for the fact that Justine was ten years Anjanette's junior, something that hadn't escaped Jan's attention when she first joined his team, which had led to a torrid romance within weeks of their meeting.

And now the roles had been reversed. Jan had dumped Justine and shifted his allegiance to Gwendolyn, who was exactly the same age Justine had been when she had started her affair with the politician. The irony of it all hadn't escaped Justine's notice.

She took a seat and ordered a coffee.

"You look tired," said Anjanette.

"I *am* tired," she said, giving a brief grimace. "Election coming up. You know what it's like."

"Jan working you to the bone again?"

"Something like that."

Anjanette waited patiently as the waiter placed Justine's coffee in front of her and moved out of earshot. "Tell me about Gwendolyn."

"Capable campaign manager," said Justine as she took a sip from her coffee. "Ambitious. Driven. Talented and with her fingers on the pulse. TikTok savvy."

"I know Jan is having an affair with her, Justine."

She stared at her former rival. Over the years, a sort of truce had been established between the two women, even though they had never openly acknowledged it. But Anjanette had had plenty of opportunities to divorce her cheating husband, and she hadn't. This led Justine to assume that Anjanette must have accepted the situation and was fine with it. Every time they had met during one of the many official engagements Jan attended with Anjanette and where invariably Justine was also present—some reception, barbecue, or opening of an exhibit—Anjanette had never given any indication of hating Justine. On the contrary, the two women had established an understanding. They even enjoyed the occasional shopping trip and visit to the hairdresser. It was probably too much to say they were close friends, but they were friendly, which to any observer was quite unusual and to some bordered on the obscene and perverse.

Justine had always assumed that after being married to Jan for twenty-five years, Anjanette had simply tired of catering to her husband's sexual whims and decided that the shop was closed, letting another woman take over that side of her married life. She had asked Jan about it, but he had always shut down any discussion of his wife, claiming it was a topic best left untouched. Let sleeping dogs lie, was his personal opinion.

He was probably right. While Anjanette might look like a placid and sweet-tempered woman, she had another side that was quite vicious, capable of lashing out in ways that had often shocked Jan. Once, during one of their many arguments, she had even bitten him on the arm, leaving a scar that was still faintly visible to this day.

These days, there were no arguments and no passion in their marriage. The marital bed had seen no activity for many years, that role having been taken up by Justine and now Gwendolyn.

"You don't have to protect him, Justine," said Anjanette, gazing at her placidly across the table. "I know, all right. I've seen them together. I've seen the looks, the little gestures, the conspiratorial smiles. I know."

Justine nodded. "It's true. He's left me for Gwendolyn."

"When did it start?"

"About a year ago? Maybe a little less, since Gwendolyn only joined us a year ago. So maybe eleven months? Ten? Something like that."

"He always was a fast worker."

"He was—he is."

"How long had you been working for him before you started seeing each other?"

Justine swallowed. This was not a topic she cared to discuss with her former lover's wife. "Maybe we shouldn't—"

"I still remember your predecessor. He wasn't in politics back then, but worked for his dad's bus company. Jack-of-all-trades: driver, mechanic, salesperson. Just like Teddy. One day, this girl started working for them. She was a mechanic, which was unusual for a woman at the time. She was young and pretty, and before long, rumors started circulating that Jan was having an affair with her. They used to disappear from time to time, and when they returned, they both looked… exhilarated. Excited. Like schoolkids who had done something naughty." She made an ineffectual gesture. "You know what I mean."

Justine nodded. She knew exactly what Anjanette meant. It had been the same way with her and Jan those first couple of months—sneaking off in the middle of the day for a quickie at her apartment or in the back of Jan's car. It had been exciting and fun.

"I was pregnant with Jayson at the time and didn't spend a lot of time at the bus company—I was in charge of admin back then—and so Jan had free rein. Or so he thought. Then at one point, Teddy decided that enough was enough—or Teddy's wife did, more likely—and they got rid of the girl, much to Jan's disappointment."

"I didn't know that," said Justine, feeling more and more uncomfortable with how the conversation was progressing. It's one thing to have an affair with a married man and quite another to discuss it in graphic detail with the man's wife.

"No, of course not. Jan never mentions his old mistresses to the new ones. Same way Gwendolyn more than likely isn't aware of you."

"Oh, I think she is. She's pretty sharp." Not to mention wily.

"I've thought about divorcing him many times, you know," said Anjanette, continuing down a path that, in Justine's estimation, would inevitably lead to more awkwardness and embarrassment for the both of them. "But in the early years, I had Jayson to think of, and then after my operation, I simply couldn't be bothered anymore."

"Operation?" She knew she shouldn't ask, but she couldn't help but feel a certain morbid curiosity. Why was Anjanette choosing to discuss their private lives? Why now, after having stayed silent about it for the past fifteen years?

"I'm not surprised that Jan never mentioned it. Shortly after Jayson was born, I developed a particularly aggressive case of endometrial cancer. I had a hysterectomy, and they also removed my cervix and my ovaries. It was a pretty invasive procedure, and I ended up suffering a lot of pain every time Jan and I tried to…"

"God, I had no idea," said Justine.

"In the end, he decided that if he couldn't get his jollies with me, he might as well get them elsewhere, and that's when he started playing away even more than he had before. Even though he didn't tell me, and he was very discreet about it, I decided that maybe it was all for the best. As a wife, I couldn't give him what he wanted or needed, and so it was only right that he would get it from another woman—or women."

"Oh, Anjanette, but that's awful."

"It wasn't a lot of fun," Anjanette said with a wry smile. "But Jayson kept me busy and I had the household to manage. And then after a couple of years, I decided to go back to work, and I derived a lot of enjoyment from that. So even though it was tough, I learned to live with it. With the lack of intimacy, I mean. Which is why I never resented you."

Justine stared at the woman. "I—I don't know what to say."

"It's fine," said Anjanette, placing a hand on Justine's and giving it a light squeeze. "I've always liked you and thought that Jan had made a terrific choice." She took a deep breath. "Unfortunately, I wish I could say the same thing about Gwendolyn."

"I despise her," said Justine viciously before she could stop herself. "She's a horrible little trollop."

Anjanette stared at her. "You see? You and I are exactly the same. We even have the same opinion about Jan's mistress. I also thoroughly despise the girl. To the extent that for the first time in years, I'm starting to consider divorcing the man. Jayson is in college now, and soon he won't need me anymore as he strikes out on his own. And Jan certainly doesn't need me—hasn't needed me in a long time. So I find myself thinking, why stay, you know? I might be better off on my own."

"I'm thinking the same thing," Justine confessed.

"You'd quit working for Jan?"

"I would. Like you, he doesn't need me anymore, and he's made it clear on more than one occasion that he finds my presence more of a nuisance than a blessing."

"He's got Gwendolyn now," said Anjanette. She offered Justine a vague smile. "I knew this was a good idea—us having a little chat. We should do it more often."

"Maybe we should."

"You can keep me informed of what my husband is up to while I make all the arrangements to get rid of him." When Justine gave her a strange look, she laughed. "Legally, I mean. Make sure I get as much out of this divorce as I put into the marriage."

"And while I start looking for a new job," she said, surprised at how uplifted she suddenly felt when considering that notion—how unexpectedly cheerful.

"You do that. And make no mistake, honey. Jan might think that he doesn't need you anymore, but the moment you quit, he'll find out how much he has relied on you over the years. In fact, it's not too much to say that you have been the making of that man."

"He won't know what hit him," said Justine.

They shared a conspiratorial smile, raised their cups, and clinked them in a toast.

"This just might be the beginning of a beautiful friendship," said Anjanette, and in spite of her initial misgivings, Justine couldn't have agreed more.

## CHAPTER 13

As Anjanette set foot for the homestead—after a quick detour at the supermarket to pick up some scampi—she realized she was pleasantly surprised by how well the conversation had gone. She had dreaded it to some extent, though clearly not as much as Justine. She hadn't lied. She could actually see a future where she and her husband's ex-mistress became good friends. They already were good acquaintances, but it was always nice to have a friend—or even an ally—especially if she was going to divorce Jan.

She hadn't mentioned this to Justine, but she was worried about her husband in more ways than one. Until recently, he'd been fully dependent on Anjanette, as her family had always supported and funded his political career. The Atkinsons were a rich family of industrialists, with Anjanette's dad having made his fortune in the shipping and container handling trade. So when Jan had decided to go into politics, Bo Atkinson had backed him and continued to do so even when he switched allegiances from the Liberal Party to Flemish Front. If Daddy found out that Jan had been unfaithful to his wife over the years, he'd turn off the spigot, and Jan would be left to his own devices.

Though Anjanette had the impression he didn't care, as Teddy had replaced the Atkinsons as the main donor of his campaign. It struck Anjanette as odd that Birt Travel would suddenly have become so flush with cash they could afford to sponsor Jan to the tune of hundreds of thousands of euros on a continual basis, as they kept the campaign going even between elections, pushing Jan as one of the Flemish Front mainstays.

She had a sneaking suspicion that Jan had decided to launch himself into national politics—as a major force of Flemish Front. One of the big contenders for a seat in the Flemish government—or even the federal one. And his new campaign manager had a lot to do with that, feeding his ambition, just as Teddy fed his campaign war chest.

Which begged the question: where was Teddy suddenly getting all of his money from?

It wasn't long before she arrived home. She parked her Tesla in the driveway, grabbed her purse and shopping bag from the passenger seat, and walked up to the house. If she divorced Jan, he'd be the one who'd have to move out, as the house had been paid for with her dad's money. Maybe he could move in with Gwendolyn, if he loved her so much.

She smiled. When a mistress suddenly becomes a wife, she might discover that Jan wasn't an easy person to live with, and her fervor would probably take a major hit. Maybe he might even cheat on her the way he had cheated on Anjanette. Karma was a bitch.

She let herself in and saw her son's head pop up over the upstairs balustrade.

"Did you see Dad's new campaign video?" asked Jayson. At twenty-one, he was looking more and more like his dad did at that age, before Jan had gone to seed—lanky and too

FIELD OF BLOOD

handsome for his own good. Lucky for her, he hadn't inherited some of Jan's more offensive traits, like a total lack of moral compass. On the contrary, Jayson was the most caring and responsible young man she knew, but then she had pretty much raised him herself while Jan was busy building his career as a politician to be reckoned with.

"No, I didn't." And frankly, she wasn't all that interested in seeing it either. "Why? Something special about it?"

"Oh, he's only calling those kids that stole the bus filth and scum and whatever other name he could come up with." He pounded the balustrade. "The man is evil, Mom. Pure evil!"

"Some kids stole a bus?" she asked. Clearly, she wasn't as up to date on the news as she could have been.

He rolled his eyes. "It's only the biggest story, Mom! Two kids stole one of Uncle Teddy's buses this morning, then crashed it and made a run for it, only for one of them to stab the other one to death."

She stared at her son. "What?"

"Murder, Mom. One kid murdered the other, and now Dad is trying to use it for his campaign, insinuating that they were drug dealers and that he's going to take care of things when he gets re-elected, and yadda yadda. You know, the usual stuff."

"I see," she said, and she did. Obviously, this was more evidence that Jan's new campaign manager was doing a pretty good job wrapping her husband around her little finger. Maybe she should get these divorce proceedings going sooner rather than later. Make sure she had nothing to do with this new version of Jan Birt and Flemish Front, which was getting more and more racist and obnoxious by the day.

"Can't you tell him to stop?" asked Jayson, still leaning over the balustrade. She laughed a mirthless laugh, and

Jayson smiled. "No, I didn't think so. He doesn't listen to anyone, does he, that wretched man?"

"He listens to his campaign manager," she said. She had almost said 'his mistress' but managed to refrain from doing so. Fortunately, Jayson wasn't aware of that part of his dad's personality. If he was, he probably would dislike him even more.

"Shall I start dinner?" she suggested, the topic of her husband's dreadful political campaign videos already making her slightly nauseous. Ever since he had switched allegiance from the Liberal Party to Flemish Front, he had started utilizing more polarizing and offensive language, and it seemed to be getting worse as the years went on. Pretty soon he'd morph into a full-blown fascist if this kept up.

She entered the kitchen and opened the fridge, drawing inspiration from the food items on display. It was just the two of them tonight, as Jan had already told her he'd be eating in town with some of his party sponsors.

She didn't mind. She was just happy that Jayson was home and that she got to spend some quality time with him. Ever since he'd gone off to college, those moments had become far and few between, so she had learned to treasure them.

UPSTAIRS IN HIS ROOM, Jayson rewatched the video of his dad's little speech and got worked up all over again. He had never had a lot of affection for his dad, but lately he found himself resenting the man more and more—the word 'hate' had even occurred to him from time to time. Especially when he posted stuff like this, which could have come from the mouth of any unhinged right-wing agitator.

He finally ended the video and surfed his feed. Plenty of anti-Flemish Front memes, some of them mocking his dad.

He laughed loudly at a particularly good one, where his dad was depicted with a Hitler mustache and haircut, railing against 'scum,' 'filth,' and 'riff-raff,' the way his dad often did.

He gave the meme a like, then changed it to a heart. His dad probably wouldn't like it if he knew that his son was batting for the opposition party, but then he probably didn't care. As long as Jayson didn't openly support the opposition he wouldn't even notice.

He sat back and thought for a moment. Now wouldn't that be something? If he became a candidate for the opposition? But just as quickly as the idea had occurred to him, he dismissed it again. It would only turn into one big circus. The media would jump on it, and he'd be forced to give interviews, and his studies would suffer. Besides, he wasn't a big fan of the opposition party either, who, in his opinion, were equally responsible for wrecking Loveringem as Dad had over the past six years.

No, he wasn't going to vote at all this time. Instead he'd boycott the election.

Not a single candidate deserved his support.

AT THE SAME moment that Jayson closed his laptop in disgust over the fiery campaign video his dad had launched, Wanda Desai, chairwoman of the local branch of the Liberal Party, stared at the same video in dismay on her phone. She had just left a meeting of her party's campaign team at their local headquarters off Town Square, and one of her campaigners had sent it to her. "My God," she murmured as she watched the number of likes and shares rise by the second. Hundreds of comments had already been posted underneath the video, most even more outrageous and obnoxious than the video itself.

A set look settled around her mouth as she sent a message

to the campaigner that they needed to post a response video, distancing themselves from the terrible rhetoric the mayor was using. They needed to point out that there was such a thing as common decency when dealing with a tragic event like the one that had taken place that morning.

Even though she had launched Jan Birt in local politics years ago, he had quickly proven himself a force to be reckoned with, displaying a tendency to grandstand and trample over his coalition partners. He had served as an alderman under her tenure as mayor but had quickly decided that he wanted to go for the mayoral sash in the next election. When she had refused to step down and give him the top position when the new election lists were being drawn up, he had quit the party and joined the then-opposition party of Flemish Front, quickly making a name for himself by organizing a pretty ruthless opposition. Every single decision she made, he opposed. And as if that wasn't enough, he also launched a vicious campaign against her on social media, trying to tarnish her reputation by painting her as soft on crime, a weak leader and tainted by corruption. Wanda's husband ran a real estate agency, and Jan had suggested a conflict of interest.

It had worked, and in the last election, he had beaten her and become the first mayor in the history of Flemish Front—a breakthrough, as the party had been locked out of power across all of Flanders since its inception in the late seventies. And now they were going for round two—or three. Only this time her advisors had told her that maybe she should take the gloves off and get down and dirty with the man. Give as good as she got. Launch attack videos against Mayor Birt and his policies every chance she got.

She had refused, arguing that if you got down in the mud with the pigs, you got dirty, and the pigs would love it. Birt's entire style was combative and hateful. If she lowered herself to the same level, he would probably win, and she would end up looking stupid.

No, she was not going to rise to the bait. Instead, she would focus on her own strengths and those of her party: humanity, togetherness, community spirit and plenty of initiatives that would improve the everyday lives of the people who lived in Loveringem. It was the only way she wanted to do politics and still be able to look at herself in the mirror.

She tucked her phone away and picked up her pace. Her car was parked right around the corner, and when she reached it, she saw to her dismay that someone had kicked off her rearview mirrors on both sides and had keyed the paintwork all along the side.

For a moment, she felt tears well up.

But then she decided to be strong and instead took a couple of pictures for her insurance and dialed 100.

She glanced up at the camera located right behind her. It wasn't the first time her car had been targeted by Jan Birt's followers, which was why she had started parking in places where she knew a camera was located.

Hopefully, the police would catch the vandals.

# CHAPTER 14

Jan Birt was washing his hands in the private bathroom attached to the mayor's office when his phone belted out a familiar ringtone. It was from *Der Ring des Nibelungen* and warned him that Daron Topley was trying to reach him.

He sighed, took his time drying his hands, and headed into his office to pick up the phone.

"Daron," he said curtly. Lately, he and the Flemish Front leader hadn't always seen eye to eye, and he had a vague idea of where this conversation was headed.

"I just saw your latest stunt," said Daron, who didn't sound happy. "I thought we agreed to run a clean campaign this time? No over-the-top nonsense?"

"All I did was point out that if these thugs think they can come to Loveringem, start dealing and stealing and murdering each other, they've got another thing coming. I don't condone that kind of nonsense in my town."

"I want you to remove the video," said Daron. "It doesn't conform to the platform we agreed on during the election congress."

"It's got three thousand likes!"

"I don't care. Get rid of it. It's going to get us in trouble with the anti-racism campaigners eager to prove that Flemish Front is a party of racists. We agreed to clean up our act, and that's exactly what we're going to do."

"But—"

"You don't run this party, Jan. I do. Is that understood? Now get rid of the video, or you can start looking for a different party to represent."

With those words, Daron ended the call.

Silently fuming, Jan considered whether to comply or not. Daron had issued a clear threat: take down the video, or I'll replace you as our candidate. Could he do that? He picked up his phone again and, moments later, was speaking to Gwendolyn.

"Can you come to my office? We've got a problem."

When Gwendolyn walked in, he noticed she had already changed her dress. During their earlier extracurricular activities in his office, it had become crumpled and stained, and she had giggled while gently scolding him for ruining her outfit. "Good thing I always keep a dress in my office," she had said. He was glad, too, because this one was even more stunning than the last and really showcased her striking figure.

For a moment, he was too mesmerized to remember why he had summoned her to his office. Then it came back to him.

"Um... I just got off the phone with Daron, and he wants us to take down the video."

"You can't do that," she said immediately, showing just how much they were on the same page. "It's already the most successful and shared video we've ever posted. It might even go viral and give a great boost to our campaign."

"That's what I told Daron, but he says the party needs to

clean up its act and stay away from anything that might create controversy."

She scoffed. "Stay away from controversy? Doesn't he know that courting controversy is the only way to attract attention in a crowded marketplace? We need to stand out. And the only way to do that is by creating videos that have the potential to go viral."

"He says he'll replace me as a candidate if I don't comply. Can he do that?"

"I doubt it. The election is four weeks away. The lists have all been made, the posters and flyers printed. Also, you're one of the most visible and popular figures in the party, Jan. As the first elected Flemish Front mayor, you're a legendary figure. He knows that if he replaces you, it'll kick up a storm of major proportions. Not to mention that any candidate he replaces you with isn't going to win the next election, and the electorate and the party members will blame him. So if I were you…"

"Yes?"

"I'd keep that video online."

He nodded slowly. He'd been thinking the same thing. "He won't be happy."

"Of course he won't. But I think we both agree that Daron is taking the party down the wrong track. And if we don't stand up to him, he'll drag us down with him. Already, the polls are predicting a significant defeat for Flemish Front, except for the Loveringem branch. So chances are, Daron will be the one being replaced if he fumbles this election."

He liked what she was saying. Even though he'd never been a brave man, he instinctively felt she was probably right about Daron being the one whose future was in jeopardy, while he had the wind in his sails. He'd already gotten messages from Flemish Front mayoral candidates in other towns asking if they could use the video on their own social media, so he knew he was onto something good here.

It still made him slightly nervous to be in direct conflict with the party leadership. But Gwendolyn was right. They weren't going to risk replacing him at the eleventh hour, especially as he was one of the party's most visible and popular candidates. Getting rid of him now would only cause a massive storm of protest among the party's members, who saw him as a rising star at the national level.

"Okay, we'll leave the video up for now. And see what happens over the next twenty-four hours."

"I think you should double down on this," said Gwendolyn. "Make more videos. Post one a day for the next couple of days. As long as the police haven't caught this second kid, stoke that fire. Go for broke. This is a godsend, Jan. An absolute gift for us, and we should milk it for everything it's worth. I can promise you right now that this is going to crush the opposition and turn you into the most popular mayor this town has ever seen."

Her eyes were glittering with excitement, and it was infectious to the extent that he found himself nodding along as she outlined her vision for the next four weeks: go from strength to strength, whip up Jan's followers until they swept him to an absolute majority. That way, he wouldn't even need to find any coalition partners and could rule undisputed—like a local god.

"I like your thinking," he said. He closed the distance between them. "I like all of you."

She smiled seductively. "You're not thinking about ruining my second dress, are you? I don't keep a third one in my closet, you know."

"We could nip over to your place for an hour after lunch?"

"Now you're talking."

He briefly glanced at the door, then risked pressing a

passionate kiss to her lips. God, what he wouldn't give to put her up on his desk for round two. But even he knew they should be careful. He was running on a family-values platform, after all. If word got out that the family man was cheating on his wife with his campaign manager, it would cost him plenty of votes.

So he restrained himself and watched her sashay out of his office, even as he tamped down the primal urges she stirred in him.

His phone belted out another ringtone—this time the theme from *The A-Team*—and he picked up.

"Ezekiel. What's new?"

In a few words, the Commissioner gave him an update on the state of the investigation into the bus hijacking and the death of Mohammed Elmaleh. The most interesting part was that the two kids had grown up together and lived in the same neighborhood, one rife with crime and drug-dealing mayhem. And now Beni was suspected of having murdered Mohammed on Loveringem soil. You couldn't make this stuff up.

He was already planning his next video. It was going to be a real doozy.

## CHAPTER 15

In Hol of Pluto, the café where all Flemish Front supporters liked to gather, André Wiel checked his phone to see if more videos had appeared on Mayor Birt's Facebook. The last one had attracted a lot of attention and provoked excited discussion among André's fellow Flemish Front adherents. They all agreed the mayor was finally taking the gloves off and saying what they all felt: that Loveringem belonged to people like them and that outsiders, like those two kids, should stay away if they knew what was best for them.

André hoped more videos would appear, and since he'd liked and shared all of the mayor's videos so far, he'd even received a message saying he was one of the mayor's biggest fans and had earned himself a badge. A badge of honor, as far as he was concerned, and he was proud of it. He'd told all of his drinking buddies at the café. It was true that he was one of Flemish Front's biggest fans. He wore a pin on his lapel, had stickers festooning his car, and posters in the windows of his home. He had even put a placard on the roof of his house, tied to the chimney, so nobody would get it into their nut to tear it down or spray-paint anti-Flemish Front slogans on it, as often happened.

Mom didn't always agree with the level of participation he was prepared to display, but that couldn't be helped. As he'd told her many times, he was working for a better future for all of Loveringem—for his kids and grandkids. If not for Flemish Front, their way of life would soon be a thing of the past. In other words: what he did was important.

He drained his beer and got up a little unsteadily. He wasn't normally in favor of getting drunk in the middle of the day when he still had a couple of hours of work left, but after that video, one of the guys at the café had bought a few rounds to celebrate, and he hadn't been able to refuse.

He walked to the door, followed by loud words of encouragement from one of his buddies at the bar. He raised a fist in acknowledgment and turned up his collar. September was often a balmy time of year and could even be warm, but the last couple of days had been rainy and cold—a definite nip in the air and a feeling of fall. He didn't mind. Fall was his busiest time, with all the leaves that needed to be collected across Loveringem's territory. Employed by the parks department, he mostly took care of the greenery. Since Loveringem prided itself on being one of the greenest towns in the region, he never stinted for work. In the springtime, all the entrance roads to the town were a riot of color from the impressive flower displays, which took a lot of work to maintain and water during the summer months.

André loved his job. It was varied, and he got to spend most of his time outdoors. Being cooped up in an office would have done nothing for him. Even though a lot of people looked down on the parks department, figuring they were a bunch of untrained ruffians on the same level as sanitation workers, he had never seen it that way. The only issue he had was that many of his colleagues were immigrants. But even they weren't all bad. He liked Ayoub, for one, and even counted him as a friend—which was quite amazing when you thought about it. But then he figured Ayoub was different from the immigrants he objected to. Ayoub was one of the good ones—the exception to the rule.

He passed the Town Hall parking lot on his way back to the parks department compound, and before long, he was riding around with his cart, picking up the leaves that had dropped in the park adjacent to Town Hall. Tonight, he was going out again with the mayor's campaign team, putting up posters and pasting over the posters of the opposition. In other words: the usual fun and games. They'd paste over the opposition's posters, the opposition would do the same to theirs, and so the long day wore on.

At one time, André had worked for the mayor's brother, Teddy, as one of the Birt Travel mechanics. But he'd gotten into a scuffle with a Moroccan mechanic, and he'd been let go. Lucky for André, by that point Jan had been elected mayor, and so Teddy had put in a good word for him, landing André, a loyal party soldier, his current job.

It wasn't all sunshine and roses, though. One major disappointment he had was that Flemish Front hadn't yet made good on their promise to put all immigrants on a boat and send them back to where they came from. He hoped they'd do it soon. If not, he'd keep stoking the fire—make sure that Birt and the party brass kept their promise.

Except for Ayoub. He could stay.

TEDDY HESITATED before picking up the phone. He'd been dreading this moment ever since Boyd had called to tell him his bus had been stolen, and also its precious shipment.

"This is Teddy."

"Where is my merchandise?" the familiar voice growled into his ear.

He blinked a few times. This was not good. "I'll get it back for you, I promise."

"That's not what I asked. I want to know where it is. Did those kids steal it when they took the bus for a joyride? Is that what happened?"

"I—I'm not sure. All I know is that it's gone. They took the bus, they crashed the bus, and when my driver got there, the shipment was gone." Boyd had discovered the theft, which had elicited a moment of sheer panic in both the bus driver and Teddy.

For a moment, there was silence on the other end, then a series of loud curses. Teddy held the phone away from his offended ear. He knew the drill. He'd just have to wait it out.

"I know where the second kid lives," he finally managed to interject.

The cursing stopped. "Tell me. And you better not be lying, Teddy."

"I'm not," he promised, and gave the other man the intel.

It came courtesy of his big brother Jan.

Information that just might save his life.

TIM WAS FILLING the tank on his motorcycle when the message came in. He tucked the nozzle back into its holder and screwed the cap on the tank before checking his phone.

All it said was a name and an address, but that was all Tim needed. He smiled. As luck would have it, he was on the ring road around Ghent, at the Lukoil gas station on the Vlaamsekaai, near Lily's chip shop. It was only a short drive along the ring to Ekkergem, where Beni Idrissi lived. This time, the kid wouldn't get away.

## CHAPTER 16

Holt stretched. He'd been checking Mayor Birt's Facebook page and didn't like what he saw—racist claptrap and highly inflammatory videos, designed to stir up the mayor's base. Too bad the man was also the head of the police force, and in a sense, his boss.

His daughter glanced up at him. "That bad, huh?"

"Of all the towns in all of Flanders, why did they have to send me to this one?"

"Because the apple of your eye lives here?"

He smiled. "You're not wrong." He gestured to his screen. "This jerk is using this tragedy to collect more votes, and as far as I can tell, it's working. Now he's even released the name of the second kid."

"I'll bet the Idrissi family will love that."

"They'll have to go into hiding." He frowned. "I wonder where Mayor Birt gets his information."

Poppy jerked her thumb in the direction of the Commissioner's office.

Holt's frown deepened. "Isn't that illegal? Leaking information from an ongoing investigation?"

"He's the head of police, so he's probably entitled to be kept abreast of our progress."

A snigger rose up behind Holt. "Abreast," murmured Leland. "Funny word."

"Oh, grow up, Leland," Georgina grunted.

"Forrester should have kept the name under wraps," said Holt. "Knowing what kind of guy the mayor is, he should've known he was going to use that information to stir up a frenzy with his cult."

"Would you call Flemish Front a cult?" asked Rasheed earnestly. "Technically, it's a political party, boss."

"I would, and I do," said Holt. He turned his swivel chair. "Any news on that ANPR search, Rasheed?"

"Well…" The techie pushed his glasses further up his nose. "I did get something… odd."

"What is it?" Holt rolled his chair over to Rasheed's desk.

"A motorbike with false plates. I mean, it probably has nothing to do with this case at all. Just thought I'd flag it, boss."

Holt studied the footage. Black bike, black-clad biker, black helmet. Impossible to get an ID. "Like you said, no way to know if it's important, but just to be on the safe side—"

"I've followed him all the way to Ghent, boss."

He smiled. "And?"

"And I lost him."

His smile fell.

"He disappeared in that warren of small streets next to the railway here." Rasheed pointed to the map where the motorcycle had last been caught on camera near Dampoort Station on the East side of Ghent.

"Okay. Could be something, could be nothing. Still interesting to keep an eye on."

He rolled back to his own desk.

# FIELD OF BLOOD

"Boss?" said Georgina, raising her hand. "You probably should take a look at this."

He got up and joined her, placing his hands on her desk. "What have you got?"

"Well, forensics looked over the bus, collecting evidence on those two kids, and they found... something pretty weird."

She blew up a picture on her screen. It depicted the undercarriage of the bus, and as she zoomed in, he frowned. "What am I looking at?"

"Some kind of boxes, sir. Attached to the underside of the bus. Four big, empty boxes. You know, like the ones you strap to the roof of a car? To store all of your extra luggage?"

"Huh," he said, scratching his head. "I'm not an expert on buses, but is that normal?"

Rasheed had also joined them, along with Leland, Poppy and Jaime. The six of them stared at the picture.

"I could be wrong here," said Poppy, "but I always thought luggage went in a compartment on the side of the bus, not underneath it."

"Those boxes—how are they accessed?" asked Rasheed, sucking on a lollipop. He was big on lollipops.

"There's no easy way to access them," said Georgina. "You'd have to crawl underneath the bus."

For a moment, they all stared, imagining how this would work.

"I mean, does Birt Travel expect their drivers to crawl under the bus to store passengers' luggage?" asked Leland.

"Doubtful," was Rasheed's opinion.

"Maybe they've got one of those hydraulic lifts?" Jaime suggested. "Like at a garage? So mechanics can work on the cars? I mean, they must have them at Birt Travel."

"I'll bet they do," said Holt. "It's not very practical, though, is it?"

"There's something else, sir," said Georgina. "When they checked those boxes, they found traces of cocaine. Could belong to one of the passengers, maybe?"

"Yeah, right," said Poppy, sarcastically.

Holt exchanged a look with his daughter. "Now isn't that interesting?" he said. "Looks like Teddy Birt has been a bad, bad boy."

He returned to his desk. "Good work, Georgina." Grabbing his coat from the back of his chair, he said, "With me, Poppy."

"Where are we going?" she asked.

"To have a little chat with Mr. Birt."

TIM PARKED his bike two streets away from the Idrissi family home, then walked the distance, slowly making his way up and down the street to ensure the cops weren't staking out the place, as they might. He kept the lower half of his face covered with a scarf. He would have preferred to keep his helmet on, but that would have drawn attention, so the scarf would have to suffice.

As far as he could tell, there was no surveillance in place. But just to be safe, he took up a position across the street from the house and waited patiently, checking for any signs of suspicious activity.

When nothing stirred, he finally crossed the street and pressed his finger on the buzzer. It wasn't long before the door opened, and he immediately pushed his way in, grabbing the woman by the throat and shoving her back before slamming the door shut.

"Where's Beni?" he demanded, pulling his knife from his jacket pocket.

The woman looked terrified, as she should, but shook her head as tears sprang to her eyes. "I don't know! He hasn't been home!"

"Liar," he said calmly. He grabbed her by the shoulder, led her to the living room, and pushed her down on a couch, pointing the knife straight at her face. Also present were two kids, an elderly woman, and a middle-aged man. He smiled. He loved a crowd.

"If you don't tell me where Beni is, I'll start slicing and dicing the lot of you. And I'll start with her," he said, grabbing one of the girls from the floor and holding her up.

"No!" the woman screamed. "Beni was here, but he left. He didn't tell us where he was going."

"He took his stuff and left," said the middle-aged man, probably the woman's husband and Beni's dad.

Tim got the impression they were telling the truth. And they'd better be, because he wouldn't hesitate to get rid of every last member of the Idrissi family if that's what it took to find the little cretin who had conspired to steal the bus and its precious cargo.

"Where did he go?" he demanded, holding the girl up and pressing the knife to her throat. A trickle of blood was already appearing where he prodded the tender skin.

"Please!" the woman yelled, holding up her hands. "He didn't tell us where he was going."

"If we knew, we'd tell you, sir," said the man.

Tim had half a mind to slice the girl's throat, just to send a message to Beni. But then he decided against it. The boss probably wouldn't like it. Too messy. So he dropped the little girl, who was shivering violently and immediately crawled over to her mom.

He'd find Beni some other way.

And so he left the scene, walked out, and made his way to the end of the street and his bike. Placing his helmet back on his head, he was soon racing off again.

Where to find Beni? What flat rock could that cockroach

have crawled under? Not his concern. His bosses would figure it out. They had plenty of resources at their disposal. He was just the tip of the spear, going where they sent him.

As he drove, he got in touch with the boss. When he told him that he hadn't been able to locate Beni, the man wasn't best pleased, as evidenced by a long string of curse words.

"I'll get back to you," said the boss finally. "Better lay low for a while. This thing is blowing up all over social media. But stay close to your phone. I may have another job for you real soon—probably tonight, maybe sooner."

"Gotcha," he said and set a course for the good old homestead, an industrial loft in the Ghent harbor. He'd get some R&R and await further instructions.

After all, he was just a small cog in a very large machine.

## CHAPTER 17

Holt and Poppy arrived at the site where Birt Travel was located. It was a sizable compound in the industrial zone between Loveringem and the neighboring town, home to dozens of small and medium-sized companies. Birt Travel operated a respectable fleet of buses, and most of them were parked in the lot. Except, of course, the bus that had been taken, which was still being investigated by the forensics department.

When they walked into the small office housed in a low-slung brick building and approached the reception desk to announce their presence, the receptionist didn't seem pleased to see them. She was an owlish woman in her late fifties, with a perpetual frown on her face and a mouth drooping at the corners. Not exactly the friendly face one would expect to see in a tour operator's main office. If potential customers came face to face with her, they'd likely run screaming instead of being encouraged to book a trip with Birt Travel.

Then again, as he understood, the company got most of its business through deals they had struck with independent travel agents located across the country and abroad and also through its website, which, he had to admit, looked pretty professional and inviting.

"Teddy, the cops are here," the woman barked into the phone. She hung up and gave them a dirty look. "He'll be right out. Take a seat over there."

Holt glanced around and saw that 'there' was a row of uncomfortable-looking molded plastic chairs. Obliging, he squeezed his form into one of them and grabbed a magazine from a side table. It was a copy of *Top Gear*, which told him the head office of Birt Travel probably catered more to suppliers and business partners than potential customers.

"How do you want to play this, Dad?" whispered Poppy, keeping a close eye on the receptionist. "Good cop, bad cop?"

"Let's play it straight," he said. "He's the mayor's brother, so if we push him too hard, he'll probably be on the phone with his brother the moment we walk out of here, complaining."

"We're not letting him off the hook, are we?" asked Poppy, looking aghast at the possibility that her dad was getting soft in his old age.

He smiled. "Absolutely not. But sometimes you have to be diplomatic when you're handling an investigation." He sighed when she gave him an incredulous look. "I know, I'm not exactly known for my diplomatic skills."

"I'll say. Unless you call punching a man who's sleeping with your wife diplomacy."

He grimaced. "Let's not go there." Just then, his phone buzzed, and he checked the display. "Well, that was quick."

She looked at the message. "Pathologist?"

He nodded. "Let's go and see him the moment we finish with Teddy Birt."

Teddy Birt must have been listening, for at that moment he walked into the small reception area, all smiles and holding out his hand to greet Holt and Poppy. "What news?" he asked. "And when can I have my bus back?"

"Do you want to do this here?" asked Holt, arching an eyebrow at the receptionist, who gave him a sour-faced look.

"No, we better take it into my office," the tour operator owner agreed, and led them along a short hallway into a cramped office.

"I apologize for the mess," he said as he cleared the debris from a chair for Holt and pulled out a second chair for Poppy. "It's been a busy couple of months."

"You do most of your business online, is that right?"

"Sixty percent," he said as he took a seat behind his desk, which was as cluttered as the rest of his office. Papers were strewn about, travel brochures, and big folders with bills opened on the desk. "The rest comes through independent travel agents we have arrangements with. We're one of the largest bus tour operators in Flanders, with a fleet of fifty buses. But you probably didn't drop by to book a trip with us."

"No, we're here because of this," said Holt, placing his phone on the desk. He pointed to a picture of the undercarriage of the bus. "Our forensics people were really curious to discover these boxes located underneath your vehicle, Mr. Birt. Could you enlighten us?"

Birt leaned in and studied the picture. Then he smiled. "I can understand why they were surprised. Not a lot of bus companies offer these. Extra luggage space for our passengers." He leaned back. "You see, the main problem we're always faced with, especially on the longer trips, is where to put all of that luggage. Birt Travel prides itself on being a customer-oriented company, as well as forward-looking and innovative. Unlike our competitors we don't like to restrict the number of suitcases our passengers can bring, so we decided to add this extra space. The boxes are custom-made and available on our first-class vehicles. And I have to say that the solution has proven extremely popular."

"First-class? I thought that Bertha was an older vehicle?"

The man's eyebrows shot up in surprise. "I see you've been talking to Boyd. I can assure you that 'Bertha' is a fine bus. Absolutely up to Birt Travel's exacting standards."

"But… how do the passengers stash their luggage in these boxes?" asked Poppy. "They can't be accessed unless you crawl underneath the vehicle. And even then it's almost impossible to open them, let alone shove any luggage in there. So what gives?"

Birt's smile crept back up his cherubic face. "Our drivers are all trained to handle this task. I'll admit it's not easy, but at Birt Travel, we like to go above and beyond for our customers. All part of the five-star service and what sets us apart from the competition."

"There's one other thing that's got us concerned," said Holt. "Traces of cocaine were found in some of these undercarriage boxes, Mr. Birt. You can see how that would raise alarm bells. How do you explain that?"

The man wreathed his face into an expression of appropriate concern. "The only thing I can think of is that some of our passengers must have carried the stuff in their luggage. There is no other explanation." He shook his head gravely. "It's a sign of the times, Chief Inspector. This poison seems to be everywhere these days. Just this morning I read a story in the paper that the amount of cocaine found in the waste water in Antwerp has doubled again. It's a major problem. But then I guess I don't have to tell you that."

"So you're telling me that the cocaine that was found belongs to your passengers?"

He held out his hands, palms up. "I see no other possible explanation."

Holt could see one explanation—one that made a lot

more sense—but refrained from voicing it for the moment. "What about your drivers?"

"What about them?"

"Maybe they smuggled the stuff on board?"

The man smiled a deprecating smile and shook his head. "Impossible. I vouch for my drivers, Chief Inspector. They don't drink and they don't do drugs. It wouldn't be safe, you see. Not to mention illegal," he hastened to add when Holt opened his mouth to speak.

"Is there a possibility that one of your drivers has been *smuggling* drugs?" asked Poppy, deciding that she'd had enough of her dad's careful approach.

The man's eyes went wide, then he laughed an incredulous laugh. "Inspector, what are you saying? That's such an outrageous accusation."

"Not an accusation," said Poppy. "An explanation for the presence of cocaine in those boxes."

Teddy closed his eyes and pursed his lips, reminding Holt of an undertaker he had once interviewed. Teddy had the same habit of looking mournful and talking in low, gentle tones as if addressing the recently bereaved. "I can promise you that my drivers—who are like family to me—would never smuggle drugs—or any other illegal substance for that matter." He opened his eyes again and gave Poppy a sad smile. "Does that answer your question, Inspector Holt?"

She returned his smile. "For the present," she said.

He seemed relieved the ordeal was over. "So when can I expect the return of my bus?"

"As soon as forensics is through with their investigation," said Holt, getting up.

"And when will that be?" Teddy insisted.

"When they're finished," Holt said, giving the man a smile of his own.

As he and Poppy walked to the car, he saw Boyd Batham,

the bus driver whose bus had been stolen that morning. The man didn't look happy as he stared after them. In fact, he looked downright unhappy. Holt wondered why. But then Teddy walked right up to the driver, and Holt saw that he no longer resembled a kindly and concerned undertaker. Instead, his face was beet-red and contorted with rage, and he was giving the driver hell.

The latter stared at his feet while he took the abuse in kind.

"I wonder what that's all about," said Holt.

Poppy looked over. "Probably telling him that we found his stash."

"Hmm."

"Did you buy that whole spiel about the coke belonging to the tourists?"

"Nope."

"There's something seriously rotten here, Dad."

And wasn't that the truth?

"We should organize a search," said Poppy. "I'll bet we'll find more of the same coke that was found underneath that bus."

"We'd need a search warrant, Poppy."

"So? Can't you get one?"

He grimaced. "I'd have to talk to the prosecutor, who'd have to talk to the examining magistrate. They'd ask on what grounds we need the warrant. And when I tell them that traces of cocaine were found on a bus, they'll laugh me out of the room. It's simply not enough to justify an investigation into Birt Travel."

"Well, it should be."

"But it's not."

"Maybe we can sneak in tonight, when the place is closed, and do some more searching? We can bring a sniffer dog."

He smiled. "We could bring Harley," he said, referring to

his and his ex-wife's French Bulldog, who now lived with him and Poppy. "He'd love that."

She rolled her eyes. "Very funny, Dad. I'm serious. We need to investigate Teddy Birt."

"And we will," he said as he got into the car. "I can promise you that right now."

## CHAPTER 18

The Ghent University Hospital housed the pathological anatomy department, where autopsies were carried out. Holt and Poppy were welcomed by the head of the forensic medicine department, Lionel Kewley, who had performed the autopsy on Mohammed Elmaleh. Doctor Kewley was a large man with a hirsute appearance: a thick crop of dark hair, thick dark eyebrows, and a full black beard. He welcomed Holt most heartily, as the Chief Inspector had plenty of dealings with Doctor Kewley back when he was still working for the Ghent police force.

"Glen," said Lionel warmly as he placed a hand on his back. "So great to see you. I heard they transferred you out to the sticks?"

"Oh, well, I can't complain," he said with a sparse smile. "This is my daughter Poppy—Inspector Holt."

"The apple doesn't fall far from the tree," said Lionel as he pressed Poppy's hand. "So nice to work together with family. I don't know if I ever told you this," he said as he led the Holts, father and daughter, along a warren of corridors until they reached his office, "but my son is studying to be a

FIELD OF BLOOD

forensic pathologist as well. Maybe one day we'll be working together too." He let them into his office. "Well, here we are." He took a seat behind his desk and positioned his computer screen so they could see what he saw.

Holt and Poppy took a seat in front of him and studied the screen, which displayed plenty of pictures the pathologist's assistants had taken of the body of the dead man.

"So what's the verdict, Lionel?" asked Holt.

"Single stab wound to the chest," said the doctor. "Long, thin blade, straight to the heart. Death must have been pretty much instantaneous. Whoever killed him knew what they were doing. Unless it was a lucky strike, of course," he added with a faint smile. "Um, healthy young male, as you can see. Apart from some traces of cocaine in his blood."

"Cocaine?" asked Holt, sitting up a little straighter.

"That's right. Which means he must have used it less than two days before he died. But we also found it in his hair samples, and since cocaine stays in your follicles for up to ninety days, that's how long Mr. Elmaleh had been using—at the very least, that is."

"Long-time user, huh?" said Holt, nodding. "Anything else?"

"Apart from a recent fracture of his left radius and ulna—the two bones in his forearm—no."

Holt frowned. "His left forearm was broken?"

"That's correct. I'd say around four months ago. The fracture had almost completely healed."

It reminded Holt of something—something pretty dreadful. He shook it off for the present and paid close attention as the doctor took them through the autopsy and the results of the toxicology tests that had been carried out. When asked about the nature of the weapon, he said that any knife with a long, thin blade would have sufficed.

As they left his office, Lionel suggested they meet up for

dinner one of these weeks—he and Trudy, and Glen and Leah—before remembering, to his intense embarrassment, that Leah was now Holt's ex-wife.

"I'm so sorry," said Lionel, his tan face coloring.

"That's all right," Holt assured him.

They shook hands, and as they traveled down in the elevator, Poppy suddenly burst into laughter.

"What's so funny?" asked Holt with a grin.

"The doctor's face when he realized that you won't be bringing Mom to dinner with him and his wife any time soon—or ever."

"Lionel is a genius pathologist, but when it comes to matters of everyday life, his grasp on things tends to be quite tenuous, to put it mildly."

They both laughed about the doctor's honest mistake, then Holt turned serious again. "That fracture of the kid's forearm—and the coke in his system. It wouldn't surprise me if he was a member of a gang."

"How can you tell?"

"There's a drug gang known for breaking the arms of anyone who trespasses on their territory. They're called Phoenix, since they operate mainly around Phoenix Street, and they're quite ferocious. Plenty of dealers who ran afoul of the gang have ended up in the hospital with broken arms. Looks like Mohammed may have been one of them."

"Is there a connection with the cocaine found in the Birt Travel bus, you think?"

"I don't know, but this whole case is starting to stink to high heaven. Which means…"

"Don't tell me. A trip down memory lane?"

He nodded morosely. "Unfortunately, yes."

"Well," she said in a faux chipper way, "we're in the neighborhood, so we might as well drop by my stepdad."

"Don't call him that," he growled. "He's just a guy."

"Who just happens to be married to my mom."

"He's not your stepdad," he said decidedly. "And besides, we don't have to see him."

He certainly hoped they wouldn't. And he was pretty sure Commissioner Bayton wouldn't mind if he didn't come face to face with his former colleague either.

"I'll just put in a call," he said as they walked back to the car parked in the lot opposite the impressive building of the pathology department. Normally, cars had to be parked in the designated car park on the edge of the university hospital, and the distance to the different departments had to be traversed on foot, but fortunately that rule didn't apply to the police, which saved them plenty of time. Time they could use if Mohammed was part of a gang. If Holt's hunch was right, they could be looking at a potential gang war with the possibility of spilling over onto Loveringem soil.

He smiled when he heard the familiar voice.

"Hey, stranger," said Chief Inspector Roy Hesketh when Holt introduced himself. "You've gone cold on me. No messages, no emails. I feel rejected, buddy."

"Keeping busy, Roy. How are things at Ekkergem?"

"Pretty boring since you left. Nobody here to punch the Commissioner in the face."

Holt placed his hand on the top of the vehicle. "I need some information, Roy."

"And here I thought this was a social call."

"Mohammed Elmaleh. Hijacked a bus this morning in Loveringem, then got himself killed."

"I know all about it. Lived right around the corner from HQ, didn't he?"

"He did."

"I thought I'd hear from you sooner or later. So what do you need?"

"I just paid a visit to Lionel. He says the Elmaleh kid had

cocaine in his blood and his left arm was fractured four months ago. What does that tell you?"

"It tells me that I'd better take a closer look at his file for you right now. Hang on. That's Elmaleh with an H at the end, right?"

"That's right. And his friend's name is Beni Idrissi. Buddies since they were kids. Beni's gone missing."

"Course he has. Probably doesn't want to stare into those pretty brown peepers of yours, Glen. Here we go. Mohammed Elmaleh. Low-level street dealer, according to my information. Associated with the Green Valley gang. Now let's take a look at his little friend, Beni Idrissi," he said as he typed in the name. He whistled. "Same thing. Picked up a couple of times for dealing."

"So why aren't they in the national database?"

"They were never arrested or brought before a juvenile court. Picked up and immediately released."

"But why?"

"Probably because they're low-level dealers and they were underage. You know the drill, Glen. If we have to process every kid we pick up, we'd be here twenty-four-seven."

"I guess," he said. "Well, if you find out more…"

"You'll be the first to know. Oh, and Glen?"

"Mh?"

"Don't be a stranger, buddy. You still owe me a beer, remember?"

"Oh, I remember."

After he ended the call, he tapped the phone against his chin.

"Trouble?" asked Poppy.

"Elmaleh and Idrissi were picked up several times but never arrested. So they don't have a record. But both are on the radar as low-level street dealers for the Green Valley gang."

"That explains the broken arm. Mohammed must have been dealing in the wrong part of town and come across this rival gang, this…"

"Phoenix gang."

"So… the plot thickens?"

"Oh, it does, Poppy. Big time."

## CHAPTER 19

Tim had been lightly dozing when his phone beeped with a message. He checked it and smirked. He should have known. He replied with a thumbs-up emoji and got up from his couch. No rest for the wicked, which in this case could be taken quite literally.

Ten minutes later, he was on his bike, roaring out of the underground car park located underneath the old factory where he had his loft on the top floor. The sun was setting, and by the time he reached Loveringem, it would be dark, which was just as well.

FLOYD TIMMER WAS FEELING on top of the world. Today was the day he'd always dreamed of—the day his ship had come in. And the funny thing was that it had all fallen into his lap with no contribution on his part. All it took in the end was being in the right place at the right time. His wallet was filled to capacity with crisp paper bills, and he had plenty more in the gym bag currently hidden behind the washing machine at home.

This presented him with a new problem: what was he going to do with all of that money? He knew from experience that it wasn't easy to spend a lot of cash. You couldn't buy a car by paying for it in cash. You couldn't buy a house or an apartment. In fact, there wasn't a lot you could buy once it cost over a couple of thousand bucks—all due to the anti-money-laundering laws the government had put in place.

It was definitely a good problem to have, though. And it beat having no money to spend at all, as had mostly been the case since he'd turned pro. He could retire now. He'd never have to work again, and he could tell his wife the good news. Though maybe he'd better not. She might want to blow the whole wad on fancy clothes, trips to the hair salon, and jewelry—lots and lots of jewelry. Suzy was crazy about bling. The more, the better. And the last thing he needed was for her to spend all of his dough on trips to the mall and the jewelry store. Then he'd be right back where he started.

No, he wouldn't tell her a thing. Besides, she might blab about it to her mother, her sisters, or one of her friends, and that might land his ass in prison. He'd been there, and he hadn't enjoyed it. Doing hard time had given him a hard time—especially with all those crazy people in there. Too many nutjobs for his taste.

He glanced in the window of a jewelry store and wondered if he shouldn't pick up a nice ring for Suzy. When they got married eleven years ago, he didn't have any money to buy her a decent wedding band. He promised her that the time would come when he would cover her in bling, so maybe he should start making good on his promise.

Before he could enter the store, a voice called out from the street. He looked up and saw a man on a black motorcycle watching him.

"Floyd Timmer?" asked the man.

"Yeah, that's me," he said.

The guy got off his bike and walked up to him. He couldn't see the man's face, as he was wearing a helmet. For some reason his sheer presence gave Floyd the creeps.

"What do you want?" he asked therefore.

"I have a message for you," the man said, and reached into his pocket.

"A message?"

"Yeah, a message from Phoenix," said the guy.

Floyd's eyes went wide when he saw the man pull a knife.

Before he could react, the knife plunged deeply into his chest.

A sharp pain lanced through him, and already he was going down.

"You stole from the wrong people, Floyd," said the guy, standing over him.

As he crumpled into a heap on the sidewalk, he saw the man mount his motorbike, swing it around and race off in the opposite direction with a distinct roar. You had to hand it to him: for a cold-blooded killer working for Phoenix he sure had plenty of panache.

As Floyd grew increasingly cold, the last thought that passed through his head was that he should have kept on driving that morning. Then he wouldn't be in this mess.

BENI IDRISSI HAD RECEIVED an urgent message from his mom that some people were looking for him and that he shouldn't come home. Good thing he'd followed his instincts then. Probably the guy who had killed Mo was still after him. But where could he go? He'd already been turned away by two members of the Green Valley gang that he and Mo had been working with for the past eighteen months. Too risky, they

FIELD OF BLOOD

had told him. News traveled fast, and they didn't want to get involved in whatever this was.

One of them had told him that the bus they'd taken belonged to Phoenix, and that's when everything became clear. He'd heard rumors that Phoenix had a new way of transporting their merchandise, involving some local tour operator, with the drugs hidden in a secret compartment or something.

Of all the buses, he and Mo had to take one that belonged to Phoenix—one of the most dangerous and ruthless gangs in Ghent. Even more dangerous than Green Valley.

It was a member of Phoenix who had broken Mo's arm that time when he found him dealing on Phoenix territory without even realizing it. These guys didn't mess around.

Lucky for Beni, he'd never faced the gang's heavies. Until now.

He was on his way to meet a friend, who would hopefully be prepared to put him up for a while. Until all this died down again. Or until he managed to sneak out of the country. He and Mo had often talked about becoming so rich they could move to Dubai, like some of the top dogs in the cartel Green Valley represented.

Now Mo was dead, and Beni was in fear for his life.

He glanced back and thought that a car was following him. It was a black BMW that looked like it might belong to a gang member. Phoenix loved their BMWs, just as Green Valley loved their Mercedeses. But the car passed him by and sped up, turning a corner at the end of the street.

He let out a breath of relief. He was too young to die. And what would his mother say if he ended up dead? She wouldn't be happy. She had told him when he got involved with Mo's brother Hassan, who was something high up in the chain of command at Green Valley, that he was making the mistake of his life.

Looked like she was right.

But then Mom always was.

Only a couple more streets, and he would arrive at Jamal's, a street dealer just like him and Mo, even though Jamal was a lot older than they were—probably around forty or something. Plus, he was a junkie and looked the part. But it didn't matter. As long as he could put a roof over Beni's head and get him off the street, that was all that mattered.

He glanced back just as a white van pulled up next to him. The side door slid open, and a man in a balaclava appeared, pointing an AK-47 at him.

The automatic suddenly started spitting bullets, and Beni was slammed back against the wall of the nearest house, his body jerking like a ragdoll as he was riddled with lead.

He was dead by the time his body hit the pavement.

## CHAPTER 20

Tamara Elmaleh was in hell. Not only had her sweet boy been killed, with the police apparently twiddling their thumbs and no closer to finding out who was responsible, but now her family was under fire on social media, being accused of all kinds of nonsense. And it wasn't just social media that had turned the Elmalehs into a target. Even her neighbors were giving them the cold shoulder. The kids at school, teachers—everyone, everywhere—seemed to have it in for them. To the extent that she had already suggested to Aamir that maybe they should take the kids out of school for the time being and go for a prolonged stay in Morocco with her parents—until this whole business blew over.

But Aamir wouldn't hear of it. It would mean giving up his job at the Volkswagen garage nearby, where he worked as a mechanic, and he might never get another job that paid as well, with bosses and colleagues that treated him with so much respect and consideration. Contrary to what the rest of the family was experiencing, he had yet to hear one bad word, and his colleagues had even organized a collection to pay for the funeral.

That's not to say Aamir didn't have his own cross to bear. He blamed the whole situation on their eldest son, Hassan, which had created a very tense atmosphere at home, as Hassan wasn't the kind of person to take such abuse lying down. He gave as good as he got. Things had escalated to the point where it had come to blows between him and his dad, and Hassan took off, swearing that he wanted nothing more to do with them. Aamir said it might be for the best, as Hassan had brought tragedy and embarrassment to the family. He was the one who had recruited both Mo and Beni to work for his gang, and now look where that had led them.

Hassan insisted it had nothing to do with the gang he worked for, but with another gang—a rival one. Regardless, if he hadn't been involved with this so-called Green Valley, this would never have happened. The only one in the family who seemed to be keeping a level head was Mustafa. He'd been a great support to Tamara and was instrumental in getting the preparations for the funeral going, among other things. He had also lodged an official complaint with the police about the online harassment campaign they were being subjected to and had even contacted a reporter from one of the big papers to complain about Jan Birt, the mayor of the small town where Mo had been found dead, and the hate speech he had been hurling at the family, stirring up his followers. The family had contacted a lawyer and were considering taking Mayor Birt to court.

No politician should be allowed to spread hate and get away with it.

She sat at her kitchen table and gazed out of the window at the tiny paved courtyard behind the kitchen. Amine had started a project of painting the gray cement walls with a mural of her own design—flowers and a garden scene. It was coming along nicely and would do much to make the space look less dreary and dreadful, brightening things up.

Amine had a knack for such things. She was the creative one in the family, which was why it pained Tamara so much that Mo's death had brought so much trouble to their family. She was terrified it might jeopardize the future of Amine and her other kids.

She picked up her phone and saw that her sister was trying to reach her. She decided to ignore her for now. All her sister wanted was to gossip about Mo and the events surrounding his death. The last thing Tamara needed right now was to be reminded of how much trouble the family was in—or to shoulder the blame the rest of the family was silently heaping on her. Even though they didn't say it outright, she knew they all blamed her for not keeping a tighter grip on her sons. If only Hassan had never become associated with that gang, things would be very different. But even though Hassan mourned the death of his brother, all he could think about was finding out who was behind it and getting revenge—which Tamara knew would only make things worse.

She saw that her boss was trying to reach her.

"Yes, Mrs. Parker?" she said.

"Tamara, how are you holding up?" the woman asked.

"As well as can be expected, I suppose," she said truthfully. "We're planning the funeral and waiting for further news from the police about who did this to Mohammed."

"I hope you get news really soon," said Mrs. Parker. "I was thinking that maybe you shouldn't come in for a little while. Until after the funeral. With everything that's happening, I think it's better this way, don't you?"

"Oh, but I want to work, Mrs. Parker," she said.

"I know you do, but I think it's better if you take a break. Let's talk again in a week or two and see how things stand by then, all right? Bye-bye, Tamara." Without waiting for a response, the woman ended the call.

Tamara's heart sank. She really needed this job. If Mrs. Parker decided to let her go, it might be very difficult under the present circumstances to find another one.

She could understand where the woman was coming from, though. Clients would probably ask her a million questions once they realized she was the mother of the boy who had been killed. And the cleaning company didn't need that. They needed her to be productive, cleaning houses, not talking about her personal situation.

She sighed and looked up when Mustafa entered the kitchen. He was holding his phone in his hand. "It's the police, Mom," he said.

"What's wrong?" she asked, panic already flooding her. "Is it Hassan?"

He shook his head. "Beni. He's just been shot and killed."

## CHAPTER 21

It had been a long day, and Holt was glad to be home. Even though technically it wasn't his home, but his daughter Poppy's. But if everything there was new to him, it was also new to his daughter, as she had recently gone through a similar experience, having just split from her boyfriend of three years. Truth be told, Holt had never been all that fond of Rupert, who ran a real estate agency in downtown Loveringem. The man had always struck him as being stuck-up and not particularly kind to Poppy, often mocking her and passing off his comments as jokes. Not funny, Rupert. Not funny at all. When he cheated on Poppy with some beauty queen, Poppy realized she was better off without him and had given him the old heave-ho. And good riddance, as far as Holt was concerned.

It was quite the coincidence that both he and Poppy had suddenly found themselves in search of a new place to live. So when he was transferred to Loveringem—his options being either that or dismissal from the force—it was Poppy who suggested they share the burden of the rent by taking a lodging together. These days, a half-decent apartment in

Ghent cost upwards of a thousand bucks, so he'd reluctantly agreed. For the time being. Until he could make other arrangements. But so far, things were working out well.

He and Poppy had worked out an agreement before he moved his stuff into the house she had found: they would share cleaning and cooking duties and split the costs right down the middle. That included heating, electric, water, insurance, and all the rest of it.

The house itself was extremely modest in size, and was part of a new development that had been erected close to the town center. Six attached houses had been built, all identical, with tiny backyards and a small space to park a car in front. Holt had noticed that houses were getting increasingly smaller, with the bedrooms barely big enough to fit a bed and a closet. Poppy said it was probably due to shrinkflation, a phenomenon that affected food items. You got a lot less Toblerone or Nutella these days for the same price as even a couple of years ago, and this must have given contractors the same idea.

The house had three miniscule bedrooms: one for each of them and a third they used as a shared office. The kitchen was part of the living room, but the location was great, with the police station only a stone's throw away—a definite bonus for the two cops.

The only thing he sorely missed was his extensive collection of comics. He'd always been a big fan of the genre, and over the years had amassed quite the assortment. It was still housed in his old place, where his ex-wife now lived with her new husband. Repeated pleas to retrieve his beloved comics had fallen on deaf ears, as Leah didn't want him anywhere near the house in case he punched her new husband's lights out again, even though Holt had assured her he wouldn't. He wasn't a violent man as a rule.

"Still worried about your comics, Dad?" asked Poppy as

she entered the living room with a glass of chilled white wine and took a seat on the couch. He was standing in front of the empty bookcase he had bought to house his collection—and it looked like it would remain empty for now.

"She's holding them hostage, you realize that, don't you?"

Poppy laughed, a pleasant sound that reminded him of Leah. "Why would she do a thing like that?"

"She doesn't want me to go anywhere near Terrence again, so she's keeping my comics to make sure I don't. Any wrong move on my part, and she'll probably throw them all out." His face clouded. "Or worse. Burn them. That woman is capable of anything."

"Mom is not going to throw out your comics, Dad. Or burn them."

"Then why isn't she returning them?" he asked, throwing up his hands. "Or maybe it's Terrence who's holding them hostage. Out of sheer spite. Revenge for that punch."

"The fateful punch. You guys still not over that?"

"Oh, I'm over it," he said. "Only I'm not so sure he is. Or she."

"Look, you're all grown-ups," said Poppy as she took a sip from her wine. It was her way of relaxing. She had kicked off her shoes and tucked her feet underneath her. "So why don't you simply talk about this like grown-ups?"

"We're not on speaking terms," he said sadly. Then he had an idea. "Maybe you can intervene? Act as our go-between? All I want," he added when Poppy started to protest, "is my comics back. That collection is worth thousands, honey. It took me years to build."

"I'm not getting in the middle of this," she said, not for the first time.

"No, I guess that's probably the sensible thing to do."

"How about Aaron?" she asked, referring to her brother.

"Maybe you could ask him to organize the move of your collection?"

"He's been ignoring my calls."

"I'm sure that's not the case."

"He has. Blocking my calls and my messages. Face it, Poppy, your brother has chosen your mother's side. Your mother and her new husband—his stepdad."

"Oh, and you believe that I've chosen your side, do you?"

"Well," he said with a shrug, "you're here and he's not."

"I have chosen nobody's side," she said firmly. "I'm Switzerland. Strictly neutral."

"Your mother doesn't seem to think so."

"I thought you weren't on speaking terms."

"During the divorce proceedings, when we were in court, she accused me of poisoning your mind against her."

"So that's why she hasn't been in touch so much lately."

Just then, Harley came waddling up to him and gave him an expectant look. Holt grinned as he bent down and patted the French bulldog on the head. "At least your mom hasn't taken *you* hostage, has she, little buddy?"

It had been touch and go, but in the end, Leah had decided that her desire to punish her ex-husband didn't outweigh her lack of affection for the lovable mutt. She could have asked the judge to let her have Harley, of course, and then gotten rid of him by dumping him at the pound. That would have hurt Holt even more than the divorce had. But in a gesture that proved she still had a heart, she had allowed him to adopt Harley. She had never liked dogs, and neither had Terrence, so that was probably the reason.

"My turn to cook tonight, I guess," said Poppy with a grimace. Even though his daughter possessed many fine qualities, cooking wasn't one of them, and the fact of the matter was that she didn't like it all that much either. When she was still with the real estate mogul, they had spent most nights going to restaurants, as Rupert hadn't been crazy about cooking either. But now that it was just her and Holt, they preferred to stay in.

"I can do it if you want," he offered.

"No, it's fine," she said. "I'll do spaghetti."

"And I'll take this fine fellow for a walk," he said. He took one step toward the corridor, and Harley was practically beside himself with joy. When Holt grabbed the leash from the coat rack, Harley started pawing Holt's leg, barking happily. Moments later, the Chief Inspector and his faithful canine companion were walking along, greeting fellow dog walkers as they went, and he thought, not for the first time, how odd it was that his life had completely turned around in just a couple of months.

Who could have predicted that he would be living in Loveringem, of all places, working with Poppy and actually sharing a house with her?

All in all, things had worked out for the best, even though he still missed his old life with Leah, his old precinct, his career. Things weren't exactly happening in Loveringem, and he often felt that maybe being kicked out of the force altogether would have been the more humane thing, instead of putting him out to pasture like this.

When his phone buzzed in his pocket, he figured it was probably Poppy, wanting to know what sauce he wanted on his spaghetti. Instead, it was Delilah Rocker, the station's desk sergeant.

"I think you'd better come in, sir," said Delilah. "A man's just been killed on Falcon Street. Fellow named Floyd Timmer. Looks like he was knifed to death. Witnesses report seeing the killer flee the scene on a fancy black motorbike."

"I'm on my way," he said curtly.

Looked like Loveringem was starting to turn into the Wild West of East Flanders, he thought. So much for being sidelined and relegated to the boonies.

## CHAPTER 22

Poppy had actually planned to go to the gym and had been hoping to convince her dad to accompany her, as he could use some exercise. Since the divorce, he hadn't been eating all that healthily, and he'd packed on the pounds, not getting any exercise either, apart from walking Harley. But she didn't consider that a proper exercise regime.

She'd been trying to convince Holt to get a membership at the same gym she attended. It would do him a world of good, get him off his couch, and do wonders for his mental health, which had taken a hit since his effective demotion. Even though they hadn't taken away his rank, his career had been cut short by the transfer and was unlikely to recover.

She had just put the spaghetti to boil when her dad stormed in with Harley waddling behind him. "Better get your coat," he said. "A man has been killed on Falcon Street."

"What, just now?"

"Yeah, just now."

"But… we haven't eaten yet."

He gave her a comical look. "Murder doesn't wait, honey."

So she turned off the heat on the pot of spaghetti, put a

lid on it, and hurried after her dad. In passing, Harley gave her a sad look. Looked like he wasn't all that happy that his walk had been cut short. But that couldn't be helped. Like her dad said, crime waits for no man—or dog.

When they arrived on Falcon Street, the area had already been cordoned off, and the coroner had arrived. It immediately became clear to her that the victim was beyond medical assistance. He lay on his back on the sidewalk with his eyes wide open, and he had a sort of surprised look on his face, as if he couldn't quite believe what had just happened to him.

Leland, Georgina, and Rasheed had also arrived, with Leland talking to an older man with a dog, Georgina interviewing a couple of teenagers on mountain bikes, and Rasheed carefully placing the dead man's phone in a plastic evidence bag.

Poppy and Holt were introduced to the uniformed officer who had been the first to arrive on the scene. His name was Quinn Errington, and he seemed duly impressed by what he had found, which was understandable, as this type of brutal killing was not what you expected in Loveringem.

"His name is Floyd Timmer," said the young officer. "I arrested him only last week when he was caught shoplifting. He has a record a mile long, but only minor offenses. Mainly he's a thief, sir, and also a fence. Nothing major. And now, to be killed like this..." He shook his head. "What's going on, sir? First that kid, and now this."

"Any witnesses?" asked Holt, preferring not to go down the road of speculating whether the two crimes were connected.

"That man over there," said the young cop, pointing to the old man with the dog who was talking to Leland. "He was passing by when it happened. He said a man on a motorcycle stopped and said something to Floyd, then he took out a knife and stabbed him in the chest. Just like that. Said it was like something from a movie."

"And the kids over there?"

"They were also in the vicinity, but too far away to see what happened. But they corroborate the witness's statement. Said the motorcycle passed by them, and they got a good look at it. They reckon it was a fancy motorbike. Kawasaki, one of the kids thinks."

"And the rider?"

"They couldn't see his face because of the helmet. Dressed in black from head to toe, they said. All leather."

Holt frowned and shared a look with Poppy. She knew exactly what he was thinking: the motorcycle with the false plates that had been flagged by Rasheed that morning when he went through the ANPR data.

"Okay, thanks, Quinn," said Holt, clapping the man appreciatively on the shoulder.

"Do you think it's the same motorcycle?" asked Poppy.

Holt shrugged. "Hell of a coincidence, wouldn't you say?"

"That would mean the two cases are probably connected."

They approached the coroner, who stood hunched over the victim, examining the wounds on the man's chest. He looked up as they approached and gave them a rare smile.

"You two are keeping me busy. Is it something in the water, you think?"

"Don't tell me, knife wound to the chest?" Holt asked.

"And now you're psychic too," said Dr. Lovelass. "Pretty soon, you won't need me at all. You'll be solving your cases from the comfort of your home, just like Nero Wolfe."

He smiled. "Except I don't have a green thumb, Tomas."

"Ah, yes. The orchids. That's a pity."

"Time of death?"

"Within the past hour, I'd say."

Holt nodded. "That corroborates the witness statements."

"If this keeps up, you'll be drowning in blood, Holt. And that in a town whose mayor prides himself on being tough on crime. Looks like the criminals don't necessarily agree with him. Or maybe they're doing this to show him who's really in charge."

"Thanks, doc," said Holt.

Lovelass gave him a sad look and instructed his team to remove the body as soon as they could. It wouldn't do to leave the poor man lying there longer than absolutely necessary.

Holt studied the body closely, as if hoping to derive a clue as to why the man had been killed in such a brutal fashion.

His phone buzzed with a tired series of beeps, signaling that someone was trying to reach him. He frowned at the display and picked up. "Roy?"

He walked off as he spoke to his former colleague. Poppy watched as the crime scene team took numerous photographs of the victim and the surrounding area. Soon, an ambulance arrived, and Floyd Timmer's body was placed in a body bag, transferred to a stretcher, and taken to the University Hospital, where the pathologist would perform the post-mortem.

She joined Georgina, who had just finished taking statements from the teenagers. "They couldn't tell me a lot," she said as she closed her notebook. "Just that they saw a guy on a motorcycle arrive and then take off again. They were pretty impressed. Said they'd never seen anything like it. They could hardly believe it was actually happening."

"You don't expect that kind of thing here," Poppy agreed.

"I interviewed Floyd on more than one occasion," said Georgina.

"Same here," said Poppy. "I think we all interviewed him at one time or another."

"Do you think there's a connection to this morning's killing?" Georgina asked.

"No idea." Poppy glanced over to her dad, who was still talking to Roy. "Let's hear what the boss has to say."

Georgina smiled. "Isn't it odd to have to call your dad 'boss'?"

"You get used to it," Poppy said. "And it's not like I call him 'boss' at home. He's just my dad."

"I'm not sure I could work with my dad," said Georgina. "Or—shudder—live with the man."

"I thought you got along with your dad really well?"

Georgina's parents ran a funeral home and had always hoped that their daughter would one day join them and eventually take over the business.

"Oh, we do get along—but the man is an absolute control freak. I used to work with him during the summer holidays, and he's a terror to work for. Great dad, horrible boss."

"Holt isn't so bad," said Poppy. "He's pretty much the same person all the time—on or off the job." Apart from all the whining about his comics collection, of course.

Holt had joined them. He looked serious. "They had a shooting over in Ekkergem," he said. "Roy just told me all about it. That's Roy Hesketh," he added for Georgina's sake.

"I know Roy," she assured him.

"Remember the second kid from this morning? Beni Idrissi? The one we thought might have killed Mohammed? Well, he was just gunned down very close to his home. Drive-by shooting. AK-47, by the looks of things. Body absolutely riddled with bullets."

"Christ," said Poppy. "What's going on, boss?"

"Roy thinks this is all part of some drug war. He told us that both Mohammed and Beni were members of a gang called Green Valley, right? Looks like someone wasn't happy with them, and Roy thinks it may have been their rival gang, Phoenix."

"The cocaine in the bus," said Poppy.

"I told Roy, and he says we probably should take a closer look at Teddy Birt. It's possible that Teddy is using his buses to transport drugs. It wouldn't be the first time. We busted a Croatian gang in Ghent that did exactly the same thing a couple of years ago. They put the stuff in hidden compartments located underneath their buses and shipped the stuff around the country. It's possible that Teddy Birt is in this up to his neck."

Rasheed and Leland had also joined them.

"What are you saying, boss?" asked Leland. "That our 'tough-on-crime' mayor's brother is secretly a drug trafficker? But surely that's impossible. He would never do such a thing," he added with a cheeky wink.

"Imagine if the mayor was also involved," said Rasheed.

"Wouldn't surprise me one bit," said Leland. "He might even be using the money to pay for his election campaign."

"If this got out, it would be the end of Mayor Birt," said Georgina.

"It would be a major scandal," Poppy agreed. "A career-ending scandal."

"All the more reason to tread carefully," said Holt. "And not make any accusations we can't back up with solid evidence."

"If we could nail Mayor Birt, now wouldn't that be something?" said Rasheed, who had never been a big fan of the mayor.

"Let's do this strictly by the book, folks," said Holt. "Because make no mistake. If the mayor finds out that we're targeting his brother, he's going to come down on all of us like a ton of bricks. Especially with the election coming up."

Looked like they had just stepped into a hornet's nest of major proportions.

## CHAPTER 23

The following morning, Holt and his team of detectives were gathered in the precinct, huddled around Rasheed's computer and intently studying footage captured by the ANPR camera that monitored the onramp to the R4—same location as the day before. It showed the same motorbike taking the onramp. Same bike, same false license plate, and likely the same person riding it.

"Better send this footage to Roy," said Holt. "So he can look out for this guy on his end."

"I lost him again, boss," said Rasheed. "This time in the Ghent harbor. Which makes me think he probably lives there."

"Very careless of him to use the same plates," said Leland. "Or maybe he simply doesn't care. Figures we'll never catch him?"

"So first he pays a visit to Loveringem to stab Mohammed Elmaleh," said Holt. "And then the same evening, he returns to stab and kill Floyd Timmer. Same MO. Same killer."

"What about the shooting of Beni Idrissi?" asked Georgina. "Do you think there's a connection?"

"Has to be," said Leland. "But what connects Timmer to those two kids?"

"This is all circumstantial," said Poppy. "We can't say for sure that this guy killed Elmaleh and Timmer, just as we can't be certain that the people who gunned down Idrissi last night are connected to Motorcycle Man."

"No, but it does point to the same people," said Leland. "This gang that the two kids belonged to. This Green Valley gang."

"What about Timmer?" asked Georgina. "Was he also a member of this gang? I mean, I could be wrong, but I don't think he was. Unless I'm missing something here?"

"Timmer wasn't a drug dealer I don't think," said Poppy. "We picked him up plenty of times, and always for stealing. We never found any drugs on his person or any sign that he was dealing."

"No, Floyd was a thief," said Leland. "And a burglar. But no drugs. Never drugs."

They had searched Floyd's place last night and hadn't found any drugs there either, or any sign that he was involved in the drug trade. So why had this gang decided that he needed to be taken out, if indeed this was a gang-related killing? And why in such a public way? A way that was designed to make a statement? Unless there was something they were missing?

"Roy better come through and find this Motorcycle Man," said Georgina. "And give us some answers."

"Even if they catch him, he probably won't tell us anything," said Leland. "These gangs rely on extreme violence to keep their members in line. If he talks, he knows he's a dead man."

Leland was right. Even though most of the drug gangs were located in Antwerp, some were also active in Ghent. Mostly, the violence had been limited to the city, but it looked like things were quickly starting to change, especially if Loveringem wasn't safe anymore.

"I'll talk to Roy," said Holt. "Make sure we work together on this." It was pretty ironic, he thought, that the gang violence was spreading from Ghent to the suburbs, forcing him to cooperate with his former colleagues.

Leland checked his watch. "We better keep a close eye on the mayor's press conference. In case he creates more bad blood with his nonsensical comments."

"The mayor is holding a press conference?" asked Georgina. "Why wasn't I told?"

"Maybe because you don't belong to his target demographic?" Leland suggested. "Last time I looked you were not an angry middle-aged white guy, Georgina."

"Excellent powers of observation, Leland." She seemed concerned. "I just hope he tones things down. The last thing we need is calls for more violence from that man."

"When have you ever known Mayor Birt to act sensibly?" asked Leland. "I can tell you right now that he'll use this new killing to prove his point: that he's the only person who can stop this violence and that we should all vote for him to make that happen."

Rasheed had surfed to the mayor's Facebook page, where the press conference would be broadcast live.

"Does he have security?" asked Poppy.

"Plenty," said Holt. "The Commissioner has sent pretty much every available officer to guard the mayor with their lives. Nothing will happen to the guy."

Jan Birt was absolutely furious. "I told her to be here!" he said as he paced his office. He had tried to call Anjanette a dozen times already, and every time the call went straight to voicemail. Clearly, she was ignoring him. Even though he and his wife had been living separate lives for years now and didn't sleep in the same bed or even the same bedroom anymore, he had always been able to rely on her support whenever an important event demanded they put up a united front as husband and wife. As a candidate who ran on a platform of family values, it was absolutely vital that Anjanette stood by his side when he gave a press conference as crucial as the one he was about to give.

Preferably, he would have wanted his son to also be present. Make it a family affair. During the last election campaign, six years ago, Jayson had been dragged along the campaign trail and had stood next to his mom and dad at every occasion that counted. This campaign, Jayson had assured his dad that the last thing he wanted was to support him and 'his fascist ideas.' And so it had only been him and Anjanette who had been present at the press meeting where he had launched his re-election campaign.

And now this.

"Maybe she forgot?" Gwendolyn suggested.

"As if. I told her last night and then again this morning. She promised me she would be here." Though she had seemed about as excited at the prospect of standing by her man as having her wisdom teeth extracted. "Maybe *you* can try calling her?"

Gwendolyn's eyebrows rose, but she did as she was told. She placed her phone to her ear but likewise had to admit defeat. "Voicemail," she said.

"Okay, I guess we'll have to do this without her," said Jan finally. He couldn't keep the press horde waiting for much longer. Not to mention his faithful army of online supporters, who would be tuning in to hear what he had to say about this spate of murders that was ravaging Loveringem. "You stand next to me instead," he said.

Gwendolyn perked up. "Of course, Jan. With pleasure."

"But not too close. We don't want people to think Anjanette is out of the picture. You know how quickly rumors get started." He checked her outfit. Appropriately dignified and modest. Gray pantsuit. Black flat shoes. Hair done up in a tight chignon. She looked like a prison warden, which was the kind of image they wanted to project: solemn and austere. He himself was donning a charcoal suit in honor of the victims—or rather, victim, as he didn't consider Elmaleh a victim but a perpetrator. Technically speaking, Floyd Timmer wasn't exactly blameless either, but at least he was one of them. So in his mind, he was a victim. He checked himself in the full-length mirror and practiced his serious face.

"How do I look?"

"Perfect," said Gwendolyn. "You exude exactly the right mix of solemnity and respect for the victims."

"Victim," he corrected her. "Only one victim here."

"Of course," said Gwendolyn.

"Though you might say we're all victims today."

He would have said more, but he was going to keep that for his speech.

He grabbed his notes from his desk, buttoned up his jacket, and strode out of the office, Gwendolyn a few paces behind him.

CHAPTER 24

Holt and his team watched as Mayor Birt walked up to the podium, accompanied by his campaign manager, Gwendolyn Lopez, and gave a curt acknowledgment to the reporters in the room. He started by reminding everyone that another citizen had been killed last night and called Floyd Timmer a man who may have had his faults but was still an innocent victim. A victim of the kind of violence that is all too prevalent in societies being overrun by rampant immigration—hordes of savages invading countries like locusts.

"Here we go," said Leland, who sat with his arms crossed as he watched the mayor deliver his address.

Jaime walked up to Holt and handed him a piece of paper. "I forgot to give this to you, boss," she said. "Wanda Desai's car was vandalized yesterday. Her side mirrors were destroyed and the side of her car was keyed. One of our officers checked it out, and it turns out the incident was caught on camera—her car was parked right underneath."

She handed him a file folder with a single picture inside.

It was a nice close-up of the person who had vandalized Mrs. Desai's car.

"André Wiel," he read from the note that accompanied the picture. "Works for the parks department?"

"That's right. I've looked him up, and he's been with them for years. Though he is also on record as one of Mayor Birt's most ardent supporters."

"Big fan of the mayor, huh?" he said with a nod. "Thanks, Jaime. Looks like we'll be paying a visit to Mr. Wiel."

She smiled and returned to her desk.

He tuned in again just when the mayor was saying something about rats and vermin and for a moment wondered if there was a pest problem at Town Hall. But then he remembered the mayor had his own unique vernacular when referring to immigrants.

"We should really arrest the guy," said Leland as he shook his head. "For hate speech. Aren't there laws against that kind of thing, boss?"

"I'm sure there are," said Holt with a sigh. "But it's not up to us. If no complaint comes in, and the prosecutor doesn't tell us to make an arrest, it's not our place to do so."

"Try to arrest the mayor," said Georgina, "and you'll probably be hung, drawn, and quartered in Town Square by the baying mob that hangs on the vile man's every word."

Just then, a kid appeared into view. It was a teenager, and Holt recognized him as the mayor's son, Jayson.

The mayor probably hadn't expected him, for he momentarily faltered, staring at his son as the latter approached the lectern. The kid was carrying something. Holt now saw it looked like a bucket.

And before the mayor could stop him, Jayson heaved the bucket over his dad's head and was emptying it on top of the man. It was some kind of thick, brown slurry, and judging from the loud howls of disgust emanating from the recipient of the slurry, it was safe to say that it probably wasn't mud.

"Oh, dear," said Poppy.

JAN WAS HOME AGAIN, and after taking a long shower, felt more or less clean again. He was still fuming, though, after his son had poured a bucket of cow manure over his head, humiliating him in front of a live audience and the entire press pack gathered at the event.

He walked down the stairs, and when he saw Anjanette, he had to check himself or he would have thrown something at her.

"What were you *thinking?!*" he yelled.

She was in their light and spacious living room, seated at the dinner table, and looked up when he approached. "You smell," she said, wrinkling her nose.

He smelled his pits and had to admit she was right. Even though he'd scrubbed and scrubbed and used plenty of soap and shampoo, the stuff was very hard to get rid of—especially the foul odor that seemed to cling to him like glue.

"You promised me you'd come! And instead, you sent Jayson with a bucket of *shit!*"

"I didn't send Jayson," she said calmly. "I didn't even know what he was up to. And as for the press conference, something came up, and I couldn't make it."

"What could possibly have come up that was more important?!" he demanded.

She made an ineffectual gesture with her hand. "A crisis at work. They asked me to deal with it, so I did."

He didn't believe a word she said but wasn't in a position to accuse her of lying either, since he was going to need her on the campaign trail. "You need to keep that son of yours under control," he said, wagging a finger in her face. "He just turned me into a laughingstock and may have ruined my chances of being re-elected." He swung his arms. "The opposition will turn this into a *meme!* For the rest of my life, all I will be is the guy who gets a bucketful of cow shit poured over his head."

"I'm sure it's not that bad," she said. "People have a very short attention span these days. Within a couple of days, something else will happen, and they'll forget all about it."

"We need to keep Jayson away from me," he said. "Far, *far* away."

Too bad the cops hadn't stopped his son when they saw him carry in that bucket. Then again, they probably figured that he wanted to show his support to his dear old dad.

For a brief, wild moment, he considered filing a complaint against his own son and having him arrested, locked up for the duration of the campaign. But if he did that, he wouldn't be much of a family man, would he? So instead, he decided to laugh it off. To say it was simply a student prank that had gotten out of hand. That Jayson had been challenged by some members of his faculty club and that the whole thing was a silly bet.

"We need to get him out of the country," he said as he paced the living room. He turned to his wife. "Maybe we can send him to England? Finish his studies over there? Just like Princess Elizabeth? What was that posh school they shipped her off to?"

"We can't send Jayson to England, Jan," said Anjanette with an eye roll. "The new school year has just begun. And besides, we can't afford that 'posh' school, as you call it."

"Then maybe we can send him to live with your aunt and uncle in Holland? We can't risk him pulling more stunts like this, that's for sure. He's gonna cost me my re-election."

"We are *not* sending him to my aunt," said Anjanette

decidedly. "I'll talk to him and tell him he shouldn't have done it. I'm sure he'll listen to me."

"I hope so. If he doesn't…" The threat was clear, and he hoped Anjanette wouldn't laugh it off. He was perfectly ready to get rid of the kid and put him on ice for a couple of weeks, until after the election. In a way that didn't look like he was punishing him, of course. Optics are everything for a politician, especially in an election year. "He can still follow his classes," he argued when his wife gave an incredulous laugh. "Long-distance learning and all of that. During corona, it was all the rage, wasn't it? Kids loved it."

"You can't ask him to skip college for a month, Jan," she said. "He'll hate you for the rest of his life if you deny him the chance to participate in college life."

"It's only for a month," he argued, but he could tell that he was fighting a losing battle. "Okay, at least make him see that he can't do this again. Next time…"

She raised a questioning eyebrow. "Next time?"

"Well, next time I'll have him arrested. And I'm not even kidding."

"Yeah, right. The mayor who has his own son arrested. That will go over well with the 'family values' crowd."

He uttered a noise of disgust. "Oh, have it your own way. But I'm not standing for this, you hear? I will *not* have you jeopardize my chances for re-election." He pointed a finger at her. "Just… *deal* with it!"

And with those words, he was off. He had a meeting planned with Gwendolyn to discuss how they could turn this disaster around—damage control. And if Gwen was up to it, they might get in some nookie. He needed it, as his self-esteem had taken a major hit.

. . .

SEATED IN HIS OFFICE, Daron Topley, Flemish Front party leader, had also been watching Birt's press conference with rapt attention. When Birt's son had poured that bucket of excrement on his dad's head, Daron had experienced what could only be termed mixed emotions. On the one hand, he was outraged that a prominent member of his party would be humiliated to such an extent. But on the other hand he hadn't been able to suppress a loud guffaw.

He leaned back in his chair and pondered the consequences of the incident. To be honest, he had watched Birt's meteoric rise in popularity with a growing sense of concern, for he knew exactly what was to follow. Birt would snag himself another six years in office, and then he would decide to enter the next party leader election and try to bump Daron out of the top spot, organizing a coup to remake Flemish Front in his image. In other words: a tougher, colder, more extreme version of the party Daron envisioned.

Birt was a proponent of the party's right wing, believing that Daron and the party leadership were too soft and pulled their punches when it came to defending the party's platform. Too soft on crime, too soft on immigration, and too eager to compromise. Under Chairman Birt, Flemish Front would be remade into a radically different beast, one that would appeal to the supporters of the mayor's approach, but would appall and alienate possible coalition partners, thereby guaranteeing that Flemish Front would remain an opposition party for years to come. Isolated and powerless to do anything about it.

Daron wanted to turn Flemish Front into a powerhouse, a party that participated in the democratic process and boasted mayors, ministers and perhaps even a prime minister in its ranks. In other words: he wanted to rise to power and make an actual difference. Birt and his ilk wanted the exact opposite: to remain a thorn in the establishment's side.

And now, with this whole drug business and those kids being murdered in what looked like a targeted hit, Birt's popularity would go through the roof, providing him with the support necessary to challenge and possibly oust Daron as party leader. He couldn't get rid of the man, as Birt was far too important to the party and way too popular. But he couldn't allow him to chip away at his position either.

Talk about a dilemma.

## CHAPTER 25

Holt and Poppy had decided to have another chat with Teddy Birt to see if they could get him to revise his earlier statement that he had absolutely no idea why two kids with connections to a Ghent drug gang would have targeted his bus. As Holt was driving them to the Birt Travel offices, Poppy was checking her phone.

"Anything interesting?" asked Holt. "The mayor giving another press conference?"

"No, this one is from the Elmaleh family," said Poppy. "They want to officially protest all the abuse that's been coming their way after Mohammed's death. Especially on social media, but also the horrible slogans that have been painted on their house."

"They should file an official complaint," said Holt, who didn't approve of this kind of vigilante justice that seemed to have gripped certain segments of the population.

"They have, and they've also pressed charges against Mayor Birt for the things that he's said about them." She held up the phone, and Holt briefly glimpsed Tamara Elmaleh, flanked by her husband and her kids. She was saying something about the irresponsible way Mayor Birt was using the murder of her son for his own personal political gain.

"She's not wrong," said Holt as he focused his attention on the road. "But I'm not sure it's going to change anything. Birt is milking this for all it's worth, and once the election is over, he'll probably calm down again."

"To the right, Dad," said Poppy as she pointed to a sign that read 'Birt Travel,' accompanied by a smiling couple with sunglasses and cameras around their necks, eager to book a trip with the tour operator.

Contrary to what Holt had hoped, Teddy Birt didn't prove more forthcoming than he had been the last time they spoke. On the contrary, he claimed that the police were treating him as a criminal and not the victim that he was. "You should be ashamed of yourselves," he said vehemently. "*I'm* the victim here, not those kids."

Holt decided to ignore the man's outburst and held up his phone. "Do you recognize this person, Mr. Birt?"

Teddy glanced at the picture of Floyd Timmer and shrugged. "Never seen him before in my life. Why? Is he the man who killed those kids?"

"This is Floyd Timmer," said Poppy. "He was killed last night on Falcon Street. Possibly by the same person who killed Mohammed Elmaleh."

"Look, I can't help you. I don't know any of these people," said Teddy. "You're wasting your time asking me a lot of questions I can't answer. And now, if you'll excuse me, I have a business to run."

Holt and Poppy saw themselves out, and Holt wondered if they didn't have enough on the guy to apply for a search warrant. But considering he was the mayor's brother, the magistrate probably wouldn't be easily convinced to give them a warrant.

As he got back into the car, he saw that Teddy was watching them from his office.

BOYD BATHAM HAD BEEN GRANTED one day off for his trouble, but the next day he was expected back at the job, bright and early. Teddy's explanation was that he couldn't afford to miss him for the week off Boyd had asked for, on account of the shock he'd endured after his bus had been stolen. Teddy was probably right, as the labor market was tight, and it wasn't easy to find qualified drivers he could rely on to keep his business going.

Despite the shocking events, there was no sign that tourists were abandoning Birt Travel. On the contrary, it almost seemed as if they were getting more bookings than ever. Teddy's wife, Anna, who mostly dealt with the booking side of the business, suggested that some of these were disaster tourists, hoping to ride on the bus that had been hijacked, hopefully with Boyd himself behind the wheel, since his name and picture had appeared in the papers. Boyd had even been persuaded by Teddy to give an interview to some local rag, even though he wasn't all that keen. 'Good for business,' Teddy had argued.

So he was a minor celebrity now. To be honest, he didn't need this kind of attention, and he liked the constant questions about what happened even less. He'd already told the story several times, yet people kept asking him to repeat it—again and again.

This time his bus was filled to capacity with British pensioners who were on a three-day cruise. Southampton, Zeebrugge and Cherbourg-Octeville in France. On their itinerary today: a visit to Bruges, the Venice of the North, and a perennial favorite. He had left the Cruise Terminal at the Port of Zeebrugge in his rear-view mirror and was on his way to Bruges when he noticed a white van trying to overtake him on the narrow road. He half considered pulling over to let the idiot pass, but then decided against it. If he had to pull over every time someone was in such a hurry they were prepared to act recklessly, he'd never get to Bruges on time. His passengers had an entire day scheduled to tour the town, lunch included, and he wasn't going to let anyone spoil it for them—or for him.

Finally, the van's driver seemed to deem it safe to pass, put the pedal to the metal, roared past him, and pulled out in front. And that's when it happened. The van's driver suddenly slammed on the brakes and skidded to a halt right in front of Boyd. It was all he could do to bring the bus to a full stop without ramming into the back of the vehicle.

Suddenly, the van's side door slid open, and a man appeared, a black balaclava obscuring his face, and pointing what could only be a machine gun at Boyd.

Instinctively, he threw his hands in the air, and as more men poured out of the van, he was forced to open the door. They stepped onto the bus while the man holding the gun stood directly in front of the vehicle, pointing the weapon straight at him. Behind him, passengers were screaming, all hell breaking loose amongst the fifty or so pensioners.

He was dragged off the bus and unceremoniously shoved into the white van. A bag was pulled over his head, his hands tied behind his back, and the door slammed shut.

As the van pulled away with screeching tires, he was thrown backward, his head hitting something hard and unyielding, and he realized that yesterday's adventure with the two joyriders was nothing compared to what was coming.

Because he knew exactly who these people were.

## CHAPTER 26

The passengers stood gathered by the side of the road. They looked terrified, Holt thought—terrified and confused. He could understand why. Watching their driver get kidnapped right in front of their eyes must have been a huge shock. One moment they were on their way to Bruges for a fun day out, and the next, they found themselves in the middle of what must have felt like an action movie: men with guns dragging their driver off the bus while aiming those guns at the passengers. Enough to traumatize anyone.

Since the bus was operated by Birt Travel, headquartered in Loveringem, local police had called in Holt and his team to assist in trying to work out what was going on.

While Leland, Rasheed, and Georgina spoke to the passengers to get a clear picture of what had happened, Holt and Poppy found themselves talking to Teddy Birt again. The owner and proprietor of Birt Travel had personally driven up there to try and calm his customers. He had brought a replacement driver and was hoping to send the bus on its way to Bruges posthaste to minimize the impact on his business. Fifty British tourists had paid for a trip to the capital of West Flanders and he didn't want to keep them waiting.

It seemed like a fool's errand to Holt, but then again, he wasn't a businessman.

"Do you think there's a connection to yesterday's events?" asked the tour operator owner. "When Boyd had his bus stolen from under his nose?"

He seemed genuinely concerned, though Holt wasn't entirely convinced he was being honest. Surely he must know this couldn't possibly be a coincidence?

"We believe so, yes," Holt confirmed.

The man brought his hands to his face. "My God. I hope they won't hurt Boyd. He's one of our oldest and most trusted drivers. The guy is practically like family to me."

"Can you think of a reason why these people would target your driver, Mr. Birt?" asked Poppy.

"Absolutely not," the man said, shaking his head sadly. "It's a complete mystery."

"What can you tell us about Mr. Batham?" Holt asked.

"Like I said, he's an exemplary worker. Very punctual, very popular with the passengers. Perfect record. Reliable and hard-working. Which is why this is all so puzzling. Maybe they made a mistake? Targeted the wrong person?"

"A case of mistaken identity?" Poppy asked.

"That's the only explanation I can think of."

"What about drugs?" asked Holt.

Teddy gave him a look of astonishment. "Drugs? I don't understand."

"Is it possible that Boyd had business dealings with a gang called Green Valley? They're operating out of Ghent, but may have expanded their territory to Loveringem."

"Mohammed Elmaleh and Beni Idrissi were both members of the gang," Poppy added.

"Is that a fact?" Teddy asked, looking surprised.

"It's possible they were both killed because of their connection to the gang."

Teddy shook his head. "I don't know anything about any gangs, and neither did Boyd. I'm absolutely sure of that."

"So you have no reason to suspect Boyd of being involved in the drug trade?" asked Poppy.

"The idea is simply ludicrous. Like I've told you before, we run a respectable business and have no connection whatsoever with any of that stuff. That goes for both myself, my wife, and the people who work at Birt Travel. To suggest such a thing is just… crazy."

"Right," said Holt, though, as before, he couldn't quite conceal his doubt at the statement.

Back at the station, Holt told Rasheed to check the bus's itinerary and see if he could find any anomalies.

"What kind of anomalies, boss?" asked the inspector.

He shook his head. "Any stops he shouldn't have made. Anything out of the ordinary. I just want to know what's going on with this whole bus business. First, those two kids steal one of Birt's buses and both end up dead within the next twenty-four hours. Now, the driver of that same bus is kidnapped. So, anything you can find, let me know. And get ahold of the guy's phone records, financial records, social media activity—the works."

"Will do, boss," said Rasheed, cracking his knuckles as he got busy.

Leland and Georgina were going through the witness statements from the passengers, but there didn't seem to be a lot to glean from them. They all told the same story: masked men brandishing big guns, driving a white van, had abducted their driver. Meanwhile, Holt and Poppy were checking the CCTV footage from the bus. Fortunately, the bus had both a camera pointed at the driver and a dash cam. It provided them with plenty of footage of the kidnapping, including the license plate of the vehicle used.

"Same vehicle used in the killing of the Idrissi kid last night," said Poppy. "So we have a definite connection between the two events."

"We better send this over to Roy," said Holt. "If these kidnappers belong to the Phoenix gang, as Roy believes, and they're engaged in a war with Green Valley, Batham must be involved somehow. And if he's involved, it's more than likely Birt is, too."

"The cocaine found in those secret boxes underneath the bus," Poppy said, nodding.

"In spite of all his protestations, I'm convinced Birt knows exactly what's going on."

"What's the connection with the shooting of Floyd Timmer?"

"I don't believe for one second that's a coincidence. Somehow Timmer must be involved as well."

"Member of one of the two gangs, you think?"

"Has to be. Though as far as we can tell, he's never had any business with the drug trade. But that doesn't mean he didn't get involved somehow."

"Boss?" said Rasheed as he raised his hand. "I think you may want to see this."

Holt and Poppy joined the technically gifted inspector at his desk.

"I've checked Boyd's itinerary, and he picked up his group of passengers in Zeebrugge to take to Bruges, right? Most of them are British tourists arriving on one of the big cruise ships that frequent Zeebrugge port. The odd thing," said Rasheed, "is that before he picked up the tourists, he parked his bus in a part of the port where, strictly speaking, he had no business being." He pulled up a map of the

Zeebrugge harbor and pointed to the location where Boyd had parked.

"How do you know he parked there?" asked Poppy.

"From the bus's satnav," Rasheed explained. "It shows us exactly where Boyd has been. Also, his phone pinged off a nearby mast. Right… here," he said, pointing again, "which confirms the satnav data."

"What's there?" asked Holt, studying the map.

"It's one of the main terminals where the containers are stored after being unloaded from cargo vessels that dock in Zeebrugge, before they're loaded onto trucks and trains for inland transportation. Compared to Antwerp, Zeebrugge is a small coastal port handling over 70 million tonnes of cargo annually, a lot less than Antwerp's 220 million. But like the port of Antwerp, it's also afflicted by drug trafficking, with drugs arriving destined for the European market. Mostly, the drugs are hidden in containers, mixed with other goods, and removed by people working for the big drug cartels."

"So… are you saying that Boyd Batham works for one of the cartels?" asked Holt.

Rasheed shrugged. "Nothing on his phone indicates that he does, but the fact that he parked his bus where it had no business suggests he was picking something up there."

"And tucking it away in the boxes hidden underneath his bus," said Holt, nodding.

"They probably have one of those hydraulic lifts so they can access those boxes and load them," said Rasheed. "The same type of vehicle lift they have at Birt Travel."

"He probably has a second phone," said Poppy. "To communicate with his bosses about his illegal activities."

"I also discovered that Boyd makes this same trip every week," said Rasheed. "Every week, he parks his bus in exactly the same location, spends about an hour there, before picking up a fresh batch of tourists from the cruise terminal, a ten-minute drive away."

"So every week Boyd picks up a shipment of drugs," said Poppy, "and also a busload of tourists. Then what? Where does he take the drugs?"

"Here," said Rasheed. He had enlarged the map and traced Boyd's itinerary. "First, he travels to Bruges and drops off the tourists for the day. Then he drives up to Antwerp, where he presumably drops off the drugs at one of the warehouses operated by the cartel he works for. The final destination is probably Holland, where most of the main European drug cartels are located. From there, they distribute the drugs across the continent."

"Nice work if you can get it," said Poppy.

Holt immediately sprang into action. "We need a warrant to search that bus, Birt Travel's headquarters—and also a warrant to arrest Teddy Birt and all the people working for him." He grimaced. "So much for Boyd Batham being a model worker."

"Oh, I'll bet he is," said Poppy, "just not in the way Teddy likes us to think."

## CHAPTER 27

While a small cadre of officers, led by Leland, combed through the Birt Travel offices, Georgina had been put in charge of tracking down the bus. Holt could have kicked himself for not impounding it right then and there. In the meantime, he and Poppy had placed Teddy Birt under arrest. The Chief Inspector had a devil of a time convincing Prosecutor Shonna Turner that arrest and search warrants were of vital importance, but in the end, he managed to persuade her of the strange goings-on at Birt Travel.

While an officer escorted Teddy Birt to the interview room, he discussed the case with his daughter over a cup of coffee. Contrary to his old precinct, the Loveringem Commissioner had invested in a state-of-the-art coffee machine, which wasn't a luxury, as Holt was a self-admitted coffee nut. Poppy, not so much. She preferred herbal tea and other strange concoctions—in other words, hot water with a funny taste.

"So as I see it," said Poppy as she took a sip of something called 'Happy Delight,' even though it smelled horrible to

Holt's delicate palate, "Teddy Birt is in league with a gang called Phoenix, allowing it to use his buses for transportation purposes. But yesterday two kids, belonging to a rival gang called Green Valley, decided to steal a bus, and for their trouble were killed by Motorcycle Man, who we have to assume is a hired gun for Phoenix."

"Seems like the most logical conclusion," Holt agreed. "Assuming that the drugs were located in those boxes when Boyd set off from Zeebrugge, and they were empty when we found the bus crashed in that ditch, Phoenix were probably extremely unhappy with Elmaleh and Idrissi, suspecting them of ripping them off and stealing the shipment for their rival gang. Same reason they've now kidnapped Boyd Batham. Which means they must suspect that Batham was working with those kids somehow."

"You think that's possible? That Batham stole a shipment and sold it to a rival gang?"

"It's the only logical explanation." He pointed his thumb toward the interview room. "And I know just the guy who can explain all this to us—if he will talk."

"Then let's make him talk… sir," said Poppy.

Holt grinned. "Let's go get him, Inspector Holt."

"Not if I get him first, Chief Inspector Holt."

Ever since Belgium had become the number-one transportation hub for the drug cartels, especially Antwerp, one of Europe's biggest ports, most of the gang violence had been limited to that city, with some spilling over to Brussels, Ghent, and some of the smaller provincial capitals. But never to the countryside, of which Loveringem was the shining crown. But then there were probably drug users everywhere now, and they had to be supplied, which meant that the gangs were steadily working to expand their network.

He and Poppy took a seat in front of the tour operator

owner, who looked slightly nervous but mostly annoyed that he had been dragged in there.

"I'll have you know that I will lodge a formal complaint with your Commissioner," he said. "And also with my brother, the mayor. You can't do this to a hard-working businessman like me. You have no right." He didn't act so smarmy now, Holt thought.

"In light of the evidence we have gathered, we have every right, Mr. Birt," said Holt.

"What evidence? What are you talking about?"

Holt placed a map of the port of Zeebrugge on the table in front of the suspect, along with several pictures of the boxes attached to the bus's undercarriage—empty. "We have reason to believe that your driver, Boyd Batham, has been secretly shipping drugs from the port of Zeebrugge to Antwerp by hiding them in these undercarriage containers."

"Nonsense," said Birt. "Boyd would never do such a thing. I've told you already that he's a model worker. Part of the Birt Travel family."

"And yet we believe that the reason he was abducted is that yesterday's shipment of drugs went missing after it was stolen by Mohammed Elmaleh and Beni Idrissi, two low-level dealers for a gang operating out of Green Valley Park in Ghent. The gang Batham works for, Phoenix, didn't take the loss of their merchandise lightly, and so they sent this man to deal with the two teenagers." He placed an ANPR picture of Motorcycle Man on the table. "We believe he's an enforcer for the Phoenix gang."

"I don't know anything about this Green Valley," said Birt, but he was staring at the picture of the black-clad enforcer, eyes bulging slightly, and clearly not at ease.

"And then there's the killing of this man," said Holt, placing yet another picture on the table. "Floyd Timmer. Killed last night by the same man who took out Elmaleh."

"We don't know exactly how Timmer fits into the scheme of things," said Poppy, "but we know he must be involved somehow."

They had managed to impound the Birt Travel bus taking the British tourists to Bruges, but by the time they did, the shipment that Batham had picked up in Zeebrugge that morning was already gone, the new driver having delivered it in Antwerp. The information had been passed on to the Antwerp police, but most likely the drugs would have been moved again. The driver had been questioned, but denied all charges.

"So now these same extremely dangerous people are holding your driver," said Holt, leaning in. "The most likely scenario is that they will torture him until he gives them the location of their missing shipment of drugs, and then they will kill him."

"So what do you have to say to that, Mr. Birt?" asked Poppy.

Teddy was still staring at the picture of Motorcycle Man. He shivered slightly. "Look," he said, licking his lips nervously. "Now look here… you… you don't know…"

Holt slammed his flat hand on the table, making Teddy jump. "What is your involvement with these people, Teddy?"

"I…" A haunted look had come into his eyes. "Look here, Holt. You can see where this is going, right? First those kids, then this Timmer guy, now Boyd. Who do you think is next, huh?" He tapped his chest. "Me, that's who. They'll come after me next! Me and my wife. So…"

"We can protect you, Teddy," said Holt.

"I'm not sure you can," said Teddy as he slumped a little. "These people are pretty ruthless, as you already indicated. If they're going to start kidnapping my drivers…"

Holt waited patiently. Cracks had appeared in the dam, and it was only a matter of time before it burst.

Finally, Teddy lifted his head and gave him a haunted look. "Did you mean what you said? That you can protect me and my family?"

Holt nodded. "In exchange for your confession."

"My confession." He produced a nervous laugh. He placed his hands on the table and thought for a moment. Finally, he nodded. "Okay, the thing you have to understand is that I had no idea what I was getting myself into when I signed up for this. At the time of the coronavirus, Birt Travel was on the verge of going under. No travel, no business, no money coming in."

"Didn't you receive coronavirus aid?"

He scoffed. "That only covered a fraction of my expenses. I had just made a big investment, expanded my fleet of buses, built an entirely new main office. I was in debt up to my eyeballs when corona struck. Banks weren't too eager to give me an extension on the loan, and so when the suggestion was made to use our buses to transport not tourists but…" He couldn't bring himself to say the word. "Recreational substances, I saw it as a lifeline. A way to pay off our mountain of debt and survive until we could restart."

"So you started trafficking drugs."

He held up a finger. "I object to that term. We never trafficked anything. We only shipped it from one place to the other."

"By hiding it in those boxes."

He nodded.

"How does that work, exactly?" asked Poppy, even though they already knew.

He gestured at the map in front of him. "One of our drivers travels to Zeebrugge to pick up a load of passengers, and in the meantime, he also picks up a shipment of merchandise. He then takes the passengers to Bruges or Brussels or whatever is on the itinerary, and while they're out visiting the city for the day, he drives to one of the drop-off locations, mainly located to the north of Antwerp, and then back."

"Only this time something went wrong. And those two kids stole your drugs."

"That appears to be what happened," said Teddy. "Though I still don't understand why they would do such a thing. Everyone in the business knows that these gangs are ruthless. Steal their stuff, and they come after you like a pack of hyenas. So those kids were either incredibly stupid, or this is a case of one gang trying to muscle in on the territory of another one, and if that's the case…" He sighed deeply. "God help us all."

CHAPTER 28

Teddy claimed that his brother had no knowledge whatsoever of these dealings with a criminal network, but Holt wasn't so sure. Jan Birt wouldn't be the first politician to cut corners in a bid to advance his political career. But he decided to tackle that particular angle the next time he interrogated the owner of Birt Travel. Right now, he was hosting a visitor. It was none other than Roy, who had come all the way from Ghent to talk to Holt.

"I'm going to put all my cards on the table, and I expect you to do the same, Glen," said Roy.

"I thought we already agreed we'd cooperate on this?" said Holt.

"I know, but I just wanted to make sure. We've been getting some pushback from your boss."

He raised his eyebrows. "Forrester?"

Roy nodded and glanced out of the window at the fields that stretched out behind the precinct. "Much better view than the one I'm saddled with," he said.

He couldn't argue with that. Loveringem was definitely a step up from Ghent in terms of the views. Miles and miles of green spread out in all directions. Cows lazily grazed in the fields, horse farms dotted the landscape, and sheep darted in the meadows. If you enjoyed going for long walks and breathe country air, there was no better place to live.

"I still miss my old stomping ground, though," admitted Holt. "The buzz of the city. The noise, the pollution, the thronging masses. Loveringem is a little too peaceful and quiet for my taste."

Though it was true that waking up to the sound of birds chirping was a novel and not unpleasant experience. Maybe Poppy was right, and he simply had to get used to the place.

Roy leaned in. "Look, I'll show you mine if you show me yours, all right?"

Holt smiled. "You know I love you, Roy, but not in that way, all right?"

Roy made a face. "I hear you've arrested Teddy Birt?"

Holt turned serious again. "He made a full confession. Turns out he and some of his drivers have been in bed with the drug mafia for years. The drivers pick up the drugs in Zeebrugge, hide them in secret containers located underneath the bus, and take them to Antwerp, where they get redistributed. Only now one shipment has gone missing, and the gang it belongs to is killing people left and right whom they think are involved."

"The Idrissi and Elmaleh kids."

"And a guy called Floyd Timmer. Though I have yet to ascertain how he fits into the picture."

"Timmer did occasional jobs for the Green Valley gang," said Roy. "Not as a dealer, but when they needed a guy to get into a place unseen. Timmer was an expert burglar."

"So Phoenix suspect him of being involved?"

Roy nodded. "They believe that Timmer took the drugs for Green Valley, along with those two kids. The kids took the bus, and Timmer took the drugs."

"So they crashed the bus on purpose? To get access to the drugs?"

"That's the theory we're working from."

"And they also believe that Batham was involved somehow?"

"Yeah, they think that he allowed his bus to be taken by Idrissi and Elmaleh. All they want is their stuff back. And if not, they'll make everyone involved pay."

"Well, I've got this for you," said Holt, placing a phone on the table. "It belongs to Teddy Birt, and it's the phone he used to communicate with his drivers and also with his bosses. It's encrypted, but he was kind enough to unlock it for us. There's plenty of stuff that I'm sure you'll find extremely interesting." When Roy reached out to take the phone, Holt placed his hand on it. "Batham had his own encrypted phone on him when he was taken. With any luck, you should be able to trace his location."

Roy nodded and snatched up the phone. "I'll get our tech team on this immediately." He held up the phone. "Thanks for this, Glen. This is pure gold."

"Let's hope you find the guy before they kill him."

## CHAPTER 29

Holt and Poppy were on their way to Town Hall to have a little chat with Mayor Birt. Even though Teddy had claimed that his brother had no involvement whatsoever with his illegal dealings, Poppy's dad wasn't so sure. And since the Chief Inspector liked to follow his gut, he had decided to confront the man in person.

Poppy wasn't sure this was such a good idea, but then her dad was more likely to follow his gut instinct than any advice anyone could give him.

It was only a short walk from the precinct to Town Hall, and they passed through some of the more scenic streets in Loveringem. They might live in a small town, but it certainly didn't lack charm. The cobblestone streets, the houses reminiscent of medieval times, and the many cozy shops and restaurants attracted tourists in droves. They might not be Bruges or Ghent or Brussels, with millions of visitors annually, but they were still one of the more charming little towns in East Flanders and could hold their own in comparison.

The standard of living was one of Loveringem's attraction points, as the town boasted a disproportionate number of lawyers, doctors, dentists, and business professionals. Once upon a time, the woods of Loveringem had been inhabited by Ghent's bourgeoisie, who built big country houses and castles. Nowadays, those castles might not be inhabited by captains of industry, but they were still there, and the castle route was famous, threading through Loveringem and surrounding towns, making people marvel at their beauty and opulence. Even right down the street where Poppy and her dad now lived, a smaller castle stood, hidden behind a wall. Every time she passed on her way to work, Poppy wondered about the people who lived there. Her ex-boyfriend, who had left her for a model-slash-influencer, had once claimed that a famous football star had lived there before he committed suicide. It merely added to Poppy's fascination with the place.

"A penny for your thoughts?" said Holt. He smiled. "You seem miles away."

"Oh, just thinking how lucky we are to be living in Loveringem," she said. They had just passed a shop that sold Christmas items and was popular all year round.

"I guess," he said. "At least before people started getting killed in droves."

"You just don't want to admit that you made the right choice, Dad."

"I didn't make any choice at all!"

"Oh, but you did. You told me that they gave you the choice between being fired or transferred here. And you chose Loveringem."

He was silent, not happy at being reminded of the events that led up to the dismissal from his old position. At least they hadn't removed his stripes, as his old boss had threatened to do: relegating him to traffic duty, to spend the rest of his career directing traffic. He would probably have preferred to get canned over that humiliation. At least *her* breakup hadn't had a lot of major consequences—just a loss of some of her illusions.

They had arrived at Town Hall and ascended the stone steps to the heavy oak doors that marked the entrance. Once inside the entrance hall, they directed their steps to the reception desk to their immediate left. For a moment, Poppy admired the burgundy rugs, the banners draped from the granite parapet, and the twin stone staircases that led up to the second floor, where the mayor had his office and where the main ballroom was located, where weddings took place and various ceremonies and receptions were held.

The secretary who met them seemed surprised when Holt expressed an urgent wish to talk to the mayor.

"But you don't have an appointment," she said, as if they had committed a capital crime.

"We need to speak to him in connection to a case we're working on," said Poppy.

"A case that involves his brother," added Holt.

The woman's eyes widened a little. "The mayor's brother?" She seemed anxious to be the recipient of more information, but when none was forthcoming, she finally picked up her phone. "Well then," she said huffily, and moments later was talking to Mayor Birt's personal assistant.

Before long, they were invited to ascend the stairs and proceed to the first office on the left. They found Justine Hallett equally curious to discover why two police officers wanted to have an urgent conversation with her boss, but once again, Poppy's dad refused to divulge more than he had to. He was keeping his powder dry for the moment they were face-to-face with the mayor himself.

It turned out they had quite a long wait ahead of them, as the mayor was in a meeting and couldn't be disturbed. Couldn't be bothered, more likely, thought Poppy, who didn't have a high opinion of their burgomaster.

As they took a seat in the waiting room, Dad flipped through a copy of *Het Laatste Nieuws*, while Poppy picked up a copy of the *Flemish Front Magazine* and wasn't surprised to discover it was just as rancid and disgusting as the mayor's videos and speeches.

Finally, she couldn't take it anymore and threw it back where she found it.

"Listen to this," said Dad as he held up his paper. "The police are still at a loss as to why a local man was killed in true mafioso style last night. Is the only town ruled by a Flemish Front mayor turning into the Wild West? We asked party leader Daron Topley, and he said that the underworld is clearly throwing down a challenge to his party, and he and Mayor Birt are more than willing to meet the challenge head-on and show these thugs that the time of permissiveness is over. 'They know that once we are in charge, their days will be over,' said Mr. Topley. 'We will clear them out like the scum that they are. When I become minister-president of Flanders, I will put more police on the streets and stop saving money on law enforcement.'" He closed the paper and gave his daughter a grin. "Looks like we'll all get a nice big pay raise once Flemish Front rises to power, honey."

"I doubt it," she said sardonically. "You know what politicians are like. Lots of promises they don't intend to keep."

"I, for one, am one of the politicians who does keep his promise," a voice suddenly piped up. When she looked over, she saw that they had been joined by the mayor.

## CHAPTER 30

Birt gave Holt and Poppy a tight smile. "Please join me in my office. Though I have to warn you that I don't have a lot of time."

He led them into his office, which was as opulent as the rest of the Town Hall, with high ceilings supported by thick wooden beams, walls consisting of exposed brickwork, and large paintings depicting bucolic feasts reminiscent of Breughel's best work.

"Take a seat," said the mayor as he lowered himself onto his ornate armchair behind a large wooden desk. He folded his sausage-like fingers on his desk and regarded them with a mournful expression. "Is this about my brother being arrested? If so, I appreciate the courtesy of being given the distressing news directly. It's much appreciated."

"Yes, that is the main reason we're here," Holt admitted. "Who told you about the arrest?"

"Does it matter? I know, and I want to express my shock and surprise that Teddy would be mixed up in something utterly disgraceful like this."

"Did you know about your brother's dealings with the drug mafia?" asked Holt, crossing one leg over the other.

The mayor shook his head. "Absolutely not. When I was told the news, I was as perplexed as you must have been. Nothing could have prepared me for this."

"You never talked about this?"

"Never. Teddy and I are very close, but this is one thing he kept from me."

"He blames his decision on financial difficulties because of the coronavirus crisis."

"It was a difficult time for all of us," said the mayor virtuously. "A lot of businesses suffered, and many didn't survive. It was a miracle that Birt Travel managed to keep its head above the water, but now that I know how, I'm appalled. Appalled and outraged."

"Birt Travel is mentioned as one of the main sponsors of your re-election campaign. Did you know that the money for your campaign was being provided by the drug mafia?"

"Absolutely not," said the mayor, drawing together his beetling brows in a vicious frown. He had pulled back from his desk and crossed his arms over his chest, clearly not pleased with the way the interview was going. "Like I said, I had no inkling of my brother's dealings with these despicable people."

"As I understand it, you're a silent partner in Birt Travel," said Poppy. "What is your role exactly, Mr. Mayor?"

This time the mayor wasn't all that forthcoming with information. Instead, he merely glowered at her for a moment, then seemed to make up his mind. "I think I'd better contact a lawyer before I answer any further questions." He got up. "And I should warn you to keep these insinuations strictly to yourselves. If I read any mention of this in the papers…" The threat hung in the air, but the mayor's meaning was clear: he wasn't going to answer any more questions, which struck Holt as significant, to say the least.

"If, as you insist, you had nothing to do with your brother's dealings—"

"Please leave," said the mayor as he emerged from behind his desk with outstretched arms in the direction of the door. He opened the door with a tight smile. "As I said, I want to answer any questions you have, but under the circumstances, I think it's better if I consult a lawyer first. You understand."

Holt nodded. He understood, all right. Though he and the mayor probably placed a different explanation on the man's sudden about-face.

As he and Poppy left the man's office, she made a face at Holt, which he answered by wiggling his eyebrows.

"Looks like we hit a nerve there, Dad," she said.

"You can say that again. Which tells me that the ties between Birt Travel and Town Hall are a lot closer than the mayor would like to admit."

"Imagine that: a mayor who prides himself on his law-and-order stance is being funded by the drug mafia. This is a PR nightmare for the man."

"I don't care. If it's true what he said about being taken by surprise by his brother's arrest, he sure has a strange way of showing it."


THE MOMENT they had set foot in the office, the Commissioner's door opened, and he said, "Glen? Can you step into my office for a moment? Now, please?"

Poppy gave him a look of concern, and Leland looked up from his computer. "Who did you hit now, boss?"

"Not funny, Leland," said Poppy. "Not funny at all."

"I thought it was funny," murmured the cop, not bothering to hide his smile.

The moment Holt entered the Commissioner's office, the man's face became a mask of concern. "Please close the door, Glen, and take a seat."

"Yes, sir," he said, and dutifully did as he was told.

The Commissioner stared at him for a moment, then launched into speech. "Guess who I just got off the phone with."

"Mayor Birt?"

"Got it in one," said the chief. "Says you've been harassing him?"

"We merely needed to clear up a few things, sir," said Holt. "In connection to his brother's arrest."

"Well, don't. The mayor is an upstanding citizen, and as far as I can tell, above reproach. If every person whose family members have crossed a line is to be persecuted…"

"I didn't persecute anyone," he said. "I merely asked him if he knew about his brother's dealings with the drug mafia. He said he didn't, and as far as I'm concerned, that's the end of it."

"Knowing you, that's only the beginning," said the chief with a touch of sternness. Then he softened. "The thing is, Glen, you're not in the big city anymore. This is the country. We do things differently here. For one thing, we don't interview the mayor as if he's a suspect when by all accounts he isn't."

"His re-election campaign is sponsored by his brother, sir," Holt couldn't help but point out. "And he did mention that he and Teddy have always been very close."

The Commissioner nodded. "So you don't buy that he wouldn't have known about Teddy's dealings with these drug gangs?"

"It seems odd, especially as Jan used to work with his brother. Birt Travel is a family firm—always has been. It was launched by Jan and Teddy's grandfather, then run by their

FIELD OF BLOOD

dad for many years. Teddy is the third-generation Birt in charge of the company. And not only is Jan a silent partner, but until he became mayor, he and Teddy used to run the company together. So the mayor's protestations all seem a little… dubious."

The Commissioner thought for a moment. "But you don't have any evidence?"

"Not yet," he admitted.

"Until you do, I think you'd do well to steer clear of the man. Jan Birt is an… unusual type of politician, Glen. For one thing, he's a spiteful and mean-spirited kind of man, and not afraid to go after the people he feels have wronged him. So unless you have an ironclad case, my advice would be to play it cool. If he gets one whiff of your suspicions, he'll come after you with everything he's got. And after your scrap with Commissioner Bayton, you don't have a lot of friends left. No one to fight in your corner, or to give you another chance." He gave him a look of concern. "You can see what I'm trying to tell you here, can't you, son?"

"Yes, sir," he said. "And I appreciate it. I really do."

The man's features relaxed. "So gather your evidence, but don't rock the boat. And once you feel you have a strong enough case, I'll back you up one hundred percent."

"Thank you, sir," he said, surprised by the man's candor and support.

"I for one am glad that you have chosen Loveringem to restart your career, Glen. Most of my colleagues didn't want you, after you hit a superior officer—no matter your reason for doing so. But like I said, your talent and your experience are most welcome here. We can sure use it, since like all towns, there are hidden dangers lurking beneath the surface. Appearances can be deceiving, and even though Loveringem has all the hallmarks of a Garden of Eden, we have plenty of problems of our own. An old warhorse like me, veteran of many battles, is perfectly placed to help guide you—if you're willing to accept my advice, that is." He smiled. "How about it, Glen? Are we on the same page?"

"We are, sir," he said, much relieved by this candid speech. "You can count on me."

"That's grand," said the aged police chief. "I'm glad we understand each other."

## CHAPTER 31

*H*olt was checking the file they had on André Wiel when the call came in. He picked up on the first ring. "Yes, Roy."

"We found him," said his former colleague. "Batham. He's banged up pretty bad, but he'll live. I'm waiting for permission from the doctors to interview him—Jan Palfijn Hospital. Wanna sit in?"

"Absolutely," he said, André Wiel and his habit of vandalizing cars that didn't belong to him could wait. He passed his daughter's desk. "They found Batham. He's in Jan Palfijn Hospital, and Roy wants us there for the first interview. Are you game?"

"What do you think?" said Poppy, and grabbed her coat.

As they walked out of the office, he saw that the Commissioner was eyeing him closely. He gave the chief a nod, which the old man returned in kind. They had an understanding, which was pretty exceptional. He and Commissioner Bayton had never seen eye to eye, even before Holt discovered that the man had been taking certain liberties with Leah. Looked like Ezekiel Forrester was cut from quite a different cloth.

Though he had to confess he had his doubts about the man's 'dangers lurking beneath the surface' talk. As far as he could tell, apart from recent events, Loveringem was a town pretty much devoid of crime. Then again, he was the newcomer, so what did he know?

He passed Georgina's desk. "If you have a moment, could you and Leland have a little chat with André Wiel? He's the guy who destroyed Wanda Desai's side mirrors."

"Will do, boss," said Georgina. "Where are you going?"

"They've rescued Batham. We're going to see what he has to say for himself."

The drive from Loveringem to the city didn't take Poppy more than half an hour, and then she was already swinging her car into the Jan Palfijn parking lot. The hospital had recently been fully renovated and expanded, and looked completely different from the way Holt remembered. His daughter had been born in the maternity wing, so he was familiar with the hospital, which boasted a history dating back to the thirteenth century.

"Third floor," said Holt as he checked Roy's instructions. Colorful arrows and lines had been painted on the floor so visitors and patients always knew where to go, as the hospital, like a lot of hospitals, was a warren of floors and corridors. With over 500 beds, 1,100 employees, and 150 doctors, it was one of the bigger hospitals in the Ghent region.

When they entered the room where Batham had been taken, he saw that the man looked pretty banged up, as Roy had already indicated. His head was bandaged, his nose was in a nasal splint, and his right arm was in a sling. He'd clearly been in the wars.

"My God, what did they do to you?" asked Poppy when she caught sight of the man.

The bus driver grimaced. "It was pretty awful," he said. "These people are animals."

Holt and Poppy took a seat by the man's side, and Roy launched into the interview.

"Tell us what happened, Mr. Batham, please."

"There isn't a lot I can tell you. They grabbed me from my bus and threw me into the back of a van, then drove me to an abandoned warehouse, from what I could tell when they took off the bag over my head. And that's when they started laying into me. There were three of them, all big nasty-looking fellas, and they just kept hitting me and kicking me and…" He sobbed, and tears appeared in his eyes. "I… I thought I was gonna die."

"What did they want from you?" asked Roy.

"They seemed to think I had misplaced something that belonged to them and didn't believe me when I told them I had no idea what they were talking about."

"I can see how that would have made them upset," said Holt. "Look, Boyd," he added, "we know all about the drugs, all right? We arrested your boss Teddy, and he's made a full confession. So we know he was using Birt Travel as a front to transport shipments of drugs from the port of Zeebrugge to Antwerp. All conveniently hidden in those compartments located underneath the bus. So you don't have to lie anymore."

"Just tell us the truth, Mr. Batham," said Roy. "That would be my advice."

The driver stared from Roy to Holt, then sighed. "Okay, fine. So they wanted to know about the shipment that was stolen from my bus yesterday. The stuff belonged to them, and they weren't happy that it was gone, as it represents a sizable investment. But it's just like I said: I have no idea who took the stuff. I sure as heck had nothing to do with it. Why would I? I mean, I'm not crazy. These people are dangerous. You don't steal from them."

"And they didn't believe you?" asked Poppy.

"They seemed to think that I had something to do with the theft. That somehow I tipped off those two kids who hijacked the bus. That they were working for a rival gang."

"Green Valley," said Holt.

"That's right. And so was I. That this Green Valley gang had paid me to turn a blind eye while the shipment was being removed. They said they'd already settled the score with the two kids and now it was my turn." He gave Roy a grateful look. "You arrived just in time, Detective Hesketh. They said they'd break all of my fingers next, and then they'd start chopping them off one by one if I didn't tell them where the shipment was."

"They were holding him in a container," said Roy for Holt and Poppy's sake. "In the old docklands. It looked like a torture chamber, with all kinds of torture equipment. We believe they've been using it on others, as well. Place looked pretty terrible."

"It was horrible," said Batham, as a tear slid down his cheek. "It was like something from a horror movie. Like those *Saw* movies, you know. My son likes those. I don't, and now even less after it happened to me. I really thought they were going to cut me up into little pieces and make me eat my own intestines or something. Ten minutes more and I'd have been a goner, because I really have no idea what happened to that shipment."

"We now believe that it was a guy named Floyd Timmer who took it," said Holt as he showed Batham a picture on his phone. "Recognize him?"

Batham took the phone and studied the picture carefully. "I think I've seen him. Maybe in Colruyt," he added, referring to one of the biggest Belgian supermarket chains.

"He was killed," said Roy. "Knifed to death in Loveringem last night. So that's three people dead, all over the same stolen shipment. And you're sure you weren't involved?"

The bus driver shook his head. "I swear, detective. I had nothing to do with it."

Holt figured that if Batham hadn't succumbed to the extreme torture methods the drug mafia had employed to make him talk, he was probably telling the truth. "It's all right, Boyd," he said as he placed a hand on the man's arm. "You rest up, and get well soon."

"We will have to place you under arrest," said Roy.

"I understand," said Batham. He sighed. "My wife told me I should never have gotten involved with these people, but Teddy made it sound like it was the only thing we could do to prevent the company from going under. And he also promised me a big payday if I participated in the scheme."

"How big?" asked Poppy.

"Ten K for every shipment? Cash. And since I make a trip most weeks, that's a lot of cash."

"That *is* a lot of money," Holt agreed. Forty K a month, just to drive some packages of drugs from Zeebrugge to Antwerp. Easy money—until it wasn't.

"I should have known that it was too good to be true," said the driver. Whether he was sorry that the money stream had dried up or that he was almost killed was hard to tell. Maybe both. He eyed the detective anxiously. "How long do you think I will get?"

"I'm afraid you will be looking at four to five years, Boyd," said Roy. "And a hefty fine on top of that."

The man hung his head. "My wife won't be well pleased. But at least I'm still alive." A look of anguish appeared in his eyes. "Am I safe now? Will they come looking for me?"

"We'll post an officer outside," Roy assured him. "It's important that you cooperate, though."

"I'll cooperate," he assured them. "You bet I will. I just want to put this whole thing behind me and get my life back on track. It was great for a while, being paid a small fortune for a simple job like that, but it definitely wasn't good for my ticker. Every time I set out from Zeebrugge, I didn't have a moment's peace until I reached my final destination. And even then I kept looking over my shoulder, expecting a knock on the door. Every time I heard a police siren, I figured you were coming for me." He gave them a sad look. "I'm just not cut out for a life of crime, detectives. I'm glad it's over."

## CHAPTER 32

"Do you think he was telling the truth?" asked Poppy as she popped a breadstick into her mouth. She was comfortably seated at the kitchen island while her dad checked on the risotto he had put in the oven. "Batham?"

"I think he was, yeah," said her dad. "I mean, if those violent thugs couldn't crack him, nothing could."

"So who knew about the deal Birt made with the drug cartel?"

"I'm sure at this point everyone did. And the routes Birt's drivers took. It wouldn't have been hard to snatch a bus and remove the shipment."

"I guess." The muscle for hire working Batham over had all been arrested by the tactical unit of the DSU, the Directorate of Special Units. As it happened, the arrest of Teddy Birt and his relinquishing of the code to crack his encrypted phone had put them on the track of Batham by tracing his phone, which had saved the driver's life. Otherwise, he probably would have met the same fate as the others. The only person they hadn't found yet was Motorcycle Man, who proved as elusive as before.

"I hope this whole drug business is over and done with now," she said as she grabbed another breadstick and stuck it into the dip sauce. Her dad followed her example.

"This is some great dip," he said. "Delhaize?"

"No, new caterer on Tram Street. They've got some delicious stuff—a little pricey, but now that there are two of us, I guess we can afford it."

He grinned. "Our two giant salaries combined, huh?"

"You make more than me, Dad," she reminded him. The salaries of police grades were fixed, so there were no surprises. Along with the seniority her dad had earned over his years on the force, they should be able to get by, even though she still felt their rent was exorbitant. But then the Ghent area was known for its extreme rental prices. No way to avoid it, unless she was prepared to transfer to the south of the country, where things were a little cheaper. But then she'd have to work on her French, as Wallonia was the French-speaking part of the country. Plus, say goodbye to her friends and family.

"Oh, they talked to this André Wiel fellow," she said. "The one who was caught on camera vandalizing Wanda Desai's car? He claimed that he had nothing to do with it until they confronted him with the CCTV. Then he said it was probably a lookalike, or someone wearing a mask that had been made to look like him."

"Very original," said her dad with a smile.

"They'll talk to him again tomorrow. I'm sure he'll have a new story by then. Maybe an alien stole his face."

"Sounds like something straight from a comic book."

She rolled her eyes. "Oh, not again with the comics, Dad. You know what? Next time I talk to Mom, I'll ask her very politely to return your collection, all right?"

"She's holding it hostage, that's what she's doing."

"And why would she do that? To what purpose?"

"To get back at me for slapping her new husband."

"That wasn't a slap, Dad. It was definitely a punch."

She had heard the story, and it was quite spectacular, getting more so every time she heard it. Very soon now, they'd make Dad sound like He-Man knocking Skeletor about.

She studied her dad and thought he looked tired, especially around the eyes. Even his hair had more touches of gray now than it had before 'the incident.' But then he'd gone through a pretty tough time. At least it hadn't affected his capacity as a police officer.

Harley came waddling up, attracted by the delicious scent wafting from the oven. He placed his paws on her leg and gazed up at her with a wistful expression on his wrinkly face. She picked him up and placed him on her lap. "Are dogs allowed to eat breadsticks?" she asked.

"You're asking the wrong person, honey. I'm not exactly a dog expert."

"And that coming from the man who's been Harley's human for years."

"What can I say? I love the mutt, but that doesn't make me a fount of knowledge on all things canine." He studied the little guy, who was whimpering now. "All I can say is that your mom and I used to feed him breadsticks all the time, and he's still alive, so…"

She rolled her eyes. "Dad!"

"Maybe you can google it?"

"I think they're allowed," she said, and held a piece of breadstick in front of her beloved mutt. The dog sniffed at it, then happily munched down on the treat.

"Looks like he's giving it the seal of approval, then."

"He knows what's good for him better than we do," she

said as she hugged him close. After her husband had cheated on her with his beauty queen, Harley had taken the top spot as the love of her life. Though he had to share that rare honor with her dad, of course. Her mom had dropped a couple of positions and now wasn't even in the top ten anymore. Possibly not even the top hundred. She definitely did not approve of Mom's new hubby.

The doorbell rang, and she looked up.

"Expecting someone?" asked Dad.

She shook her head. "Nope."

"I'll go."

He walked to the intercom and checked the little camera. "Looks like one of those Deliveroo guys," he said, and pressed the speaker button. "Yes?"

"Delivery for Holt," said the person.

"I didn't order anything," he returned, but that didn't seem to bother the delivery man, who turned and walked away. Moments later, they heard the telltale sounds of a scooter racing off.

Holt shared a look with her, and she shrugged. "Wrong delivery?"

"Let's have a look," said her dad, and stepped outside to check.

She fed another piece of breadstick to Harley, who seemed to enjoy it less this time, probably waiting for the good stuff.

When her dad returned, he was carrying a HelloFresh box.

"Oh, goodie," she said.

"It's definitely addressed to us. Which is weird, since we didn't order anything."

He placed the box on the table and opened it, then stared at its contents for a moment before stiffening.

"What is it?" she asked, but he held up his hand.

"Don't," he advised. But since she was the curious kind—no doubt a trait inherited from her dad—she approached anyway. Inside the cardboard box, a plastic container had been placed, and inside the container lay a small piece of red meat.

"What is it?" she asked again.

"A heart," he said.

She frowned. "It's very small for a heart, Dad."

He shook his head. "It's an animal heart. Probably a rat." He picked out a note and held it up. A single sentence was written there.

*'I haven't forgotten.'*

"What's going on, Dad?" she asked. "What is this?"

Her dad's jaw tightened. "It's not the first time I've received one of these. Remember Brian Parnham?"

"The Gentbrugge Butcher?"

"He's been sending me these from time to time. Always in a HelloFresh box, always the heart of a rodent inside, and always with the message, 'I haven't forgotten.'"

"But that's disgusting. Is it a threat? What?"

"Oh, you can bet it's a threat. What he means to say is that he hasn't forgotten that I caught him and got him locked away for life."

She shivered. "Christ, what a freak."

"You can say that again."

She gestured to the door. "We have to arrest that delivery man."

"It won't do us any good. I've talked to some of them, and they have nothing to do with this. Someone offers them money to pick up an order and deliver it to my address. That's all they know. Orders always come in by phone—untraceable. The voice is always robotic—unrecognizable. Pick-up point is a depot in the harbor."

"But someone must be behind this."

"One of Parnham's cronies, since he's still behind bars—I checked."

She leaned on the table and felt a little queasy. "There must be something you can do to stop this."

The oven timer started beeping, and her dad hurried over to the kitchen. "If you can think of anything to make this guy stop, be my guest. Actually, it's been a while since I got one of these. A year, probably."

"Maybe Parnham didn't have your new address."

The idea that a serial killer like Brian Parnham knew where they lived was pretty scary, and the fact that he enjoyed cutting open animals even more so. But she consoled herself with the knowledge that he was serving a life sentence and couldn't possibly target them.

"Let's hope his associate, whoever he is, isn't cut from the same cloth as Parnham himself," she said as she grabbed a pair of plastic gloves from the cupboard beneath the sink. She carefully picked up the box and its contents and placed them inside a plastic bag. Tomorrow she would drop it off at the lab.

"They won't find anything," said her dad as he took the risotto from the oven. "I've had a couple of the previous deliveries tested. No fingerprints, DNA, or anything that could give us a clue about who sent these."

"Still," she said. "Even maniac killers make mistakes."

"Okay," said Dad with an apologetic look. "Let's eat, if you're still hungry?"

She gave him a reassuring grin. "It takes more than that to put me off my feed, Dad."

And so they filled two plates, Dad poured two glasses of wine, and they settled on the couch, turned on the TV, and got ready to enjoy a new episode of *The Masked Singer*, one of Poppy's favorite shows, and one her dad was slowly starting to appreciate as well.

## CHAPTER 33

Mayor Birt was seated behind his desk and noticed that Gwendolyn had shed another item of clothing. She was now dressed in some exceedingly enticing lingerie—the very lingerie he had personally gifted her, which looked exactly as he had hoped it would.

She quickly divested him of his own clothes, and moments later the two lovers gave themselves up to those all-consuming throes of passion they had become accustomed to.

Unbeknownst to Jan, his erstwhile mistress Justine, located in her office, had a front-row seat to the moans, groans, and occasional grunts of pleasure emanating from her former lover's office. She rolled her eyes in disgust and thought, not for the first time, that she should probably give her notice sooner rather than later. If Jan thought that he could humiliate her like this, he had another thing coming.

She turned off her computer, grabbed her bag, and walked out of the office. Even though there was still plenty of work to be done, she wasn't going to stay there for even one second longer. The man was simply repulsive—a swine, a horrible pig, a monster.

As she thought up a few more epithets she could use to describe her soon-to-be ex-employer and ex-lover, she pulled the door closed with a bang. Jan and Gwendolyn didn't even break stride but continued their lustful escapades unabated and undiminished.

Her high heels click-clacked on the stone steps as she furiously descended the stairs. Never in her life would she work for a man like Jan Birt again. The moment she arrived outside, she grabbed her phone from her handbag. Moments later, she was in communication with her new best friend.

"What has he done this time?" asked Anjanette.

"He's only going at it hammer and tongs in his office. Right under my nose!"

"Forget about the man, Justine. He's not worth it. And I say that as the woman who married him twenty-five years ago."

"There has to be something we can do to make him pay," she said as she made her way to her car, parked in the Town Hall parking lot. "Something to get back at him?"

"Oh, there is," Anjanette assured her.

So she listened with a rising sense of relief as Anjanette described the plan she had hatched to get back at her husband and Justine's ex-paramour.

ANJANETTE TAPPED her phone against her chin. She had found a new friend in her husband's ex-mistress. Though maybe it wasn't such a great surprise, as the two women were alike in a lot of ways. The only difference between them was the fact that Justine was ten years her junior. And now Gwendolyn, another lookalike and another decade younger.

If this kept up, Jan would be seventy and dating a woman Jayson's age.

It was her son she was mostly concerned about, as the incident with the bucket of crap had proven. This whole business with Jan running for mayor again on such a radical platform was starting to affect the boy's future. Her biggest fear was that Jayson might even be ready to throw it all away. And for what? Just because his dad was a moron?

She couldn't let that happen. Jan needed to be stopped. For Jayson's sake as well as her own. Already she was losing friends, who considered Jan some kind of neo-Nazi and were pulling away. Even though Flemish Front had always been a party on the fringes of the political establishment, they had never gone overboard to the extent that Jan had.

He was taking things too far.

The plan she had outlined to Justine was a bold one, but she thought they could pull it off, the two of them.

She just hoped Jayson wouldn't get into any more trouble. That would really break her heart.

"Time for payback," she muttered.

LYING ON HIS BED, his hands behind his head, Jayson Birt was staring up at the ceiling, at the Starship Enterprise mobile that had been hanging there since he was a kid. It had been a gift from his dad, back when the old man was still cool and seemed to give a damn about his family. Back when he hadn't decided that his life's ambition was being a raging fascist. Back when they'd watched *Raiders of the Lost Ark* together and cheered when all those Nazis had been burned to a crisp. Little did Jayson know back then that one day his dad would become one of them. That he would consider Hitler a great leader who had made a couple of mistakes but could generally be described as a misunderstood genius.

Jayson had found a copy of *Mein Kampf* in his dad's study not so long ago. A copy with plenty of post-its, its pages marked up and clearly read with a lot of interest and affection.

He picked a baseball up from his nightstand and threw it at the mobile, sending it crashing against the wall and to the floor. Even though it hurt his heart to look at the wreckage, he couldn't wait to dump the remains in the trash. Or maybe he could pack it up and give it to his dad. Though with the way things were going, the old man probably wouldn't even understand the significance—the message his son was sending him.

He understood what Jayson was trying to say when he dumped that bucket of cow shit over his head, though. It seemed to be the only way to get through to the man.

Wasn't there something he could do to sabotage Dad's re-election campaign? Something to make sure he'd never be mayor again? There had to be something…

THE HOUR WAS LATE, and Gwendolyn had left, but Jan Birt was still in his office when his phone belted out the *Der Ring des Nibelungen* ringtone again. He cursed. It had been doing that steadily all night, as Daron tried to reach him. Unable to ignore his party's chairman any longer, he finally brought the device to his ear. "Daron," he practically barked.

"Oh, I'm glad you finally decided to pick up," said the party leader. "For a moment there, I thought you were going to keep ignoring me."

"I'm not ignoring you," said Jan, though he had been. "What is it?"

"We've been discussing your strategy, and I'm afraid it's not working for us, Jan."

"What do you mean?"

"What I mean is that you sound more like a candidate for the Nazi Party than Flemish Front. Your use of language is divisive and frankly revolting. And it wouldn't surprise me if it's illegal, opening us up to all kinds of issues. I've consulted with our legal department, and they have urgently advised us to sever all ties—out of self-preservation."

"I'm the only candidate who has ever managed to get into power, *Daron*," he snapped. "And you'd do well to wonder why that is. Maybe it's got something to do with that oh-so-divisive language of mine, perhaps?"

"I don't want us to get sued. And as I understand it, the family of one of the kids you see fit to insult on a daily basis has already retained a lawyer, and they're ready to drag you to court."

"I don't care! That kid was a drug dealer!"

"Be that as it may, you've opened up a whole can of worms and I don't think—"

"Look, if you're too much of a coward to see this project of ours through, so be it. But don't expect me to pull my punches just because things are getting heated. In fact, I think if we were to go to the polls today, you wouldn't have a majority, and I would."

"I'm sure that's not—"

"I'm more popular than you, Daron!"

"I don't want to discuss this with you. The decision has been made, and we would like you to officially step down as our candidate. If not, I will be forced to replace you."

"Oh, get lost, Daron," he said viciously, and disconnected. That's just what he needed—a nervous nelly who couldn't handle some criticism from the parents of a drug dealer. It only strengthened his determination to run for party leader and transform Flemish Front in his image and according to his personal vision.

. . .

DARON COPLEY STUDIED the latest poll numbers on his phone. The study department had sent them, and they were shocking. Daron had asked them to make a simulation and project how they would poll if Daron stayed on as party leader versus Birt. Much to his astonishment, the party polled about twenty percent better under Jan Birt as party leader.

He ground his teeth as he considered his options. He had asked the people carrying out the poll to keep the result under wraps for now, but he knew what they were like. Before long, the numbers would be out there, spread among the members of the party council, and they would start piling on the pressure. Not for Jan to drop out of the campaign, but for Daron to resign as party leader and clear the field for Jan.

He couldn't let that happen. Somehow, Jan Birt had to be stopped.

WANDA DESAI WAS WATCHING a news item on television. Reclined on her couch, her husband next to her, it was all about the surprising rise of Flemish Front in the polls and the prospect that they would take the country by storm. The one person they focused on was Jan Birt. They had done street interviews in Loveringem and had come to the conclusion that Birt was more popular now than he was six years ago. Most of the people who had voted for him then said they felt he'd done a great job and expressed their intention to vote for him again.

It was quite the turnaround, for the general consensus six years ago amongst all the different parties had been that they would allow Birt and Flemish Front to take over one town and let them rule it for six years. The idea being that they'd make a mess of things and people would see that in spite of all of their promises, they couldn't deliver. And that would be the end of the strange fascination a lot of people had with Birt and his ilk.

Wanda had hoped that these experts were right, but had secretly feared they weren't. That once Flemish Front was allowed to rule, they would never go away. And so it was proving to be the case. The reporter even claimed that Birt's success was inspiring other candidates of Flemish Front in other towns across the country to go for broke, and it now seemed likely that a mass breakthrough of Flemish Front across the line was imminent. With it, the complete destruction of the old guard, chief among which was the Liberal Party, reduced to less than ten percent. A party that had stood proud for over a hundred years—relegated to the scrapheap of history. Annihilated by Birt's stormtroopers.

"This is a nightmare," said her husband. "You're not gonna let this happen, are you?"

She slowly shook her head. No, she was not going to let this happen.

But how do you stop a man who was proving unstoppable?

Mustafa knew he shouldn't, but he simply couldn't help himself. The videos of Mayor Birt were all he watched on Facebook, over and over again. The words sliced across his heart and soul every time they were uttered: *filth, scum, vermin*. The mayor was talking about Mustafa's family—about his mom, his dad, his brothers, his sisters. Even though they had lost Mohammed, Birt kept using Mustafa's brother as a punching bag. Pummeling a dead kid. It was cruel and simply inhuman what he was doing.

The lawyer the family had contacted had told them that it would be very difficult to get a case going against the mayor. What he said, even though it was offensive in the extreme, was most likely protected by the law. Mustafa didn't understand, and neither did the rest of his family. How could anyone say these things and get away with it?

He looked at his mom, silently crying on the couch. His dad, somberly looking at the television with dead eyes. His sisters, unable to come to terms with the gaping hole Mohammed's death had left in the heart of their family. Mo had been a good kid—sweet and kind—until he had been ensnared by those gangsters and made to work for them. The price he had to pay had been his life, but that hadn't bothered those monsters.

Hassan was also to blame, of course, but then he was a victim too. All he wanted was to make some good money and try to improve his family's living standards—get them out of the shabby house they had lived in for the past thirty years and into something decent and clean. In doing so, he had unwittingly written his little brother's death sentence.

He could tell that Hassan was wracked with guilt over his role in Mo's downfall, but when he tried to quit the gang, he discovered that he couldn't.

They had their hooks in him and wouldn't let go—not ever.

Hassan wasn't living with them anymore. He'd gone into hiding after Mo was killed, and then Beni. He claimed that the killers would come after him next.

He held up his phone and watched the latest clip Mayor Birt had posted again.

*Filth, scum, vermin.*

His jaw worked as he imagined Birt dying a gruesome death, being visited by all the plagues known to man. If there was a God, surely he would make it so?

## CHAPTER 34

Jan was working late in his office. He wasn't normally the kind of person who was first to arrive and the last one to leave, but these were strange times. After Gwen had left, he decided to put in some extra work on his campaign speech. He had a major rally coming up in a couple of days, and he wanted to seize the moment. Ride the momentum and make a big splash. He wasn't a religious man, but over the course of the last few days, he had decided that he was being propelled to a role of great importance by a power larger than himself. Why else would two immigrant kids have decided to snatch Teddy's bus and end up dying such a gruesome death, massacred by organized crime? Surely it was serendipity. Someone up there wanted him to play a major part in the history of his country. God, in his eternal wisdom, wanted him to be the messiah the people needed.

As he settled back in his leather office chair, taking a puff from his cigar and watching the smoke plume toward the wooden beam ceiling, he envisioned himself as the next minister-president of Flanders, or even prime minister of

Belgium—and then on to president of Europe, maybe. Why not? He was blessed, and since he firmly believed that chances needed to be grasped when they presented themselves, he was determined to strike while the iron was hot and make the most of these stunning events. To that end, he had written what was probably the most fiery speech of his career. Also the most important speech—the one that would guarantee him a place in the history books.

He glanced at his Patek Philippe watch and decided that it was time to call it a night. Tomorrow was another day to work on his campaign. So he closed his laptop, grabbed his jacket from the coat stand, and glanced around his office in case he'd forgotten anything. He had a feeling that he wouldn't be mayor of Loveringem much longer. First, secure a resounding success and make himself incontestable, then challenge Daron at the next party leader election, topple the federal government, run a successful federal election campaign, and become the first prime minister for Flemish Front, creating real change.

It was a neat little program he had written for himself—a wish list of accomplishments. With his drive, energy, and charisma, he was sure he could make it happen.

He carefully locked his office door and pocketed the key, then walked down the stone steps, watched over by the portraits of all the mayors who had gone before him. A bunch of losers, in his humble opinion, who had always adhered to the status quo. He had promised he'd blow the cobwebs off this dusty old town, and he had. Now he would do the same to the country and maybe even the entire continent.

There's no limit to what a man can accomplish when he's got history on his side.

He passed through the heavy oak doors of Town Hall. Moments later, he was crossing the parking lot, where his

Tesla awaited. He unlocked the doors with his key fob and dropped his bag on the passenger seat before lowering his tubby form behind the wheel.

Something caught his eye, and he thought he saw movement next to him. As he looked up, he saw a dark figure hurrying toward him, carrying some object. He frowned as he realized that the object was some kind of candle, a small flame flickering at the top.

As he wondered what was going on, the candle was hurled in his direction.

"Hey, what do you think you're doing?" he yelled as he tried to ward off the object being launched at him. By the time he realized it wasn't a candle but something much more dangerous, it was too late. The object exploded against the side of his head, and immediately it was as if the world was set alight, a sea of flame engulfing him.

He tried to crawl out of the car, but the person who had thrown the petrol bomb—for that's what it was—kicked him in the gut, then slammed the door shut, locking him in.

The fire quickly filled the small space, turning him into a living torch, fully aflame.

He cried out as he felt his face melting, searing heat making his nerve endings scream.

As he was being burned alive, the last thought that flashed through his head was that the gods weren't on his side after all. Why else would they allow this?

## CHAPTER 35

The fire had reached the battery, which had partially exploded, and it would take several hours before the fire was finally extinguished, or so the fire chief had told Holt. All the major bigwigs were there: the Commissioner, the leaders of all the local parties, and even the leader of Flemish Front, Daron Topley. Considering that Jan Birt had been the only member of the extreme-right party who had succeeded in entering the hallowed halls of power—albeit at the local level—his death was nothing short of a disaster.

Holt wasn't much bothered by the presence of all those movers and shakers. He was more concerned with finding out what exactly had happened and if there were any witnesses to the tragic event. It was one o'clock at night, so chances were that most of the people who lived in houses and apartments overlooking the Town Hall parking lot had been fast asleep when the mayor's car had burst into flames. However, that didn't stop him from feeling fairly optimistic that someone must have heard or seen something.

The noise of the explosion must have been pretty deafening and had woken up half the neighborhood, many of whom had spilled out of their homes and into the street to find out what was going on and if the world had ended. So he had dispatched his team and uniformed officers to talk to as many people as they could and take witness statements.

The fire chief now walked up to him, face grave. "What caused the fire?" Holt asked.

The man shook his head. "Too soon to tell, but early signs point to what looks like a Molotov cocktail having been thrown into the car."

"A Molotov cocktail?" Now this was news. "So the fire was deliberately set?"

"Seems that way. Though, like I said, it will take a while before we can be sure."

"Is it the mayor?" he asked. Even though everyone seemed to be convinced that it was, because it was his car, it was important to ascertain whether this was the case or not.

"Seems that way," said the fire chief. "As long as the fire hasn't been put out, we won't be able to get the body out of there. But it was the mayor's car, so…"

Both men stared at the vehicle that was still burning. "Tough to put out, these electric cars, huh?"

"You can say that again. Might take us another couple of hours to get that battery to stop burning."

"I didn't know that car batteries could explode," he said, deciding to risk the man's derision for being so ignorant.

"A lot of people don't know," said the fire chief, "but batteries can detonate under the right circumstances. And if it's true that a Molotov cocktail exploded inside the vehicle, it's no surprise this would be the case."

Poppy walked up to them, a determined look on her face. "A witness saw a person running away from the parking lot, boss," she said. "Dark hoodie, couldn't see the face. The person was running in the direction of the park."

"What time was this?"

"Midnight. This was just before the car exploded."

"So this could have been our perp," said Holt.

"I'll leave you to it," said the fire chief. "We're getting in some expert help on this one—fire forensic specialists—to determine the exact chain of events that led to this."

"Thanks, Mike," said Holt.

"So this wasn't an accident?" asked Poppy.

"Nope. Looks like someone threw a Molotov cocktail into the mayor's car."

"Another murder? That makes four in a matter of days, if we add the Idrissi kid."

"This is a different kettle of fish, though."

"You don't think this is connected to those other killings?"

"Too soon to tell, honey." He didn't like to formulate a lot of theories before all the facts were in. But it certainly was a strange coincidence that the mayor would be killed so close on the heels of those other killings.

Commissioner Forrester walked up to him, shaking his gray head. "This is bad, Glen."

Holt remembered that Forrester had told him only yesterday that the seemingly peaceful town of Loveringem hid a much murkier reality lurking beneath the surface. Looked like he hadn't been kidding. So much for the small-town fairy tale.

"I know, sir," he said. "It would appear the mayor was targeted deliberately."

"A political assassination? Well, that's a first for Loveringem," said the police chief. He gave him a look of concern. "Any idea who's responsible?"

"Not yet," he said. "Though if it is the mayor in there… I can imagine that a man like Jan Birt had a lot of enemies, sir."

They both turned to the group of party leaders, all busy on their phones.

"Yes, he wasn't a very popular man in certain circles," the police chief agreed. He gave him a kindly look. "Tread carefully, Glen. This case will attract a lot of attention, not least from the media. So please keep me informed, and if there's anything you need, just ask."

"Thank you, sir," he said. "I will."

From the corner of his eye, he saw that Daron Topley was making a beeline for him, and he wondered what he would have to add.

"Chief Inspector Holt? I understand that you're in charge of the investigation into the death of Jan Birt?"

"That's correct," said Holt, even though he wondered how long it would be before the investigation would be transferred to the Federal Police, who often stepped in when it was deemed local police were in over their heads. Then again, maybe Forrester would let him keep the case. His words had certainly given Holt the impression that he would.

"I'm sure I don't have to tell you this," said the party leader, who was dressed in a snazzy suit, this time under an expensive overcoat, "but Jan was under attack lately."

"Under attack?" he asked.

"He was an outspoken politician with strong opinions, and that kind of thing often provokes a strong reaction in people who don't agree with what he has to say."

"You mean those videos he posted?"

The party leader nodded. "It won't be a surprise to you that he got a lot of criticism for those videos. Lots of nasty comments on his social media, hate mail, people calling Town Hall and being verbally abusive. He told me in confidence that things had gotten steadily worse since the start of the campaign, and that even he, a veteran of many campaigns, had never seen anything like it. So I hope you will take a close look at these people. Because it is my absolute conviction one of them is responsible for this attack."

"Thanks for bringing that to my attention," said Holt courteously. Even though he didn't agree with the political opinions of Jan Birt, that didn't mean that the man deserved to die. "We will look into it."

"If you need anything, or if you get any pushback, this is my direct number," he said, offering him a card. "And if you could keep me apprised of any developments, I'd be most appreciative. Jan was our rock—Flemish Front's sledgehammer—and his death is a blow to all of us who tirelessly work in the trenches to make Flanders a better place."

He walked away, and Holt thought that the politician looked pretty upbeat for a man who had just lost his best and most popular candidate. Of course, he could be mistaken.

## CHAPTER 36

The next morning, bright and early, a bleary-eyed team of detectives sat at their desks while they watched Holt, who looked fresh as a daisy, give them their assignments.

"Okay, listen up, people," he said. "Last night, Mayor Jan Birt was murdered when someone threw a Molotov cocktail into his car while he was inside it. The fire has since been extinguished, and the investigation into the circumstances of the fire is ongoing, so unfortunately we don't have a lot of information yet. But at least we know Mayor Birt was the victim, and we also know that this wasn't an accident. The car didn't spontaneously burst into flames or any of the nonsense that people have been spreading online."

"I just read in *Het Laatste Nieuws* that the mayor may have committed suicide because his poll numbers weren't great," said Leland.

"My advice? Don't read *Het Laatste Nieuws*," said Holt dryly. "It's more detrimental to your health than a petrol bomb."

"*Het Laatste Nieuws* is the only paper where Leland doesn't need a dictionary to read all the articles," said Georgina with a straight face.

"So what do you read, smarty-pants?" asked Leland.

"Haven't you heard? Nobody reads the paper anymore. It's a new age, my friend."

"*I* still read the paper," said Jaime, who had been listening in. "I read *Het Nieuwsblad* every morning. How else are you supposed to know what's going on?"

"There is such a thing as the internet, Jaime. I don't know if you've heard of it?"

Jaime rolled her eyes and returned to the stack of witness reports she was putting into the computer. They had collected dozens and dozens of those last night.

"Okay, so today we continue our neighborhood canvass," said Holt, eager to get the briefing back on track. "And let's also start working out a timeline for the mayor's movements yesterday. Rasheed, you look into that. And also check the mayor's phone records, social media activity, and try to get his bank to cooperate on those bank statements so we can build a picture of the man in his final days and weeks."

"Warrants?" asked Rasheed as he jotted down a note.

"All being arranged," Holt assured him. "The Commissioner has deemed this a number-one priority, and he's fast-tracking all the necessary paperwork. How about CCTV of the parking lot? Leland?"

"Nothing doing, boss," said Leland. "Camera out of order."

"But I thought we caught Wanda Desai's vandal on camera?" asked Poppy.

"That was a different section of the parking lot," said Leland. "Further away. The mayor parks closer to Town Hall. Unfortunately, the cameras were out of order."

"How long have they been out of order?" asked Holt.

"Months," said Leland. "The whole system is in line to be upgraded."

"Okay, that means we can rule out sabotage. It does suggest that our killer may have known about the cameras and chose that particular location on purpose."

He made a mental note of this and moved on to the next item on his list. "And then there's the mayor's social media campaign, which was getting a lot of attention."

"He had been posting some pretty controversial videos," said Georgina. "Maybe it wouldn't be a bad idea to check out the comments under those videos?"

"Rasheed," said Holt. "Check for hateful comments. See if anything jumps out. Daron Topley told me last night that the level of hate the mayor was subjected to lately was unlike anything he'd ever seen. So maybe we should look for our man in that crowd."

"The level of support for the mayor is also beyond anything I've ever seen," said Georgina. "The last video he posted has hundreds of comments, most of them painting the mayor as a martyr for the cause."

"What cause would that be?" asked Poppy.

"Oh, you know. The usual," said Georgina. "Mostly white supremacy stuff. Birt really used a bazooka to target anyone who wasn't white or didn't adhere to his point of view, which can be summed up as racist, misogynistic, homophobic, and all the rest of it."

"He was a real sweetheart, wasn't he?" said Rasheed.

"He wasn't my mayor," said Jaime, piping up again.

"No, he wasn't my mayor either," said Holt. Which didn't mean he wouldn't do his utmost to find his killer. "Even so, that doesn't give anyone the right to go and kill him."

"How did the killer know Birt was going to be there at that time of night?" asked Poppy.

Holt pointed at his daughter. "We better talk to the guy's secretary—"

"Personal assistant," Leland corrected him.

"—and find out if Birt leaving his office at midnight was a regular thing for him. This attack took some preparation, so the killer may have been keeping tabs on Birt to determine the best moment to strike."

"Couldn't it have been an opportunistic attack?" asked Georgina. "A spur-of-the-moment kind of thing?"

Now it was Leland's turn to grin. "Nobody walks around with a Molotov cocktail in their pocket, Georgina. Unless maybe you do?"

"No, Leland, I do not," she said sweetly. "I guess that means we can assume that the killer had been planning this for a while. How hard is it to make a Molotov cocktail?"

"Not hard," said Rasheed. "Basically, all you need is a bottle, gasoline or some other flammable liquid, and a wick. A rag works well, or a sheet cut into ribbons. You attach the wick with Scotch tape and—"

"Okay, we don't need a lesson on how to make a Molotov cocktail," said Holt. "I'm sure there are plenty of instructions on the internet, so anyone could do it."

"Could there be a connection with the deaths of Elmaleh, Idrissi, and Timmer and the abduction of Boyd Batham?" asked Leland. "It seems like a major coincidence that first Teddy Birt is arrested, and now all of a sudden his brother is killed."

"The drug mafia is known for their fondness of Molotov cocktails," Georgina added.

She was right. In Antwerp, those attacks were a real plague. Mostly they used grenades, but also petrol bombs, to target the homes and businesses of people they accused of being traitors or working for the competition. Sometimes they shot up a home by mistake, and plenty of innocents had been killed as a consequence of these wars.

"It's possible," said Holt. "Though I have to admit I don't see the connection yet."

"Unless Jan Birt was somehow involved in Teddy's dirty dealings with the drug mafia?" Georgina suggested.

"Like I said, it's possible. So let's keep an open mind and see where the evidence leads us. It's early days, and there's a lot we don't know yet." He got up from the edge of his desk where he had been perched. "Okay, let's get this show on the road, people."

Leland and Georgina would be organizing the neighborhood canvass with officers of the uniformed police, while Rasheed stayed at the precinct to dig into the mayor's finances, phone history, and social media activity. Meanwhile, Holt and Poppy would pay a visit to Birt's campaign manager, who reportedly was the last person to see him alive.

## CHAPTER 37

Holt and Poppy met Gwendolyn Lopez in her office at Town Hall, located two doors down from the mayor's office. The woman was a mess. She had obviously been crying, for her eyes were bright red and so was her face. She looked raw, and Holt was surprised by the woman's devotion to her employer.

"Our sincerest condolences for your loss," he said dutifully, even though he hadn't expected to use these words until they spoke to Birt's widow.

"It's such a terrible loss," said the woman. "Not only for the people of Loveringem, but for the country. Jan was going to do great things for all of us. He was the greatest man I've ever worked with. Certainly the most inspiring one. He inspired me every day. He pushed me to work hard for the people. That's who we did it for, you know: the people."

Holt and Poppy had taken a seat in the small salon located underneath a stained-glass window in the corner. Stacks of campaign posters were on a nearby table, and a large whiteboard gave an overview of the weeks of campaigning to come—now all in vain.

"I don't understand," said the woman as she pulled a tissue from a box and padded her eyes. "Teslas are supposed to be safe. Jan told me so himself. He was always going on about me buying one for myself, and when I told him I'd seen reports of cars going up in flames, he laughed and said that was all nonsense."

Holt shared a look with his daughter. Clearly, the woman hadn't been informed yet that her boss's death wasn't an accident.

"I'm sorry to be the bearer of bad news, Miss Lopez," he said. "But the fire that killed Mayor Birt wasn't an accident."

She stared at him. "I don't understand. The fire wasn't an accident? Then what was it?"

"Someone threw a Molotov cocktail in the mayor's car," said Poppy gently. She was already moving her chair closer to the campaign manager's in case she had to support her upon being informed that her boss had been murdered.

Miss Lopez blinked. "A… a *Molotov* cocktail?"

"It's a bottle filled with gasoline," said Holt. "They light it and then throw it. The bottle breaks, and the fire quickly spreads. It's like a homemade bomb. A petrol bomb."

"And… someone… threw it at Jan?" She still didn't seem to fully grasp the situation. She was gazing at a campaign flyer on the table in front of her. It showed Jan Birt in all his glory, smiling at the camera and holding up two thumbs. The caption read, 'Jan Birt for mayor. Let's do it again.'

It didn't seem like a winning slogan to Holt, but then what did he know about politics?

"Yes, someone threw it at the mayor's car, with him in it," he confirmed. "Which means we're treating this as murder, Miss Lopez."

"My God," she said, burying her face in her hands. "Who would *do* such a thing?" Poppy placed a hand on the woman's back and rubbed it gently. Finally, her shoulders stopped shaking, and she gratefully accepted more tissues, wiping her eyes and nose.

"This is the worst day of my life," she said, sniffling. "Jan was more to me than just a boss, you know. We had become friends. I admired him. His political views, but also his wisdom and his determination to make a difference. He was a force of nature." She swallowed. "And now he's gone." She looked up at Holt. "Who did this, Chief Inspector?"

"That's what we are going to find out," he promised.

"Can you think of anyone who could have done this to the mayor, Gwendolyn?" asked Poppy. "Someone bearing a grudge against him?"

"Where do I begin?" she cried helplessly. "A man like Jan has many enemies, Inspector. Every great man does. Just look at President Kennedy or Martin Luther King."

Holt cut a glance at his daughter. He could tell that she, too, would be hard pressed to consider Jan Birt in the same league as Kennedy or King, exactly.

"You should see the death threats he received on a daily basis," Gwendolyn continued. "Not that it phased him. He said it was a sign we were doing something right." Her face crumpled like the used tissue clutched in her hand. "He was such a brave man!"

"What death threats had he received?" asked Holt.

"Most of them were posted on social media," said Gwendolyn. "Though some of them arrived in the mail." She got up to grab a tablet from her desk and showed them some of the more concerning comments on his posts. She wasn't kidding. They were actual death threats.

'I WILL KILL YOU!'
'YOU DESERVE TO DIE!'
'EVERYBODY HATES YOU!'

Those were some of the more straightforward ones, and

Rasheed would get busy trying to determine who had posted them. But Gwendolyn also showed them some of the messages people had sent him, emails, and even actual letters —long ones, outlining specific ways people wanted to torture and murder the mayor, in gruesome detail.

"These are very… specific," said Holt as he held up one of the letters that had a drawing of a medieval torture machine with big wooden balls that would fall down on the mayor's head and reduce it to a pile of mush. Another depicted the mayor with arrows sticking out of his back. It all looked pretty gruesome. "When did they arrive?"

"Oh, they've been coming in over the past couple of months," said Gwendolyn. "Though Jan told me he's always been the target of a lot of hate mail. He kept all of them in a file in his office, just in case he ever wanted to press charges. He talked to your boss about this, and he said there were so many of them they probably needed a whole team to go through them. In the end, he decided it wasn't worth it. He figured that everyone who's trying to make a big change gets a lot of flak, and it just goes with the territory. Though I have to say, politics has become a lot tougher these last couple of years."

"Can we hang on to these?" asked Holt. "And if you have more of them, I would like to have those as well."

"Be my guest," said Gwendolyn. "Anything to help you catch Jan's killer." At these words, she burst into tears again. The poor woman was obviously devastated, Holt thought as he leafed through some of the letters. He couldn't imagine that people despised Birt so much they would go to the trouble of actually putting pen to paper and sending him these hateful missives. The question was, had one of them decided that words weren't enough and taken action?

"There's one other thing we need to ask you, Miss Lopez,"

he said. "Could you tell us where you were last night? Let's say around midnight?"

"It's a routine question," Poppy clarified. "To rule you out of our inquiries."

"Of course, I understand," said Gwendolyn. "I probably left Jan's office around eleven—we had worked late on some ideas I had for the campaign. I got home a little after eleven and went to bed."

"Can anyone vouch for you?" asked Holt.

"Vouch? Oh, you mean… No, I live alone." She gave him a weak smile. "This job is pretty full-on, Chief Inspector. During campaign season, it's twenty-four-seven. No partner would be happy with that."

"Thank you, Miss Lopez."

Poppy asked if they could contact someone to be with her, but the campaign manager assured them that she would be fine, so they took their leave.

"This is tough," said Poppy as they descended the stairs to return to the entrance hall. "Poor woman."

"Yeah, she clearly was a big fan of the guy."

"I can understand how she feels. If you've worked so closely with a person, it must come as a great shock when he's suddenly gone. Especially as the campaign was so intense. It must have drawn them very close together. Made them a tight team."

"They were up against it, that's for sure."

"Some of those messages and letters are pretty gruesome, Dad. Gruesome and detailed in their awfulness. Like something out of a horror movie."

"We need to go through the entire pile and find out who sent those letters and who posted those messages—every single one. Then we're going to talk to those people and find out if they carried out their threats."

Poppy nodded. "Where to now?"

"Anjanette Birt. She's expecting us."

If Gwendolyn was a mess, he expected to find Birt's widow in an even worse state.

## CHAPTER 38

It was the first time that Poppy had been to the mayor's house. She hadn't known what to expect, but it was definitely a lot nicer than she had imagined. It was one of those modern houses, with plenty of glass and concrete, and furniture that seemed to come from the future.

"I wouldn't mind living here," she told her dad as they waited for Anjanette to open the door. She glanced in through one of the floor-to-ceiling windows and thought she saw the curtain twitch. Someone was definitely home— probably checking to see if whoever had killed the mayor was back to go after the rest of the family as well.

Finally, the door opened, and a well-dressed woman in her late forties appeared. Contrary to what Poppy had expected, Anjanette Birt didn't look sad or devastated at all. No signs of tears on her face or runny mascara, like with Gwendolyn Lopez. In fact, she looked very composed and even cheerful as she invited them in.

"I thought you'd show up sooner or later," she said. She led them into the living room, which was as spacious and modern as Poppy had expected. She would have bet that the whole house was wired with the latest state-of-the-art smart technology. The kind where all you have to do is clap your hands and the lights go out, the curtains automatically close when the sun goes down and open again in the morning, or where your fridge automatically orders food when it detects that you're running low on cream cheese or yogurt. Wouldn't that be something? To live as if you were a woman of the future who had traveled back in time. No more shopping, no more opening and closing the curtains.

She tuned back into the conversation, momentarily putting any thoughts of smart homes or women from the future aside.

"I'm not sure what I can tell you, Chief Inspector," Anjanette told Holt with a light shrug. She was dressed like a woman of the future should, Poppy determined: a beige pantsuit that looked great on her. In fact, she looked more like a model than a mayor's wife—though, in all honesty, Poppy had no idea what a mayor's wife should look like. But definitely not as glamorous as Anjanette did. She could have been beamed here straight from the London, Paris, or Milan catwalks. Not only was she dressed in the latest fashion, but her hair was done to perfection in a pretty bob, her face was devoid of any wrinkles that Poppy could detect, and the light makeup she had applied was so skillfully done you could hardly tell it was there. There was nothing vulgar about Mrs. Birt. All class, all the way.

"Did your husband have any enemies that you can think of?" asked Holt, who seemed oblivious to the woman's class or the stylish home. No Flemish insignia, Poppy couldn't help but notice, or pictures of flag-waving nationalists eager to take the country by storm.

The woman displayed a slight smile. "My husband had a lot of enemies, Chief Inspector Holt. And that was exactly the way he liked it. A politician without enemies is probably doing something wrong—that was his motto. A day that he hadn't managed to stir up some kind of controversy was a day he hadn't lived. Jan loved to kick up a fuss."

"Anyone in particular that you can think of?" asked Holt. "Your husband's campaign manager already showed us some of the messages and letters that he received. Lots of people who hated him for the things he said and believed."

Anjanette shook her head. She still hadn't offered them a seat on one of the pretty cream-colored leather sofas in the living room or any refreshments. Maybe she wouldn't. Those couches looked pristine, as if no one had dared use them for fear of soiling them.

"Nobody I can think of. But then my husband very rarely discussed his work with me. He liked to come home and forget about his day, and I supported him in that. Otherwise, he would have been 'on' all the time, and no one can keep that up." She gestured around. "This was Jan's safe haven. The place he came to relax. And so I don't remember him ever mentioning anyone who he thought could do him harm. At least not like this."

There was a clatter of footsteps on the wooden stairs leading to the second floor, and Poppy looked up when a teenager appeared. Like his mother, Jayson Birt wouldn't have looked out of place in a fashion show or a shoot for a glamorous swimwear brand. He was lanky, with perfect features and a muscular physique—a young David Gandy.

"This is my son, Jayson," said Anjanette, introducing the young man.

Poppy caught herself staring and snapped out of it just in time to give the teenager a nod in greeting. He didn't look anything like the dung-dropping teenager she had seen on Birt's Facebook feed. But then the quality of the imagery hadn't exactly been high-def.

Contrary to what she had expected, the young man

draped himself across one of the couches. So they were being used after all. She now noticed the oversized flatscreen TV on the wall and wondered if the Birts had been like any normal family, settling in on the couch of an evening to watch a movie or a show. Somehow, she couldn't picture it.

"The only person I can think of who bore a grudge against my husband," said Anjanette, "apart from weirdos on social media, is the leader of the opposition."

"Mom," said Jayson. "Wanda would never torch Dad's car with him in it."

Like his mom, he didn't seem wracked with grief, Poppy couldn't help but notice.

"I'm simply answering the Chief Inspector's question," said Anjanette. "He asked me if your dad had any enemies—people who wished to do him harm. And the only person he ever mentioned was Wanda. She and Jan went head to head during the last election."

"Long before that," said Jayson. "They were at loggerheads all through the previous term, when Wanda was mayor and Dad was the leader of the opposition." He grinned. "As a young kid, I was very interested in politics—a lot more than I am now—and so Dad took me to attend the weekly cabinet meetings from time to time, where he held long speeches railing against everything Wanda Desai stood for. Even back then, he was a pretty gifted speaker. And Wanda hated it. He could really drive her up the wall."

"And then, of course, my husband won the last election," said Anjanette. "But in spite of that, Wanda was all set to lead a coalition between her party and two of the other main parties—the Socialist Party and the Christian Democrats. Only at the last possible moment, Jan made a deal with the Flemish nationalists, and together they had a majority. There was nothing that Wanda could do, and it's been bugging her ever since."

"I really don't see her as a violent person, though," said Jayson. "Resentful, yes, and frustrated, but not violent."

"No, I don't think she would actually try to kill a political opponent," Anjanette conceded. "But you never know. She really did hate Jan from the bottom of her heart. In politics, you never know if what people are saying is real or just for show, but with Wanda, I believe there was a deeply seated hatred directed against my husband."

"If you want to know what I think," said Jayson, who had made himself comfortable on the couch and didn't seem to have a care in the world. In Poppy's mind, she saw him modeling for a swimwear shoot, aiming smoldering gazes at her, his perfect body glistening with sweat. In reality, he *was* looking at her, but not all that smoldering. Instead, he seemed eager to convey a theory about his father's killer. "It's probably some nutter who had it in for my dad. The way he spoke about people, calling them all kinds of names. All it takes is one crazy person to get triggered, and this is what you get."

"You weren't too keen on your father's politics, were you, Jayson?" asked Holt.

"No, I wasn't his biggest fan, that's true," Jayson admitted.

"The cow dung incident comes to mind," said Holt.

"Yeah, I probably shouldn't have done that," said Jayson. "But he had it coming, you know. Talking so much nonsense these last couple of weeks. I really couldn't take it anymore. So I decided that someone should teach him a lesson he wouldn't forget."

"Oh, he got the lesson, all right," Anjanette assured her son.

"I doubt it," said Jayson. "Dad was stubborn. And he was going places. Did you know that his ultimate goal was to become president of an independent Flanders?"

"Jan always was extremely ambitious," said Anjanette with

a vague smile. "He wanted to go all the way. First mayor, then party leader, then prime minister, and finally president of an independent Flanders. I told him he was crazy, but he believed he could pull it off."

"He might have done it," said Jayson. "Though to be honest, I wouldn't have liked to live in a Flanders where he was in charge. It would have been a pretty horrible place to live."

He fixed Poppy with an intent stare, and she felt strange stirrings in the pit of her stomach.

"Okay, I'm afraid I have to ask where you both were last night," she said, in an effort to break the spell. "It's a routine question," she explained.

"I understand," said Jayson, waving a hand. "I've watched plenty of cop shows. We were here last night, weren't we, Mom?"

"Yeah, we watched a movie, Jayson and I."

"What movie?" asked Holt.

"*Die Hard*," said Jayson immediately. When Poppy raised an eyebrow in his direction, he shrugged. "What can I say? We love a classic."

## CHAPTER 39

Holt and Poppy sat in the car while the latter tried to find Wanda Desai's address.

"You don't really believe that Wanda killed Birt, do you?" asked Poppy.

Holt scratched his beard. "I doubt it, but then again, you never know. If she really was as angry as Birt's widow and son make her out to be…"

But Poppy wasn't convinced. "I know that politicians are always complaining that politics is turning into a blood sport, but they don't mean that *literally*. They don't actually go around *murdering* each other."

"We still need to check it out," said Holt. "At the very least, she might tell us if she knows of anyone else who had a motive to get rid of her political opponent."

"Got it," said Poppy, and expertly typed the address into the vehicle's satnav. Much to their surprise, Birt's nemesis lived right around the corner. A ten-second drive, and Poppy was parking the car in front of a farmhouse-style home of impressive dimensions. In the front yard, a large placard displayed a picture of the Liberal Party front-runner smiling back at them. A single word summed up what she stood for: 'STRONGER!'

"I wonder what that means," said Poppy. "Does she want us all to become stronger? But in what sense? Does she propose to subsidize free gym subscriptions for everyone?"

Holt rolled his eyes. "I *said* I would think about it, Poppy."

His daughter laughed. "This gym business is bugging you, isn't it? It's a suggestion, Dad. If you don't *want* to live a longer and healthier life, that's perfectly fine with me."

"Let's not go there," he said as he got out of the car. They had a murder to solve, and the jury was still out on whether going to the gym was a good idea or not. As far as he was concerned, it was definitely a no-no. People got hit by dumb bells or whatever those things were called on a daily basis. He'd once attended a fatal accident in a gym in Ghent where a guy had practically decapitated himself when a barbell fell on his neck. He didn't look so healthy after that little contretemps had cut his life expectancy down to zero.

"Look, I'm not saying that *you* shouldn't go," he argued as he and Poppy walked past the sign that admonished them to be 'STRONGER!' "but I really don't see the point. I mean, every time I go to the gym, all I see are these guys who look as if they've been pumped up with a bicycle pump. It's all steroids and illegal drugs and whatnot."

"Those are the exceptions to the rule, Dad," said Poppy. "Most people who go to the gym are like me. And do I look like I've been pumped up with a bicycle pump?"

"I guess not," he had to admit. His daughter looked just fine. Not too big or too small. Perfect, in other words, but then every dad probably thought that about his offspring.

"And I don't take drugs either, so there's absolutely no excuse." She dug her index finger into his collarbone a couple of times. "No. Excuse. Whatsoever!"

"Ouch," he murmured as he pressed the bell. "That's a surprisingly strong finger you've got there, honey."

"Working out three times a week will get you there, Dad. Trust me."

"I'm not sure that's the incentive I need to start going," he said as he rubbed his collarbone.

They patiently waited for the lady of the house to appear.

"She's probably not home," said Poppy. "Politicians are always out and about in the weeks before an election. Visiting markets and ringing doorbells of potential voters."

Much to their surprise, it wasn't long before Poppy's words were proved wrong. A woman who looked a lot like the one on the placard in her front yard opened the door and gave them a suspicious look.

Holt held up his badge, and so did Poppy. "Chief Inspector Holt," he announced. "And this is Inspector Holt. We're with the Loveringem police. Can we come in for a moment, Mrs. Desai?"

"What's this about?" she asked, studying their badges for a moment. "Holt and Holt? Are you related, by any chance?"

"Father and daughter," Holt confirmed. "We're investigating the death of Jan Birt."

"Oh, right," said Mrs. Desai. "Of course. Please come in." She led the way into the living room, which was pretty messy, with posters strewn about everywhere and tall stacks of flyers.

"I'm running my campaign from here," she explained when she correctly interpreted the look he gave the place. "Me and my husband." She removed a stack of flyers from one of the couches and invited them to take a seat while she cleared a chair of some of the clutter and joined them. "I'd offer you a cup of coffee or tea, but I'm afraid I'm out. My husband has run down to the shop for some groceries. We had a sort of rally last night with all of our party members

FIELD OF BLOOD

and volunteers—calling potential voters, putting flyers in envelopes, that sort of thing." She smiled. "You know, rallying the troops."

"So it's safe to say you were here all evening?" asked Holt.

The opposition leader's smile vanished. "You don't think *I* killed Jan Birt, do you?"

"Just a routine inquiry," Poppy quickly assured her. "We're talking to everyone who knew Mr. Birt, trying to put together a picture of the man and who may have held a grudge against him."

"Well, I guess you could say that *I* held a grudge against him," said Mrs. Desai. "In the sense that he was my political opponent."

"You didn't see eye to eye with the man?" asked Holt.

"He and I occupied diametrically opposite sides of the political spectrum."

"Is it true that you felt he cheated you out of being mayor six years ago through some shady shenanigans?"

She thought about this for a moment. "I wouldn't call what he did *shady*, exactly. We both tried to form a coalition. Only he managed to beat us to it, and in the end, I accepted my defeat and took up the role of leader of the opposition for the past six years." Before Holt could continue his questioning, she quickly added, "This time we're on track for a resounding victory, though, so there won't be any question of a repeat of what happened last time. Birt has made such a mess of things that people are quite sick of him and his party. They want change, and I'm here to offer them exactly that."

"You're *stronger* this time," said Poppy, referencing the woman's campaign slogan. It was written on all the flyers surrounding them, as well as the posters and other election material. Holt could even see keychains, pens, and flags with the image of Wanda Desai and the same slogan.

"Yes, I guess you could say that," said Mrs. Desai with a

tight smile. She had placed her hands in her lap and didn't exactly seem like the kind of person who would go around hurling Molotov cocktails at her opponent. As if she could read his mind, she added, "So you see, I had absolutely no reason to kill Jan. I was ready to beat him fair and square at the ballot box, and that would have been the end of this terrible experiment."

"What experiment would that be?" asked Poppy.

"Why, the first Flemish Front mayor, of course. The end of the cordon sanitaire. It should never have happened, and I blame it all on the Flemish nationalists, who broke their promise never to form a coalition with Flemish Front."

"Ah yes, the famous cordon sanitaire," Holt agreed. He didn't have a lot of interest in politics as a rule, and even less in local politics. But even he knew what the cordon sanitaire was. An agreement all the other parties had entered into, to never allow Flemish Front, which they considered a threat to democracy, to rise to power. Until the last election, it had worked well. But then the local branch of the Flemish Nationalist Party had gone against the national party bureau's dictum and decided to form a coalition with Flemish Front anyway, thereby breaking the cordon sanitaire for the first time in history.

"So do you have any idea who could have done this?" asked Poppy.

Wanda Desai thought for a moment, then shook her head. "Jan Birt was a controversial and divisive politician, who inspired a lot of hatred. Hatred in his followers against the people he targeted, but also hatred in his victims. When I heard the news this morning, the first thing I thought was that the families he targeted had decided to get back at him."

"What families would that be?" asked Holt.

"Well, the families of those two kids that were murdered. He was very cruel when he said those things about them, calling them filth and vermin and scum and all of that." She shrugged. "Frankly, I wouldn't know, but that was my first thought. And then of course there were all of the scandals surrounding him."

"You mean with his brother Teddy being arrested?"

"That, but also the affairs." When they both stared at her, lack of comprehension written large across their faces, she smiled. "I take it you didn't know about that?"

They both shook their heads.

"Looks like your visit to me hasn't been in vain after all." She leaned forward and seemed quite amused to be the one to break the news to them. "Jan had a long-time mistress, and then he also had a recent mistress."

"He had two mistresses?" asked Poppy, taken aback.

"That's correct. He cheated on Anjanette with Justine Hallett."

"That's his secretary," Poppy clarified for her dad's sake.

"I know who Justine Hallett is," said Holt.

"And he cheated on Justine with Gwendolyn Lopez."

The information took Holt by surprise. The last thing he had expected was that Birt would be such a ladies' man. He certainly didn't have the looks of a Casanova.

"So… he cheated on his wife with his mistress, and he cheated on his mistress… with a second mistress?" asked Poppy, intrigued by the news. But then she was an avid reader of the Flemish tabloid *Dag Allemaal* and read the thing cover to cover every week. There wasn't a single piece of gossip about a Flemish star that she wasn't aware of, much to Holt's consternation, since he didn't know half these people and rarely watched the shows they were in—except for *The Masked Singer*. Now that he was living with his daughter, he was being subjected to a lot more Flemish showbiz than he cared for.

"I know," said Wanda. "It's a lot to take in."

"And did these women know?" asked Poppy, eager to get to the bottom of the story.

"I'm sure that Anjanette knew about Justine, as the affair had been going on for fifteen years. I mean, *everyone* knew about it—it wasn't a big secret. I'm not sure she knows about Gwendolyn, though. You'd have to ask her. I'm willing to bet that she did, though."

"It's certainly a motive for murder," said Poppy.

Wanda nodded. "That's what I would have thought."

## CHAPTER 40

Before they had another chat with Gwendolyn—who had failed to mention that she was having an affair with the mayor—Holt and Poppy decided to pay a visit to Justine Hallett and confront her with this new information. They found the loyal personal assistant in her office, sitting ramrod straight with red-rimmed eyes, staring at her computer screen. She looked up when they entered, wiped her eyes with the back of her hand, and mustered a faint smile as she stood up to greet them.

"Detectives," she said, without needing them to show their badges. "Any news?"

"Nothing so far, I'm afraid," said Holt. The last time they had met was when they interviewed Birt in connection to the drug business with his brother and Birt Travel. Justine struck Poppy as an efficient and no-nonsense type of person and, frankly, she couldn't really see her falling for a man like Birt, who was a blowhard in her personal opinion. But then she had once read that power eroticizes, so maybe that's what had happened here? Though fifteen years ago, Birt hadn't been in power, as far as she knew.

Maybe he'd been a lot fitter back then? Less of a jerk? She tried hard to imagine Jan Birt as a handsome, normal person, but in the end, her imagination simply wouldn't play ball.

Justine took a seat again, looking numb with grief. "I don't understand," she said. "Who would do such a thing? Jan was an acquired taste—there were plenty of people who didn't like him—but I think everyone will agree he didn't deserve this." A flicker of hope animated her features. "Are you sure it was him in that car? Maybe someone else..."

"I'm afraid it was him," Holt said.

She slumped again, and Poppy wondered how they should approach this. They couldn't just come out and ask her about her affair with Birt, could they? That would be insensitive. Then again, these were questions that needed to be asked. As she was trying to think of a way to broach the topic tactfully, her dad decided to barge right in.

"It has come to our attention that you and the mayor were having an affair, Miss Hallett. What can you tell us about that?"

Poppy held her breath, waiting for the woman to respond.

But Justine merely shrugged. "I think it's common knowledge at this point. Though, lately, things had cooled down considerably between us. In fact, it's probably fair to say that our relationship had ended."

"And why was that?" asked Holt, Mr. Sensitivity of the Year.

The personal assistant looked him straight in the eye. "Because he had started an affair with Gwendolyn Lopez, and that took all of his time and stamina, if you catch my drift."

"So... if I understand you correctly, Mayor Birt was cheating on you with his campaign manager?"

"I'm not sure if you can call it cheating," said Justine as a thoughtful wrinkle appeared between her brows. "Is it cheating when your lover has an affair with another woman? Or does that term only apply with respect to his wife?"

"It is certainly an unusual situation," Poppy suggested carefully.

Justine offered her a tired smile. "I guess you could say that."

"And what did his wife think about all this?" asked Holt.

"Oh, Anjanette was fine with it," Justine assured them. "Anjanette and Jan had an understanding. She lost interest in him years ago, and if he didn't blab about his affair and remained discreet, he was free to see me."

"Why did she lose interest in her husband?" asked Poppy, who couldn't help but find this all wildly fascinating.

"You'd have to ask her," said Justine. "I'd be betraying confidences if I told you."

"But she told you?"

Justine nodded. "Strange as this may sound, Anjanette is a friend. When Jan first started cheating on me with Gwendolyn, she was understandably upset."

"That her husband was cheating on her with yet another woman?"

"No, that he was cheating on me. She didn't mind, but she knew that I did, and so she was upset with Jan."

Poppy and Holt shared a look of confusion. It certainly was a strange situation. But was there a motive for murder to be found? Poppy thought there was. And her dad obviously thought the same thing, for his next question didn't come out of the blue.

"Could you tell us where you were last night around midnight, Miss Hallett?"

"Oh, so now you think *I* killed Jan, do you? Well, I can assure you that I didn't. I loved that man—that hopeless, insufferable, boorish man." At this point, she uttered a loud sob that welled up from deep down her throat, and moments later she was weeping with great hacking wails.

Holt gave the woman a helpless look, then turned to Poppy and gestured for her to do something. Poppy quickly crouched down next to Justine and put her arms around her. For a few moments, the secretary's shoulders shook, but then slowly the sobs subsided.

Poppy handed her a tissue from the box on the desk, and the woman took it gratefully.

"I don't know why I'm crying," she said between sniffs. "The man was a terrible human being. But I guess love has no reason."

"No, I guess not," said Poppy, who had to admit that she had never known a love so great that she would be crying buckets when the guy passed to the other realm. When she and Rupert had called it quits on their marriage, she had been sad, sure, but not like this. Not this heartbreaking despair that Justine Hallett was displaying. Then again, fifteen years is a long time to be with a person, and as Poppy understood, she had been Birt's actual partner, much more than Anjanette had been.

"If you must know," said Justine finally, "I was home last night. Alone. So make of that what you will. But I can assure you that I didn't murder Jan. I loved him."

"Love makes people do strange things," said Holt.

"I know, but I didn't kill him. You have to believe me."

Holt nodded. "Any idea who did, Justine?"

"All I can think is that one of the people who sent him threatening messages on the internet must have done it. Some of those messages were really hateful. If I were you, I'd look at the people who sent them."

There was one thing that Poppy didn't understand. She gestured to the portrait of Jan Birt that stood on the woman's desk. "If you were so upset that Jan was cheating on you with Gwendolyn, why didn't you quit, Justine?"

She gave her a watery smile. "As it happens, I was going to. Anjanette and I both were. We were both so fed up with the way Jan was treating us—or treating me, mostly—that we had decided that we would both quit. She as his wife and I as his personal assistant. A double whammy of revenge for what he had put us through over the years."

"And did you tell him that?" asked Holt.

"We were going to. Anjanette had engaged a divorce lawyer, and I was looking at job offers. We wanted to time it so that when she announced her plans to divorce him and take the house, I would tell him to go and find himself another assistant. We figured it would have made him sit up and think. For a moment, at least. Jan was never one to think long or hard about the consequences of his actions. Or his statements, for that matter."

## CHAPTER 41

Holt felt a little unnerved by their recent encounter with Justine Hallett, and even though he knew they had to have another chat with Gwendolyn Lopez, he wasn't looking forward to it. Good thing Poppy was there, as they hadn't taught him how to deal with grief during his training. Mostly, he just stood there like a pillar of salt, wondering whether to offer a hug or a kind word, and in the end, he mostly kept on standing there.

"Okay, so you neglected to mention when we talked to you earlier that you and Mayor Birt were in a relationship," he told the campaign manager.

They had found her in Birt's office, in exactly the same spot they had left her. She seemed blindsided by the question. "I, um… who told you that?" she asked finally.

"Just answer the question, Miss Lopez."

She got up and walked over to the window that looked out over Town Square. There was a balcony outside, where possibly mayors of yesteryear would walk out and greet the crowds of cheering citizens. Though if he remembered correctly, Jan Birt had done a balcony scene himself after his surprise election win six years ago. The footage had traveled around the world and had even been on CNN, the BBC, and plenty of other global news networks. There had been plenty of Flemish flags being waved in the crowd and loud cheers as the mayor appeared for his victory speech.

"I wasn't there last time, you know," she said quietly. "Six years ago? But I saw it on the news, like most people did. And I was so impressed that I swore I would be by his side for his next election win. I was a lot younger then, of course. Still in college. But I've never forgotten what a powerful impression his speech made on me. And so when my agency told me that Jan Birt was looking for a campaign manager, I immediately put my name forward. Lucky for me, I was selected in the first round, and we hit it off straightaway. And then, as the months passed, and we worked so closely together day after day, and all of those late nights, I guess we grew close." She turned, and an uncertain look appeared on her face. "I know what people think. That he was old enough to be my father. But when you know, you know. When you're in love, things like age simply fall away, and you see the person behind the facade—the soul inside the man. And Jan had a beautiful soul. I know he had a reputation as being something of a political firebrand, a loudmouth and a boor, but few people know that he was also a poet and an artist."

"An artist?" asked Poppy.

Gwendolyn crossed the room to her desk and opened a drawer. She took out a sketchbook and flipped it open to the first page. On it, a sketch of a woman had been drawn. It looked a lot like Gwendolyn, Holt thought. Her next words confirmed this.

"He liked to draw me," she said as she flipped through the book. "I used to sit for him in the evenings when everyone had left and Town Hall was quiet. He said that as a young man, he wanted to be an artist, but his parents told him there was no money in it and convinced him to join the family firm instead. And so he did, but in his heart of hearts, he never abandoned his dream of one day being known more for his art than his career."

Next to some of the drawings, little poems had been written. Holt caught a glimpse of a naked Gwendolyn, but she quickly closed the sketchbook and clasped it to her chest. Her cheeks had reddened, and her face displayed a mixture of pride and sadness. "I will cherish these drawings for the rest of my life. A testament to the love Jan and I shared."

"So last night?" asked Poppy.

"I was here—with him." She shook her head, and tears sprang to her eyes afresh. "I should never have left. If I hadn't, he might still be alive."

"Or you could have died alongside him," said Holt.

The wistful look that came into her eyes told him she probably wished she had.

She replaced the art book in her drawer and glanced up at Poppy. "If I were you, I would take a closer look at the family of that kid—the Elmalehs. Jan told me last night they were lawyering up. Take him to court for inciting hatred against them and calling them names. Libel and slander. He thought it was a good thing, as it would probably benefit our campaign by focusing everyone's attention on what was really at stake."

"And what did he think was at stake?" asked Holt, who was reminded of Anjanette's statement that she also thought the families might be behind the assassination.

"Nothing short of our way of life, Chief Inspector," said Gwendolyn decidedly. "It's either us or them. Either we take control of our country and get rid of the filth and scum that has littered it and is destroying the soul of our people, or we succumb to the destruction that they're wreaking on us."

So she might love poetry and art, but she was just as

much of a nutjob as her boyfriend, Holt thought. No wonder those two had fallen hard for each other.

He thanked her for her suggestion, and they took their leave.

"She's pretty radical, isn't she?" asked Poppy as they descended the Town Hall steps. "I thought she was just a campaign manager, but she seems to be fully on board with Birt's extremist ideas."

"Must be all those long nights in the office together, with her posing for him."

"Do you think she's right about the Elmalehs? Could they be behind this attack?"

"We better have a chat with them," said Holt, who thought that the notion that the Elmalehs had resorted to violence to get back at Birt was probably too far-fetched to be plausible. Then again, stranger things had happened. Maybe Hassan Elmaleh had finally decided that enough was enough, or his brother Mustafa.

"Let's go over there now," he suggested. "And see what they have to say for themselves."

"What about the Idrissis?"

"The Idrissis, too."

"Don't we need permission from…" She glanced up at him.

"No, we don't." The last person he was going to ask permission from to interview a possible suspect was Leah's new husband. "We don't even have to tell them we're talking to the families," he explained.

"But it's their jurisdiction," Poppy argued. "Aren't we going to get in trouble?"

"No trouble," he assured her. "We're looking into the murder of the mayor. They're looking into the death of those two kids and their links to organized crime."

Even though, of course, both investigations were linked.

At some point, a meeting would have to be arranged between Holt's team and Roy's, but not now. And since he knew that his nemesis would also be present at that meeting, he hoped to postpone the inevitable for as long as possible. Which was why he wouldn't tell Roy they were talking to the Elmalehs and the Idrissis.

## CHAPTER 42

"Are you nervous about coming face to face with Terrence again?" asked Poppy, who was no fool.

"Not nervous, exactly," he said. "I just don't think it's a good idea, that's all."

"You mean, like two planets that accidentally drift into each other's path, collide, and destroy each other?"

He grinned. "You have a way with words, honey—did anyone ever tell you that?"

"Maybe I should become a poet, like Mayor Birt."

"Yeah, right. I'll bet he copied all of those poems from a book." He had glanced at one of the scribblings and thought he'd recognized it from his high school English course.

They were on the road to Ghent, with Poppy behind the wheel. Even though Holt didn't adhere to the tradition that Chief Inspectors were driven by their inspectors, it was fine with him, as he could use the time to check his emails and talk to the rest of the team.

"Yeah, Leland," he said now as he picked up the phone.

"I've been talking to the witness who saw the mayor's

attacker run away, boss," said the inspector. "And trying to figure out where he could have disappeared."

"The witness said he escaped in the direction of the park, right?"

"Yeah, so I traced their steps and talked to some of the people who live close to the park. Unfortunately, no one saw anything, which I understand, as it was late. One man was walking his dog, though, and he remembers seeing the same figure running full speed out of the south gate of the park and then in the direction of Barnaby Street. So I was thinking that maybe we could send a team of uniforms to start ringing doorbells?"

"Go for it," he said. He appreciated when his people showed initiative, especially if it yielded new information.

He ended the call and rang Rasheed's line. He picked up on the first ring.

"Any luck?" he asked.

"Well, I've been looking into the connection between the mayor and his brother's company. Turns out that Birt Travel sponsored not only Birt's last election campaign but also the present one. Money was withdrawn from the Birt Travel business account and showed up as cash deposits in Jan Birt's account. Probably to avoid a direct connection."

"Correct me if I'm wrong, but political candidates aren't supposed to accept money for their campaigns, right?"

"No, they are not. All monies for campaigns come from the party, and they get their money from official campaign funds—as paid for by the taxpayer—you and me, in other words. So private donations are considered illegal."

"Looks like Teddy hasn't been completely honest with us, and neither has his brother."

"Oh, and I also looked into the mayor's phone records. His last call was from Daron Topley. This was at twenty minutes to twelve and lasted for ten minutes."

"I wonder what that was about," Holt grunted. "Any luck with the social media trawl?"

"Oh, just the usual nastiness," said Rasheed. "It's soul-crushing to read so much garbage, boss."

He grinned. "Don't tell me you want to apply for hazard pay?"

"I honestly had no idea of the level of hatred people are capable of until I started going through Birt's social media. Both for and against his political views, by the way."

"But nothing that stands out? No recent death threats?"

"Oh, plenty of those. I'm trying to create a list of the worst offenders and apply for their IP addresses. I could use a helping hand, chief."

"Ask Jaime," said Holt. "Maybe she can take care of the applications to the social media companies for you."

"Thanks, boss."

He tapped his phone against his teeth as he processed the information. It was all looking promising, he thought. But it was going to take time. And time was exactly what they were short of. When a high-profile figure like Mayor Birt is killed, the pressure is on to make an arrest. If they didn't move on this soon, the Commissioner would start feeling the heat from his higher-ups. And when that didn't speed things up, the old man would have no other choice but to apply to the Federal Police to take over the investigation.

"Any news?" asked Poppy.

In a few words, he updated her on the state of the investigation. She agreed that they were moving briskly forward in the right direction. "If Leland can find a witness who saw the killer escape last night, we might get lucky."

"Or we might get unlucky." Even though he firmly believed that true police work mostly consisted of the plodding kind, he wouldn't mind a lucky break.

Poppy swung the Renault Megane in between a Toyota

Yaris and a rusty old Peugeot, and they got out. Across the street, the house looked quiet, but Holt knew that looks can be deceiving and that behind the decrepit facade, an entire family lived. The Elmalehs were still grieving, but that couldn't be helped.

He pressed his finger on the bell, which jangled jarringly, and moments later the door was yanked open, revealing Mustafa Elmaleh. He didn't look happy to see them.

"Any news of my brother's killer?" he asked.

"I'm afraid we're not here for that," said Holt.

"A different team is handling that investigation now," said Poppy.

Mustafa stepped aside so they could squeeze past him into the house. It smelled just as musty as Holt remembered from last time, and he wondered how people could live like this. Then again, he and Leah had also lived in an old row house during the first years of their marriage, and so had Poppy, though she probably didn't remember. A police salary only goes so far, and it had taken a couple of years before they were able to afford something decent.

As before, the living room was full of people, with the Elmalehs' grandparents on the couch looking up at them, kids watching television, and the lady of the house in the kitchen cooking. The man of the house was absent and probably at a nearby café. Hassan wasn't there either, which was a problem, as they needed to talk to him as well.

"Okay, so tell me what's going on," said Mustafa. He was looking at them tersely, his arms crossed.

"Mayor Birt was killed last night," Holt said.

"Good," said Mustafa immediately. "I hope he rots in hell."

Holt grimaced. "I can understand how you feel, Mustafa—after the murder of your brother. But see, statements like that make it hard for us not to consider you a suspect."

"I was here last night," said Mustafa. He swung a hand to

encompass the rest of his family. "Ask them. They will confirm it. We were all here last night—no exception."

"Your dad?" asked Poppy.

"He was also here."

"Hassan?" asked Holt.

Here, Mustafa paused. "No, Hassan was out. But then he's always out. It's hard to know if he even considers himself a member of this family anymore."

"Any idea where he was?"

"You'd have to ask him, but probably staying with one of his friends, as usual." He said it in a harsh tone, and it was obvious that he blamed his brother for bringing this calamity upon his family. And he was right.

"We were told that you were considering legal action against the mayor," asked Holt, "for the stuff he said about you in that press conference of his?"

"I guess that's out the window now, with the mayor dead. Though we might still sue his party."

"Flemish Front."

"They reposted the things that Mayor Birt said on their social media and also on their website. We want all of that gone, and we want them to pay us for the moral damage."

"Have you been in touch with the Idrissis?"

"Yes, we're doing this together. The two families acting as one. Mo and Beni were best friends since they were kids, so it's only right that we would join forces." He glanced at his grandparents. "This has hit our family very hard. Not to mention that we're still being regarded with contempt by the people of the neighborhood. Not only Belgians but also Moroccans. They seem to see us as a family of drug dealers now."

"People are narrow-minded sometimes," said Poppy.

Mustafa nodded. "Anyway, we would never get back at Mayor Birt in this way. We're not killers, Chief Inspector. We were going to take him to court, not throw Molotov cocktails at his car. That's not who we are. And also, it isn't what Mo would have wanted. Now is the time when we should all come together, not think about revenge."

"Do you think your brother Hassan feels the same way?" asked Holt.

Mustafa smiled. "Hassan can only think of one thing these days: collect as much money as he can to buy himself another luxury car, date another hot girl, or buy another loft. He dreams of moving to Dubai and live like a prince. He doesn't care about Mayor Birt any more than he cares about what happened to Mo. My brother may not be addicted to drugs, Chief Inspector, but he's addicted to something even more pernicious: money."

CHAPTER 43

When Poppy and Holt arrived at the Idrissis, they weren't the only cops on the premises—Roy Hesketh was also present, along with one of his colleagues. They were still looking into Beni's death, trying to determine whether he'd ever been seen with any known members of the Green Valley gang by showing the Idrissis some mug shots. It didn't feel like the right time to bombard them with questions about Mayor Birt, but Holt still managed to speak with Beni's father, Adil.

He looked extremely tired, Poppy thought, which was hardly surprising, given that his son had been gunned down practically on his doorstep.

"I never met this Mayor Birt," Adil said as he studied a picture Holt showed him. "But I know he said some very bad things about my family. I never look at social media, so I didn't see it myself, but my good friend Aamir told me."

"Aamir Elmaleh?"

"Yes, Aamir and I have been friends for a long time. Our boys grew up together." A wistful smile lit up his features. "It's so sad it had to end like this. And all because of Hassan.

He lured our boys into the drug business. I know it, and Aamir knows it. That's why we're both more upset with Hassan than with the people who killed our boys. When you get too close to a lion, you know you will get hurt. That's not the fault of the lion, who can't help being who he is: a wild animal. It's the fault of the person who tells you to get into the enclosure with the beast and leaves you to fend for yourself."

"And that person is Hassan Elmaleh?"

Adil nodded. "Yes, that person is Hassan. He's the one who made our boys' heads spin with promises of big money, fast cars, and girls, girls, girls. And now look what happened. They're both dead, and our families are destroyed."

"Can you tell us where you were last night, Adil?" Holt asked.

Adil looked up. "Is that when this Mayor Birt was killed?"

"That's right. Around midnight."

"Well, I was here. With my family. You can ask my wife or anyone here. We were all together. Afraid to go out. Afraid of how our neighbors and friends would react. And afraid of getting shot by these bloodthirsty maniacs."

"Thanks, Adil," Holt said, placing a hand on the man's shoulder in support.

Poppy thought he was probably right. When you get mauled by a lion, it isn't the lion who's to blame, but the person who told you it was a good idea to go near the animal.

Holt chatted with Roy for a moment, but there wasn't much progress to be gleaned from the investigation the detective was pursuing. They still hadn't found Motorcycle Man, and Boyd Batham was still in the hospital, with a guard stationed outside his door. Until the entire gang was apprehended, he would need protection, as they might try to retaliate against him for allegedly stealing their drug shipment.

Teddy Birt was locked up in Loveringem, so he was beyond the gang's reach, and Teddy's wife and family had been placed in a safe house for the time being. All in all, it was a pretty tense time.

But since Roy Hesketh and his team were mostly on top of that case, it left Poppy's dad free to focus on the investigation into Mayor Birt's murder. While it might be related to the drug case, he didn't seem entirely convinced.

"You don't think there's a connection?" she asked as they drove back to Loveringem.

"I don't know, honey," he said. "It's possible, especially considering the murder weapon. These gangs love to throw Molotov cocktails at the homes of people they consider traitors or rivals. But..." He shook his head. "This feels different somehow. And also, Birt wasn't as involved in the whole scheme as his brother was."

"We know that he received funds from his brother," she countered. "Illegal campaign financing, paid for with dirty money from the drug mafia."

"I know, but why would they go after him? So what if he profited from Teddy's links to the Phoenix gang? He wasn't directly involved, and he had nothing to do with the disappearance of that last shipment. So why would they target him?" He shrugged. "But, like you said, there may be a connection, so I'm definitely not ruling it out."

Her dad was big on following his hunches, and oftentimes they had served him well over the course of a long and successful career. Until his fateful fracas with Poppy's new stepdad, he had never put a foot wrong, and his clearance rate was second to none. That was probably the reason he hadn't been kicked off the force, but instead dumped in Loveringem to spend the rest of his career dealing with minor offenses. Until the biggest case ever to happen in the small town had landed in his lap. Which was pretty ironic.

He definitely was the right man for the job, though. No question about it.

Holt's phone beeped, and he checked the display. When he grumbled something under his breath, she assumed the news wasn't good.

"What is it?" she asked.

"Prosecutor wants a meeting. Better step on it, honey. She wants to meet in my office."

"When?"

"Now."

Poppy activated the siren and blue lights, and stepped on the gas.

The prosecutor wouldn't have to wait long.

## CHAPTER 44

Shonna Turner wasn't waiting in Holt's office, since he didn't have one. The only person who did was the Commissioner. The rest of the staff occupied open-plan rooms, with the detective's department benefiting from a separate room from the traffic police—at least they had that. They also had their own desks, unlike some precincts where officers used any available desk and a rolling set of drawers for personal possessions, or a locker.

Most of Holt's colleagues had pictures of their families on their desks. He didn't—he could look at his daughter all day long, as she sat across from him. He didn't want to look at a picture of his wife, since she wasn't his wife anymore. As for his son, Aaron, they were currently not on speaking terms. What Holt did have was a large framed picture of Harley, his beloved French Bulldog, and a portrait of his parents, Mitch and Bettina, taken at their most recent wedding anniversary. It was part of a larger family picture, but since Leah had been standing next to Holt's mom, he had cropped her out. Or rather, Poppy had, and had the picture printed and sent to him. You could do that nowadays.

He met Shonna in the meeting room, along with the Commissioner.

"You didn't have to come all the way from Ghent," said Ezekiel. "We could have come to you, Shonna."

"Oh, it's fine," said the prosecutor. "I had to be in the area anyway, so I decided to pop in for a chat." She was a handsome woman in her early forties, her hair slicked back from a high forehead, her dark eyes intense and inquisitive, her ebony complexion flawless. She folded her hands, and Holt noticed the slight discoloration on her finger where her wedding ring used to be. Rumor had it that her husband had been cheating on her with Shonna's substitute, who, understandably, was no longer a substitute and had been unceremoniously fired. In that sense, her situation resembled his own, though Shonna being Shonna—and not Holt—hadn't hit her second-in-command in the face.

"So, what have you got for me, Glen?" she asked.

"Well, as far as I can tell, Jan Birt wasn't a popular figure—except with his supporters, that is. He had made a lot of enemies over the years, some of whom haven't been able to provide us with an alibi for last night." He gave her a brief overview of the people they had interviewed and touched upon the angle of the hate mail and online threats targeting the truculent and controversial politician.

Shonna seemed displeased, if the wrinkle in her otherwise smooth brow was anything to go by. "I thought you were focusing on the drug angle? With Teddy Birt's confession, I would have thought this was a slam-dunk case."

"You mean the drug mafia?" Holt asked.

"Absolutely. A Molotov cocktail is one of their preferred methods of dealing with members of a rival gang. These… Green Valley and Phoenix gangs. Surely Birt is just another victim in the war that's been raging between the two outfits?"

"I'm afraid I don't see it that way, Shonna," he said. "I

mean, it's possible, of course, and it's one of the lines of inquiry, but before we pin ourselves down on the drug angle, I'd like to widen the scope of our investigation and look at all the possible suspects. For one thing, the last person to talk to Birt was Daron Topley. So I think it's important to—"

"Surely that's a matter of course," Shonna interrupted, leaning forward and fixing Holt with an intense look. "Topley is the leader of Birt's party. The election is four weeks away. Of course they would be talking on the phone. What makes you think this particular phone call is significant?"

He shrugged. "Call it a hunch," he said, repeating what he had told his daughter. "I just don't think this killing is connected to the gang war."

"You don't?" She seemed incredulous.

"I mean, it's possible, but it seems unlikely. These gangs usually target members of a rival gang in a turf war scenario. In this case, Phoenix suspected Green Valley of stealing a shipment of their coke, so they killed the people responsible for the theft and kidnapped and tortured the driver who was on duty when the shipment was stolen. But Mayor Birt wasn't directly involved in any of that. Okay, so he took money from his brother to illegally finance his election campaign, but we haven't found any evidence that he was aware of the operational aspects of his brother's shady dealings. That was all Teddy."

"All the same," said Shonna. "I think it's important to focus on the drug angle. So I'd like you and your team to focus on Floyd Timmer, while Roy Hesketh handles the investigation into Green Valley and Phoenix and the Elmaleh and Idrissi murders."

"It's the Molotov cocktail, Holt," said the Commissioner. "Everyone knows they are the weapon of choice for these gangs. These people don't think the way we do. They don't say, 'Oh, it was Teddy Birt who's responsible for losing our shipment and not his brother.' They figure the Birts stole their drugs, so the Birts have to pay. They take a scattershot approach and don't care that maybe they got the wrong guy."

"Exactly," said Shonna. "Jan Birt was a victim of a hit by the Ghent drug mafia. Collateral damage, maybe, but that's for you to determine. I'd talk to Teddy again. I'm sure Jan was more involved in his drug trafficking business than he's letting on. Otherwise, why target him?"

Because he wasn't involved at all, Holt thought, but since it was obvious Shonna had already made up her mind, he merely nodded.

"And you're not to go anywhere near Daron Topley," the prosecutor added. "Let's limit the scope of this investigation to the people actually involved."

"The drug mafia," the Commissioner added helpfully, giving the prosecutor a grateful smile. "This has been very enlightening, Shonna," he said as he got up.

To Holt, it had been more disappointing than enlightening, but since he wasn't in a position to throw his weight around, he also stood, shook Shonna's hand, and watched her leave.

"Great lady," said the Commissioner appreciatively. "Whip-smart." He turned to the Chief Inspector. "So you've got your marching orders, Holt. Focus on the drug mafia."

"Yes, sir," said Holt.

## CHAPTER 45

Holt stood bent over Rasheed's desk. The technically gifted inspector had discovered an interesting lead. "See, sir?" Rasheed said, pointing to his screen. "The same name keeps coming up. This person kept warning Birt not to go 'soft' on him and urged him to keep fighting the good fight. Then, a couple of months ago, he turned against Birt, accusing him of being a traitor to the cause."

Holt read the message 'Wheely Bin' had written under one of the mayor's posts.

*'You promised to kick out every last one of those maggots, and guess what? They're still here! All of them! You're a traitor, Birt! You're betraying your own race!'*

"Yeah, he didn't seem happy with the guy," Holt agreed.

"It gets better, sir," Rasheed continued. "Last week, he wrote this comment."

*'Traitors get shot, Birt. So you better watch your back.'*

Holt nodded. "Great job, Rasheed. Any idea who this guy is?"

"Actually, yes, sir," Rasheed said, glowing with pride as he pulled up the person connected to the IP address used to write the comments. "We already know this guy. It's the same man who destroyed Wanda Desai's side mirrors."

"André Wiel," Holt read the name aloud. "Well, I'll be damned." He turned to Leland. "Didn't you and Georgina talk to this guy?"

"We did, boss," Leland confirmed. "He claimed it wasn't him who destroyed Mrs. Desai's side mirrors but a lookalike, remember? Or someone wearing a mask that looked like his face."

"Did you ever follow up with him?"

"I'm afraid we didn't. With the mayor being killed and all, Mr. Wiel kinda slipped through the cracks."

Holt's lips tightened into a thin line. "Better go and pick him up. You and Georgina. This time in connection with the mayor's murder."

"Yes, boss," Leland said, grabbing his coat.

"But first, I want to update you all on the state of the investigation. So gather round." Sitting on the edge of his desk, he briefed the team on his discussion with Shonna.

"So… we're focusing on the drug angle from now on, boss?" asked Georgina.

"No, we're not," Holt replied. "Frankly, I don't think Mayor Birt's death has anything to do with drugs."

Jaime, who had been listening intently, raised her hand. "Sir? What does the Commissioner think?"

"The Commissioner agrees with the prosecutor," Holt said. "But that doesn't mean much. He's not running this investigation—I am. And I say we continue looking into the suspects we've identified so far."

"But aren't we going to get in trouble?" Jaime asked.

He smiled. "I'll take full responsibility, Jaime. So if either the Commissioner or the prosecutor gives you any trouble, just refer them to me, all right?"

"Yes, sir," she said, her cheeks flushing. She was a timid girl, not comfortable speaking in public, but she was a hard worker, and he liked having her on the team.

"Okay, so let's talk suspects."

He had asked Poppy to wheel in a good old-fashioned whiteboard, and he now wrote the following names on it: Wanda Desai, Anjanette Birt, Jayson Birt, Justine Hallett, Daron Topley, and the Desai and Idrissi families.

He pointed to the first name. "Wanda Desai. Leader of the opposition and, until six years ago, mayor of this fair town. She felt stabbed in the back when her coalition party was seduced by Birt to form a coalition with him. This year, she wanted to beat him at the polls, but it wasn't looking good. Another six years in the opposition didn't sit well with her."

"So her motive is taking out the competition?" asked Georgina.

"That's correct. If you can't beat them, kill them."

"Very funny, sir," said Leland with a grin.

"Alibi?" asked Rasheed.

"Home with her husband."

"So no alibi," said Georgina.

"Next, we have Anjanette Birt, Jan's wife. We now know that Jan had been having an affair for the past fifteen years with his personal assistant, Justine Hallett, and for the last couple of months with his campaign manager, Gwendolyn Lopez. Something Mrs. Birt neglected to mention when we interviewed her."

"So she killed her husband because he'd been having an affair for the past fifteen years?" Georgina asked, sounding doubtful.

"Justine told us that Anjanette was going to file for divorce," said Poppy. "And that Justine was going to look for another job. Both women were fed up with Jan."

"Even less likely that either of them would have killed

him," Georgina insisted. "It's easier to divorce the guy than to murder him, surely."

"Wait, how does Justine know about the divorce?" asked Leland, always sharp-eyed.

Poppy smiled. "As unlikely as it sounds, she and Anjanette are close friends."

"Huh?" said Georgina. "Now that is kinda weird. Isn't it?"

"I think the fact that Jan hooked up with Gwendolyn drew them closer," said Holt. "They were both cheated on and united in their sense of betrayal."

"Okay, so I guess it's possible they decided to get even with the bastard," Georgina said with a shrug. "Alibis?"

"Anjanette was watching *Die Hard* with her son, Jayson," said Holt. "And Justine was home alone."

"Both Christmas movies," Rasheed murmured.

"What was that, Rasheed?" asked Holt. "Speak up."

"*Home Alone* and *Die Hard*, sir. They're both Christmas movies."

"She didn't *watch Home Alone*," said Georgina. "She *was* home alone."

"Yeah, I got that, inspector," said Rasheed. "It was a pun? You know... like, like a joke?" he said uncertainly when Georgina gave him a blank look. "A play on words? She was home alone, but *Home Alone* is also the name of a movie so…" His voice trailed off.

Georgina closed her eyes and shook her head. "So lame," she determined.

"I would argue that *Die Hard* is not a Christmas movie and *Home Alone* is," said Leland, adding his two cents. When Georgina threw a paper ball at him, he shrugged. "Just saying."

"Can we get back to the investigation now?" asked Holt.

"Yes, sir," said Rasheed, his cheeks coloring. "Sorry, sir."

"So what about Jayson Birt?" asked Georgina. "What's his motive?"

"Well, he hated his dad with a vengeance," said Holt. "Dumped a bucket of cow shit all over him during that press conference and had a few choice things to say about the man, none of them complimentary. I think it's safe to say he wasn't his dad's biggest fan."

"*Die Hard* though, sir," said Rasheed. "You can't argue with John McClane."

"Was *Die Hard* even on last night?" asked Poppy.

"*Die Hard* is always on, Poppy," said Leland. "It's only one of the seminal movies of our time. A true classic. I could watch it every day of the week."

Rasheed quickly checked the TV guide and confirmed, "Yes, it was on last night. On VTM. But it didn't last until midnight. Started at nine and ended before eleven."

"Anjanette claims that she was home all night, and so was Jayson," said Poppy. "So they're each other's alibis."

"One of them could have snuck out," said Leland. "Done the deed and then snuck back."

"Or they could both have done it," said Georgina. "If they hated Birt senior that much. Mother and son organizing a family barbecue."

"Georgina!" Rasheed said, aghast. "Language!"

"What? I'm just saying they could have done it."

"What is Daron Topley doing on the board, boss?" asked Leland.

Holt tapped his marker next to the party leader's name. "He was probably the last person to talk to Birt. Call made at twenty to twelve. Lasted ten minutes."

"Why would the leader of the Flemish Party kill his star candidate? Birt put that party on the map," said Georgina.

"Beats me," said Holt. "But I'd still like to have a chat with the man." Even though Shonna had strictly told him not to, he wasn't going to mention that to his team. If he got in trouble over it, he wasn't going to drag them into it. Though he might ask Poppy to tag along. She could always claim he hadn't told her about Shonna's directive.

"Okay, so we have one more person to add to the list," said Leland. "André Wiel. Once one of the mayor's biggest supporters, but lately he'd grown disappointed with him for —and I quote—*'not kicking out the maggots like you promised.'* He also wrote in a comment that *'Traitors get shot, so you better watch your back.'* Looks like he had gone off the mayor."

"There's probably dozens of people who hated Birt," said Georgina. "Maybe even hundreds or thousands. Are we going to talk to all of them?"

"No, we're going to focus on this short list of people for now," said Holt. "If that leads nowhere, we widen the scope. I don't want to waste our limited resources on a wild-goose chase. Tracking down everyone who left a scathing comment on Birt's social media is a major job, and frankly, we don't have the manpower. So let's dig deeper into these persons of interest. You know the drill—background checks and everything that entails."

"What about the Elmaleh and Idrissi families?" asked Rasheed.

"We'll leave them to Roy Hesketh and his team," said Holt as he pushed himself up from his desk. "Leland and Georgina will bring in André Wiel, and Poppy and I will pay a visit to the pathologist."

Poppy made a face. "Is the autopsy done?"

"The autopsy is done, Poppy," said Holt. "Let's go find out the verdict, shall we?"

## CHAPTER 46

The problem they now faced was that they couldn't apply for search warrants for the persons of interest they had identified so far, since Shonna had specifically told Holt to focus on the gang war angle. To get a warrant, he had to go through her, as he couldn't very well tap the examining magistrate directly by going behind her back. He had to follow procedure, and that meant that unless he unearthed some very compelling evidence, he was effectively stuck.

"I can't believe she actually told you not to go anywhere near Topley," said Poppy after he had given her the gist of his meeting with Shonna. "I mean, it's almost as if she's protecting the guy. What is he, her boyfriend or something?"

"He's the leader of one of the main political parties," said Holt. "So it probably stands to reason she doesn't want to trouble him unless it's strictly necessary." He also felt that she had limited the scope of his investigation to such an extent that she hadn't given him any wiggle room to speak of, thereby curtailing his agency as a detective. How was he supposed to handle the investigation if he was corralled in like that?

"It's not fair," she said. "It's your investigation, Dad, not hers."

He smiled at her youthful impetuousness. It reminded him very much of the way he had been as a young cop—always tilting at windmills, gung-ho to the max. Now that he was old and gray—or older and grayer—he had calmed down a lot. But that didn't mean he wasn't annoyed with Shonna. "That's the way it is, I'm afraid. The prosecutor is in charge of the investigation, and she decides the direction it should take." Though most of the time, prosecutors gave police plenty of leeway to conduct their investigations as they saw fit. As long as it led to results—in other words: actual convictions in court.

He and Poppy were on the road again, back to the University Hospital, where they were meeting Lionel Kewley—the second time in as many days. The medical examiner saw the humor in the situation. "We have to stop meeting like this, Holt," he said with a twinkle in his eye. He then led them to the fridge where he had stored the body of Mayor Birt. "I'm afraid there wasn't a lot of him left, but I still managed to make a positive identification." He slid out the drawer and peeled back the sheet that covered the mayor.

Holt stared at the blackened figure in front of him while Poppy reeled back.

"Yuck," she muttered as she turned away. "Excuse me," she added, hurrying away from the scene, possibly to get some fresh air or find a bathroom.

"Like I said, not much left," said the pathologist. "Burned to a crisp. Temperatures can reach extremely high levels, and by the time the fire department managed to douse the flames, most of the body had been consumed. His dental records were on file with his dentist, though. And if that hadn't worked, a DNA check would have done the job."

"So the cause of death is probably pretty obvious?"

"You would think so, wouldn't you? I still carried out a full autopsy just to make sure. Sometimes bodies are burned by the perpetrator to hide the actual cause of death and to destroy evidence. But in this case, he died from the effects of the fire. Heat or burn shock, in fact, because the Molotov cocktail was thrown directly at him. The remnants of the glass were found all over the victim's body, as well as on the driver's seat and the footwell of the car. Mostly, burn victims die from asphyxiation— inhaling carbon monoxide mixed with other toxic by-products of combustion. Or they die from pulmonary edema and spasm of the epiglottis due to inhalation of super-heated gases. But Birt died because his tissues and organs were deprived of adequate oxygenated blood."

"The attacker threw the Molotov cocktail directly at him?"

"Indeed," said the doctor. "And then he closed the car door, locking his victim inside the vehicle and thereby sealing his fate. Death was inevitable at that point."

"Still, it's a pretty risky proposition. The bottle could have bounced off the mayor and ricocheted back on the killer. Or he could have missed him altogether."

"Yes, it's not a very efficient murder method," Lionel agreed. "And it could have backfired in any number of ways." He displayed a fine smile. "No pun intended."

Holt pictured the sequence of events. "The bottle broke, so that means it must have hit a solid object. If it had been thrown at the mayor's torso, it wouldn't have shattered."

"The point of impact presumably was the mayor's head," said the doctor. "It's the only explanation that makes sense. It's hard enough to cause the bottle to break on impact. Like you said, if it had been thrown at his torso, most likely it wouldn't have shattered. I found glass shards embedded in what was left of the mayor's scalp, so the only explanation is that the bottle hit him in the head."

"God, that's awful," said Holt.

"Yes," said Lionel as he studied the mayor's remains in rather a dispassionate manner. "I'd say that whoever killed him must have held quite the grudge against this man."

## CHAPTER 47

"So what did he say?" asked Poppy.

"That whoever did this didn't like the mayor. They threw the Molotov cocktail straight at his head with enough force that it broke, dousing him in flames. Then they slammed the door of his car, locking him inside the vehicle while he burned to a crisp." He shuddered to think of Birt's final moments. It must have been pretty hellish.

"I'm so sorry for bailing on you like that, Dad. It's just that the moment I saw the body, my stomach did a backflip. I practically vomited all over him."

"It's fine, honey," he said. "It wasn't a pretty sight."

"How Lionel can do what he does is beyond me."

"Yeah, I have often wondered how he manages."

They were in the car, with Poppy waiting for instructions on where to go next. Holt had been consulting his notebook and held it up for her.

"Rose Drive. Who lives there?" she asked as she entered the address into the car's satnav.

"Daron Topley."

She gave him a look of surprise. "But I thought…"

"I just want to have a chat with the guy. I'll be gentle—I promise."

She grinned. "Yeah, right." She started the car. "Okay, Dad. But if he files a complaint against us for harassment—"

"It's on me, I promise." He didn't think the party leader would file any complaints, though. He didn't know that Shonna had announced him off-limits, did he? So how would she ever find out? It would just be a friendly little chat—off the record. He wasn't even going to put it in his report. "It's an itch," he explained.

"I get it, Dad."

"An itch I need to scratch."

"Okay, fine. Scratch away. I don't mind."

He couldn't explain it, but as long as he didn't talk to the party leader, he felt he couldn't move the investigation forward. Shonna wouldn't understand. In fact, very few people would. Maybe Roy, but then he was something of a maverick cop.

"So what about fingerprints on the bottle?" asked Poppy.

"No fingerprints were found, unfortunately."

"Destroyed by the fire, right?"

"Well, Lionel explained that fingerprints aren't necessarily destroyed by fire. In some cases, they can be retrieved, even on petrol bombs used to light the fire. But not in this case. Which means—"

"That either the perp wore gloves or that the prints were destroyed in the fire."

He smiled. "Exactly."

"So no prints. What about DNA?"

"No usable DNA was retrieved from the scene."

"Great. So no CCTV, no fingerprints, no DNA."

"We still have the house-to-house," he reminded her. "That might yield a lead."

Though to be honest, he didn't hold out much hope. It

had been after midnight, after all, and the perp had taken precautions to hide their features. So even if they found a second witness, it was unlikely that they would be able to make a positive ID.

Still, it was worth a shot.

The party leader lived in downtown Ghent, which was a nice change, as the leaders of other political parties all lived either in Brussels or Antwerp, with the Walloon leaders residing in the country's capital, Liège or Charleroi. Topley occupied a nicely renovated bel étage in the more expensive part of Ghent, next to one of the many canals that traversed the city.

Topley greeted them heartily, possibly hoping to convert them into voters and supporters of his brand of Flemish nationalism. He would have found a tough convert in Holt, who wasn't all that interested in politics, and definitely not of the sort Topley and his ilk dealt in. The man's living room was as stylishly appointed as the house's facade had suggested, with several paintings adorning the walls. All reproductions of Flemish masters—or perhaps they were the real deal?

A Flemish Front pin was attached to the party leader's lapel, and as usual, he was dressed in a suit, his hair neatly coiffed, looking like everyone's favorite son-in-law. But behind the smooth-shaven, boyish features lurked a pretty shrewd operator, Holt knew.

Topley invited them onto his balcony, which looked out across the park, and beyond it the Ghent skyline, with its three famous towers: the Belfry, Saint Nicholas Church and Saint Bavo's Cathedral. It was certainly impressive.

"Great view," said Poppy.

"Yeah, it's quite something," said Topley. "My wife actually found this place. We had been renting for the last couple of years, and we were looking to buy. Once this popped up on her radar, we both knew that this was it. We didn't need to look any further."

"Must have cost a pretty penny," Holt couldn't help but mention.

"Lucky for us, my father-in-law decided to chip in," said Topley. "Otherwise, we'd never have been able to afford it. Not on my salary and my wife's schoolteacher's income. But then prices in downtown Ghent are through the roof at the moment, which is a crying shame. And something we really need to address, as the government is letting us down in that regard by not curtailing this rampant speculative behavior by the real estate mafia."

Holt smiled but didn't respond. They weren't there to let themselves be drawn into a political argument, though it was obvious Topley felt strongly about this. "I wanted to ask you about Jan Birt," he said, deciding to launch into the reason for their visit.

"Yes, of course," said the young party leader as he gestured to a white leather couch. He took a seat across from them and gave them all of his attention. It was a knack that he had mastered well, Holt thought, and one that he quite appreciated. Too many people seemed distracted these days by their phones, but not this guy. Holt and Poppy were the only people that existed for him at that moment, which was a nice change of pace from some of the other people they had interviewed. "Such a tragedy. We've already set up a memorial site, and the condolences are streaming in. Any news on who was responsible?"

"The investigation is ongoing, I'm afraid. But we are following several promising leads."

"I hope you're looking into the people who had been targeting him? Like I told you last night, Jan was under attack."

"We are looking into that," he assured the man.

"So the thing is that the last phone call that Jan Birt received was from you, sir," said Poppy. "A call that came in at twenty to twelve and lasted around ten minutes?"

"Could you tell us what you and Mr. Birt discussed?" asked Holt.

"You may very well be the last person who talked to him."

The party leader frowned. "Yes, I do remember phoning Jan. I hadn't realized that I was the last person to talk to him. Surely that wasn't the case?" But when both Holt and Poppy continued to look at him expectantly, he shook his head. "Terrible. I mean, it's hard to imagine that only moments after our phone call... Absolutely terrible."

"So what did you talk about, sir?" asked Holt.

"I really don't see how that is important, Chief Inspector."

"It might be. At the very least, it might shed some light on his state of mind."

"Oh, his state of mind was fine," Topley assured them. "Combative, you know. He knew that he was on the right track and he was determined to win this election and win it in such a big way that would leave our enemies scrambling. The thing is that no other party wants to form a coalition with us, and so we need to win in such a big way that we become impossible to ignore. And that was Jan's ambition: to become even bigger than last time. He told me that he thought he might even get an absolute majority."

"Was that in the cards, you think?" asked Holt.

"Absolutely. Jan was even more popular now than six years ago, and he got close to the forty percent mark then. Which is probably why he was killed. He was too popular."

"So that's what you talked about in his final phone call? The strategy to win the next election?"

Topley nodded. "That's correct. I told him that the entire party was watching him and cheering him on. He told me he was eternally grateful for all the support. We also talked about police protection. I suggested it, in light of what I told you last night, but he refused. He said he wasn't a coward and he wasn't going to let his enemies intimidate him." He sighed. "Now I wish I had broached the topic sooner and that I had insisted. Maybe he would still be alive today if I had."

"He didn't want police protection?" asked Poppy.

"No, he said that it would make him look weak and might lose him votes."

Holt decided to try a different tack. "Did he mention the scandal involving his brother?"

"Scandal?" asked Topley innocently. Then he added, "Oh, that business with the drugs, you mean? No, I didn't see the need to discuss it, as it didn't involve Jan."

"I see," said Holt, and he did see. There was no way that Birt hadn't discussed the potential ramifications of his brother's arrest with the leader of his party. But then Topley wouldn't tell them if that was the case. "It may surprise you to know we have discovered a direct link between Teddy Birt's dealings with the drug mafia and Jan's campaign."

The lawyer raised his eyebrows. "Oh?"

"Money was flowing from Teddy's account into Jan's. Not directly, but indirectly. So effectively, Teddy was funding his brother's re-election campaign with drug money."

Topley didn't even blink. "And you can prove this?"

"The evidence is incontrovertible, I'm afraid."

"Well, that certainly paints Jan in a different light." He thought for a moment. "If this is true, that means Jan deceived all of us, and most of all me. And to think I even offered him more money from the party coffers."

"You were offering him more money?"

"His campaign was extremely important for the party. If he could hold on to his position, win the election, and rise to power, that was a big win for us. But now you tell me that he had alternative sources of income—income that he failed to declare to us."

"Illegal campaign financing," said Holt, spelling it out.

A flicker of annoyance momentarily marred the party leader's smooth countenance. Blink and you would have missed it. The man would have made a great poker player. But then he had been a defense lawyer for many years, so he had learned to keep his emotions in check and work an audience, making them do his bidding.

He leaned forward and gave Holt a look of grave concern. "So do you think that the people who killed Jan were members of the same gang that killed those kids?"

"It's possible," Holt conceded.

"I see." He leaned back again and shook his head. "If what you're telling me is true—"

"It is."

"—then I'll have to call a party council meeting. We will have to address this before the media puts their own spin on it." He gave Holt a quick glance. "Has this information been released to the press?"

Holt shook his head. "If it has, it didn't come from me."

"Well, thank you so much for giving me a heads-up, Chief Inspector," said the party leader, getting up and buttoning his jacket. "I will call an emergency meeting immediately. Looks like Jan Birt has betrayed my confidence in the gravest way possible and put our historic victory in jeopardy."

Holt and Poppy also got up. It looked like their audience was at an end. It hadn't gone exactly as Holt had hoped, with the party leader giving absolutely nothing away. But then he probably should have expected that he'd be a tough nut to crack. "One final question, sir," he said. "Can you tell us where you were last night around midnight?"

"I was right here," said the party leader immediately.

Clearly, he had given this some thought before they arrived. "Ask my wife. She will confirm I was home all evening."

"So that call to Birt, that was made here?"

"Yes, on my mobile."

"Thank you, sir."

If need be, they could get a warrant for the man's phone records and location data. But only if they could get the prosecutor onside, and that wasn't likely at the moment.

They took their leave, and he could tell the party leader was rattled. A scandal of major proportions was brewing, and once the story broke, he'd be the one to contend with the fallout.

Truth be told, Holt didn't much care whether Flemish Front weathered the storm or went down in flames. All he cared about was finding Birt's killer, and he wasn't sure if his chat with Topley had brought him closer to the truth or not. He had a feeling it hadn't.

They had only just commenced their return trip to Loveringem when Shonna called.

The prosecutor did not sound happy.

## CHAPTER 48

"I'm running out of patience with you, Holt," said Shonna. "Didn't I specifically tell you not to go anywhere near Daron Topley? And what is the first thing you do? Go and pay the man a visit. I mean, what's wrong with you?"

"He called you, did he?"

"What does it matter?"

"He went running to you and complained about me like a crybaby."

"He was concerned about the allegations of illegal campaign financing your investigation has dug up, and so he wanted to find out if we were going to pursue the matter now that Birt is dead, and if we were communicating the story to the media."

"And what did you tell him?"

"That our media strategy was none of his concern, and that the decision on whether to look into the allegations hasn't been made yet."

"So basically, you told him to bugger off."

"Something like that." She sighed. "Look, Holt, nobody is

denying that you're an excellent detective, but you're also your own worst enemy sometimes. Please don't make the mistake of also making an enemy out of me, is that understood?"

"Yes, ma'am," he said.

"In your current situation, you need all the friends you can get. Unless you want to remain stuck in Loveringem until the end of your career, which might be upon you sooner than you may think."

"Understood, ma'am."

"So focus your investigation on the drug angle and stay away from Daron Topley. He may not look it, and his party may not be to everyone's taste, but the man has friends in high places." And with those words, she disconnected.

Looked like he had overstepped the mark—again.

"What did she say?" asked Poppy, who was steering the car back to Loveringem.

"That if I go anywhere near Topley again, I can kiss my career goodbye."

"So maybe you better do as she says this time?"

He shrugged. "We've got as much out of Topley as we possibly can, so there's no need to bother the guy any further." He stared straight ahead of him. "He was extremely concerned about the illegal campaign financing business, though. Which tells me that he may know more than he's letting on."

"But does it have a bearing on the case?"

"Of course it has. Birt's campaign was being financed by the drug mafia. I don't see how that *can't* have a bearing on the case. But in her wisdom, the prosecutor has decided that it behooves us to let Topley off the hook. For the present."

"Better listen to her. Unless you want to be transferred to a precinct even worse than Loveringem?"

He scoffed, "What can be worse than Loveringem?"

"Oh, I don't know. They could send you to the Westhoek. To some outpost manned by two cops and a goat?"

He grimaced. "Yeah, I guess there's that." Though it was far more likely they would simply kick him off the force this time. No more transfers—just straight out on the street.

"Please behave, Dad," Poppy said as she shot a quick glance at his profile. "I like the way things are right now. With the two of us working together. We're fine, aren't we?"

"Yeah, it's worked out very well," he agreed.

He hadn't thought that living with his daughter would be a good idea. But he had to admit that they got along like gangbusters. Then again, they always had, even when she was little. She had always been his little princess. So, even though people thought it was weird that he and Poppy would share lodgings, it was working out surprisingly well.

"Okay, I'll behave from now on, I promise," he said.

"Good. We don't want to lose one of the best detectives Loveringem has ever had. Though I still contend that you're overqualified for the job, and I hope that at some point the powers that be will give you a chance to redeem yourself and put you where your talents are more useful." She smiled. "And when that happens, I also hope you'll put in a good word for me, so I can move right up the totem pole along with you."

He was touched that she had said that. Mostly, kids want to get as far away from their parents as they possibly can, and most definitely don't want to work side by side or, *gasp!*, live under the same roof with them. So, he must have done something right.

"When that happens—*if* that happens—I'll be sure to give you a glowing recommendation, honey," he promised.

They had arrived back in Loveringem, and Poppy swung the car into her designated parking spot.

The time had come to talk to André Wiel and to see what the man had to say for himself.

Leland and Georgina had decided to hold off on interrogating Wiel until the boss arrived, and so it was Holt who now sat across from the parks and recreation worker in the small interview room. Next to him, Poppy sat, a stack of printed-out Facebook posts in front of her. When she showed them to the man, he smiled.

"That was a good one," he said as he tapped his own comment. "I was on a roll there."

Holt frowned as he grabbed the printout. "'You are a traitor to your own race, and you will be punished accordingly. Traitors get shot, and that's what's going to happen to you, you piece of...' Proud of this, are we, Mr. Wiel?"

"Very," said the guy as he leaned back in his chair, not a care in the world. Even though most suspects get unnerved after being locked up in a holding cell for a couple of hours, this man didn't seem fazed at all. Quite the contrary. He appeared to enjoy all the hullabaloo tremendously. As if it was the highlight of his week, which maybe it was.

"You threatened to kill Birt," said Poppy. "Many, many times. A constant barrage of verbal threats. You also knew exactly where the mayor parked his car, and that the CCTV camera covering that part of the car park was out of order."

"What are you implying?" asked the man.

"I'm implying that you first threatened the mayor, and then when that didn't have the effect you were hoping for, you took matters into your own hands and killed him."

Wiel laughed uproariously, rocking back and forth as he did. Some spittle flew from his lips and landed on the pages laid out in front of him. "You're crazy! Me? Kill Birt? That's just nuts."

"But you just said you're proud of the death threats that you wrote. It's obvious that you hated the man."

"Are you crazy? I'm one of his biggest fans. Ask anyone. I'm Team Birt all the way. I even put one of his placards on my roof. I would have done anything to get that man re-elected." He tapped the table with an angry index finger. "But he made a *promise*—he said he was going to kick *all* the immigrants out of Loveringem and send them back to wherever the hell they came from—*every* last one. *No* exceptions. It's been six years, and as far as I can tell, he hasn't kicked out a single one. Not one. On the contrary, more and more are arriving every day. When I walk around, I don't feel at home in my own town. The town I was born in and where I grew up. All I see are strangers looking back at me. And I blame him—the guy who was going to fix all of that and ended up fixing *nothing*."

"So why the hateful messages and the death threats?"

"All I did was try to keep the guy on message! Make sure that he made good on all the promises that he made." He slapped his chest. "I was Mayor Birt's guardian angel!"

Holt picked up the list of death threats. "'I WILL KILL YOU!' 'YOU DESERVE TO DIE!' 'EVERYBODY HATES YOU!' You don't sound like Birt's biggest fan, Wiel."

"Someone had to make sure he didn't get sucked up by the system."

"A little harsh, though, wouldn't you agree? Not to mention completely unhinged."

"I talked to Birt many times at the Hol of Pluto, reminding him of his promises. Every time he told me I needed to be patient. Have faith. And I did. I think I was very patient. But after six years of no change I got real frustrated. So I decided to try a different tack. And it worked. His speeches were getting more radical, and also his campaign videos."

"So why did you kill him?" Poppy asked.

"I didn't! I never went anywhere near the guy."

"Where were you last night around midnight?" asked Holt.

"Was that when he was killed?" He thought for a moment. "I was at the Hol of Pluto last night. I don't know until what time. But after that, I went straight home. It must have been really late, though, because Mom had already gone to bed. She usually waits up for me, but she was fast asleep by the time I got home."

"You live with your mother?" asked Poppy.

"My mother lives with me," he corrected her. "After Dad died, she found it hard to live by herself, so I took her in."

"You didn't sneak over to Town Hall and throw a petrol bomb at the mayor, did you?" asked Holt.

He made a scoffing noise. "I think I'd remember if I did. I was pretty wasted, but not *that* wasted. And besides, I would never hurt the mayor. Like I said, I was one of his biggest fans." When Holt tapped the list of threats he had made, he repeated, "All I wanted was for Mayor Birt to do the right thing, because I knew only he could do it—nobody else comes close. Birt was all we had, and now he's gone, and that terrible Desai woman will probably be our new mayor. She'll destroy Loveringem even further with her inclusion and diversity programs and her woke nonsense. Rumor has it she wants to open an asylum seekers center. Which means this town will be destroyed. It'll be the end of us."

"Is that why you destroyed her side mirrors?" asked Poppy.

He shrugged. "And what if I did? She's destroying our way of life, so what are a few stupid side mirrors compared to that?" He looked up when they didn't respond. "Next thing you'll accuse me of trying to murder *her*. I would never do that. I'm a peaceful person—just ask my mother. She'll tell you."

"We will ask her if she remembers you arriving home last night and what time that was," said Holt.

"Like I just told you, she was fast asleep, so that won't do you a lot of good."

"I hope for your sake that isn't true, Wiel," said Holt. "Because right now, she's the only person standing between you and prison."

"But I didn't do it!" he cried, his complacency a thing of the past now that he realized how much trouble he was in.

After Wiel had been returned to his cell, Holt and Poppy discussed the interview.

"Do you think he was telling the truth?" asked Poppy.

"Maybe," Holt said. He had struck him as pretty convincing. Also, he had the impression that André Wiel wasn't the kind of guy who possessed a great capacity to deceive. What you saw with him was pretty much what you got. And if he *had* killed the mayor, he would have been boastful. Like he was proud of those nasty messages he had posted.

"He wouldn't jeopardize his mother's well-being," said Poppy. "That's what I think. And if he's arrested and sentenced for the mayor's murder, his mother would have to go and live in a retirement home, and I've got a feeling he's attached to his mom."

"Yeah, not a lot of people take their elderly parents to live with them. It's a rare thing these days."

They had returned to the main room, and he told Leland to organize a search of Wiel's house. If they were lucky, they might find evidence proving his guilt—or innocence. For the time being, he would remain in custody.

## CHAPTER 49

Rasheed had sent Holt a list of other 'regulars' on Birt's social media, some of whom had criminal records. Nothing that stood out, though. Mostly minor stuff, and it seemed like a major leap from petty crime to murder. Still, he went through the list, trying to determine if one of these people could possibly be implicated. He was just opening the crime scene report that Lionel had sent him when his phone rang. It was Roy Hesketh.

"We got him, buddy," said his old-time collaborator.

"Got who, exactly?"

"Motorcycle Man. We finally managed to trace him back to his place. Neat loft up north. He didn't put up much resistance when we showed up to collar him."

"Good work, Roy," Holt said, and he meant it. Professional killers like Motorcycle Man can be hard to pin down.

"His real name is Timmothy Warmington, and oddly enough, he's never been arrested before. Though we have reason to believe he's been active for a while."

"Warmington. Doesn't ring any bells with me."

"Wanna be there when we question him? Not in the room, but as an observer?"

"Absolutely," he said, but then realized this would mean he'd be in the same precinct as his former boss. "Where is Bayton?"

"He's around. Just try and avoid him, all right? And try not to take a swing at him."

He grimaced. "As long as he doesn't take a swing at me. Can I bring Poppy?"

"Sure. See you in half an hour?"

He hung up as Leland appeared at his shoulder.

"Boss? Uniform has turned Wiel's house upside down and haven't found anything suspicious. No jerrycans filled with petrol or materials to make a Molotov cocktail. All they found was Wiel's elderly mother, who wasn't too happy about all the mess and the inconvenience."

"What about her son's alibi?"

"Says she was asleep by the time he got home and didn't hear him come in."

"Hmm," Holt said.

"So, should we let him walk?"

"No, hang on to him for the moment. I want to have another crack at him later today or maybe tomorrow. He's still our number-one suspect."

He grabbed his jacket and told Poppy about the phone call.

"Oh, that's great news," she said. "Does Roy believe he's also responsible for the attack on the mayor?"

"I guess we'll find out."

This time Holt was behind the wheel, with Poppy riding shotgun. "If this keeps up, we should probably get a desk at Ekkergem precinct," she said. "We seem to be spending more time there than in our own precinct."

"I *had* a desk there," he said. "Although in recent years

there was some contention, as they decided to go with this new desk-less craziness, and we all had to grab any desk that was available on a day-to-day basis."

"Let me guess, you kept your own desk anyway."

He grinned. "They touched my desk at their own peril."

"I should have known. That probably went over well with Terrence?"

"Oh, he *loved* it," said Holt sarcastically. "Though he shouldn't have complained, since he got to keep his office. Now, if they had instigated a no-office policy and made the top brass grab any office on a daily basis, *that* would have been fair, but the new policy was limited to the grunts only."

Poppy's phone beeped, and she checked the message. Her face clouded as she put her phone away.

"Who is it?" he asked.

She shook her head. "Nothing."

He knew better than to pry, so he kept quiet.

"I don't believe this," she finally said. "Lynn is pregnant."

Lynn was Rupert's new girlfriend. Poppy and Rupert had been trying to have a baby for years, but it never happened. "I mean, how long have they been together? Three months? And already she's pregnant." She frowned. "I wonder how far along she is..." The implication was obvious. Rupert had officially met his new girlfriend six months ago, while he was still together with Poppy. "If she's more than six months along, I will..." She balled her hands into fists, and a determined look crossed her pixie-like features.

"Who sent you the message? Rupert?"

She nodded. "Gloating."

"I'm sure he simply wanted you to know before you found out some other way."

"He's a jerk, Dad. A rotten jerk, and I, for one, am glad it never happened for us. Imagine sharing a child with that man."

"I share two kids with your mother, and I haven't regretted it for a single moment."

"That's different. You were together for a long time. Rupert and I..." Her voice trailed off, and he could tell that despite her determination not to dwell on the past, she was far from over her ex-husband, who had walked out one day in a shocking development that had knocked the ground from under her feet. Even though the exact circumstances were still a little hazy to Holt, he could vividly picture the scene.

He placed a large hand on hers and gave it a squeeze. He felt for her, and all he could think of saying were some lame comments about there being more fish in the sea and all that. Since he didn't want to come across like a jerk himself, he decided it was better to keep his mouth shut.

Finally, she wiped a tear from her eye and swallowed. "I should have destroyed his collection of Star Wars figurines when I had the chance. Or buried them where he could never find them."

He quirked an eyebrow in her direction. "Like your mother is keeping my comics hostage, you mean?"

She gave him a watery smile. "That's different."

"How is that different from you destroying Rupert's figurines?"

"I don't know, but it is," she said determinedly, and there was no arguing with that.

They had arrived back at his old stomping grounds, and out of sheer habit, he swung the car into his old spot, which happened to be available.

Timmothy Warmington was a man Holt's age, but thin and sinewy, with a pockmarked face and long black hair. He was dressed in jeans, a T-shirt featuring death metal band Anwynn, and a leather jacket. The neckline of his T-shirt revealed part of a tattoo. Holt had a feeling the rest of his body would be similarly covered in ink.

"Tough guy," Roy commented as they both studied the man for a moment. Roy had a file folder under his arm and took a deep breath. "Wish me luck," he said.

"You don't need it, buddy," said Holt. "You got this."

Holt and Poppy watched from the next room, where they had a perfect view of the interview room through the one-way mirror.

Holt felt oddly unnerved being back at his old precinct, where he had spent so many years. He'd been where Roy now sat, confronting a suspect, so many times that he wouldn't have minded joining his old colleague in there now. But it wasn't his case, so he had refrained from making the suggestion. He was grateful Roy had invited them to observe.

Next to Roy, another detective sat, and together they confronted Timmothy Warmington and his lawyer, who was there to ensure his legal rights were observed.

"Mr. Warmington," said Roy, addressing the suspect, "what can you tell us about the events that led to the death of Mohammed Elmaleh?"

"Never heard of the guy," said Timmothy.

"And yet you were seen in the vicinity of the place where he was killed," Roy said, placing a picture on the table, taken from the ANPR camera, of Timmothy presumably fleeing the scene of the crime. "This is you, I take it?"

Timmothy glanced at the picture. "If you say so."

"This is your license plate, is it not?" asked Roy, placing another picture next to the first. "We took this picture in your garage. You should have changed plates."

Timmothy gave Roy a stony-faced look. "No comment."

"So, now that we've established you were near the location where Mohammed Elmaleh was killed, we move to your next achievement: the killing of Floyd Timmer."

"Never heard of him either."

"He was stabbed to death, also in Loveringem, and once again, your motorcycle was seen in the vicinity."

"So I like riding around Loveringem. Taking in the scenery. That doesn't mean anything."

"It's a mighty big coincidence, though, isn't it?"

"You said it, chief," said Timmothy. "One big coincidence."

"We also retrieved this encrypted phone from a search of your loft. We've managed to crack it and found plenty of messages back and forth between you and Abdellatif Abourouphael. We've arrested Mr. Abourouphael and are talking to him as we speak." He jerked his thumb toward the next room. "He's right there, if you must know."

For the first time, Timmothy's face betrayed some measure of concern.

"As the head of the Phoenix gang, Abourouphael has been instrumental in helping us create a list of people who work for him—in exchange for a sentence reduction," Roy added meaningfully.

"Abdellatif is... talking?" asked Timmothy with a frown.

"Singing like the proverbial canary," said Roy with satisfaction. "Frankly, I hadn't expected him to, but fortunately for us, we found quite a load of incriminating evidence during our search of his place and those of his lieutenants. That helped loosen his tongue. From a further search of your phone, we've been able to get a good idea of the kind of work you do for Abourouphael. So far, we've linked your name to a dozen assassinations. So there's no question about it, Timmothy—you are going to do time. How much time depends on how cooperative you decide to be. But I have to warn you, time is running out. Like I said, Abourouphael is eager to make a good impression on us, and I, for one, am very impressed. So, what about you, huh?"

Timmothy glanced over at his lawyer, who nodded.

Finally, the guy sighed and placed his elbows on the table. "What do you wanna know?"

"Did you assassinate Mohammed Elmaleh on the instructions of Abdellatif Abourouphael?"

Timmothy nodded.

"Speak up, Mr. Warmington."

"Yes, I did."

"Did you assassinate Floyd Timmer on the instructions of Abdellatif Abourouphael?"

"Yes, I did."

"Did you assassinate Jan Birt on the instructions of Abdellatif Abourouphael?"

"No, I didn't."

Roy looked up at this. "Are you sure about that?"

"Quite sure," said the hired gun.

Roy glanced in the direction of the one-way mirror and happened to lock eyes with Holt. He turned back to the suspect. "But Jan Birt was implicated in Abourouphael's business, was he not?"

"Indirectly," said Timmothy. "No reason to kill him, though."

"What about Teddy Birt? Did you have a reason to kill him?"

Timmothy shrugged. "Beats me. I never got the kill order for Teddy Birt, so I guess he was off the hook."

"So why were kill orders given for Mohammed Elmaleh, Beni Idrissi, and Floyd Timmer?"

"The two kids stole a shipment from Abdellatif, and so did Timmer. All three of them worked for Green Valley, so a message needed to be sent. Also, Abdellatif wanted his shipment back, which represented a nice chunk of change."

"And what about Boyd Batham?"

"What about him?"

"Were you involved in his kidnapping?"

"Nope. That was a different team."

"Why wasn't he killed outright?"

"I guess they figured he might be able to put them on the track of the missing shipment. In the end, he couldn't, claiming he had no idea where the stuff ended up."

"So what do you think happened to that shipment?"

Timmothy studied Roy's face for a moment, then seemed to feel that he didn't have anything to lose by sharing his personal thoughts on the matter. "As I see it, those kids didn't steal the bus on behalf of Green Valley. They took it because the opportunity presented itself, and they decided to go for a joyride. Little did they know that a shipment was on board. In the end, they paid the price for their stupidity. They crashed the bus, and next thing, this Timmer fella happened to pass by. He saw the secret compartments, unloaded the shipment, loaded it into his van, and took off. Then he tried to sell it to Green Valley, who, for obvious reasons, made a deal with the idiot. Only by now, we were on the guy's track, so he was a goner, and so were the two kids."

"So... You're telling me it was all one big coincidence?"

Timmothy nodded. "That's what Abdellatif told me. And he had it straight from the horse's mouth—Green Valley. They came to an arrangement last night. Decided that neither side benefited from a turf war, so they talked things through." He grinned. "Pretty funny, if you think about it."

Roy seemed incredulous. "Four people died!"

"Could have been worse. Many more would have died if this kept up. I had my orders, and there were plenty more people on the kill list. So in a sense, it was bad for me that they buried the hatchet."

"What happened to the shipment?"

"It was returned. And thus ended the war. Though now that you've picked up Abdellatif, it will probably start all over again, with Phoenix blaming the arrest on Green Valley." He shot Roy another grin. "You've stirred a hornet's nest, detective, and things are about to get pretty rough."

"So what about Jan Birt?"

"What about him?"

"You insist that you didn't kill him?"

"I take pride in my work, detective. In that sense, you and I are much alike. But what I don't do is take credit for things I had nothing to do with. And I never touched Birt."

"So who did?"

"No idea."

"You didn't pick up any chatter?"

"Oh, plenty of chatter, but nothing concrete. As far as I can tell, his murder had nothing to do with us or Green Valley."

"Wanna know what I believe?"

The hitman made a face. "Not really."

"I believe that you killed Mayor Birt as a warning. Don't mess with us, or you die."

"You believe what you want to believe," said Timmothy with a shrug. "I told you what I know, and if you don't like it, that's your problem." He placed his hands on the table. "Now how about we work out a deal, huh? And police protection. Because if I'm going to talk more, I need to know that you've got my back. These people don't mess around. I should know—I did their wetwork for years. They're probably already arranging for both me and Abdellatif to be taken out by my replacement before this thing goes to trial."

## CHAPTER 50

"So what do you think?"

Poppy and Holt had been joined by Roy.

"I'm not sure," said Holt. "He seems pretty convincing."

"I think he's lying," said Poppy. "Clearly, the mayor was one of the people the gang targeted. Okay, so maybe Warmington wasn't involved in his murder, but it fits the same MO I mean, Warmington wasn't involved in the assassination of Idrissi, was he?"

"No, we don't think he was," said Roy. "They used a different team for that. And also for the kidnapping of Boyd Batham."

"So most likely they had the same team that took out Idrissi target the mayor," said Poppy. "It all stands to reason."

"It does," Roy agreed. "And I'm sure that if we continue uncovering the truth, it will all come out in the wash." He clapped Holt on the back. "Looks like I solved your murder for you, buddy boy."

Holt grimaced. "Forgive me if I'm not convinced. I mean, Birt wasn't directly involved in his brother's drug business.

So why target him? They must have known he had no involvement in the disappearance of that shipment."

"Do you believe Warmington when he claims that the whole thing was a fluke?" asked Poppy. "That Idrissi and Elmaleh just happened to hit a bus that contained a shipment from their rival gang?"

"I don't buy that for one second," said Roy. "I think Green Valley put out that story to appease Phoenix and stop the gang war they had going on. I'm sure they knew exactly what was on that bus and decided to muscle in on their rivals' turf."

"I don't know, Roy," said Holt. "It might be true. Idrissi and Elmaleh would have known that stealing a shipment from a rival gang would land them in a heap of trouble. So why go ahead and risk it?"

"Because they got their marching orders, and since they were loyal foot soldiers, they did as they were told."

Poppy studied her dad's face. She knew that mulish expression well. He had his own opinion and wasn't going to budge, even though it meant their investigation was over and that the mayor's murder had been solved.

"I think this calls for a celebration," said Roy. "How about we take it to the Koevoet?"

"Maybe some other time," said Holt as he held up his hand. "We've got a man locked up on suspicion of the mayor's murder and need to determine what to do with him. Not to mention a mountain of paperwork to deal with."

Roy didn't seem well pleased by what he must have seen as a snub, but he shrugged. "Have it your way. But if I were you, I'd release that suspect. The case is closed. I closed it." And with those words, he walked off. Moments later, he was re-entering the interview room to discuss the terms of the deal he was about to make with the hired gun.

"I don't think it's right," said Poppy. "To offer this man a deal. He killed several people."

"No, I don't think it's right either," said Holt. "But then that's the way Bayton likes to operate. It's not my way, I can tell you that. But I guess I'm surplus to requirements at the moment."

"Let's get back to Loveringem," Poppy suggested. "And put this case to bed."

"Yeah, let's," Holt agreed.

They walked out of the office and almost bumped into a large and imposing man, who seemed about as surprised to see them as they were to see him.

"Holt," said the man coldly. It was none other than Poppy's new stepdad, Commissioner Terrence Bayton. The man resembled a captive balloon, with a head as big as a melon, and it never ceased to amaze Poppy what her mom saw in the guy.

"Terrence," Holt acknowledged.

The Commissioner took a step back, possibly to avoid being punched again by the man whose wife he had been having an affair with for the past couple of years behind Holt's back.

"What brings you here?"

Holt gestured with his head in the direction of the interview room. "Roy has brought in most of the Phoenix gang. According to him, they're responsible for the murder of Jan Birt."

"Don't tell me. You don't agree?"

"Well…"

The Commissioner frowned darkly. "Don't you go and make trouble for my people, Holt."

"I'm not making any trouble," said Holt. "I just don't happen to agree with Roy's assessment that Birt was killed by the Phoenix gang, that's all."

"I should have known," said the Commissioner. He couldn't hide his disdain for his former love rival. "You were never a team player, were you, Holt? Always wanting to do things your way, with nary a thought of the consequences for the rest of the team."

Holt stood his ground. "I don't think that's fair."

"You should be grateful to Roy!" the Commissioner spat, momentarily forgetting to keep his distance.

"Oh, but I am grateful," Holt assured him.

"You have a funny way of showing it." He studied Holt for a moment, then finally waved a hand. "Get lost. You're not even supposed to be here. Crawl back into your hole."

Poppy opened her mouth to say something, but Holt gave her a warning look, and she swallowed her words.

When they were outside and walking back to the car, she exploded. "You shouldn't let him talk to you like that, Dad!"

"Oh, who cares? The guy is a blowhard, and he's frustrated that he couldn't get me suspended. He hates me for it, and it shows."

"But you *are* a team player, Dad. You're very much a team player. It's him that isn't."

Holt grinned. "Now look who's getting all worked up. If I had let you, you probably would have told him a few home truths."

"I would have told him that he was being disrespectful and demand an apology."

Holt laughed. "An apology! Terrence Bayton! The man doesn't know the meaning of the word. No, if you want an apology from Terrence, you will wait a long time." He pressed the beepy thing on the key fob and gestured to the door. "Let's do as he suggested and return to the hole we both crawled out of, shall we?"

"Oh, that man!" Poppy cried as she got into the car.

She understood now why her dad had punched his lights out. He hadn't hit hard enough, in her opinion.

Moments later, they were en route back to the 'hole.' And glad of it. At least the case was closed now, although with Holt in charge, she wasn't sure if that was true or not.

When questioned on the subject, he demurred, saying that it wasn't up to him.

Somehow, she doubted that he would allow the prosecutor to close the case if he still had doubts.

Though he might not have a choice.

## CHAPTER 51

Back at the station, the team watched the press conference the Elmaleh and Idrissi families gave. They were accompanied by their lawyer, but mostly Mustafa was the one doing all the talking. He said that the police had been in touch and that the killer of his brother had been found and locked up.

"I hope that he will go away for a long time," he said, while Holt thought that he might be in for a nasty surprise on that front. "I want to thank the police for bringing justice to my brother, and I want to thank all the people who have shown their support in these difficult times for both our families."

Then it was time for Adil Idrissi to address the gathered journalists and also thank the police department, especially Chief Inspector Roy Hesketh and his team, for working around the clock to make sure that the people responsible for his son's murder were arrested and jailed.

The two families then announced they were launching a new organization that would try to keep young kids off the street and out of the claws of the drug mafia.

"Too many lives have been destroyed already," said Mustafa. "And so we will honor the memory of my brother and his best friend, Beni, by working hard to make sure that what happened to them doesn't happen to others."

The families took questions, and the gathered press corps fired off a bunch of them, with most of the questions being answered by their lawyer. The gist was that they felt that Mohammed and Beni had been victims of the drug gangs more than criminals themselves. No mention was made of the role Hassan Elmaleh had played, which was probably for the best. Mo's eldest brother was conspicuous in his absence. Perhaps he'd also been scooped up in the wide net that Roy Hesketh's investigation had cast, along with the rest of the small fry.

"I wonder if Anjanette Birt will also give a press conference now," said Leland, "thanking Roy Hesketh and his team for arresting her husband's killer."

"He's denying it," said Poppy. She was seated on the edge of her desk while they all watched Rasheed's screen, where the press conference was being displayed. "Timmothy Warmington? Says that he never went near the mayor."

"But Roy thinks differently, right?" asked Leland. "So chances are that it was the Phoenix gang that killed the mayor?"

"What do you want us to do with André Wiel, boss?" asked Georgina. "Release him or keep him here?"

But before Holt could respond, Commissioner Forrester stuck his head in the door and beckoned Holt to follow him into his office. Holt gave his daughter a comical look. "It's my day for talking to the top brass."

And then he was gone, leaving them all to speculate about what the Commissioner was going to say.

It wasn't hard to guess.

. . .

"Take a seat, son," said the Commissioner warmly. "Another case solved, eh? Well done, Glen. Well done indeed. And in record time, no less. Quite the achievement."

"I take it Commissioner Bayton has been in touch, sir?"

"He has, he has. Told me the good news just now." His face clouded. "Sad about the loss of life, of course, but that's the drug mafia for you. Vicious killers, one and all. Nasty people who go for the jugular with no rhyme or reason. Let's hope we've seen the end of it."

"Yes, sir," said Holt, who could see which way the wind was blowing. He still felt compelled to give some pushback. "I was there when Chief Inspector Hesketh interviewed his main suspect, and the man denied having any involvement in the hit on Mayor Birt, sir. He also denied any knowledge that it was the same gang that is responsible for the killing of Mohammed Elmaleh, Beni Idrissi, and Floyd Timmer to also have had a part in the murder of Mayor Birt. So I want to keep an open mind, sir."

The Commissioner gave him a look of confusion. "You don't believe that it was the drug gang that killed the mayor? Is that what you're saying?"

"I'm saying I don't know," said Holt. "The suspect hasn't confessed, and so it's only conjecture on Chief Inspector Hesketh's part at this point."

"Right," said the Commissioner thoughtfully. "I see. So what do you suggest, Glen? That we don't close the case?"

"It's not up to me to decide what direction the investigation needs to take, sir. But if it was, I would advise not to be too hasty. There are still several leads we can—"

The Commissioner closed his eyes. "But Commissioner Bayton has assured me he has the killer in custody. It's only a matter of time before they get a confession. His words."

"Be that as it may, I still would like to continue to look at the several leads that we haven't explored yet. Not to mention we have a solid suspect in custody ourselves."

"Yes, André Wiel," said the Commissioner doubtfully.

"He wrote some extremely disturbing messages on the mayor's Facebook page," said Holt. "Death threats, sir."

"Yes…" He didn't seem convinced. Then he gave Holt a fatherly smile. "Why don't we leave this to Prosecutor Turner to decide, mh? After all, she's the only person who has all the different pieces of the puzzle in her possession, so she is best placed to know what the best way forward is."

"And in the meantime?"

The Commissioner held out his hand. "Oh, it's your investigation, Glen. So you do as you see fit. Far be it from me to interfere. But if Commissioner Bayton thinks that he's got his man, then I don't see…" Holt's face must have betrayed his emotions, for the Commissioner regarded him commiseratively. "Now I know that you and Terrence have history, Glen. Bad blood. And I don't blame you. If a man went behind my back and had an affair with my wife, I would be just as cross with him as you are with Terrence. But what we can't do is allow things of that nature to cloud our professional judgment. So why don't I call a meeting with Shonna and we can thresh this whole thing out, hm?" Before Holt could respond, he nodded. "Yes, that's what we'll do. I will let you know what she says."

He frowned and waved his hand in the direction of the door, his way of indicating that the meeting was over.

## CHAPTER 52

Mayor Birt's funeral, held at the Church of Our Lady, was a pretty big affair. Not only had half the townsfolk of Loveringem come out, but there was plenty of interest from the rest of the country, and the media were out in full force. Flemish Front flags were prominently placed next to the altar, and the innocent bystander might be excused for confusing the funeral with a meeting of the extreme-right party.

The church itself was full to capacity, so large screens had been placed outside for the people who were unfortunate enough not to find a seat inside to follow the service.

It had taken some effort to find a priest to officiate the funeral, as Mayor Birt may have been popular with a lot of people, but he wasn't popular with the local cleric. A priest had been trucked in from elsewhere. He was a family friend and had known Jan all his life, so that was all to the good. The only drawback was that he was also a Flemish Party member and, in that sense, a proponent of certain edicts from the Bible that support the idea of 'an eye for an eye and a tooth for a tooth,' which was the central theme of the man's eulogy.

Jan's wife was there, along with his son Jayson, though oddly enough Anjanette wasn't dressed in black as befitted a grieving widow, and neither was Jayson. The latter was dressed in jeans and a T-shirt that proclaimed, 'End Fascism Now!' It depicted his dad's face with a red cross over it.

Lucky for him, he was seated in the first row, so the majority of the people he was so eager to provoke were behind him and never got to see the T-shirt.

Next to Anjanette, Justine Hallett was seated, and across the aisle, keeping a safe distance, was Gwendolyn Lopez. Of the three women, only Gwendolyn cried bitter tears throughout the service. She was also the only one who was dressed appropriately: a nice charcoal ensemble. She even wore a hat with a veil. Connoisseurs recognized her outfit as an original Edouard Vermeulen, the favorite couturier of Queen Mathilde. Before and after the service, she was extensively interviewed by reporters from all the major papers and appeared on camera for both VTM and VRT, the two major Flemish TV stations. One might be confused into thinking she was Mayor Birt's widow, and some of the reporters were. She didn't bother to correct their mistake, possibly drawing some consolation from the fact. She could have been married to Jan, after all, if his life hadn't been cut short.

Anjanette didn't mind. Gwendolyn could act as if she were Jan's partner as much as she wished. The only reason Anjanette had shown up for the service was that not doing so would have created quite a hullabaloo, and she didn't need the aggravation. Better to sit through an hour of boring speeches, press a million hands, and listen to people offering their condolences than contend with a lot of prickly comments and other nonsense.

Jayson thought the same way, though he seemed to have found a happy medium between attending the service as the lesser of two evils and getting some of his own back.

Justine was there because Anjanette had invited her. The two women were each other's support, their friendship having deepened even further through their shared ordeal.

"I don't believe this guy," whispered Anjanette when the priest admonished all those present to let Jesus into their hearts and embrace the values and principles Jan had stood for. "He's even more hardcore than Jan was."

"They had to look hard to find him," said Justine. "Most of the priests they approached didn't want to come near this funeral. For a while, there was even talk of organizing it at the funeral home—a civil service, you know. But the party insisted on a church service."

Justine had handled the funeral, as she had handled all of Jan's affairs over the course of their long association. Anjanette had told her she didn't have to do it, but apparently, the woman had loved Jan even more than Anjanette had, and she had said she wanted to do it. Besides, if she didn't do it, who would? Anjanette didn't want to, and Gwendolyn would have turned the whole thing into a circus, with her at the center of all the hoopla.

"I'll be glad it's finally over," said Anjanette.

"Me too. This has been a pretty rough couple of days."

Officially, she hadn't been informed that Jan's killer had been caught, but unofficially, she had been approached by a woman named Shonna Turner. She had introduced herself as the prosecutor in the case and said she was convinced that Jan's murder was connected to a drug gang war in Ghent that had spilled over into nearby Loveringem. It wouldn't be the first time that big-city crime had affected their otherwise peaceful little town.

"So what's the word about the investigation?" asked Justine. "Has Jan's killer been arrested or not?"

Anjanette shrugged. "No idea. The prosecutor has told me that charges will soon be brought, but so far, nothing."

She had noticed that the Chief Inspector in charge of the case was also present. He was seated a couple of rows behind her, but since she hadn't heard from him, she assumed that the case had yet to be successfully concluded. It was all very strange, she had to say—almost as if the police didn't have a clue. Or maybe this was the way they always worked?

"Have they spoken to you?" she asked Justine.

"No, after that last interview, I haven't heard from them. He's here, though. Glen Holt? And also his daughter."

"That's odd, isn't it? Father and daughter working together? Isn't that considered a conflict of interest or something?"

"I doubt it, honey."

She had to admit that she had more or less lost faith in the police. If they had the gall to accuse her and Jayson of murder, they clearly had no clue. Then again, she wasn't all that interested in finding out who had killed her husband—except for the fact that it was hanging over their heads. At least the body had been released, which was a sign that things were probably moving along. After taking one look at the remains, the funeral director had told them that an open casket would be quite out of the question, and there would be no visitations. Apparently, not much was left of the body. "Charred beyond recognition," the director had told her in confidence and warned her not to look.

She had no intention of doing so. After all, she had seen plenty of Jan while he was still alive—too much, in fact. If she never laid eyes on the man again, it would be fine by her.

The director had also advised her on the choice of casket, remarking that it had to be one equipped with excellent isolating qualities so as not to let the awful burning smell escape. He would try his utmost to mask it, but there was only so much he could do.

She glanced back and caught Chief Inspector Holt's eye. She gave him a slight nod, and he returned it in kind. Not an unfriendly man, she thought. And certainly very handsome—tall and built like an ox, with a full crop of dark hair. She wasn't so sure about the beard, but then she had never been into men with beards. Give her a clean-shaven specimen every day. As far as she had been able to ascertain, Holt wasn't married, his wife having left him for a colleague. Silly cow.

Jayson was wagging his foot again, driving her mad, so she placed a hand on his leg and he stopped. He was nervous, and she didn't know why. She hadn't forced him to attend, though she had told him that if he didn't, he might regret it later on. He may not have liked his dad, but he was still his father, and he was only going to be buried once.

And so he had agreed to come out, but only if he didn't have to wear a suit. He'd worn a jacket before they entered the church but had taken it off to reveal the T-shirt. Not a good idea, with so many Nazis attending. She hoped he would have the common sense to put his jacket back on when they left the service and zip it up tight. It wouldn't do for him to get attacked and killed at his dad's funeral. He was all she had left now.

Except for Justine, of course. Her new best friend.

At least something good to come out of this whole mess.

## CHAPTER 53

Holt had been fully prepared to offer his condolences to the family, but since he didn't want to impose, the opportunity never presented itself. As the church emptied after the service, he stood to the side, observing those present. Anjanette was accompanied by her son Jayson, who wore a strange outfit—if Holt wasn't mistaken, it was a T-shirt with something about fascism on it. He couldn't quite make it out, as his mother zipped up his jacket before he got a chance to read the message—much to the kid's disappointment.

Jayson wasn't the only one who was trying to use the funeral as a way to send a message. Daron Topley was also very active, networking like an expert. He seemed to be the most popular person in the church, which was filled with Flemish Front loyalists. It was the first time Holt had ever attended a funeral that felt more like a party meeting than an opportunity to pay respects to the deceased. Even the priest was in on it, more interested in spreading his personal beliefs than providing succor to the mourners.

Not many tears had been shed. In fact, the only person

Holt had seen looking remotely sad was Gwendolyn Lopez. Birt's campaign manager had a hard time holding back the tears, not wanting to ruin her mascara. She found a lot of support in Daron Topley, who was on hand to console her. The party leader and the PR expert seemed to get along like gangbusters, and Holt wondered if he was witnessing the start of something beautiful. The man was married with kids, but that hadn't stopped Gwendolyn before.

As he stood watching the church empty out, and a select few gathered to accompany the family to the graveyard, Wanda Desai happened to drift into his view.

"Quite the spectacle, isn't it, Chief Inspector?" she said.

"You can say that again. For a moment there, I thought I was at a Flemish Front rally instead of a funeral."

"It was probably to be expected that Daron would hijack the service," said Wanda, who didn't look all that happy with the way things had gone. "Jan was one of the party's stalwarts, so it stands to reason Daron wants to milk this for all it's worth. Especially with all the media present."

"I'm surprised that you decided to attend," said Holt. "I would have thought you'd want to stay as far away from your opponent's funeral as possible."

She smiled. "And now you think I've come to gloat."

"Oh, no, absolutely not. It's just surprising, that's all. You and Birt haven't exactly been on amicable terms."

"No, you can say that again. I should probably be glad he's gone, but oddly enough, the battle we had gave me focus. The man may have had a lot of faults, but he sure knew how to keep me on my toes. The best moments of my political career —and I don't say this lightly—were when Birt and I sparred during council meetings." She sighed. "Things will be a lot more boring from now on."

"Whatever he was, Mayor Birt wasn't boring," Holt agreed.

Though he'd never been all that interested in politics—and definitely not local politics—if his investigation into the death of Jan Birt had taught him one thing, it was that the man had been a force of nature. When he shared these thoughts with the leader of the opposition, she heartily agreed.

"He definitely was that. He was a very, shall we say, virile man?"

Holt smiled. "You mean the whole situation with his mistresses?"

"It was common knowledge. And in that sense, he was part of a legacy of political leaders known both for their insane ambition to succeed and their insatiable sex drive."

"Surprising then, that he only fathered the one son," said Holt, watching Jayson sullenly stand next to his mother as they accepted condolences from a long line of well-wishers.

Wanda gave him a sideways glance. "Oh, but he fathered more than one child, Chief Inspector."

"He did?"

"We're entering the realm of pure gossip now, I'm afraid. But I guess it doesn't matter anymore, now that the man is dead and will soon be buried." She lowered her voice and became quite conspiratorial. "You didn't hear this from me, but rumor has it that Jan Birt was an avid visitor to the fertility clinic as a young man."

"You mean he was a sperm donor?"

Wanda nodded. "And a very active one. For a couple of years, he made good money from sowing his seed." She said it with a certain relish, as if she enjoyed shedding light on an unknown side of her erstwhile nemesis's personality.

"You don't say."

"I do say. One of the secretaries at Town Hall once told me. Apparently, it's common knowledge among the cognoscenti."

"What's the name of this secretary?" he asked. "Not Justine Hallett?"

For some strange reason, the information that Wanda had just divulged sent a tingle dancing up and down his spine.

"It wasn't Justine," said Wanda. When Holt gave her an expectant look, she seemed startled and produced a nervous laugh. "I probably shouldn't have told you."

"I won't tell her it came from you," he assured her.

"Well, in that case... ask for Jeanie Stockwell."

"Jeanie Stockwell. I will, thanks."

"Secretaries do love to gossip. They're always present on the scene, inconspicuous in the background, and they often know more than we think they do." She gave him a curious look. "Why? Do you think it's important?"

"No idea," he said truthfully.

"I thought you had nabbed the killer? It was those drug gang people, wasn't it? At least, that's what it said in the paper."

"That seems to be the accepted opinion, yes," he said.

"But you don't believe it?"

He shrugged. "I find that the most logical answer isn't always the right one, and so I like to keep digging until I'm absolutely sure I've got the right person behind bars."

She nodded. "I heard about the circumstances of your departure. And I have to say, Ghent's loss is our gain."

He smiled. "Thanks… Madam Mayor."

"Oh, it's much too soon for that. But maybe."

He was sure there were no maybes about it. With Jan Birt gone, Flemish Front didn't stand a chance of coming up with a new candidate who would prove as popular as the late local leader. Wanda Desai was a shoo-in for mayor.

Which meant she was still a suspect. But he wasn't going to ruin the moment by reminding her of that. She must have read his mind, though, for she said, "I really was home with my husband the night Jan was killed."

"I know. He told me."

"But you don't believe him?"

"It's my job to keep an open mind, Mrs. Desai."

"Wanda, please." When he didn't respond, she added, "So what do I call you?"

"Holt," he said. "Just Holt."

## CHAPTER 54

Holt didn't waste time after the service and headed straight to Town Hall to try and confirm the story Wanda Desai had just told him. He considered calling Poppy and asking her to accompany him, but then thought better of it. The case was in a strange sort of limbo—not officially closed, but on the verge of getting there—and he wasn't sure if he could still task his team with investigative actions. If he went alone, he could simply ascribe his probing to personal curiosity if questioned.

He found Jeanie Stockwell in her office. She was responsible for issuing driver's licenses, and when he knocked on her door—after being pointed in the right direction by one of her helpful colleagues—he saw she was about the same age as Holt's own mother.

She smiled when he entered her office.

"Do you have a ticket, young man?" she asked.

"Oh, but I'm not here for a driver's license," he said. He flashed his badge. "Chief Inspector Holt. I'm conducting the investigation into the death of Mayor Birt."

Her face lit up with excitement. "Oh, do come in and take

a seat, Chief Inspector. I'm working behind the scenes these days." She smiled again. "They don't like to wheel me out in front of the public anymore. Too old and wrinkly. Mayor Birt wanted all of his personnel to project a dynamic and youthful image. I guess I didn't fit the profile."

Holt had noticed that all the people manning the counters were quite young. So Birt hadn't just been a racist, but also an ageist.

"So, if you're not here for a driver's license, what are you here for?" asked Mrs. Stockwell, wasting no time getting to the point—in other words a woman after his own heart.

He took a seat in front of her desk. "It has come to my attention that Mayor Birt used to be a frequent visitor at the fertility clinic. And it was also brought to my attention that you might have more information about that part of his life."

"Oh, do I have more information," she said as she put down the stamp she had been using with surprising agility and force. "Well, it's certainly true. Jan Birt used to boast that he was probably one of the most active sperm donors in the country. Certainly in this town. Though that probably isn't saying much, as I can't imagine a lot of people being in the habit of donating their sperm. But he did, and he was proud of it."

"It's the first I've heard of it," he admitted.

"This was years ago, Chief Inspector," she said. "What did you say your name was?"

"Holt."

"I think I've heard about you. Weren't you the one who got kicked out of the force because you hit your boss?"

"Something like that," he said. "Though I wasn't kicked out, just transferred to Loveringem."

"Same difference," she said. "Relegated to the sticks, huh? Well, I'm sure you had your reasons for hitting that man."

"I found out he was having an affair with my wife," he felt

compelled to point out, lest she think less of him. For some reason, he liked this woman, and her opinion mattered. Which was silly, of course, since mostly he didn't care what people thought of him.

"That *is* a good reason," she said, nodding.

"So, about Mayor Birt?"

"Oh, yes. Birt's sperm," she said, rolling the words around her tongue with some relish. "Like I said, he used to boast about it a lot, but this was years ago, long before he became mayor. He was a young whippersnapper back then, working here during the holidays."

"Birt used to work here as a student?"

"That's right. Birt senior was a civil servant here. He pretty much ran Town Hall behind the scenes. So when his son wanted to earn an extra buck, he foisted Birt junior on us." She shook her head, causing her little white curls to bounce. "He wasn't well liked. Always gave me the creeps, that kid. Cruel to animals and children, if you know what I mean. Not," she added, holding up her hand, "that I ever actually witnessed him being cruel to animals or children. It's just an expression."

"Interesting," said Holt.

"He once told me that he wanted to become the man with the most kids in the world. There was a story not so long ago about a sperm donor with a thousand kids. Well, Jan Birt boasted that he had fathered hundreds." She made a face. "Like I said, an extremely unpleasant youth."

"Any idea what fertility clinic he used?"

She thought for a moment, tapping a pencil against her lips. "There was an article at the time about this whole sperm donor business. People were fascinated by it. And I seem to remember that Jan was interviewed for the article. He was very proud of seeing his name in print."

That tingle dancing up and down his spine returned. "You

wouldn't happen to have kept a copy of that article, would you?"

She smiled. "Why don't I look it up for you? I'm sure I've kept it somewhere." She sat up a little straighter. "You're looking at Loveringem's number-one archivist. Before they put me in charge of the driver's licenses, I was the official archivist for many years. So you've come to the right place, Chief Inspector Holt. Give me your email, and I'll see what I can do. It might take me a while, but I will do my best."

# CHAPTER 55

Poppy walked into the coffee shop, unsure of what to expect. Her dad had sent her a message asking her to meet him there, which struck her as a little odd. Why didn't he just come to the station like a normal person? But then again, Holt wasn't a normal person. He didn't always follow the book—sometimes he tossed it out altogether if it suited his purpose.

The coffee shop was warm, and the scent of freshly baked pastries made her mouth water. The coffee machine sputtered, and patrons sat around tables, quietly chatting and enjoying the atmosphere along with the baking prowess of the coffee shop's owner, who also owned the bakery next door.

She spotted her dad sitting by the window, facing the door as always. *Never let them take you by surprise, kid.* Advice to live by. And he clearly did.

She sat down and checked the menu. Hot chocolate with plenty of cream and chocolate sprinkles on top. Now we're talking, she thought.

"What's up?" she asked. "Why all the cloak and dagger?"

"I think I may be onto something," he said, sliding his phone across the table. She picked it up and frowned. "Why are you showing me an article about fertility clinics?"

"Recognize the guy being interviewed?"

"Jan Birt? Not *the* Jan Birt?"

"One and the same. Turns out the guy had a burning ambition to become the most prolific sperm donor that ever lived. This was years ago, though, when he was in his early twenties. I guess he dropped the project when he became politically active, and it was never mentioned again. This article is probably the only time his opinions on the topic were recorded. And even then, it's for an obscure magazine that went out of business years ago."

"So where did you find it?"

"A Town Hall secretary named Jeanie Stockwell sent it to me. She remembered Jan working at Town Hall as a student. His dad had arranged the job. Apparently, he couldn't shut up about this sperm donor business. Struck more than a few people as weird and icky."

"I'll bet it did. But what's the significance, Dad? So what if he was a creep as a teen? What does that have to do with anything?"

"I'm not sure," Holt said, taking a sip of his coffee. "But I've got this tingle."

She rolled her eyes. "Not the tingle again!"

"I can't help it. The moment Wanda Desai mentioned it, I knew I had to know more."

A waiter appeared by her side, and she ordered a hot chocolate with lots of cream and a couque suisse, her favorite pastry. She knew Koen ran the best bakery in town, and she might as well take advantage. "This is your treat, right?" she asked, just to make sure.

"My treat," he confirmed.

"Add a slice of strawberry pie," she told the waiter.

Holt smiled. "Got quite the appetite, don't you?"

"While you were gossiping with Jeanie Stockwell about Birt's sex life, the Commissioner had us all on paperwork duty. Writing reports and more reports."

"Looks like I had a lucky escape."

She gave her father a look of concern. "So what's going on with this investigation, Dad? I mean, are we done or what?"

He shrugged. "Beats me. Officially, I'm still in charge, but I've got a feeling that Shonna has quietly transferred the entire investigation to Roy and his team and folded it into their drug bust."

"So, Mayor Birt was collateral damage?"

"Something like that. Just one of the many victims of this gang war between Green Valley and Phoenix."

"But you don't buy that?"

He grimaced. "I have my doubts."

Her hot chocolate had arrived, with a majestic tower of whipped cream on top, a side dish with more whipped cream, chocolate sprinkles, and chocolate dusting. For the next few seconds, she closed her eyes and savored the treat. Then she took a big bite of her couque suisse, warm with vanilla cream inside, and was ready to discuss the case some more. She knew her dad often had his own ideas about the cases he worked on, and they didn't always align with Shonna's. Probably one of the reasons he'd been transferred, along with the fracas with Terrence Bayton. But she also knew he was a brilliant detective, so she was willing to hear him out, no matter how far-fetched it might sound.

"So, you really think this fertility business is connected to his murder?"

"I have no idea. But what kind of a detective would I be if I didn't at least find out?"

"So, what do you want to do?"

He tapped the article on his phone. "The University Hospital Department of Reproductive Medicine is mentioned in the article. So, I was thinking maybe we could go talk to the person in charge."

"I'll bet those records are confidential, though."

"They are," he confirmed, wriggling his eyebrows. "But with a little luck, maybe we'll convince them to let us take a peek at the file they have on Jan Birt."

"And if not, we can get a warrant, right?"

He made a face. "Doubtful. Unless I can convince her it's important to the investigation, Shonna won't even consider it. And since she's already made up her mind that Birt was killed by Timmothy Warmington..."

"So, we're going rogue?" she asked, licking the cream from her lips.

"We're going rogue," he confirmed with a smile.

"Goodie." She hoped he would at least let her finish her hot chocolate—and especially that strawberry cake. Solving a murder was one thing, but this cake was to die for.

## CHAPTER 56

Since Holt knew it would probably be impossible to get any information from the Department of Reproductive Medicine without a warrant, his first port of call was Lionel. When he and Poppy walked into the pathologist's department, he looked surprised.

"Did someone else die in Loveringem that I'm not aware of?" he asked. "Not that I would mind, of course."

Lionel was one of those people who lived for his job, Holt knew, and he never minded if more work was piled on his plate. What his wife thought about that was probably a different matter, considering how often she had to go without a husband when he decided to work well into the evening or even the night.

"I wanted to ask you for a favor, Lionel," said Holt.

The pathologist gave him a puzzled look. "Go on. I like a mystery. What's this favor?"

Holt explained the predicament he found himself in.

"I see," said Lionel finally, rubbing his chin. He thought for a moment, then led them into his office. "Take a seat," he said as he picked up the phone.

Holt and Poppy did as instructed. Holt looked around. Apart from the skeleton located in a corner of the room and the many anatomical posters adorning the walls, the office was pretty sparsely decorated. No plants or personal items in sight—not even a potted plant or a goldfish in a bowl. Lionel definitely seemed to favor the dead over the living.

Lionel spoke on the phone for a few minutes, then checked his computer. "I see," he said. "Thanks, Margaret. I owe you one." He hung up. "Well, it seems your information was correct, Glen. Birt was quite the regular. Came in at least once a week to make a donation. And that's not all. According to Margaret, who pretty much runs the fertility clinic—and has for the past twenty-five years—he also donated at other fertility clinics, not just here in Ghent but all over the place. At least that's what he claimed at the time."

"She remembers?" Poppy asked.

"She doesn't. But she's an excellent record keeper, and she records everything in a person's file. Jan's file mentions that he boasted about donating everywhere he could, including clinics in Holland and Germany."

"But… isn't there some kind of rule against that?" asked Poppy.

"There is now, but there wasn't at the time," said Lionel. "It was pretty much the Wild West before 2007, when a law was passed that restricted sperm donation to a maximum of six different families. Before that, nobody seemed to keep track. So people who wanted to take advantage, could."

"So… it's entirely possible that Birt has dozens of kids walking around," said Holt.

Lionel arched an eyebrow. "Probably hundreds. A donor as active as Birt was back then could easily have had his sperm used to impregnate hundreds of women."

Holt thought about the implications. "And he was a regular at many of the clinics?"

"That's what he claimed at the time. Like I said, what he did isn't possible today, and for good reason. The chances of meeting a sibling are too high. And we all know that siblings have a higher genetic risk of passing on a recessive disease to their offspring. We're talking physical deformities and defects. So it's important to limit the chances of that happening. That's why they're thinking about changing the law again. Right now, it's impossible for a person to find out whose sperm was used in their conception, even though it's on record. In the future it will be easier to find out—just in case."

"It's also the reason that these super-active donors need to be weeded out," said Holt, who had read up on the subject.

"In the article, Birt says he wants to make the world a better place," said Poppy. "Make sure every family has a chance to have kids."

"That's nonsense," said Lionel. "Most of these super donors don't do it out of the goodness of their own heart but simply for the money—or as an ego boost. And knowing Jan Birt, I think in his case it was the latter."

"He never mentioned it, though," said Holt. "The only time he did was in this article, but if I hadn't accidentally found out, I would never have known."

"It may have been trendy to boast about being a super donor twenty years ago," said Lionel. "But it isn't anymore. He probably knew full well this could be used against him, so to further his political career, he decided to bury the story and hope no one ever found out."

"I wonder if this has any bearing on the investigation into his murder, though," said Poppy. "I mean, I don't see how." She was watching Holt closely. "And don't start about the tingle, Dad. I don't want to hear about the tingle."

Lionel was amused. "The tingle? Is this something we need to be concerned about?"

"It's not a medical condition," Holt assured the doctor. "Just a hunch, you know."

"Ah, yes, the famous hunch," said Lionel. "All good detectives get it, or so I've been led to believe."

"I don't know about that. But I just felt it might be worth looking into." He still felt that way. And as he listened to Lionel explain the ins and outs of the fertility program at the hospital, he started to experience the annoying sensation that there was something nagging at the back of his mind. Somehow this whole discussion reminded him of something. But for the life of him, he couldn't remember.

No matter. It would come to him. Hopefully.

## CHAPTER 57

They had just gotten back into the car when Holt received a call from Shonna. He frowned. Did she know that he was paying a visit to the fertility clinic? But how?

"Shonna?" he said cautiously.

"Holt. I'm organizing a meeting in the examining magistrate's office. I want you to be there. We're discussing the gang war business and also the murder of Jan Birt."

"When?" he asked.

"In one hour. Can you make it?"

"I'll be there," he said. He knew the way.

"What did she want?" asked Poppy nervously.

"A meeting with the examining magistrate. They want to discuss the case. Probably want to lay it to rest and talk about the upcoming court case with the judge."

"Can I come?" she asked.

He smiled. "I'll ask. Why?"

"I've never met the examining magistrate," she said with excitement.

He would have told her to prepare for disappointment,

FIELD OF BLOOD

but since he didn't want to cloud her judgment, he refrained from doing so. Instead, he entered the address of the Ghent Tribunal of First Instance into the satnav. Frankly, he wasn't exactly looking forward to the meeting, as it would mean that the case was officially going to be closed.

Which meant he and his team wouldn't be allowed to work on it anymore.

It certainly was a quandary he now found himself in. If he didn't tell Shonna and the examining magistrate that he might have discovered new evidence that threw a potentially different light on the case, he wouldn't get a chance to follow this line of inquiry. But if he did tell them, and they dismissed his arguments out of hand, that would be the end of the line. Also, they'd want to know how he had accessed the information.

All in all, it was quite the predicament.

The old Palace of Justice, a protected monument, was located right in the heart of town. Nowadays, it was used by the Court of Appeal and the Federal Police, operating the cell block located there, while the other courts and administration had all moved to a new location, which was a steel-concrete-and-glass monstrosity, offering modern accommodation to the judges and lawyers working there. The examining magistrate also had her office there, and this was where Holt and Poppy now found themselves. Nancy Blackthorn was a middle-aged woman of stern aspect whose demeanor demanded respect. She was seated behind her desk, her court clerk at an adjoining desk, making notes and ready to look stuff up on his computer or offer her any needed documents.

Across from her sat Holt, Shonna, Roy Hesketh, and... Commissioner Terrence Bayton. Behind them, where a row of chairs had been placed against a glass partition, Poppy had taken a seat along with a member of Roy's team. All in all, it was a full house.

Holt had been unpleasantly surprised to see his old boss, and the feeling had obviously been mutual, for Terrence didn't give him a handshake or a nod in greeting.

"Okay, so we're here to discuss the case against the members of the Phoenix gang," said Judge Blackthorn as she consulted her papers. "Madam Prosecutor, you recommend that charges be made against Timmothy Warmington, Abdellatif Abourouphael and other members of the Phoenix gang for the murders of Mohammed Elmaleh, Beni Idrissi, Floyd Timmer, and Jan Birt, and also the kidnapping, unlawful confinement, and torture of Boyd Batham, as well as their involvement in the supplying of drugs—"

"Can I interrupt for one moment, ma'am?" asked Holt, deciding to go for broke.

"Oh, here we go again," Terrence grunted.

"You mentioned the murder of Jan Birt. Only I'm not convinced that his murder was committed by members of this gang."

"Holt, we've discussed this," said Shonna, none too pleased.

"I believe I have since uncovered fresh evidence that throws an entirely new light on the matter," Holt insisted.

"What evidence?!" Terrence cried.

"That's what I would like to know," said Shonna.

"Evidence that suggests that Jan Birt was a serial sperm donor," said Holt.

Silence reigned for a few moments before Terrence burst out, "Have you lost your mind?!"

"What's this about a serial sperm donor?" asked Judge Blackthorn with a frown.

"Don't listen to him, ma'am," said Terrence. "The man is a fantasist and a liar."

The judge gave him a tight smile. "What makes you say that?"

"Isn't it obvious? Ever since the investigation into Mayor Birt landed on my desk, he's been giving us grief. He hates that he's been sidelined, and this is his way of getting back at me."

"I suggest you leave the personal accusations at the door, Commissioner Bayton," said the judge as she fixed him with a stern look across her reading glasses. She then turned to Holt. "Now please explain what you mean by 'serial sperm donor.'"

Holt took a deep breath. "When Jan Birt was in his early twenties, he had one ambition in life, and that was to become Belgium's premier sperm donor. To that end, he visited every fertility clinic in the country, and also across the border in Holland and Germany. Allegedly, he donated hundreds of times and possibly fathered hundreds of children. It is my belief we should look further into this matter, as it might have a bearing on the case."

"But how?" asked the judge, who seemed genuinely interested and ignored Terrence Bayton's groans.

"I'm not sure yet," Holt admitted. "But if you let me, I intend to find out."

"I see," said the judge.

"Oh, this is all nonsense!" Terrence exploded again.

"I have to agree with Commissioner Bayton, ma'am," said Shonna. "All the evidence in the case points to a revenge hit by the Phoenix gang. Even the Molotov cocktail fits their MO to a T. There have been plenty of documented cases where the drug mafia has used a similar weapon to attack and intimidate people they consider their enemies."

"Of course it's the drug mafia," said Terrence. "And Holt knows this. He's just messing with us."

Holt shrugged. "If I wanted to mess with you, Terrence, you would feel it."

Terrence's face took on a darker tinge of purple. "Is that a threat? Madam Judge, you heard it! He threatened me!"

"Oh, please be quiet," the judge snapped. "What is this? Kindergarten? If you can't leave your petty grievances at the door, you have no place in my chambers. Is that understood? And if you don't like it, you can leave now."

Terrence silently fumed, cutting glances at Holt that were designed to maim and kill. Holt didn't let it bother him. Even though his fists itched to give the man a taste of his medicine, he knew that it would be the career-ender that Terrence wanted it to be. He was simply goading him, hoping Holt wouldn't be able to keep his temper under control.

"I have to admit that I find this angle of the serial sperm donations quite interesting," said Judge Blackthorn. "So what do you suggest?"

"Give me a week, ma'am," said Holt. "If I haven't been able to dig up any evidence that points to a different killer than the one Roy's team has dug up, I will gladly agree with his theory. And if not…"

The judge nodded slowly. "Mayor Birt was a prominent political figure. I think it behooves us to go the extra mile and make sure that we have examined every possible avenue so no one can accuse us of not having done our due diligence and followed every lead. So I will grant your request, Holt. But if you don't come up with something, your investigation will be folded into Chief Inspector Hesketh's investigation."

"That's fine with me, ma'am," he said.

He glanced over at Roy and got the impression that his former colleague wasn't too happy with him at that moment, and neither were Shonna or Terrence. But that couldn't be helped. He had to go where the evidence led him—and his tickle, of course. But he wasn't going to mention that to the judge.

She would laugh him out of the room.

## CHAPTER 58

As Holt and Poppy walked to the exit, Roy came hurrying after them.

"Wait up," he yelled, and Holt turned. Once the detective had caught up with them, he said, "I don't get it. I thought we had this thing in the bag. And now you're going off on some wild goose chase? I mean, serial sperm donors? Come on, Holt! This is bullshit!"

"Maybe it is, and maybe it isn't," said Holt with a shrug.

"It's the drugs, man! You know it and I know it!"

"Look, you yourself told me that Abourouphael believes that Idrissi and Elmaleh took that bus on a whim. That this whole thing was nothing but one big coincidence. The kids took the bus, Floyd Timmer happened to pass by and saw an opportunity to make some money—or a lot of money—and things got pretty ugly for a while. There was no big conspiracy from Green Valley to rip off Phoenix. Just a misunderstanding. And if that is so, and we have no reason to doubt it, that means they had no reason to kill Jan Birt."

"You're really going out on a limb here, Holt," said Roy,

shaking his head. "I mean, you just pissed off Bayton in a big way."

"Bayton will always be pissed off with me, whatever I say or do. There's nothing I can do about that."

"You've got a point there," Roy admitted. He eyed Holt curiously. "You're not doing this to get back at me, are you? For not standing by you when Bayton gave you the boot?"

"There's nothing you could have done, Roy. If you had gone to bat for me, we would both be stuck in Loveringem now, and Irene would have hated that and so would you."

"Who knows? She may have loved it. Loveringem sure is a lot more peaceful and lovely than Ghent. She even asked me once if I wouldn't consider a move there."

Holt clapped his old friend on the back. "You know what you need to do to get there, buddy." He balled his fist and pretended to give the detective a punch in the teeth.

Roy grinned. "Don't tempt me. One of these days I might just do it. Though with my luck, he'll probably get me canned. And I've got two kids in college, so I can't afford to get canned." He sighed. "Just keep me informed, all right? And I'll do the same for you."

BY THE TIME they got back to Loveringem, it was pretty late, and Holt decided not to return to the precinct but to go home. Tomorrow was another day. The clock was ticking, though. The judge had given him one week to prove that his theory had merit, and then it was game over, and the investigation would be taken away from him. So he'd better make every second count. Since he'd always found that he could think a lot better when he was walking his dog, he decided to do just that.

Poppy had offered to cook, and while she was busy

working her magic in the kitchen, he drove over to his mom and dad's house to pick up Harley.

"He farts," said his mom the moment she opened the door. "Smelly farts."

"Impossible," he said. "If he did, I would have smelled it. Or Poppy."

"Well, he does. He was in your father's office, and he stank the place up. We had to open a window."

He smiled and crouched down to pet the dog. "So you've been stinking up the place, have you, buddy?"

The dog regarded him stoically, then licked his lips. He didn't seem overly concerned with his lack of bowel control.

"I'm sure he's fine," he assured his mom.

"You probably should take him to the vet," she said, a wrinkle of concern appearing on her smooth brow. Even though she said she believed in aging gracefully, Mom had secretly become a frequent visitor to their local beauty clinic, where they weren't averse to doling out the odd Botox injection.

His dad came ambling up. "You're off work early," he said, a hint of reproach in his voice. When Holt was a kid, his dad had never been home before eight o'clock, sometimes even much later, and even then he'd often brought his work home with him. Holt took after his old man in that regard, and so did Poppy. But if he thought that was the reason Leah had left him for Bayton, he was probably mistaken, since Bayton was also a cop.

"Can I ask your opinion about something, Dad?" he asked.

"As long as you leave Harley out of my office, I'm all ears," said Dad as he headed toward the back of the house, where he had his 'office.' Once upon a time, this was where he would work on his cases long after the sun had set, but these days, well into his well-deserved retirement, all he did was devote his time to the hobby he had picked up. He was the chairman of the local nature preservation society, and most of his time was now spent organizing nature walks and making sure that the local government didn't give in to the demands of real estate developers to destroy every last piece of greenery for yet another luxury condo.

"What is it, son?" asked Holt senior. He could have been Holt's lookalike, only twenty years older than he was and a lot grayer on top. But he was still an imposing presence, even though he was a little bigger around the midsection nowadays. He still went for his daily run, though, and could probably outrun Holt himself, who didn't have the time.

"Did you know that Jan Birt was a serial sperm donor?"

Holt senior frowned. "I seem to recall that there were some rumors about that floating around the precinct at the time, yes. Why do you ask?"

"I'm not sure, but I've got this feeling that it might have a bearing on the case. I'm not sure how or why, but the investigating magistrate has given me a week to find out."

Dad leaned against his desk and folded his arms across his chest. "Birt always was a nasty piece of work. Even as a kid, he wasn't well-liked and had some strange ideas. He also liked the ladies a little too much."

"He still liked the ladies a little too much."

"I don't see how that could have led to his death, though. I mean, this was years ago."

"Yeah, when he was fresh out of college. A way to make some extra money. He must have fathered hundreds of kids, though, if the information I received from the fertility clinic is to be believed."

"I see. So what you're saying is that someone found out and didn't like the fact that Birt was their father?"

"Something like that. Imagine if you disliked Birt with all

your heart, and then one day you discover that he's actually your biological father? That could be a trigger."

"A trigger for murder, though? The person must have really, really hated the man."

"He wasn't well-liked, Dad. We found plenty of people who had good reason to get rid of him."

"I know, but even though you don't like a person, there's a big difference between that and actually murdering them. Something in the person's personal makeup must have led to their normal sense of self-preservation being breached. Merely finding out that Birt is your daddy doesn't cut it." He held up his hands. "At least that's my personal opinion."

"Hmm," said Holt. More food for thought. "So what's all this about Harley stinking up the place?"

Dad smiled. "I think your mom has been feeding him cookies again."

"Dad!"

"I keep telling her she shouldn't, but she can't help it. She takes one look at that cute little face of his, and all of her good intentions go out the window." He gave his son a wink. "He seems to prefer her home-baked gingerbread cookies."

"Sugar isn't good for dogs, Dad."

"Sugar isn't good for humans either. And still we eat it. It's a drug, buddy, plain and simple. Just as bad as cocaine. Only sugar is a legal drug. That's the big difference."

"Okay, I guess that makes me an addict."

"It makes us all addicts! And it's the food industry's fault. They're the drug pushers."

"I know, Dad," he said, hoping his dad wouldn't go on another one of his rants about the food industry trying to poison everyone. It was one of his favorite bugbears.

Dad fixed him with a look. "I've just thought of something."

"What?"

"What if your mom made sugarless cookies? Would that be bad for Harley? He probably wouldn't taste the difference."

"I'll bet he would," said Holt. "Harley is pretty smart."

"A smart farter," Dad grumbled. "Just my luck."

Holt joined his mom in the kitchen. Dad's talk about those freshly baked gingerbread cookies had given him an appetite. But when he tried to pick one up from the baking tray, she slapped his hand away. "Not before dinner, Glen."

"Just an appetizer," he said.

"You'll spoil your appetite."

"Considering Poppy is doing the cooking, consider it spoiled already." His daughter might be a lot of things, but cooking was not her strong suit. She didn't have the aptitude or the inclination. Not that he minded. Most of the time, he did the cooking, and she was eternally grateful that he did. He had a sneaking suspicion that her lack of talent might have inspired the breakup between her and Rupert, a gourmet if there ever was one, and afflicted with a conservative streak where he considered a woman's place to be in the kitchen. When he discovered that Poppy hated cooking, it put a damper on his fervor.

Probably there had been other reasons, like the fact that he had decided that being unfaithful was a good idea.

"Was your father able to help you out?" asked Mom.

"I think so," said Holt. "Yeah, he was."

She pressed her hands to the sides of his face and squeezed, causing his lips to protrude into a pout. "I'm sure I told you this before, but I'm so proud that you have decided to follow in your father's footsteps, and so is he."

"You have told me this many times before," he reminded her.

"And I will keep saying it. That's how proud I am."

"Thanks, Mom," he muttered.

"Now I'm going to fill a bag with cookies, but you have to promise me that you won't touch them until after dinner, and you're going to share fair and square with Poppy."

"Absolutely," he said. "Though considering that I'm bigger and heavier than Poppy, not to mention older, I was thinking more along the lines of a seventy-thirty split?"

"Fifty-fifty or you're not getting anything. And don't think I won't check."

He grinned and watched his mom dump a sizable amount of cookies into a paper bag. She always loved to spoil the members of her family—even Harley.

"I just heard the weirdest thing today," she said conversationally. "Marva's granddaughter has a crush on her cousin. She says they're going to get married when they grow up."

"How old are they?"

"Six," said Mom as she aimed one last cookie into the bag.

Dad had entered the kitchen and frowned when he saw that the stack had diminished. In spite of his protestations about sugar being a drug, he loved his wife's baking.

"Don't worry," said Mom. "I'll bake more later."

"Good," Dad grunted. "You shouldn't spoil the lad. Look at him. He's getting fat."

"Look at yourself!" Mom cried with a laugh.

Dad slapped his protruding gut. "The good life," he told his son with a wink. "And I blame you, by the way," he told Mom.

"So Marva's son had to have a talk with his daughter about cousins not being allowed to marry each other because if they do, their kids might end up being handicapped or might even die in childbirth. Marva made such a fuss about the whole thing."

That tickle was back, and suddenly Holt remembered what had been niggling at the back of his mind all this time.

*Could it be?*

He grabbed the bag of cookies, gave his mom a kiss on the cheek, his dad a hug, and then he was off.

"Where are you going?" asked Mom, her jaw dropping.

"Following a hunch!" he said over his shoulder.

"It's all that sugar," Dad grumbled as he picked up a cookie and took a big bite. "Makes them all go loony."

## CHAPTER 59

Poppy hadn't expected to see her dad in such a state. She had been wondering what to cook, but in the end she simply didn't feel like it, so she had taken something from the freezer and was ready to pop it into the microwave, fully prepared to endure her dad's comments. It was rare to have a father who was also something of a gourmet cook, especially when her own culinary talents were extremely limited. It wasn't that she couldn't cook. It was simply that she couldn't be bothered. It seemed like such a waste of time—you spent an hour or so getting everything ready, and then you ate it in minutes.

The time investment just didn't seem worth it.

So when he came charging in with a bag of cookies in one hand and Harley under his arm, looking quite excited, she felt a certain reluctance and decided to let him down easy. Maybe a glass of wine would do the trick? Mellow him out and soften the blow. Clearly, he had expected her to prepare a meal fit for a god, and instead, he was getting something more akin to prison food. Then again, she could have pointed out to him that she had other talents. She couldn't have listed them off the top of her head at that moment, but she knew they existed. For instance, she was a good swimmer. Now that was always a handy skill to have, wasn't it? Not when you were starving, obviously, like her dad now was.

"Um... dinner will be ready soon," she told him and gestured to his favorite armchair. "A glass of wine, maybe?"

He had set Harley down, and the dog waddled straight into the kitchen to see if, by chance, she had dropped something into his bowl. He returned five seconds later, took up a position in front of her, tongue wagging, and gave her a reproachful look.

Now she had two males to feed. Tough crowd!

"I think I've got it," her dad said as he accepted her offer and dropped into the armchair. She switched on the television, hoping it would distract him.

"You've got what?" she asked.

"I think I may have just cracked the case."

"Is that a fact?" she asked, suddenly distracted from the food dilemma and doing a double take. "You have?"

"Well, it's only a theory at the moment—just like all the other theories we've been working from. But it's a theory with promise—I can feel it in my gut," he added, slapping his stomach. His empty stomach, she couldn't help but notice.

She wavered for a moment but then figured this was exactly the respite she had been looking for. So, she took up position on the couch, her leg slung over the armrest, and gave him her full attention. Dinner, such as it was, could wait.

It wasn't long before she realized her dad was clutching at straws. It saddened her to some extent. He had always been her hero—the brilliant sleuth. As a kid, she had imagined her dad was more akin to Sherlock Holmes or Hercule Poirot than her friends' dads, who were all accountants and lawyers. His move to Loveringem must have done a real number on him because what he was telling her now did not make sense at all.

"Are you sure about this, Dad?" she asked carefully.

He shrugged. "Like I said, it's just another theory. But we still need to check it out."

"Let's do that tomorrow," she advised, then gave him her best smile. "And why don't we go to the pizza parlor? My treat."

He stared at her for a moment, then held up the bag of cookies. "Your grandmother has been baking again. And I have to say, they taste absolutely delicious."

He sure was in a good mood. She hated to spoil it, so she repeated her suggestion that she'd pay out of her own pocket for pizza at their nearest pizza place. Still, he didn't seem all that eager. And then she understood why. When her dad had one of his brainwaves, he lost all sense of space and time and could think of nothing else. So, it wasn't a big surprise when next he was getting up again, the bag of cookies still firmly clutched in his hand.

"I'm going back to the office for a moment," he announced.

"But Dad, you haven't eaten."

He held up the bag of cookies. "This should tide me over."

For a moment, she was at a crossroads. She had a fine spaghetti Bolognese defrosting that she only had to pop in the microwave to provide them with all the nutritional benefits they needed. Or she could join him at the precinct and prove or disprove his latest brainwave.

In the end, she decided that a compromise was probably for the best. So, she grabbed the spaghetti Bolognese, put it in a bag, and accompanied her dad to the office, where they had a perfectly functional microwave in the canteen.

She might as well humor him and dig into the possible solution he had unearthed. The cookies could serve as dessert. Even though she loved her grandmother's baking, she would never substitute cookies for real food. Even she knew that much.

Ten minutes later, she was heating up her and her dad's meals in the precinct's microwave, while her dad was already at the computer.

She passed by her colleague's desk and remembered that she hadn't come in to work, having taken a sick day. A niggling sense of concern worried her, so she asked her dad, "Did you share your latest theory with anyone?"

"Nope. Only you. And I'd like to keep it that way for now —for obvious reasons."

She glanced over at the whiteboard, where pictures of all the different suspects had been placed, along with some of the theories they had considered over the course of the investigation. Then she saw it: written on the edge of the whiteboard was the 'serial sperm donor' theory they had been working on, with a copy of the article placed there.

Could it be that her doubts about Dad's theory weren't justified after all? She glanced from the whiteboard to her colleague's desk. Then a terrible thought occurred to her.

"Dad?"

"Mh?"

"Guess who didn't come in today."

He looked up. "Did she give a reason?"

"Sick day."

He sat back and frowned. "She didn't look sick yesterday."

Poppy chewed her bottom lip and locked eyes with her old man. An unspoken communication passed between them, as it often did. Finally, he nodded and got up.

"Let's go," he said, and they were already on their way out the door before she remembered that she had put the spaghetti in the microwave. The appliance dinged just as she closed the door of the main room behind her.

Looked like they'd have to go without dinner.

## CHAPTER 60

Poppy had suggested calling in backup, but Holt didn't think that would be necessary. After all, there might be a perfectly good explanation for why their colleague hadn't come in to work that day. It could just be a coincidence. He didn't think so, though, and clearly Poppy didn't think so either. She had always been closest to the young woman, having worked with her longer than Holt had.

"I hope she's all right," said Poppy, her face pinched.

He didn't say anything. Whether she was all right or not, the main thing was that they needed to get to the bottom of what was going on. Maybe they should have brought along a psychologist, he thought, since that wasn't exactly his strong suit. Then again, he did spend a few months on a shrink's couch after his marriage broke down. It was part of the deal that allowed him to keep his job. Non-negotiable, the Chief of Police had determined.

It hadn't been as bad as he'd imagined. The shrink had been really nice, and he'd learned a couple of things about himself he hadn't been aware of. She had also taught him some techniques he could use in his everyday life to better cope with the challenging circumstances of his profession—dealing with grief and loss, for one thing. And he had a feeling their upcoming encounter would give him a chance to put those skills into practice.

They arrived at the house in question, and he saw that the lights were on in the living room, which told him that someone was home.

"Let's go," he said as he made to open the car door.

"Wait. How do you want to handle this?" asked Poppy.

He shrugged. "We just do."

"No, but we need a strategy, Dad. We need to break down her defenses. Make her confess. So how do we go about that?"

"Like I said. We just do." And with those words, he got out of the car. Poppy was of a generation that had been taught that before you entered a situation, you needed to have everything figured out. But he knew from experience that in situations as potentially volatile as this, there was simply no way to plan everything out. It was better to play it by ear and trust his instincts.

Poppy followed him reluctantly as he made his way across the street and up the stone path to the front door. Before he could press the doorbell, she placed a hand on his arm. "Maybe you should let me do the talking, Dad. I've known her since she started working for us."

He nodded and then pressed the bell.

They waited patiently, Poppy looking distinctly ill at ease, and Holt wondering if he had made the right call. Poppy might know the woman, but that didn't mean she would be ready to confide in her—considering the consequences.

The door finally swung open, and they found themselves looking into the familiar eyes of Jaime Lett. She didn't seem surprised to see them, but she wasn't happy either.

Poppy painted her most engaging smile onto her face. "We were worried about you, Jaime," she said. "Maybe we could come in for a moment?"

"I'm fine," said Jaime as her eyes darted from Holt to his daughter and back. "Just a stomach bug, that's all. I'll be back tomorrow—or maybe the day after tomorrow."

Behind her, a loud voice yelled, "Who is it?"

"People from work, Mom!" she yelled back.

Holt remembered reading in Jaime's file that she lived with her mom, who'd had a heart attack a couple of years ago after Jaime's dad died. It wasn't an ideal situation, to be sure, and he now wondered if perhaps they shouldn't bring her in for a proper interview.

But before he could suggest it, Jaime stepped aside and invited them in. "Walk on through to the living room," she said.

And so they did. Holt let Poppy go first and brought up the rear. As he followed, he studied some of the framed photographs that adorned the hallway walls: pictures of Jaime with her husband and their baby boy. Plenty of pictures of the baby himself. And also pictures of Jaime with her dad. It looked like they had been particularly close.

It made the task at hand not much easier.

He took a seat on the living room couch and found Jaime's mother studying him intently. The woman looked particularly sickly, like a shrunken elderly version of Jaime herself, even though she was probably only in her forties. The tragedies that had befallen the family must have hit her hard, and then there was her heart condition, of course.

"Ma'am," he said, nodding in greeting.

"So you're Jaime's boss, are you?" asked the woman. "You look exactly as I imagined—a big brute of a man."

"Mom!" said Jaime, then gave Holt an apologetic look. "Pay no attention to her, boss. She's been diagnosed with early-onset dementia. She doesn't always know what she's saying."

Holt nodded. "Don't worry about it, Jaime. You're all right."

For a moment, no one spoke, then Poppy cleared her throat. "So, is that why you didn't come to work today, Jaime? Because of your mom's diagnosis?"

"No, she was diagnosed last fall. Things have been gradually getting worse, though, so I've asked someone to come and look after her during the day while I'm at the office." She gave her mother a look of concern. "She's proven to be quite the difficult patient, though, and if this keeps up, I may be forced to look for an alternative solution."

"You mean, put her in a home?" asked Poppy gently.

Jaime nodded. "I can't afford one, though. Not on my salary."

"Doesn't your mom have a widow's pension?"

"Yes, she does, but it's not enough. These places are insanely expensive." She lifted her hands and let them drop into her lap. "I'll probably have to sell the house. It's Mom and Dad's, but I moved in when…" She swallowed. "When my husband died and then my dad."

Jaime had been hit by misfortune after misfortune, Holt knew. First, she and her husband lost their baby, then her husband took his own life, and finally, Jaime's dad, wrecked with grief over the death of his grandson and his son-in-law, suffered a fatal heart attack and died at the age of forty-five, leaving Jaime and her mom as the sole survivors of what had once been a happy family.

Jaime stared down at her hands, then finally looked up. "You'd better tell me why you're really here, boss," she said quietly. "I know it isn't because you're worried I didn't come in today."

Holt hesitated. "The thing is, Jaime, I don't think it's a good idea to talk about this in front of your mom."

"You can say anything you want in front of her. She won't understand most of it," said the administrative aide. "And besides, if it's what I think it is, it's probably best to get it out of the way." She swallowed with difficulty. "So just go ahead, Chief Inspector."

He nodded. "You know we've been looking into the claims that Jan Birt made years ago about his ambition to become the country's most prolific sperm donor?"

The corners of Jaime's lips curled down. "Yes."

"And you also know that the main reason the law was changed in 2007 was to prevent one man from fathering as many children as Birt claimed he had?"

"That man should never have been allowed to do what he did," she said bitterly.

"I've contacted the fertility clinic where Birt was most active, and I specifically asked to look for one parent pair." He gestured with his head to Jaime's mom. "Your mom and dad. I haven't heard back from them, but I think it's safe to assume they used that clinic?"

Jaime squeezed her eyes shut. "They did, yeah."

"And if I dig a little deeper, I'll probably discover that your in-laws also used a fertility clinic?"

"I had no idea. I mean, neither of us did."

Tears were rolling down her cheeks now, and she struggled to hold on to her crumbling composure. "It was only after…" She let out a loud sob, and her mom, who had been staring intently at Holt in a not-so-friendly way, gave her a look of surprise.

"My darling, what's wrong?" she asked.

"Nothing, Mom," Jaime said.

Poppy had hurried into the kitchen and returned with a

roll of paper towels. She tore off a sheet and handed it to Jaime, who nodded her thanks. "I only found out after Juro died. The doctors told us he suffered from a rare hemoglobin disorder. When he died… it destroyed us both. Marco… well, he thought that maybe we did something wrong. I thought maybe it was the breast milk... But the doctors assured us there was nothing we could have done. And then one night, we saw this documentary on television, about a guy who boasted that he had fathered a thousand babies. They had experts on, who explained the dangers of allowing sperm donors like this guy to go unchecked. They mentioned…" She swallowed again. "They mentioned hemoglobin disorders in babies when the parents are related, along with other birth defects."

"My God," said Poppy.

"I knew that Mom and Dad had used a fertility clinic, and Marco told me that his parents had also used a fertility clinic. And so that got us thinking... and looking... At first, they didn't want to give us the information, but when we threatened to sue, they finally did." She looked up, a haunted look in her eyes. "Turns out that we both had been conceived with sperm from the same donor."

"Jan Birt," said Holt.

"So Marco and I were half-siblings. We didn't know. Our parents didn't know. But when we told the doctor, he said this was most likely the reason Juro had died."

"Jaime, I'm so sorry," said Poppy sincerely.

Jaime was wringing her hands, shredding the paper towel as tears fell from her eyes and dripped onto the carpet. "After we discovered the truth, Marco fell into a deep depression. He felt that it was all his fault. If only he had known sooner, maybe he could have saved Juro's life. Or maybe he and I should never have gotten together. He drove himself crazy.

Six months after Juro died, I came home one morning and found him… hanging… from…" She sobbed, and Poppy moved closer, putting an arm around her shoulders. "It was that man," she wailed.

"Yes, it was," Holt agreed softly.

"He was a murderer. Because of his greed, his stupidity, and his big, fat ego, he killed my baby boy, my husband, and my dad—and now he's killing my mom! And me!"

"So you killed him," said Holt.

"He didn't deserve to live. After what he did to us, he didn't deserve to go on living."

"So you decided to end his life by throwing a petrol bomb at him."

Jaime looked up at him and gave him a defiant look through her tears. "I'm not sorry. He destroyed our lives, and probably countless others that we don't even know about."

"You could have taken him to court, Jaime."

"You know as well as I do that he didn't do anything wrong in the eyes of the law. Back then, a man could donate as much as he liked. There was nothing we could do to make him pay. Nothing at all." She balled her hands into helpless fists. "So I took matters into my own hands. For Juro, for Marco, and for Mom and Dad. And for Marco's parents, who are also going through hell right now."

She fully broke down, and Poppy hugged her close, rocking her gently in her arms. Jaime's mom seemed extremely confused and increasingly distressed by the scene, not knowing what to do with herself. After a moment, she began wailing loudly and thrashing about. Holt had to go and restrain her before she hurt herself.

"You big brute!" the woman yelled. "I knew you were a bad 'un from the moment you set foot in here! You monster!" She freed a hand and slapped him across the face. It took him by surprise, and he had to use his body weight to prevent her from doing it again.

He pulled his phone from his pocket.

Looked like they'd need that backup after all.

## CHAPTER 61

It didn't take long for the other members of Holt's team to arrive, as well as an ambulance for Jaime's mom. As Jaime was placed under arrest and led away, with plenty of neighbors watching, it was clear that Poppy's dad wondered if he should have handled things differently by bringing her in earlier. It would have saved her the embarrassment of being arrested in front of the entire neighborhood.

"We did the right thing, Dad," Poppy assured him. "If we had brought Jaime in, maybe she wouldn't have told us what happened."

"Yeah, I guess," he said.

They watched as Jaime's mom was taken away in the ambulance. She had been sedated and seemed out of it. A paramedic had examined the claw marks on Holt's face, disinfecting them and concluding that no permanent damage had been done.

Leland, Rasheed, and Georgina stood next to them on Jaime's doorstep. None of them spoke, and the mood was somber. After all, one of their own had killed the mayor, and like Poppy, they found it hard to feel vindicated now that the killer had been arrested. None of them had been particularly fond of Mayor Birt, and the whole thing felt like a Pyrrhic victory.

"I'm sure the judge will take Jaime's circumstances into consideration," said Holt, addressing what he knew they were all feeling. "And that the jury—if this ever goes to trial—will observe leniency when determining her punishment."

"She shouldn't be punished at all!" Leland exclaimed. "She didn't do anything wrong."

"She did kill a man, Leland," Rasheed pointed out. "And it's against the law to kill people."

"Birt killed people. He killed a lot of people. We should open an investigation into his actions. Maybe other people have died because of what he did."

"It's not up to us to do that," said Georgina. "But I agree, the guy had it coming." She glanced quickly at Holt. "Which doesn't mean I condone murder, boss. Like, at all."

"Look, Jan Birt was a scumbag," Holt said. "There's no two ways about it. His politics, his womanizing, the way he used drug money to fund his campaign, and this nonsense about becoming the biggest sperm donor in the country—I think it's safe to say the guy did more harm than good, and the world is probably a better place without him. But…"

"I knew a 'but' was coming," Leland muttered.

"That still didn't give Jaime the right to kill him."

"It's against the law," Rasheed insisted. "And we're here to uphold the law."

"Thanks, professor," said Leland darkly. "Still, I can't help but feel sorry for Jaime."

"I think we all feel sorry for Jaime," said Poppy. "And we'll do what we can to get her the right representation and make sure she gets a fair trial."

"I have a feeling it won't come to that," said Holt. "The

prosecutor was already on the phone, and when I told her the story, she was as struck as we all are by Jaime's situation."

"You think they won't prosecute?" asked Georgina.

"They have to prosecute," said Rasheed. "It's the law."

"Oh, shut up about the law for a minute, will you?" said Leland. "We know it's the law and all, but it's Jaime, you know."

"Yes, I also feel for her," said Rasheed as he pushed his glasses up his nose. "And I also wish things were different." He gave his boss a hopeful look. "So there will be no trial?"

"They'll probably make some kind of deal," said Holt. "I know for a fact that Anjanette wouldn't want Jaime prosecuted. So let's see how things shake out."

"What will happen to Jaime's mom?" asked Poppy, clearly concerned.

"Hopefully Jaime will be able to come home soon," said Holt. "Maybe they can arrange for an ankle bracelet to serve out her sentence." He turned to Poppy. "I suddenly remember you said something about making dinner? Or did I imagine that?"

"Dinner!" Poppy said, startled. "I totally forgot!"

"I didn't," her dad said. "I could eat a horse."

"Why don't you all join us?" suggested Poppy. "It's only spaghetti Bolognese, but we've got enough in the freezer for everyone."

"I love spaghetti Bolognese," said Georgina.

"My favorite," said Leland.

"Is it homemade?" asked Rasheed.

"Um… it's from Delhaize?" admitted Poppy.

"Delhaize is good," Rasheed said magnanimously.

And so it was that the entire team ended up seated around Poppy and her dad's dinner table, enjoying a late-night meal of microwave-heated Delhaize spaghetti Bolognese. Even Rasheed seemed to enjoy it, despite his claim that there was nothing better in the world than Indian food, and that next time they closed a case, he'd invite them all to the Indian restaurant his aunt and uncle ran nearby.

He and Holt shook hands on it, even though Poppy knew her dad hated spicy food.

They discussed the case and speculated on what might happen to Jaime. Poppy suggested they launch a petition to get her released, but Holt said it was probably not a good idea—coming from one of the cops who had put her under arrest. It might give people the wrong idea. She had to admit that her dad probably had a point there.

Leland suggested that Jaime not be replaced—out of respect for their colleague—and expressed the fervent hope that she would come back to work. When they all gave him a strange look, he added, "She could work with an ankle bracelet, right? Why not?"

"Because she murdered Mayor Birt, you doofus!" said Georgina as she slapped him on the back of the head.

"Maybe she could work from home?" Leland tried, but Poppy saw that he knew he was fighting a losing battle.

By the time they all returned home, it was way past midnight, and she and her dad started clearing away plates and putting everything in the dishwasher.

"I'll cook something decent next time it's my turn," she told her dad. "I promise."

"No, that's fine," he assured her. "It was pretty tasty."

"Not as tasty as the stuff you come up with," she said.

He gave her a smile. "I thought it was great, honey."

Somehow, she didn't feel like turning in. After the events of the evening, she felt too jazzed and doubted she would be able to sleep. Her dad seemed to feel the same way, so they decided to catch some Netflix. They settled in on the couch, and she got to pick the show. She chose a Scandi-noir crime show that had gotten some great reviews, and before long, her dad was fast asleep.

She got up and tucked him in with a blanket, placed a pillow under his head, then turned off the TV and headed upstairs.

Time to put this case to bed.

# EPILOGUE

The scandal that enveloped the Birts was mostly of their own making. The prosecutor, along with the investigating magistrate, had agreed not to turn the case into a media spectacle out of respect for Jaime's family. It was Teddy Birt who decided that his brother wasn't getting the justice he deserved and called a press conference. In the aftermath, the story came out, including some of the less savory aspects, such as the fact that Teddy had allowed his company to be used as a drug mule, Jan's predilection for sleeping with other women, and finally, the man's boastful claim that he had fathered hundreds of kids.

As a consequence, more people came forward, demanding a full investigation into Jan's serial sperm donor activities, the results of which showed quite a few surprises. Fortunately, no other fatalities were unearthed, but there were a lot of demands being made that the law on fertility clinics should change again to avoid what happened to Jaime and her husband.

Jaime herself had been found guilty, but there wouldn't be an assizes trial, as a deal had been struck between the prosecution and Jan's family, represented by Anjanette. The girl would be allowed to serve a reduced sentence at home with an ankle bracelet and be in a position to keep caring for her mother.

A documentary maker had gotten wind of the amazing story and had contacted Jaime, asking if he could turn her life story into a feature documentary. The matter would be handled with the utmost delicacy and respect, and Jaime was actually excited to be able to tell her side of the story. The money she would be paid was greatly welcomed.

The Elmalehs and the Idrissis had launched their organization and were working hard to prevent other vulnerable kids from being snagged by the clutches of the drug mafia. It was an ongoing battle, but as Mustafa Elmaleh had voiced it, every kid who didn't end up a drug dealer was worth it.

At the next election, Wanda Desai won a majority of the vote, with the Flemish Front candidate being obliterated at the polls. She promised to be the mayor of all the people, not just her own party supporters. When she was finally sworn in as mayor, the applause she received from the members of the Town Hall administration was overwhelming and well-meant. Jan Birt, in spite of being mayor for six years, or maybe because of it, had never been able to win over the hearts of the people who actually worked for him.

Daron Topley suffered a serious setback when his party lost quite a lot of voters in the election. Instead of making the great breakthrough he had hoped for, Flemish Front was cut down to size. The scandal that his most popular mayor had suffered had sunk Topley's reputation, and after the election defeat, he was forced to step down as party leader. He returned to the lawyer's practice where he had been picked up to become the country's youngest party leader five years before. The new party leader was a hardliner determined to raise the party's profile, though analysts thought that unlikely.

Justine Hallett decided to stick around for a couple more years until her retirement. She had wanted to quit, but Wanda Desai had personally asked her to stay. She and Justine had worked together well before Jan Birt had rocketed onto the scene, and even though Justine had thought that Wanda would harbor a grudge against her for not quitting her job when Birt became mayor, she discovered this was far from the case.

She and Anjanette Birt remained firm friends. Jayson decided to launch himself into politics, with the support of his mother. Not for Flemish Front or the Liberal Party, but the Greens. Anjanette was nervous about losing another member of her family to the great game of politics, but it soon became clear Jayson had inherited all of his father's ambition and talents, but not his faults. She knew he'd make a great leader and make her proud.

Meanwhile, her brother-in-law was serving his time in prison, and Birt Travel was now being run by Teddy's wife. No drugs were allowed on the premises. She had decided to retain Boyd Batham, who had always been an extremely reluctant drug smuggler. He'd served a short prison sentence and was back to work trucking tourists around the country.

Almost every day, he passed by the spot where Mohammed's body had been found. A permanent reminder in the form of a small memorial had been placed there. Fresh flowers were frequently laid by passersby and neighbors. Mo and Beni would never be forgotten.

ONE EVENING, a week after the election that had shaken Loveringem and returned Wanda Desai to power, there was a ring at the bell at Poppy's house. She hurried to open the door and saw, to her surprise, that it was her mom. Before she could express her surprise, her mom had opened her arms and was enveloping her in a tight embrace.

"Darling!" she cried. "You're looking well." She released her daughter and glanced beyond her into the hallway. "Is your dad home?"

"Um… yeah, he is. Why?"

Mom gave her a dazzling smile. "I've brought him something."

A sense of alarm shot through her. "You didn't bring… Terrence?"

Mom laughed. "Are you crazy? Of course not. Those two are better kept apart. It's like worlds colliding, you know? Or the stuff that makes an atom bomb. Once those elements get too close—kaboom!"

Holt came ambling up. He looked none too pleased to see his ex-wife. "Leah."

"Glen," she said with a curt nod. "I come in peace."

"Is that so?" he grunted.

"I've even brought you a gift." She gestured to her car, which she had parked behind Poppy's squad car. "It's in the trunk," she added as Holt gave her a confused frown.

He wandered over, and Poppy and her mom watched as Holt opened the trunk, then froze for a moment before looking up and giving Mom a look of surprise.

"A peace offering," she shouted.

He nodded and picked up a box from the trunk and carried it over. As he drew closer, Poppy saw that it was filled with comic books.

"They're all there," Mom assured him. "I asked Terrence to put them in boxes. He was glad to be rid of them."

"He always was a barbarian," Holt grumbled. But Poppy could see that he was pleased. He gave her a curt nod.

"Thanks, Leah. That's very…" He frowned for a moment before muttering, "I'd better…" and disappeared inside.

"That's probably all the thanks I will ever get," said Mom. "But then I knew he was a grump when I married him." She seemed to realize she was talking to Holt's daughter and quickly added, "A lovable grump, though. Absolutely lovable."

"Thanks, Mom," said Poppy. "He's been going on about those comics for months."

"Yeah, I figured I might return them and put a smile back on the man's face for your sake. Though now I realize that's probably physically impossible. Your dad is one of those medical anomalies who was born without the facial muscles needed to smile." When Poppy rolled her eyes, she held up her hands. "I'm sorry. It's just that when I see your dad's face, it all comes back to me."

"The years of marital bliss, you mean?"

Mom smiled her brilliant smile. She certainly had all the right muscles. "I miss you, you know, darling. Are you sure you're all right living with your father?"

"I'm fine, Mom. We get along great."

"Working together, living together. How you manage is beyond me. But then I guess he always enjoyed your company more than he did mine."

Holt had passed a few more times, carrying boxes into the house, until he announced, "That was the last one."

"Great," said Mom cheerfully. "I'd stay, but there's somewhere I need to be."

"There always is," Dad said acerbically.

"Same old Glen," Mom replied, placing a hand on his cheek, earning herself another scowl from the man. "Right. I'll be off. Have fun reading your comic books, Glen." She made it sound as if he were a child, and that was probably her intention. She gave Poppy a kiss on the cheek. "We have to go shopping one of these days. It's been too long."

"I'll call you," said Poppy.

"You'd better."

They watched as she drove off, with Poppy waving and Holt just standing there like a block of ice.

"That was nice of her, wasn't it?" said Poppy.

"Hmm," said Holt noncommittally.

"She could have chucked them out."

"They're my property," he said. "So she had to give them back eventually. Or I would have accused her of theft and had her arrested and thrown in the slammer."

"Of course, Dad," she said, patting him on the back.

She had just closed the door again when there was a knock. When she went to look, she saw that a box of Hello-Fresh stood on the doorstep.

She carried it into the house and locked eyes with her dad.

They opened it together this time.

Inside was a small heart and a message:

*'I haven't forgotten.'*

## THE END

**Thanks for reading! If you want to know when a new Nic Saint book comes out, sign up for Nic's mailing list: nicsaint.com/news**

# ABOUT NIC

Nic has a background in political science and before being struck by the writing bug worked odd jobs around the world (including but not limited to massage therapist in Mexico, gardener in Italy, restaurant manager in India, and Berlitz teacher in Belgium).

When he's not writing he enjoys curling up with a good (comic) book, watching British crime dramas, French comedies or Nancy Meyers movies, sampling pastry (apple cake!), pasta and chocolate (preferably the dark variety), twisting himself into a pretzel doing morning yoga, going for a brisk walk, and spoiling his feline assistants Lily and Ricky.

He lives with his wife (and aforementioned cats) in a small village smack dab in the middle of absolutely nowhere and is probably writing his next book right now.

www.nicsaint.com

Printed in Great Britain
by Amazon